Traitor

by

Murray McDonald

First Published by Kennedy Mack publishing

Traitor

ISBN 978-0-9574871-7-8

Chapter 1

The sound of the gunshot reverberated through her entire body. Her sole purpose in life was to ensure that wouldn't happen. She crashed through the door and was met by the sight of her colleague stemming blood from a chest wound. Unfortunately it wasn't his own.

"Shots fired, POTUS is down, I repeat POTUS is down," she said calmly into her mic. Years of training had taken over.

She swept the Yellow Oval Room as more agents came crashing through the door. Trauma kits in hand, they rushed to the President's aid.

"Bill?!" she shouted, looking at her colleague, pressing his hand into the President's wound. The room was clear, except for the President and Bill Jameson, the head of the President's Secret Service protection team. A National Intelligence Cross lay on the floor next to the President; its recipient was nowhere to be seen. Frankie began to panic. Her training had not covered the loss of a loved one.

"Balcony!" replied Bill urgently, the President's blood spurting between his fingers as he tried to maintain pressure while handing over to the medics who were flooding into the room.

Frankie rushed across the lounge and burst onto the second floor balcony, her gun at the ready. It was empty. The corner of her eye caught a movement on the railing that ran around the perimeter of the balcony. A thin wire was attached to the railing and trailed down to the ground below. Frankie moved across and watched a man unclip himself from the wire and take off at a sprint.

"Bill! Who's Nick chasing?"

"Chasing?!"

"Who's he chasing?! Where's the shooter?!' she shouted, scanning the grounds for whoever had taken the shot.

"He's not chasing, he's running!" replied Bill, as he joined her.

Frankie lined up her shot. He was already beyond pistol range but still within her capability. The image of the morning they'd had had flashed through her mind. She should be taking the shot, but it wasn't right. She could still feel him inside her.

She hesitated. "Are you sure?!" she asked, taking aim.

"Shoot him!' screamed Bill, lining up his own shot.

They both squeezed off shots. They both missed, although only one wasn't intentional.

"Shit! We missed him!" said Bill, watching Nick disappear around the side of the White House. Bill turned back towards the scene in the lounge and spoke into his mic. "All agents, the shooter is Nick Geller, DIA agent, last seen on the southeast corner of the residence, heading towards Kennedy Gardens. He is armed and extremely—"

A massive explosion interrupted Bill, lifting him and Frankie off their feet and slamming them into the railing. As heavy dust filled the air, the entire West Wing of the White House lay in ruins. The President was holding on by a thread and Frankie held her stomach, praying to God that the baby of the President's would-be assassin was safe.

Chapter 2

The White House - East Wing
Presidential Emergency Operations Centre (PEOC)

Frankie took the seat indicated to her. Her mind was still racing. Barely thirty minutes had passed since the shooting and the explosion. The President was on his way to the Walter Reed National Military Medical Centre. His condition was described as grave. She looked around the room. For every face she recognized, there was another she didn't. Everybody remained silent. No hum of chatter, just the deathly silence of shock.

From the faces she knew, she was the only Secret Service Agent in the room. She was also, at least she assumed, the only person in the room with intimate knowledge of the suspect. She focused on the word 'suspect'. She was still struggling to accept that Nick was capable of the deceit involved in the acts he was alleged to have committed. She had no issue believing he was capable of the acts themselves, they were what he had been trained for, that's what he did - just not to his own President or country.

The arrival of the FBI's Deputy Director and Bill Jameson, Frankie's immediate boss, silenced the already quiet room completely. Bill sought her out and, with a flick of his head, summoned her to him. Frankie got up and walked across the room, conscious of every pair of eyes in the room following her closely.

"Could you just give us a few minutes, Frankie?" whispered Bill in her ear. His apologetic tone made it clear that he did not agree with her having to leave the room.

Frankie opened the door to leave just as the Deputy Director's voice boomed across the room.

"Ladies and Gentlemen, you've been selected as the brightest and finest in your organizations, and you're here to lead the hunt for Nick Geller."

Frankie closed the door behind her, tears pouring down her cheeks, as she realized that she was not just closing the door to the room. Her life, her career, everything that made her who she was, had just ended. She had also been one of the brightest and finest operatives in the organization. She was the Deputy Lead Agent in charge of the presidential protection detail. No one had ever reached that position at her age and, more surprisingly, not with her background. Her professionalism and ability were without equal and nobody doubted Frankie had a long and illustrious career ahead of her. Had it not been for Nick Geller, Frankie would have been representing the Secret Service on the Task Force. In all likelihood, she was about to be labeled a potential accomplice and conspirator. She began to shake with panic. She hadn't even considered that prospect.

With her legs no longer able to support her weight, she slid down the wall and pulled herself into a tight ball. The questions poured through her mind, all unanswered.

How did I miss the clues? How could I have trusted him? Will anyone believe me?

Every question had the same answer. A blank. The more she asked of herself, the less sense it made and the more she realized she was going to be suspected.

Nick Geller. She had loved him. She still did. Love didn't just stop. They had first spotted each other six months earlier, flirted with each other professionally, both knowing they wanted more. She was delighted when the flowers arrived at the White House addressed to 'The President's hot guard'. Embarrassingly, they were handed to her. She wasn't the only female member of the President's protection detail. However, it seemed the mailroom were in little doubt and directed them straight to her.

He was everything she wanted from a man. Handsome, well mannered, well travelled, intelligent and, most importantly, she actually felt he could protect her. His eyes pierced into her, opened her up like no one had ever managed before. He had a raw power and energy that very few possessed. There was no doubt in her mind that Nick Geller was a very special man. The man for her. She shared her house, her life, her body and soon a child with Nick Geller. She hadn't even had a chance to tell him about the test she had only taken that morning, or its positive outcome. She banged her head back against the wall in frustration.

Would he have still done it if I had told him?

It was irrelevant. She hadn't thought he was capable of anything like this to begin with.

Frankie felt the floor vibrate as a herd of shiny leather shoes thundered towards her with purpose. She pulled herself together, stood up and wiped her eyes as best she could. The thunder rose to a crescendo as the posse appeared at the end of the corridor. Secret Service agents flanked their protectee so well that Frankie could not even see who was coming. She assumed it was either the Vice President or the First Lady, given the size of the protection detail and the entourage in tow.

Her first glimpse of the protectee made Frankie realize that the worst day of her life had just gotten worse. The Speaker of the House drew to a stop by her side. The Chief Justice, Frankie could see, was still pushing his way through the entourage, a bible held high above the crowd, as he maneuvered his way towards the Speaker.

"Aisha Franks?" asked the Speaker, looking at Frankie.

Frankie winced at the Arab name her Muslim mother had insisted on giving her. A name that very few knew existed.

Chapter 3

Fort Detrick, Maryland
United States Army Medical Research and Materiel
Command (USAMRMC)

Brigadier General Harold F. McLennan watched the horror at the White House unfold on the 24/7 news channels. With each passing minute, another of his senior staff joined him as the news of the attack on their President and the world's most prestigious address filtered through. They were all desperate to know how their Commander and Chief was doing and whether any of their departments could assist in any way.

Between them, they controlled and developed the most advanced medical research and procedures in the world for battlefield injuries, diseases and biological weapons. If there were any people in the world who could help in that situation, the professionals crowding General McLennan's office were amongst the very few who could. The General had made a call to Walter Reed Hospital the moment he had heard the President had been shot. His people were ready to help in any way they could. The offer was noted and much to McLennan's concern and frustration, they did not update or offer any details of the President's condition.

His answer, therefore, remained the same to each of his concerned subordinates. Walter Reed would call if they needed them. In the meantime, all they could do was hope and pray for the President and all the other casualties.

An audible gasp silenced his office when the first aerial shots of the White House were broadcast across the world. The West Wing, the executive branch of the federal government, lay in ruins. The main body of the house remained undamaged but it was a very different silhouette that would be adorning the Washington skyline for some time to come.

The new skyline faded out, replaced by a somber-faced White House spokesman in front of a hastily prepared podium on the East side of the White House, out of view of the rubble and debris that littered the previously pristine White House lawns.

General McLennan hit the volume button on his remote and bathed the office in the background sounds of emergency sirens a few hundred miles away.

"Ladies and Gentlemen," began the spokesman, "I will be brief. At approximately 9:55 this morning, a gunman shot and injured the President. The President is responding well to treatment and is expected to make a full recovery." The spokesman paused as the relief was absorbed by reporters and audiences at home. "To aid his escape, the gunman triggered an explosive device that has damaged the West Wing of—"

The office door burst open and grabbed everyone's attention away from the TV screen. A breathless and panting Colonel Valerie Barnes, a sight that, without the dramatic entrance, would have got their attention anyway, stood almost unable to speak.

"General," she gasped, between attempts to re-oxygenate her lungs.

General McLennan was already up and helping her into a seat before she collapsed.

"Val?" he asked, concern deep in voice.

"W-we've got a Level 4 b-breach!" she stammered.

Level 4 was the highest biosafety hazard category involving highly infectious diseases with high fatality rates and no known cures; it was not an area in which you ever wanted to suffer a breach. A number of her colleagues in the room openly moved away from her.

"Not a leak, a *theft*!" she said, making it clear she thought this situation far worse. She could control a leak.

"Impossible," replied the General, calmly. "This facility is as secure as Fort Knox and anyway, security would have alerted me by now."

"I've only just discovered it!" she said, tears welling in her eyes. The implications of her failure were catastrophic.

"I'm sorry to say that so far we have been unable to locate the Vice President." The voice of the spokesperson cut through the chaos in the room, as the enormity of the announcement caught their ears.

"What did he just say?" asked the General, turning back to the TV.

"It looks as though the Vice President was in the West Wing when the explosion was triggered," explained one of his subordinates.

"Sorry, what explosion?" asked Val.

"The President has been shot and the gunman blew up the West Wing as part of his getaway," replied the General succinctly.

"Oh my God! Is he okay?'

"It appears so. Now, what is it you think is missing?"

"I don't *think* anything is missing," she replied angrily. "I *know* that fifty doses of *Zaire Ebolavirus* have been stolen!"

"You must be mistaken," argued the General, shaking his head. However, his demeanor changed.

"What's the big deal?" asked one of the few non-medical members of the team.

"You know the movie *Outbreak*?" replied Val. On receiving an affirmative nod, she continued, "*Zaire Elboavrius* is like the disease they faced but much worse and with no magic serum to cure it!"

"Oh shit!"

The TV was issuing an alert in the background and caught Val's attention: *"We ask all citizens across the city and beyond to look out for this man. Please do not approach him. He is armed and extremely dangerous. If you do see him, call 911, lock all doors and windows and wait for the emergency services to attend. His name is Nick Geller…"*

Nick Geller's photo appeared on the screen.

"Holy fuck!" said Val. Her heart almost stopped as the image burned into her retinas.

"What?" asked the General, turning to the screen and seeing Geller's face.

"He was here yesterday!" Val managed to say. "Oh fuck! What has he done?!"

The General ran to his desk and picked up the phone. "Get me the Chairman of the Joint Chiefs now!!" he commanded. "Whatever he's doing, get him on the phone now!!"

While he waited to be put through, he turned to Val. "Get to DC immediately. I want the White House and Walter Reed Hospital quarantined. Nobody gets out of either building until we have an all-clear and I mean nobody!"

Chapter 4

"Yes, Madam Speaker," replied Frankie.

"The President wants you in on the investigation," she said gruffly before barging into the Operations Center. "The President is alive and will recover," she announced loudly, walking to the seat at the top of the table. The Speaker was on the opposite side of the political divide from President Mitchell and she made sure he knew it.

A cheer echoed throughout the room but was quickly stifled as the Speaker continued. "I'm afraid that's the only good news. The Vice President is believed to have been in the West Wing. From the initial reports of the damage, it is unlikely that he has survived. The President is currently incapacitated and as such I will take office while he recovers."

A more somber audience watched the Chief Justice step forward and swear in the Speaker of the House as the Commander and Chief of the United States for the first time in its history. Maria Lopez became the first Speaker, female and Hispanic, to ascend to the highest office in the land.

"Madame President," concluded the Chief Justice before leaving the Operations Center.

"Miss Franks?"

Frankie stepped forward from the doorway and into full view of the table of attendees when President Lopez said her name.

"As I said, the President—sorry, President *Mitchell*," she corrected, "wants you to be fully involved in the investigation. As such, you will be the Secret Service's representative on the task force. Please take a seat."

A few grumbles echoed around the table, none of which President Lopez made any attempt to stop, making it abundantly clear that she herself disagreed with Frankie's involvement. Bill, however, smiled warmly and gladly gave up his seat for her before leaving to resume his normal duties.

"So what do we know?" asked President Lopez.

To her right, the Deputy Director of the FBI, Paul Turner, stood up. A headshot of Nick Geller was displayed on the bank of screens that surrounded the room.

"This man," he said, looking directly at Frankie, "Nick Geller, while receiving the National Intelligence Cross for services to the country, suddenly and without warning, produced a weapon, shot the President, and fled via the Truman balcony to the grounds below. From there, he made his escape under cover of a massive explosion that has all but demolished the West Wing of the White House."

Hearing it out loud for the first time still did not make Frankie believe it was true. There had to be a catastrophic mistake.

"Run VT," said Turner.

Any lingering suspicions of Nick's innocence were instantly quashed. The video feed from the presentation of Nick's medal played out before them. President Mitchell, smiling warmly, walked towards Nick, the medal in his hands ready to be placed over Nick's head. Bill stood off to the side, relaxed in the presence of the President and a man who had proved to be beyond reproach. He was a man who had risked everything for his country. He was a hero.

Frankie gasped when Nick dropped his hand and in a flash produced a small pistol-like object. He fired it once directly at the President, who fell immediately to the floor. Nick dropped the pistol and ran for the balcony door. Bill rushed forward to assist the President, simultaneously drawing his gun. He managed one shot towards Nick as he desperately tried to stem the flow of blood from the President's wound. Frankie rushed through the door, her gun drawn and was directed onto the balcony. That was the last scene before the screen went blank.

It was also the first time Frankie realized that the shot she had reacted to had not been Nick's but Bill's. Whatever weapon Nick had used had not only been undetectable to the scanners but it was silenced. It also put an end to any doubt about Nick's guilt.

"Tell me more about this Geller guy," prompted President Lopez.

"Up until 9:55 a.m., Madame President, I would have said he was the all American hero. A former Ranger and Delta Force soldier, he moved into the DIA's Defense Clandestine Services where he's been for a number of years as a specialist in the war on terror. Most recently he infiltrated and assassinated the recently appointed head of Al Qaeda."

The murmurs around the table started as this revelation came to light. Geller's assassination of the Al Qaeda leader had been a closely guarded secret and the reason for Geller's private presentation ceremony by the President of the highest award to an intelligence officer: the National Intelligence Cross. Nick Geller had been about to join the ranks of very, very few elite. Along with his previous Medal of Honor, the National Intelligence Cross would have elevated him to the equivalent of a double Medal of Honor winner.

The President motioned for quiet, shaking her head in bemusement. "Do we have any idea how on earth…" she began but struggled to find the words to convey how bizarre the situation really was.

A few heads turned questioningly to Frankie, who didn't look up, not wanting to engage with anyone on the inner mind of a man who up until a couple of hours ago she would have sworn she knew inside and out.

Before anyone could offer an opinion, the door swept open to reveal another entourage of suits. The Director of National Intelligence led the group and held up a DVD as though it were his invitation to crash the party.

"Madame Speaker," he interrupted, before noting the very subtle but deliberate shake of Deputy Director Turner's head. "My apologies, Madame *President*," he corrected, "I think you will want to see this and I'm sure it will answer a few questions for you." He handed the DVD to an aide on her left.

While the room waited for the DVD to be cued up, all eyes were on the TV screens displaying news broadcasts from the grounds of the White House. Buried deep in the ground, out of reach of every conceivable manmade weapon, there was no safer place for them to be.

"Don't press play!" commanded the President. The sound in her voice conveyed the fear that all in the room shared.

Before she could say any more, the red phone in front of her began to ring. A direct link to the Pentagon and the military sat at her fingertips. She looked at the TV screen showing hermetically-sealed biohazard-suited soldiers surrounding the White House perimeter.

Frankie watched in horror as the newly pronounced and acting President of the United States listened, failing to hide her terror at whatever was being conveyed to her by the military chiefs. She slowly replaced the receiver and turned from the screens to her captive audience.

"Well, things just got a whole lot worse," she said nervously. "It appears that we may all have been exposed to a highly contagious and deadly virus. It seems Mr Geller may not have failed to kill the President after all."

Frankie began to shake; it was too much. Nick loved her, he hadn't been faking it, *couldn't* have been, but he knew she would be there. If he had exposed the White House to a deadly disease, he had inevitably exposed her too.

The President looked directly at Frankie. "Miss Franks?" she asked coldly.

Frankie shook her head, she had to pull herself together. "I don't know…I feel fine, Madame President," she said.

"That's yet to be proved," said the President. "They want to check you first, you're potentially patient zero. Mr Geller may have used you as the delivery method." The President paused, watching Frankie break down into floods of tears, before adding with little feeling. "Unwittingly, of course."

Chapter 5

Leesburg Executive Airport
30 miles NW of Washington D.C.

The Gulfstream G650 touched down and taxied the short distance to the small terminal building. The pilot looked again at the runway and winced; it was going to be very tight. He would have to do a rolling start, build up some speed on the apron before turning sharply onto the runway and continuing the takeoff. It was the only way with a full tank of fuel. The prince had insisted on filling up. He didn't do refuels. The Leesburg officials wouldn't like it but he doubted they'd ever grace their runway again. The G650 was the smallest of the prince's planes and one he seldom used, certainly not for a transatlantic trip. With a fleet of private aircraft at his disposal, which included a Boeing 747 and an Airbus A380, it had been a surprising choice but the prince was not a man to be questioned, especially not at the exorbitant salaries he paid his staff. What the prince wanted, he got.

The prince, a great nephew of the king, was worth almost fifteen billion dollars and was one of the wealthier members of the Saudi royals. However, he was also one of their more visible and challenging members. His wealth had skyrocketed through the financial crisis. His father's death, just prior to the economic crash in 2007, had left him an inheritance valued in the hundreds of millions, almost entirely in cash. The crisis had allowed him to leverage his cash strength to great advantage and resulted in his meteoric rise in wealth. With wealth came influence and with influence came power. It was a mantle the prince was happy to accept. Power suited him.

The short hop from New York to pick up their precious cargo had been an unexpected one. An afternoon lunch in New York had somehow resulted in the prince spending the night in Washington. The pilot had no doubt they'd hear all about it during the flight home. The prince enjoyed telling his staff how important and powerful he was.

The helicopter arriving to his left caught the pilot's attention as he ran through the final checks with his co-pilot. They both hurried their progress. The prince was too important to wait for such mundane tasks, or so he told them. The pilot had previously explained how important such checks were, only to find his bonus curtailed that month. Losing fifty grand in a month was not something he planned to do very often, or ever again.

A knock on the cockpit door preceded the entry of one of the three most beautiful women the pilot had ever set eyes on. The other two were already on board as they prepared the rest of the cabin for their employer.

"He's just landing," said the stewardess. "Can I get you anything?"

The pilot could think of many things but unfortunately none of them were appropriate. He shook his head, as did the co-pilot.

After the door closed behind her, a knowing look between the pilot and co-pilot conveyed more than words ever could; a special language between men, for men.

The pilot watched the two bodyguards exit the helicopter and check the area before opening the door for their prince. The pilot waved to his employer, unnoticed, as the man walked directly onto the plane. More movement from the helicopter caught the pilot's eye. This was unexpected since the prince had journeyed alone. An elderly woman struggled out of the helicopter. She was covered from head to toe in a black burka. Her walking stick managed to hold her upper half from falling forward. Even without the burka, all you would see was the top of her head, such was the degree of her stoop. The woman struggled unaided towards the aircraft. The pilot unclipped his seatbelt and was about to rush to her aide when one of the bodyguards finally turned back to assist her. The pilot observed that the bodyguards attended to the prince before the elderly lady who was probably the prince's mother or an aunt. He shook his head in disgust. The prince's self importance knew no bounds.

He wondered again if a tax-free salary of a million dollars a year was enough. He turned away from the scene and completed his safety checks in record time.

Two knocks on the cockpit door confirmed the cabin was ready for takeoff. Leesburg had become far busier in the last hour but their departure time had been booked and a healthy donation to the airport's development fund would ensure a prompt and priority departure, befitting the prince's status.

Less than three minutes from securing his seat belt, the wheels were up, the sleek G650 jet was heading east, and Nick Geller, the most wanted man in the world, was making his escape.

Nick stretched out and removed the burka, tossing it into the corner of the cabin. His muscles and bones slowly recovered from his enforced stoop and he was able to stand up to his full six foot two inches.

"Now tell me, Mr Geller, why I am saving you and not having you killed, like the dog that you are?" hissed the prince.

Nick smiled. "Because of this." He handed the prince a DVD, the very same recording that the acting President had been handed in the White House.

Chapter 6

The screen burst to life. Although grainy, one half of the image clearly showed Nick Geller facing the camera. The other half of the image was the face of the man Nick Geller had assassinated just two months earlier. The man that had led to Nick being regarded as the all-American hero. The man that Nick had killed to receive the highest honor in the land from the most powerful man in the world.

The man was the self-proclaimed Caliph of Al Qaeda. His full name was Caliph Zahir Al Zahrani and he had replaced Osama Bin Laden. He had immediately pronounced Al Qaeda as a Caliphate in the hearts of all its followers, in honor of their fallen leader. The Caliph smiled warmly at Nick before turning to face the camera.

"Following the death of our great founder, leader and father, Osama Bin Laden, our struggle has weakened. Our successes are a distant memory as the non-believers continue their daily lives, disrespecting Allah. My friends, it is time to strike back, avenge our father and breathe fear into the hearts of all non-believers."

The Caliph paused and turned once again to face Nick, before turning back and smiling into the camera.

"This man is a gift from Allah himself. He will rain death and fear onto the hearts of our enemies. They think he is one of them but he is one of us, a true believer in the will of Allah."

The Caliph paused again and his smile disappeared. "Sacrifice is the greatest gift we have for the furtherance of Allah's will," he said, his rhetoric building. "Sacrifice is something that I and our father before me have asked of many of our brothers. Sacrifice is what our father did for us. And what I must do for you!"

"In the name of Allah, I have asked Nick to assassinate me. I do this for Allah and you, my brothers. A plan to rid the world of non-believers is in motion and I ask you, my followers, and all true Muslims to help our brother Nick fulfill my dreams and those of our father and Allah."

The Caliph stood up and faced Nick, taking his head in his hands. "I ask that you do my bidding in the name of Allah. I ask this of you as a son of Allah and a true believer in Allah."

Nick nodded, a tear clearly running down his cheek and said "Allahu Akbar, Allahu Akbar…"

The tape ended.

The prince rewound the tape and replayed it, moving closer to the screen and analyzing every frame closely. He replayed it again, this time watching every movement. Convinced it was genuine, he turned to Nick and smiled.

"Whatever I can do to help my Caliph, I am yours. My monies, my properties, anything, just ask. The Caliph is a genius! This is genius!" he proclaimed.

"We had to keep it a secret," Nick said. "The Caliph felt terrible about not making you aware of his plan. You were like a son to him, the son he never had. I was to reach out to you before any other person. He made me promise that you would know before anyone else that his death was his doing and his plan to fight back in the name of Allah."

"Anything, my brother, anything!" the prince said, hitting the play button again. The man who had been his childhood tutor, the Caliph, came back to life. The man who had been more of a father to him than his real father spoke to him from beyond the grave. The prince stood up and wiped the tears from his eyes and knelt at Nick's feet.

***

Frankie left the room. Hearing the words from Nick's mouth was too much. She staggered into the corridor, barely able to hold her own weight. The biohazard-suited soldiers filling the corridor were only too happy to help her into a seat. They had a blood sample to retrieve and she was top of the list. Frankie's arm was held out as medics accompanying the soldiers took a sample of her blood. She winced when the needle punctured her arm. It wasn't the pain of the needle, it was the pain of what that needle may uncover— a deadly virus and the child of a murdering traitor.

The image on the screen faded, and the silence in the room lingered. Any doubt that Nick Geller would not have infected them with a deadly virus had just been dispelled. They had trusted Nick, some had worked with him for years and yet he had just exposed himself as one of the greatest traitors in the history of the nation, or even throughout history, period.

"It's been thoroughly checked by the NSA. It's real," confirmed the Director of National Intelligence, removing any remaining hope that it was all a mistake.

A knock on the door preceded the entrance of a biohazard-suited team who made their way towards the President.

"Madame President," the DNI turned to face the acting President, "would you please follow these gentlemen?"

"Why?" President Lopez asked as calmly as she could.

"You're going to be placed in a secure room while we ascertain whether or not the virus has been released. You may still be free from it and we do not want you to catch it while the checks are ongoing."

Acting President Lopez was about to discover that, when it came to her wellbeing, she was not in charge of her own destiny. The freshly drafted in and safely suited Secret Service agents placed a mask over her head and removed her from the potentially hazardous environment. A small office at the back of the Emergency Operations Center was awaiting her arrival. Airtight seals and a fresh smell of bleach welcomed her to her new home for the foreseeable future.

After the President left the room, the DNI turned to the FBI Deputy Director.

"Mr. Turner, I'm sure I don't need to say it but whatever you need from the intelligence community is at your disposal. This man Geller has to be tracked down and brought to justice. If anyone gets in your way call me, 24/7," he commanded before leaving the room with his entourage.

The message was as much for Turner as it was for the roomful of senior members of the intelligence community. The FBI was the lead and everyone was to jump to its tune.

Turner looked around the room at the team he had been given for the task. Some of them he recognized, others he had heard of, and others he had no idea who they were or which clandestine or secretive part of the community they worked for.

Before he had a chance to address them, the door opened and another biohazard-suited person entered the room. However, this time, the person took an empty seat and sat down.

"I'm Colonel Valerie Barnes, I've been seconded to this team," she announced to the group through her glazed mask.

"On whose orders?' asked DD Turner.

"The Secretary of Defense and the Chairman of the Joint Chiefs."

Turner nodded his approval of two people he would allow to trump him.

"I head up the USAMRIID unit at Fort Detrick," Colonel Barnes said.

Blank faces stared back at her.

After explaining what that meant, Colonel Barnes became the most popular person in the room. everyone clamored for information on what the disease was and the likelihood of their catching it.

With no confirmation that anyone was in fact infected, Colonel Barnes played down the impact of the disease as much as possible. The reality would come soon enough. However, even the sugar-coated version was enough to scare the life out of her captive audience.

Chapter 7

Nick removed the DVD from the player, replaced it carefully in its holder and returned to his seat. The prince stared at him throughout, his eyes transfixed on the man who had martyred his tutor.

"Can you tell me the plan?" asked the prince, struggling to hide the awe in his voice.

Nick closed his eyes. "No. The Caliph was explicit. Nobody should be made aware of the plan, only what is required of them. That way, even if we have a traitor in our midst, they will not be able to stop us. Even the scale, which I assure you will honor our dead Caliph, will remain a tightly guarded secret."

Nick sensed the prince's disappointment. He opened his eyes and stared deep into the prince's eyes. "But what I can tell you is that what we have planned will destroy the western world and lead to the birth of the one true global Caliphate." He smiled conspiratorially.

"So where can I take you?" asked the prince, wiping tears of admiration from his eyes and breaking into a smile.

Nick pulled a slip of paper from his pocket and handed it to the prince. "This is all I need of you just now but rest assured, My Prince, you have a very important role to play but your day has yet to come. The Caliph was explicit as to how vital your part in his plans would be."

The prince took the paper in his hands and saw two numbers. One he recognized as a bank account number. A Swiss bank that he himself had an account with. The other number was a sum of money, $250,000,000.00, one quarter of a billion dollars. The prince nodded as though this were small change. "It will be there tomorrow," he said, without a second thought or question as to how the monies were to be used.

Nick nodded and once again closed his eyes. He had a few hours to kill during the transatlantic crossing. After that, sleep was going to be hard to come by. With the devastation he had left behind in Washington, there would not be a stone left unturned in the hunt for him. He knew the American and Western agencies inside out. He knew how effective they could be and how personally they would take the attack on the President and the White House. They were not to be underestimated but, more importantly, he knew their weaknesses.

The plan was a complex one but at its core it was stunningly simple. He had no illusion that it would be easy, nor that he would definitely succeed. Many obstacles lay before him. Tracking down and uniting the leaders of the world's Islamic terrorist groups to launch a holy war on the United States was not going to be a walk in the park. The Caliph had laid down the groundwork. His initial conversations with his counterparts across the Arab world had set Nick in motion and only through the Caliph's death could the plan ever hope to succeed. His sacrifice would unite jihadists like never before. Nick had one chance to strike a blow that would make the western world finally realize its days were numbered.

Uniting the cause was key. Al Qaeda, although a thorn in the US's side, was not capable on its own of defeating the might of the US forces and capabilities. A jihadist force, combining the Islamist factions and groups to unite as one, with a common goal and leader, was the Caliph's vision, a vision that he had tasked Nick with delivering.

With sleep pulling at him, Nick began to relax for the first time that day. As his mind and body began to de-stress, regret suddenly surfaced. Despite all the planning and preparation, one problem had emerged. Aisha Franks. Frankie. She had never been part of the plan. Their relationship had exploded from nothing, a mutual attraction that had just blossomed into something far more. He knew his plans would mean it could never be but he'd never verbalized that out loud, caught in the moment, caught in the closeness of a real relationship, a relationship he had never before experienced. They clicked. In another life, they'd have been perfect, destined to be together. Nick thought back to the hug and peck on the lips, as Frankie had run out that morning, the coffee he had prepared for her in one hand and a wicked smile etched across her face. She'd promised him a surprise that night that would trump the day he met the President, as she had closed the car door.

Nick hadn't had a chance to think about those words until that moment. The moment the car door had closed behind her, he had raced to get ready for the biggest day of his life. What would become of his beautiful Frankie? She'd be labeled a suspect, a potential collaborator. Her career would be over. That was a given. Who would trust her to protect them after her boyfriend had shot the President? He fell asleep, saddened by the loss of his first true love.

It was his only regret.

Chapter 8

"Let's calm down people, we have work to do!" Turner shouted over the din. "While we wait for the results, we'll assume we're all clear. Let's worry about things we can do something about."

A few knowing nods agreed and the room silenced.

"Okay, I think that's it for interruptions. Let's start by introducing ourselves and then getting down to some work and catching this traitorous son of a bitch."

Frankie's timing was impeccable, reentering the room just as Turner described her boyfriend. She looked at him impassively, her reddened eyes incapable of any more tears, and sat down at the table.

With nearly twenty people in the room, it took some time for each person to stand up, give their name, title and the organization they represented. Frankie listened carefully as various investigative branches of the US government were rhymed off.

When it came to her turn, Frankie stood up and introduced herself, although it was obvious that everybody in the room had been made aware of who she was. They just weren't aware that she was also a senior and highly respected member of the Secret Service, responsible— ironically, given her murdering boyfriend— for the safety of the President of the United States.

The door opened as she was speaking and a man entered the room silently, taking a seat against the wall rather than joining the table. Frankie noticed an almost imperceptible nod of recognition to Turner as the man, in his early sixties, took his seat.

A hand shot up as Frankie sat back down. "Given Miss Franks' relationship wi—"

"Miss Franks is here at the request of the President," interrupted Turner, silencing the man who had recently introduced himself as Brian Jones from ATF.

However, once again, the tone in Turner's voice failed to hide his agreement with Jones and his bewilderment at the President's order. He obviously would have liked nothing better than to get Frankie into an interrogation room and find out every piece of information she had on Geller.

With Frankie avoiding all eye contact, the remaining members of the group stood up and introduced themselves. The FBI was the most heavily represented of all the agencies with three agents on board, whereas the ATF, CIA, DIA and Homeland had each supplied two agents. The Department of Justice had supplied an attorney that would clear any legal obstacles, while Transportation Security Administration, the Coast Guard Investigative Service, Immigration and Customs had all supplied an agent to ensure Nick Geller wouldn't escape the confines of the United States.

Turner stood up when the last attendee finished his introduction. Frankie, along with a number of other attendees, looked at the man seated against the wall at the back of the room. He sat impassively uninterested in their stares. He had no intention of introducing himself.

"The gentleman some of you are looking at is Mr. Carson," intervened Turner. "He's a representative from the Secretary of Defense's office. He'll be privy to the investigation but will play no active role in it. He'll be the Secretary's liaison on the task force. The Secretary has made it clear to me that the full might of all our forces are at our beck and call."

"Whatever you need, I'll make it happen," said Carson. A quiet assurance in his demeanor filled everyone with the confidence that he meant exactly what he said. "And please, everyone, just call me Harry," he added with a smile before leaning further back into his seat, signaling clearly that everybody should move on.

"Thank you, Mr. Carson. Sorry, Harry," continued Turner. Frankie had noted Harry's disproval when Turner had called him Mr. Carson, a simple lift of the eyebrow and Turner had reacted instantly. Frankie read people. Turner may be in charge but the power in the room was the mysterious Harry Carson.

"Before we begin, here's a quick update on where we are with the search so far. Within minutes of the shooting, a highest priority alert for the arrest of Nick Geller was issued to every law enforcement agency in the country. Through our colleagues at Transport, Borders and Coast Guard, the United States is effectively on lockdown, certainly for Mr. Geller. We're currently tracking down leads to residences, family, friends, and so on."

Frankie didn't look up but felt eyes burning into her from around the table.

A sneeze from Harry Carson drew attention away from Frankie. He extracted his handkerchief and a long, sustained blow into it had everyone in the room turning to the masked Colonel Barnes for signs that Harry may have just contaminated them all.

Frankie watched Harry, who winked at her as he replaced his handkerchief in his breast pocket.

"It was just a sneeze people," said Turner agitatedly looking at Barnes himself for confirmation.

"I'd now like to hand you over to my colleague, Special Agent Sarah Reid. She's currently head of the National Joint Terrorism Task Force. What she's about to disclose is not, I repeat *not*, to leave this room. Some of you will already be aware of what she is about to disclose but for those of you who are not, unless specifically authorized, it is not to be shared with anyone—and that includes your bosses or even the heads of your agencies. "Do you understand?" asked Turner, reacting to the half-hearted nods and murmurs of agreement that followed.

An affirmative response from everyone followed immediately.

"Special Agent Reid," said Turner, handing the floor to his colleague.

Reid cleared her throat. "Approximately eighteen months ago, there was a sharp increase in terrorist chatter. Since then, levels have continued to escalate to the extent that we're now experiencing five fold levels over anything previously experienced. Most of you will have been aware of this fact, as we maintain a high state of readiness across our law enforcement agencies. However, one part you will not be aware of is how coordinated these communications have become. In essence, terrorist organizations are not only talking amongst themselves, they're talking to each other and we have no idea what they're saying. Within ten minutes of the shooting this morning, the chatter increased again. Ladies and Gentlemen, we think this morning's shooting and bombing are merely a precursor to a far bigger attack by a coordinated group of international terrorists."

"And you don't consider having stolen and perhaps delivered the most deadly hemorrhagic fever to the President, the White House and God alone knows how many thousands or millions of people might be the far greater attack?" asked Colonel Barnes, struggling to hide her anger.

The suggestion that millions were at risk and the words 'most deadly' focused everyone in the room on the disease specialist.

"Perhaps I should have been more forthcoming with this information. However, until we know if we have an outbreak, I didn't want to panic you any more than you have been," she said. "As I mentioned, the Ebola virus is deadly in some cases. Ebola Zaire is deadly in approximately 90% of cases. The strain of the Ebola Zaire virus that has been stolen is I'm afraid nearer 95% deadly and is also highly contagious. You were all correct when you were concerned at Mr. Carson's sneeze. If he had the disease, the particles he deposited into the air through that sneeze would have infected most of the people in this room. Mr. Geller knew exactly what he was stealing when he stole this strain of the vir—"

"Colonel Barnes is correct," Harry Carson interrupted. "The fight for our survival may already have begun." His unspoken message to her was loud and clear. She had already said too much. He'd stopped her before she disclosed that the strain was not an entirely natural occurrence. The stolen strain had been the remnants of a long forgotten biological weapons program, enhanced to increase its contagion and deadliness. The biggest problem had been just that, its deadliness. With no known cure, it would kill foe and friend alike.

With panic once again catching hold, Turner stood up. "Settle down, we've got a man to find and a nation to protect, people. Let's worry about what *has* happened, not what *may* happen."

The red phone at the top of the table rang and the room instantly silenced. Turner lifted it tentatively.

The room held its breath as they watched Turner listen to whatever was being said. Turner shook his head. "I'm not entirely sure what you're telling me," he said into the mouthpiece. He looked at Colonel Barnes, beckoned her towards him and handed her the phone as she approached. "The first test results are in," he said, his tone one of great concern.

Frankie felt a shiver run down her spine. A sudden sweat soaked her shirt and her eyes struggled to focus on Colonel Barnes.

Shivers, sweating, blurry vision.

All symptoms of Ebola.

Chapter 9

"Madame President?" said the Secret Service agent holding out the telephone." "I have President Mitchell for you."

Acting President Maria Lopez smiled broadly. Her first experience as Commander-in-Chief was not one she wished to prolong. In the past half hour, the barrage of requests and issues that had crossed the desk of her airtight cocoon was eye watering. A national crisis was on the brink of becoming a global pandemic and an international disaster. Overwhelming was not even close to describing the situation she was in.

"Madame President," said President Mitchell warmly, an emotion he had never felt when conversing with Maria Lopez. She had been, without doubt, his biggest pain in the ass since winning the presidency.

"Mr. President, it's so good to hear your voice," she replied, equally warmly. The feeling was mutual. She did not normally enjoy hearing his voice.

It was evident to both of them that, at times of crisis, political differences were set aside. Although they sat on opposite sides of the political spectrum, a truce would be maintained for the security of the nation.

"I just wanted to thank you for stepping up for me," he said with pain evident in his voice.

'Of course, Mr. President, whatever I can do." The pain in his voice worried her. She had assumed he was calling to retake control.

"Can you bring me up to speed?" he asked.

Maria spoke for the next ten minutes, describing the aftermath of the attack, the lockdown of the White House and Walter Reed, the task force being formed and the actions put in place to ensure Nick Geller did not escape the country. She informed him of the countless calls from heads of state from across the world who had called to offer their support to the United States and condolences for the Vice President.

"It sounds as though you've been thrown in at the deep end," said President Mitchell when Maria drew to a close.

"It's why we enter politics, Mr. President," she replied, giving a true politician's answer.

"If it's any consolation, I'm fairly certain we're all clear on the Ebola front," he offered.

"Have you had your results?"

"No, no just common sense. If he infected us, he would have been infected himself. Why go to the bother of blowing up the West Wing and escape if you've exposed yourself to a deadly disease?"

"That does make sense, Mr. President. But why is he doing this? Did he say anything before he shot you?"

"Just the usual Allahu Akbar stuff and then he pulled the trigger on a ridiculous looking little pistol. It was made out of some sort of plastic, probably made on a 3D printer. He walked straight through all our scanners without so much as a beep."

"Thank God his aim was off," she said wholeheartedly. She respected the office of the presidency above all else and would never wish ill of any president, no matter how much she disagreed with his politics.

"One sixteenth of an inch, that's how close he was. One sixteenth of an inch to the right and I'd have been dead in seconds. I'm told it was an exceptional shot from the makeshift pistol. Its lack of power meant he had very few kill shots and he missed his by one sixteenth of an inch," he said again, still coming to terms with how close he had been to dying.

"God was on the side of the good, Mr. President!"

"I hope he stays there. I think we have a storm coming and I pray he keeps us safe."

"He will, Mr. President, he will. I'm sorry, sir, but you sound tired."

"I've been tired since I took office two years ago." He couldn't help the subtle dig at how hard she had made his presidency. "I called to thank you and let you know that now I'm out of surgery and been given the all clear, I'm fine to take back the presidency."

Maria didn't need to be asked twice. She had future plans and taking the reins for even two hours was going to be a massive boost to her career when the time came.

"Of course, Mr. President," she replied without missing a beat.

"Thank you, Madame Speaker," replied President Mitchell and with those four words, he was back in charge of a country in crisis.

By the time she had replaced the handset, her Secret Service guard had halved. She was surprised it hadn't entirely disappeared until she realized she was still just a heartbeat from the big ticket. Without a Vice President, she was next in line should the President's health deteriorate.

Less than a minute later, the TV screen cut from the scene of biohazard-suited soldiers guarding the White House to the President of the United States. His left arm was pinned by a bandage across his chest and the Walter Reed logo was clearly visible above his head. The presidential seal was prominently displayed on the podium in front of him. His face was pained but his features and his stance were strong and resolute.

"Today, we suffered a great loss. A great American, a great man, a great friend has been slain by our enemies. Vice President Donald Brodie was killed during the attack on the White House. I'm sure you have all seen the images and you may be surprised to hear that, as far as we are aware, Vice President Brodie was the only fatal casualty in the explosion. Although his loss is devastating to the country and to me personally, I thank God that many more were not killed alongside him. As you can see, I have suffered a small wound to my shoulder. It is nothing more than that, a small wound and at no time was my life in any danger. I would like to thank Speaker Maria Lopez who took over the duties of President while I was incapacitated during a short operation. I am proud to say that our great country can now say that it has had a female President."

A few smiles from the reporters assembled in front of the President suggested that the comment was taken in the lighthearted manner it was intended to be.

"As for the bio-hazard suits surrounding the White House, please do not be alarmed. That is merely a response that any terrorist attack on the White House will illicit. It is standard procedure and I assure you, it is nothing to be concerned about."

***

Throughout all their disagreements and political fights, one thing had comforted Maria Lopez about President Mitchell - his honesty. Their views may have been very different but at least he was always honest about them, or so she thought. The blatant lie, so easily told and so convincingly delivered, had just altered her entire impression of him. If he wasn't the man she thought he was, what else had he lied about? Before she had a chance to digest the information, the desk phone interrupted her.

"Yes," she snapped.

"Madame Speaker, I'm pleased to say, we have the all clear, everybody has tested negative for the virus." The caller ended the call. He obviously had many other calls to make.

Maria relaxed, although she didn't know what was more comforting, the fact that the President hadn't so easily lied or that she hadn't contracted Ebola.

***

"And God bless the United States of America," said the President as he ended his address.

Walking away from the podium, a cell phone was passed to him and the same message Speaker Lopez had just received was delivered to him for the first time.

Chapter 10

The news sent a rush of relief through her body. The panic attack she had been about to succumb to instantly abated. Nick had not given her a parting gift to end all gifts.

As soon as Colonel Barnes received the news, she removed her mask and smiled broadly. No words were needed.

"Alright folks, we're going to move from here and reconvene in one hour in the National Joint Terrorist Task Force offices at the National Counter Terrorism Center," announced Turner. "That's going to be our base of operations. Passes and ID badges are being prepared for you as we speak."

As comfortable as the President's operations center was, it was hard to get over the fact that it was simply a very large safe buried deep in the ground, not really a place where any normal person would wish to spend a great deal of time. The room emptied quickly and left Frankie alone with Harry Carson, who seemed perfectly comfortable in the tomb-like environment. Frankie, it seemed, was going to be the kid nobody wanted to play with.

Carson stood up and walked over to Frankie. He offered her his hand to help her up from her seat where she sat as dejected as she had ever felt in her life.

"He fooled many more people than you and I," he said, pulling her up both physically and mentally. "It's nothing to be ashamed of or embarrassed about." He smiled at Frankie trying to put on a brave face.

"Thank you," she said.

He held the door for her. "So how long were you seeing him?" he asked nonchalantly.

"About five months, three weeks and four days," she replied. "Give or take a few hours." He nodded acknowledgment. "Why?"

"Nothing to do with you, it's just… nothing, sorry, I shouldn't have asked."

"No, if there's something you're trying to say, just please say it," she insisted.

"I promise you, it's nothing to do with you. He just never informed his department of a relationship, something he should have done. It came as a shock to us that he was involved with you, that's all."

Frankie stopped and looked more closely at Carson. "Why on earth would he have to inform his department?"

Carson looked around to check that no one was listening. "As I said, he fooled a great number of people. Nick Geller had security clearance as high as it goes. He was one of our most trusted and capable agents. His actions and the danger he poses to us are without precedent."

"He did want to keep our relationship quiet," she said. "But I couldn't." She smiled and as quickly as the smile came, tears began to flow once again.

Carson led her by the shoulder towards the elevators. The last of the task force had already left without waiting for the two stragglers.

"I should resign," blurted Frankie.

"Don't be ridiculous," replied Carson.

Frankie knew she couldn't. As long as her country had a use for her, she would give it her best. She wasn't a quitter.

Boarding the elevator, Carson turned to her. "Ready?"

She knew he was meaning more than just pressing the button for 'up'.

"Yes," she replied confidently.

Chapter 11

Carson insisted on driving, which was just as well. The massive explosion that had wiped out the West Wing had emanated from the car she had shared with Nick that morning. The parking spot that he had selected had been perfectly planned. The shaped and directional charge of an experimental explosive, still in testing, had meant that the damage to everything except the West Wing was minimal. Almost the entire force had been sent directly into the building, destroying its structure and bringing it down on itself. How more people had not been killed was being described as a miracle. The fact it was a Saturday morning had of course made a big difference. The fact that the Vice President had made it clear that he had wanted his videoconference to be private and confidential had also helped. His security detail had left him to it. After all, he was in one of the safest and most secure buildings on the planet.

"Would you mind if we swung by my house?" she asked Carson. "I'd love to grab a change of clothes. It's on the way to McLean and the NCTC."

Carson checked his watch. "I'm not sure we've got time."

"Please," pleaded Frankie. What she really wanted was to get out of the clothes she was wearing. They smelled of Nick. His aftershave hung on her collar where he had nuzzled her that morning, laughing and joking on their way to the White House.

Carson looked at her puppy dog eyes and as much as he wanted to say no, she reminded him of his daughter. He could never say no to her either. He also didn't know how to tell her that things were going to be very different. He decided it was easier if she just saw for herself.

"Where to?" he asked.

"Just head towards Wesley Heights," said Frankie. "I'll direct you from there."

With little traffic heading out of Washington - it seemed everybody wanted to see the missing West Wing - they pulled up to Frankie's address in no time.

Carson whistled as the gates to the property swung open and revealed a spectacular country estate.

"Holy shit!" he said, as the full splendor of the house came into view, along with what seemed like fifty or so law enforcement vehicles, from crime scene vans to local police vehicles and FBI sedans.

"Turn here," barked Frankie on seeing the unwelcome guests.

Carson followed her instructions and turned down a small lane tucked into the heavily wooded drive. As you approached the house, the angle obscured its existence. Driving back from the house, you couldn't have missed it. Carson followed the tight wooded drive for what seemed like half a mile, arcing round the perimeter of the main house. The darkness of the drive gave way to a far smaller house, built in a similar style to the far more opulent main house.

"We're here," said Frankie awkwardly.

A garage sat off to the left. A Toyota Prius was parked next to a Porsche 911 convertible. The two couldn't have looked more awkward next to each other. The door into the house looked more like a back door and, as they exited the vehicle, Frankie led Carson around the side of the house. A large terrace led out to one of the most beautiful pools Carson had laid eyes on. A grand staircase at the far end of the pool swept up to the main house.

"The guest house," said Frankie, watching Carson struggling not to gawp in wonder. The home, pool grounds and landscaped garden were immaculate and beautifully maintained.

Carson was as old in the tooth as they came and was not easily impressed. He had signed off the search warrant himself and it did not cover a guest house. They simply had a house number on University Terrace NW for Aisha Franks' home address. He hadn't thought they'd need to search more than a small apartment or home. He certainly hadn't thought she'd be living in a house that rivaled the White House, or, he corrected himself, living in its guest house. He began to consider that Aisha Franks was a far smarter young woman than he had given her credit for. He was also beginning to see why Aisha Franks had been assigned to the case.

"I really shouldn't let you in there," he said, taking his cell from his pocket. He needed to get the team into the right house. He could see the high visibility vests of the team tearing through the main house and winced at what the bill was going to be to fix whoever's house they had just trashed.

"I'll stay here if you can just get me a change of clothes," said Frankie. "I…I smell of Nick," she confessed awkwardly and uneasily.

Any doubts he had had instantly evaporated. The look of utter betrayal and loss in Frankie's face could not have been faked.

"Wait here," he ordered and taking her key, opened the main door and walked into a photo shoot straight from the world's most luxurious homes. Despite being just the guesthouse, it was a four-bed six-bath mini mansion with only the best quality fittings, furniture and craftsmanship.

In less than two minutes, he was back and had to avert his eyes as Frankie was showering in her underwear in one of the outside showers that skirted the pool.

"Sorry, I just need to get rid of his aftershave."

Carson nodded and continued to avert his gaze. She was an exceptional looking woman and from her physique, it seemed she was used to using the pool. He tried really hard not to look. He had a daughter her age but couldn't help notice that the tone of her skin was natural. Either she had an incredibly even tan or an exceptionally good tanning salon. However, her long, dark, wavy locks hinted towards a Middle Eastern heritage, despite her height and bone structure and most importantly, her blue eyes that suggested a European, Dutch or Germanic heritage. Whatever the case, he could see why Nick Geller would have been interested. Hell, he was past it and didn't have a chance in hell but *he* was interested.

He passed her a towel he had retrieved for her from the house. ""Do you mind if I ask how you afford this place?"

"It's free," she replied, drying off as he averted his eyes again. "They like having me in the grounds."

"Free, as in nothing?" He looked again at the guest house which on its own was easily worth two million dollars.

"I suppose having a Secret Service agent as a guard dog is no bad thing," she smiled.

Carson looked at her, spotting the lie, or more correctly, the lack of the whole truth.

"Who's the owner?"

Frankie shrugged awkwardly. "My mom and dad."

"I thought your dad was an accountant at a small firm?" said Carson, giving away more than he wanted to about how much he had looked into her.

Frankie squinted at the realization of how much interest she had generated since Nick's actions. Carson had hung back to get her alone, he had insisted on giving her a lift. Frankie had no doubt her house would have been searched the moment Nick was the suspect. It wasn't exactly why she had suggested going there but it had played a part. Perhaps it was time to give Carson something more interesting to think about.

"He is but he did marry a Saudi princess," she said, dropping her towel and getting dressed as Carson struggled to compose himself from the two bombshells that had just hit him.

Chapter 12

Nick woke up to a small vibration on his right wrist. His GPS alarm had activated. He opened his eyes and was assaulted by the vision of an inanely smiling prince looking directly at him.

"You're awake," announced the prince excitedly.

Nick closed his eyes again and shook his head and not for the first time wondered if his choice of benefactor may have been misjudged.

"Would you like a drink, sir?" offered a stewardess who had appeared on hearing the prince's voice.

"Just a glass of water, thank you," replied Nick.

"Would you like…?" asked the prince, gesturing towards the stewardess.

Nick was not entirely clear on the prince's meaning.

"There is a bedroom through that door," he winked.

Nick, much to his own surprise, shook his head in disgust. Not that the stewardess was not attractive— she was stunning, just like his Frankie. He mentally corrected himself, she wasn't his any more.

"No, of course not," he said. Once again, his only regret from that day's actions raised its head.

"I apologize," said the prince, suitably chastised by Nick's look of disgust.

Nick looked out of the small window and was pleased to see the view. Land lay ahead to the left. After five hours of continuous ocean, the firm prospect of escaping the confines of the aircraft and the prince was a welcome sight. The prince meant well and was obviously elated at the news that his Caliph had died as a martyr to further their cause, but to say he was somewhat full on about it would have been an understatement. Nick liked his space and had it not been for the quarter of a billion dollars he needed, he would have taken it happily.

"I need to speak with your pilot," announced Nick. "Can he be trusted?"

The prince shook his head. "I'm afraid not but he can certainly be bought."

The stewardess reappeared with Nick's water and from the look on her face, she had heard and not appreciated his rejection. Nick looked at the glass and noticed the other two stewardesses looking on from bedroom door. He was well aware of the immediate laxative effects eye drops could have on drinks and as such, laid the glass down on his armrest, untouched.

"Thanks, maybe later," he said with a smile, before turning to the prince. "I'll just grab a word with the pilot."

Nick opened the door and entered the small cockpit. The view across the horizon was of Northern Europe. The pilot was surprised to see Nick, something he didn't make any attempt to hide.

"Who the hell are you?!"

"I'm a guest of the prince," replied Nick evasively.

"But he only got on board with an old woman!"

Nick shrugged. "You must have been mistaken. Anyway, I'm afraid I need to get off."

"Our flight plan is direct to Riyadh," replied the pilot, confirming it with a look at his co-pilot, who nodded agreement.

"I'm afraid that doesn't work for me. The heat may be a little too much at the moment," said Nick, not referring to the weather.

He explained what he wanted to do.

"Not a chance in hell," replied the pilot.

Nick left the cockpit to get the prince involved. Five minutes later and two million dollars richer between them, the pilot and co-pilot began the descent to an impromptu and unscheduled drop off.

The National Counter Terrorism Center, NCTC, was located in Mclean, Virginia, just a stone's throw from Tysons Corner in a modern custom built complex. As a direct result of 9/11, no expense had been spared on the building or the capabilities of its inhabitants. With expertise from across the law enforcement spectrum, the building housed the National Joint Terrorism Task Force, which would take the lead on tracking down their current number one target, Nick Geller. Further strengthened by their most recent additions, the team had access to over a hundred similar teams across the nation in regional sites.

The sight that met Carson and the freshly showered Frankie was of organized chaos. Or at least chaos, they just hoped it was organized.

Desks were being doubled up. Space was at a premium. Phones and computers were being hooked up as fast as technicians could keep up with the additional bodies that were flooding in as a response to the attack. Deputy Director Turner stood on a gangway that skirted around the three-story main intelligence room. He was looking down at the activity below, a captive audience who was reacting to him as he barked out orders.

Turner spotted Carson and beckoned him up. Carson took Frankie by the elbow and led her up the stairs with him.

"We have a lead," said Turner, walking them back towards his office. "And we need some assets."

"Of course," replied Carson, following Turner into his office with Frankie in tow.

"A Saudi prince," Turner said, causing Carson to stop him and look at Frankie.

Frankie stepped outside, closing the door behind her.

"What was that?" asked Turner.

"I'll tell you later," said Carson.

"A Saudi prince, Prince Abdullah Bin Fahd Al Khaled, left Leesburg Executive Airport about forty minutes after the attack and explosion. Two people boarded the flight, an Arab woman in full burka and the prince."

"And?"

"We have no idea who the woman is. It was believed to be his mother or aunt, but both have now been accounted for elsewhere."

"Shit, where's the plane now?" asked Carson.

"That's the thing, they filed a flight plan direct to Riyadh but they've just commenced a descent towards an airport on the northern French coast."

"Get me a phone. I'll have the flight intercepted. That is exceptionally fast work!" congratulated Carson.

Turner pointed to the phone on his desk. Carson walked across the room and lifted the receiver. "What do we know about the prince?"

"Very wealthy, bit of a playboy, and up until now nothing other than a few rumors of funding a few militant groups but all covered as humanitarian support for refugees and the displaced. Nothing has ever been proved and to be honest, he has a number of friends on the Hill."

"How much time until they land and where?"

Turner checked his computer screen. "Twenty minutes at Le Touquet, Northern France."

Carson retrieved his cell, scrolled though his contacts and dialed a number that got him through to the Supreme Allied Commander of NATO forces in Europe. After a brief and exceptionally frustrating catch up, Carson finally got around to requesting the interception of the prince's plane.

"How connected is this prince within the royal family?" asked Carson of Turner, removing the handset and covering the mouthpiece.

Turner checked his watch. They were down to ten minutes before the landing.

"What difference does it make?"

"Don't be so naïve," countered Carson sharply.

"He's more connected here than in Saudi Arabia. He's pretty much an outsider there from all reports."

Carson relayed the information, giving the commander the 'go'.

"All done," he announced, replacing the handset.

"They'll be landing in eight minutes," said Turner, checking his watch again.

"No they won't," smiled Carson confidently.

Chapter 13

RAF Lakenheath was concealed deep in Thetford Forest, less than sixty miles from London and just 117 miles from Le Touquet, on the northeastern tip of France. Travelling at sixty miles an hour, it would take the same in minutes as the measurement in miles. However, a McDonnell Douglas F15 on afterburners will cover almost thirty miles for every minute, travelling at over two and half times the speed of sound, or 1,700 miles per hour.

Although called RAF Lakenheath, it was in fact almost exclusively manned by USAF personnel and equipment and was home to the 48th Fighter Wing. With two fighters on constant patrol, the two F15 pilots allocated the task by the Supreme Commander of European Forces had little to do but point their jets in the right direction and hit the afterburners. They would be on site in time to intercept the prince's jet before landing and before hitting the French mainland, with two minutes to spare. Not that they had any issue with crossing over onto mainland France – the French would be more than happy to assist. They just wanted to minimize collateral damage wherever possible.

***

Nick readied himself for a fast exit. There wasn't going to be lot of time. The pilot had made it very clear how unhappy he was. The money had convinced him to do it but no amount of money was going to make him happy about it. Fortunately, the pilot and co-pilot were blissfully unaware that Nick was the most wanted man on the planet. Once that came to light, the prince was going to have to dig even deeper into his pockets. Of course, there was the fact that if they ever did open their mouths, they would be admitting that they had not checked the identity of one of their passengers before departure. Nick had a sneaking suspicion that it may not take that much more money to keep them quiet. After all, pilots tended to be highly intelligent individuals.

He checked his backpack again, along with the slim metal briefcase that secured one of the most lethal viruses known to man. Nick did not enjoy carrying it around and looked forward to securing it in a safety deposit box as soon as physically possible. Maximizing the virus' effectiveness required very precise timing and conditions. It was one of the last phases of his plan and until then, he just had to make sure the seals and the contents remained secure.

"You ready?" Nick asked the prince.

The prince's face said no but he nodded. Nick turned to the stewardess who sat in the jump seat by the exit door. "Ready?"

She nodded, double checking her straps were properly secured.

Nick checked the door through to the bedroom. It was shut and the other two stewardesses were also strapped in and the cockpit door was secure.

"We've just been hailed by two American fighters," came a panicked announcement by the pilot over the internal P.A. system. "They're going to shoot us down if we don't do what they say!"

"Okay, now!" Nick yelled to the stewardess, as a rush of air blasted into their faces.

***

"So why did you react when I mentioned the Saudi prince?" asked Turner nodding towards Frankie out on the gangway. The silence, while they waited for an update, was deafening.

"How much do you know about her?" asked Carson warily.

"Other than she's a Secret Service agent, obviously trusted by the President, despite her boyfriend trying to kill him and blowing up his house, and the fact that he insists she is part of the investigation, very little."

"Well I suggest we learn a lot more very quickly. Her mother's a Saudi princess."

Turner's head snapped back again to look at Frankie. "No fucking way!"

Carson nodded. "I've got her file being sent to me as we speak. I've just been to her house, trust me, it's not bullshit. She lives in a mini palace behind Mom and Dad's full sized one."

"Do you think…" Turner didn't want to finish what he was about to say.

"Honestly, no. However, Nick Geller is a very smart cookie and he may just have been using her for more than a booty call," interrupted Carson.

"We're just about to debrief her but it may all become a bit irrelevant very shortly," suggested Turner, checking his watch again for the tenth time in less than two minutes. Almost on cue, the desk phone rang. Turner let Carson answer it.

Carson listened for a few seconds before replacing the handset.

"We got them," he smiled triumphantly.

"So are the French going to hand him straight over to us?"

Carson looked at him strangely. "Why would the French have them?"

"Because they just captured them at Le Touquet," replied Turner, somewhat confused.

"No they didn't, we just stopped them getting to France!" said Carson.

"I thought you sent a team to get them when they landed?' asked Turner, his mind spinning.

"Le Touquet's in the middle of fucking nowhere. Do you think we've got Special Ops teams all over the world, ten minutes from anywhere?" asked Carson irritably.

"No but—"

"I sent two fighter jets to stop them landing in France and getting away."

"Fighter jets? What the fuck have you done?" Turner shouted. He worked for the FBI. They followed process, they followed the law. They were not judge jury and executioner.

Carson laughed awkwardly. "I guess you'll find out soon enough," he said cryptically before leaving an infuriated and dumbfounded Turner to stew.

Chapter 14

"Come with me," ordered Carson, slamming Turner's door behind him.

Frankie looked at the infuriated Turner before quickly following Carson.

"Where are we going?" she asked.

He turned into an office at the end of the gangway. A plaque stamped DOD adorned the front of the door. Two officers sat at two of the four desks that took up half the room. The other half had a conference table with ten chairs.

"Out!" barked Carson at the two officers.

Neither questioned the authority with which he had evicted them. They just assumed and correctly, that if somebody barked an order at them, it was presumably someone of a higher rank.

"Sit," he ordered Frankie, pointing to the conference table.

Frankie stood her ground.

Carson glared at her, she glared back. Carson smiled sarcastically, she smiled sarcastically back. Carson smiled warmly. "My apologies, please could you take a seat?"

Frankie sat.

Carson took a seat opposite her and put his hands up in surrender. "I'm sorry, Turner just really pissed me off."

"What did he do?"

Carson laughed. "You know, I'm not really sure. He just acted like an FBI guy does, you know?"

Frankie smiled. "Hmm, yes," she said nodding. "Like we're all beneath them and their standards."

"Exactly," said Carson snapping his fingers and pointing at her. "He assumed I had the prince's plane shot down, like I'm some sort of trigger-happy lunatic."

"Did he apologize?"

"What for?"

"Being wrong."

Carson smiled wickedly. "I didn't tell him he was," he shrugged. "If that's what he thinks of me."

"So what have you done with it?" she asked wondering what had become of Nick.

"We're just about to find out," he said, hitting a dial button on the teleconference machine that sat in the center of the table. "Either, they're on their way back to Lakenheath or…" he shrugged again.

"Or they shot it down?" she gasped.

"Only if the pilots failed to follow directions," explained Carson, realizing he had in fact given the order Turner had accused him of so outrageously. "I suppose we have a reputation for good reason."

Frankie held her breath as the confirmation came through. The Gulfstream had followed directions and would be landing at Lakenheath within the hour.

Carson killed the phone line and retrieving a laptop from one of the desks, pulled up an email that had been sent to him in the previous few minutes.

"Okay, Frankie," he said, "it's time we find out a little more about you and Mr Nick Geller."

Frankie shifted uncomfortably. "I assumed I'd be speaking to the FBI."

"You will, I just want to know you're telling them the right thing."

"I'll tell them the truth," she replied quickly.

"Of course, I'd just like to hear it first please," he said.

Colonel Valerie Barnes slipped into the room quietly and took a seat next to Carson. Frankie eyed her carefully while Colonel Barnes smiled at her warmly.

"Colonel Barnes," said Frankie nervously.

"Please, just Val. I'm a doctor who just happens to work for the Army."

"Doctor Barnes," corrected Frankie.

"Does he know?" asked Val.

"Does who know what?" asked Frankie, looking from one of them to the other.

"Does Nick know?"

Frankie's barrier broke and she shook her head, tears trying to flow once again. Frankie pushed them back. She wasn't a crier.

Carson was struggling to keep up when he finally understood. "Shit!"

"It's the hormones, they're raging inside you at the moment. They'll calm down," promised Val.

Frankie removed another piece of toilet tissue to dry her eyes.

"But how did *you* know?" asked Carson.

"The blood test for the virus," she replied.

"You see," said Carson, "there's something the FBI don't need to know and not telling them isn't not telling them the truth."

Frankie looked at him warily. "But why?"

"Nick Geller was one of ours," he said. "The fallout is going to be huge and the Secretary of Defense and the President would like me to manage that. Politics is a difficult enough power game. Let's just say there are some within the corridors of power who may try and use this situation to their political advantage. There are many in Washington who would like to see the Defense Department on its knees, irrespective of how it makes us look to our enemies or even how it affects the security of our nation."

"Okay, but I want to see President Mitchell first."

Chapter 15

The Gulfstream jet drew to a stop as indicated by the ground controller. A section of Lakenheath's apron had been sectioned off specifically for its arrival. The welcoming party that awaited them caused instant panic inside the prince's jet.

The pilot grabbed his mic. "Your Highness, just what the fuck is going on?" he asked across the internal P.A. system, the panic in his voice evident.

The prince unbuckled himself and rushed into the cockpit. The sight of dozens of men dressed in full biohazard suits was not a sight anyone wanted to see, particularly when you weren't wearing one yourself.

The prince, although panicking, tried to regain his composure. His Caliph needed him. His Caliph had *selected* him.

"Just stick to the plan," he said, looking intensely into the eyes of the pilot and co-pilot. "I'll double what we've already agreed!" They may be mercenaries but even they had their limits. "Okay, ten times!" the prince blurted. The subtle smiles told him he had just hit theirs.

The Prince drew himself to his full royal stature and made his way to the exit where the stewardess opened the door. He was greeted by a wall of armed men dressed in hazard suits.

"What is the meaning of this!" he shouted in his most indignant voice. He did indignant very well. "This is an outrage!"

The Base Commander stepped forward. "We have reason to believe that you are harboring a wanted fugitive on board."

"If any of my staff are international fugitives, please take them away," he said angrily. "But I seriously doubt that any of them have done anything to warrant this treatment. I demand to see the Foreign Secretary!"

"If you and your staff will exit the plane, I'm sure we can sort this out very quickly," replied the Colonel.

"Of course, but I must ask, is it safe?' he asked, looking across at the field of hazard suits in front of him.

"These are to protect us from the fugitive."

Outwardly, the prince didn't flinch. Inwardly, his intestines wanted to explode. What the hell had he been exposed to? A whisper from behind him asked "Double again?"

He nodded slightly before walking down the steps ahead of his pilot and co-pilot who had just earned a $40 million bonus between them. The stewardesses followed next, and behind them a woman dressed head to toe in full burka.

"Feel free to check," announced the prince waving the armed guards towards the plane.

Base Security searched the plane, every square inch, before exiting and with a shake of the head towards the Colonel, confirmed it was empty.

The Colonel checked the photo of Nick Geller once again against the two pilots, the stewardesses, and the eyes of the woman behind the burka. He called a female airwoman over.

"Your Highness," he asked, "would you mind if my female colleague took the lady aboard and confirmed she is not who we are looking for?"

The prince looked at the Colonel in disbelief. The burka, although covering the woman's body and face, could not hide her eyes. They were as beautiful as any woman's eyes could possibly be, emerald green and sparkling.

"You obviously have a different type of man where you live," he snorted and waved his acceptance with one sweep of his hand towards the plane.

The airwoman and burka-clad woman boarded the plane before reappearing shortly after the woman in the burka had shown her face to the airwoman. The airwoman, unsurprisingly, shook her head as she exited the plane.

"May I ask why you wanted to change your plans and land at le Touquet?" asked the Colonel politely.

"I do not see why it is any of your business," snapped the prince haughtily. "But if you must know, my friend," he said, pointing to the lady in the burka, "has been unwell and a plane is no place for a beautiful lady to be sick."

The Colonel nodded and excused himself for a few moments to make a call. After speaking to a furious and highly embarrassed Supreme Commander, he was routed directly to Deputy Director Turner, the man in charge of the investigation. Carson was nowhere to be found.

"Deputy Director Turner," said the Colonel, "I'm the Base Commander at USAF Lakenheath in Engla—"

"It's your guys that shot down my suspect?" Turner cut in disgustedly.

"Shot him down? What the hell are you talking about? They were in a civilian aircraft!"

Turner stopped in his tracks and revisited the conversation with Carson. He hadn't ever said he was shooting it down, just that he was not letting it land in France.

"Sorry, it's been a long day. How can I help?"

"You can help by telling me why I have just diverted a seriously pissed off member of the Saudi royal family for no good fucking reason!"

"You've got them there?" Turner asked excitedly.

"Touched down a few minutes ago," he confirmed. "We've searched the plane, your man's not there."

"He has to be!"

"He's not."

"He was disguised in a burka," said Turner.

"Well he's had the best sex change operation in history, because trust me, under that material is a very beautiful, and I mean *very* beautiful woman."

"But the woman in the burka was bent double and struggled to board the plane here."

"The prince said she was unwell earlier," replied the Colonel.

"Shit! And the two pilots and three stewardesses aren't talking?"

"No, they're just standing there wondering what in the hell we crazy Americans are… wait a minute, you said *three* stewardesses?"

"Yes, three!"

"There are only two here," said the Colonel, rushing back to the plane.

***

Nick hit the water hard. The cold Atlantic waters bit into his skin and deep into the bone. His breath left him as the water began to drag him down into its depths. The water-logged parachute weighed over twenty times its dry weight, the perfect anchor for the disposal of unwanted bodies. Nick managed to grab the knife from his belt and slash at the cords. The parachute drifted down towards the ocean bed and he was propelled upwards. When he breached the surface, he gasped desperately for every breath of air.

The prince's Gulfstream jet was already a dot on the horizon when the first fighter jet screeched overhead. A sharp bank brought it around, closing the distance on the world's fastest corporate jet as though it were hovering stationary, such was the difference in speeds. A second jet appeared as the first's sonic boom hit him. His ears felt like they would explode and another boom was about to hit. He ducked under the water, the cold almost as shocking and damaging to his ears as the noise.

He checked the metal briefcase was still strapped across his chest and broke the surface once again, checked the small compass on his wrist, and started the long, slow swim ashore. Best guess, he was three to four miles from the shore, a good two hours' swim. With darkness falling, the lights on shore would help keep him on course.

***

The Colonel returned a few minutes later to the call with the exasperated Turner.

"They claim one of the stewardesses was so unwell before they took off that they left her behind," explained the Colonel.

"Bullshit!" spat Turner.

"All their stories are consistent. They've even given the hotel room and details of where you'll find her in Washington."

"Of course they have! Some stand-in, no doubt. Do you believe them?"

"Nope," replied the Colonel.

"Is there anywhere they could have landed and dropped him off?"

"I doubt it. The timings suggest they flew directly here. And according to where you started tracking them, there was nothing but ocean below."

"And they never reached France?"

"Intercepted before then."

"Shit!"

"What do I do about the prince? He's starting to have a shit fit here," said the Colonel.

"Nick Geller is definitely not on board?"

"Definitely not. We've searched everywhere feasibly and unfeasibly possible for a person to be. The prince is demanding to see the Foreign Minister here in the UK or failing that, the US Ambassador."

Turner thought for a second before making the biggest mistake of his career. "I suppose we'd better let him go on his way," he said, resigned to the fact that the hunt was back on.

Turner replaced the handset and set off to find Carson. He had an apology to make as well as informing him they still hadn't got their man.

After five minutes of looking, he was advised of Carson's imminent departure to see the President with Frankie. He ran to the helicopter pad and caught them just as they were about to board.

He dragged both of them back towards the building, struggling to be heard over the noise of the helicopter's engines. He quickly brought them up to speed.

"So he must have gotten off mid-flight," said Carson matter-of-factly. Turner looked at him, confused.

"You can't just open a door and jump out of a jet," said Turner.

"What do you think parachutists do every day of the week?!"

"Even if he did, how the hell would we ever find him?" asked Turner. "They flew over 2,500 miles before we stopped them."

"Easy," replied Carson. "The black box will tell you exactly where and when they opened the door."

"Fuck!" said Turner, his head dropping.

"What?"

"They just left!"

Chapter 16

Frankie boarded the chopper and let Carson take the front seat. A very pissed off Turner stood and watched their departure. He had made it clear he wanted to interview Frankie immediately. Carson, keen to control the political fallout and flow of information, was going to get Frankie on board whatever it took, even lying that the President had asked to see her. As Carson pointed out to Turner, he had more pressing priorities: a plane to re-catch and a black box to retrieve.

The helicopter climbed and with Turner safely out of sight, Frankie could speak. She leaned forward to speak into Carson's ear on the far side of the pilot.

"You made out you knew nothing but you knew everything that Turner told you?" she asked quietly. Carson had received a call just prior to Turner's arrival from a very unhappy Supreme Commander of European Forces.

Carson nodded.

"You didn't suggest the black box either when you were told."

Carson turned around to face Frankie. "To be honest, it just came to me."

"If you had thought of it faster, you could have stopped the plane leaving."

Carson nodded.

"So you are as much to blame as Turner?"

Harry Carson had worked for four different administrations over the previous thirty years, nobody ever really knowing what he did or who he worked for. He was the quiet guy at the back of the room, the guy who was always invited but nobody knew by whom, the guy who seldom spoke but when he did everybody listened. Harry Carson's contact list read like a who's who of the most powerful individuals over the previous three decades, yet he had never run for office nor been voted into any position of power by the American public. Harry Carson had that very special gift very few people had. He made things happen in the corridors of power. He delivered.

He smiled back at Frankie. "Maybe, but only you and I know that," he winked. Turner was going to take the flak for the fuck-up. Carson never took the blame for anything, only ever the credit. He had thirty years of eating Turners and spitting them out for breakfast.

"You told him the President wanted to see me?"

"I'm sure he does. He'll need cheering up and I'm sure he'd be delighted to see you," replied Carson.

"But what if Turner checks?"

"The President will tell him he wanted to see you," said Carson confidently.

Frankie shook her head. "But he doesn't."

Carson simply smiled.

Frankie sat back in her seat. "What is it you do exactly?"

"I'm just someone who helps out when required," replied Carson.

"Helps out who?"

Carson smiled and turned back to the window and the view of the approaching Walter Reed Hospital.

***

President James Mitchell sat up in the hospital bed as they entered. The pain in his face made it clear that the TV address earlier that day had been staged. At least in the respect that they had hidden just how badly injured the President really was.

"Mr. President." Frankie maintained her professionalism despite her instincts to rush over and hug the man she'd been in close contact with over the previous few years.

"It's good to see you, Frankie," he said warmly, biting back the pain.

"I'm so sorry, Mr. President, I can't believe he fooled me." She broke down in to tears again. *Jesus*, she thought, fighting them back. She hadn't cried since she was a child until that day.

The President beckoned her towards him and placed his good arm around her to console her.

Bill and Carson watched on as one of the most highly trained female law enforcement officers in the land, experienced in all forms of self defense and trained to kill when required, approached the man who, just a few hours earlier, had almost been killed by her boyfriend. Neither flinched or thought it inappropriate. Aisha Franks, daughter of a Saudi princess, hugged the President and wept on his shoulder.

There could have been no greater show of trust and faith in her as an innocent caught up in a terrible tragedy.

Frankie stood up. Her tears were finished. "What can I do for you, Mr. President?"

"Trust Harry."

Chapter 17

Turner watched the helicopter disappear out of view and more importantly, out of earshot before hitting the dial button on his cell phone. He paced while the phone rang and rang. Nobody picked up. He killed the line and rushed back to his office. He grabbed his desk phone and dialed the number again. He consoled himself with the thought of the time it took to refuel, taxi to the runway and get clearance for takeoff, it had only been about nine minutes. The line rang and rang again.

The Colonel answered, gasping for breath as he rushed to grab the ringing phone.

"Keep them there!" blurted Turner.

"What? Who is this?" replied the Colonel catching his breath and taking a seat.

"FBI Deputy Director Turner."

"They are gone *Mister* Turner," replied the Colonel coldly.

"Well get your planes up and get them back!" ordered Turner.

"On whose authority?"

"Mine!"

"I've just had a new asshole chewed into me by a Saudi prince who assures me he has the connections to kill my career. He's already promised I'll be in the Arctic for the rest of my career. What can you promise me *Mister* Turner?"

"You'll still *have* a career," said Turner boldly.

"Unfortunately for you I believe him far more than I do you, and the sad thing is I think you know that's true."

"The black box on the plane will tell us where they opened the doors and let the suspect escape."

"And you know for an absolute fact that happened?"

"We assume—"

"Assume! What a very appropriate word, makes an *ass* of *u* and *me*" interrupted the Colonel.

"We can't see any other explanation."

"I can. Perhaps the stewardess did get ill and she did leave and nobody noticed her going."

"Look, we know the prince is tied up in terrorist activity."

"Yet we let him fly in and out of America and have contact with senior officials?"

"Well, we don't have any actual proof, we just know." Turner winced at how weak he sounded.

"*Mister* Turner, I am going to end this call. If the President or the Secretary of Defense or State orders me to retake that plane with their written authority, it will be done without hesitation. Anyone else, not a chance. We can't just order planes out of the sky with threats of violence, particularly when we know the suspect is not on board. Goodbye."

"Fuck!" screamed Turner into the empty line. There wasn't a chance in hell that anyone was going to allow him to pluck the plane out of the sky again. Certainly not based on a hunch that a man may have jumped out of the plane at some point over the Atlantic. But you'd need to be jumping somewhere and the middle of the ocean wouldn't be somewhere, it was nowhere.

He hit his intercom and connected with his assistant.

"Get me a large scale map of the Atlantic Ocean and Northern Europe, an aviation expert and anyone in the building who was trained to jump out of planes!"

Chapter 18

With every degree rise in temperature, Nick knew he was just that little bit closer to shore. The depths of the ocean gave way to the sands of the shoreline and he approached the shore, checking for any passersby. It was approaching midnight in France. The beach was deserted. He had visited the same beach three months earlier. The vast expanse of sand stretched for miles but, in the almost forgotten northeast of France, even in the height of summer, the beaches were never filled.

He checked his bearings. Merlimont Plage was just a half mile north. After a two-minute breather, he began the walk along the beach, picking up the pace as the first sounds of helicopters began to break through the stillness of the night. A bright spot a few miles to the north, just off shore from Le Touquet, was all he needed to know that they were looking for him. Another bright spot appeared in the sky, only nearer. Searchlights glared down on the ground and sea below.

Nick knew that was the least of his worries. The chances of them picking him out in the spotlight were minimal to nil. His biggest worry was the infrared and thermal imaging devices that would be accompanying the light. The spotlight was the secondary tool to pinpoint what they had already seen.

Nick made it into the small seaside village while the search was still concentrating a couple of miles to the north. He smiled at the small green Renault Clio, almost ten years old, that had received a number of polite messages to move it. Although parked perfectly legally, the apartment owners who assumed ownership of the spaces in front of their beachside apartments during the summer were obviously perturbed at the length of time the mystery car had been parked in front of their building. Nick bent down and retrieved the key taped inside the small tailpipe. He opened the car, popped the hood and connected the battery. The car, thanks to its age and simplicity, started on the first turn of the ignition key, despite being inactive for over three months. Nick checked his mirror and pulled away.

He retrieved the roadmap from the glove box and glanced at his chosen route - the direct route to Paris would be using the main A16 toll road. However, at that time of night and in that area of France, he'd be one of the only vehicles on the road. They were already looking for him off the Le Touquet coast, which meant there was every chance they may also check the roads, especially the main road.

Nick took the back roads option and began the long drive to Paris. It was in contrast to the race he had undertaken three months earlier to place the car without being missed. Catching an earlier Eurostar service between Paris and London, he had hopped off at Calais and purchased the Clio for cash before driving it back down to Merlimont Plage and leaving it there. He'd then jogged the few miles back to Le Touquet, took a taxi back to Calais to catch the next Eurostar train, and arrived in London at the time he had arranged to meet his colleagues from DIA. With all purchases in cash and no time unaccounted for, nobody had been any the wiser.

The dark and empty roads allowed perfect thinking time for Nick. His meticulous planning and preparation had finally come to fruition. The adrenaline was pumping through his body. Although just over a year, it felt so much longer since that fateful day in Afghanistan.

Memories had been triggered as he watched the scene unfold before him. Young children played carefree while their mothers prepared the evening meal, chatting and joking as they watched over the young ones. A few shouts echoed across the hillside as warnings were issued to keep the children away from harm.

All the time constant updates were being fed into Nick's ear. His hilltop vantage point was one of many spread across the Kunar province, one of the main smuggling routes between Afghanistan and Pakistan. His job was to spot drugs leaving and munitions entering, and call in air strikes when necessary. Over the previous ten years, between his time in the Rangers, Delta Force and the Defense Clandestine Service, he had spent nearly six years in the region and had witnessed more than any man ever should. The sight of the children playing so innocently filled him with hope that one day it may finally be over.

With the sun hanging low in the sky and evening approaching, the families began to gather around a fire that had been prepared. It seemed a celebration was under way. The village was nothing more than a few ramshackle buildings built around a small communal area at its center. Nick watched the celebrations commence. They were for a wedding. His headset burst to life, his call sign was followed by a notification that a drone strike was inbound.

Nick requested the details of the strike. He was informed that information had come to light of a gathering of senior Al Qaeda and Taliban leaders at the village. After confirming the wedding that was taking place contained the villagers and that no visitors had arrived over the previous few days under his watch, he requested the strike be cancelled. The request was denied.

Nick broke cover and ran as fast as his legs would carry him across the rocky terrain. With literally seconds to spare, he cleared the village and saved the fifty innocents that would have been slaughtered. Caught in the blast, he suffered a concussion and woke up the following day in a camp surrounded by the fighters he had spent the last six years hunting.

Nick Geller couldn't have been happier.

Chapter 19

Carson held the door for Frankie as they arrived back at the NCTC. The activity level had increased above the already hectic pace from when they had left. Frankie headed straight for Turner's office, Carson following close behind. Frankie's meeting with the President had given her a newfound energy. The toxic feeling that had plagued her all day was brushed aside by the one man whose opinion truly counted.

Turner barely acknowledged their presence as he pored over a map with a group of agents.

"Did you get the black box?" asked Carson, looking at the large scale map of Northern France and Southern England.

"No," said Turner, "but we think we may not need it. Lieutenant, can you explain?" he asked, turning his attention back to the map.

A fresh faced young man stood upright and turned to face Carson and Frankie. "It's quite simple really, they couldn't open the door at high altitude as they'd have to depressurize the cabin, killing everyone inside. Therefore, the only opportunity to leave the plane was at any point they dipped below the point at which the cabin pressure was equal or above that of their surroundings. The aircraft was a Gulfstream G650 which maintains cabin pressure at an altitude equivalent to between 2,850 feet and 4,850 feet, depending on the altitude of the plane. So for example, if they were flying at anything up to 41,000 feet, the cabin pressure inside the plane would be maintained at 2,850 feet which is very low. Most commercial planes have the pressure in the cabin at the equivalent of about 8,000 feet. The lower the pressure, the more comfortable the ride."

"Okay," nodded Frankie, following the logic.

"So we have tracked the plane's route and the only point at which they flew below this level was as they approached Le Touquet."

"Or just after takeoff?" suggested Carson.

"Well, yes, technically," replied the Lieutenant awkwardly.

"But that makes no sense," smiled Carson, patting the lieutenant on the back. "It's good work, Lieutenant, very good work."

"So what's the area?" asked Carson, pushing into the group to get a clear view of the map.

Turner pointed towards a large oval drawn over the English Channel, stretching from twenty miles out to sea to three miles from the coast.

"We're concentrating efforts at the last point before the F-15s had them in sight," he said, pointing to three miles from shoreline. "From their reports, there was no way anything fell or left the aircraft once they were on scene. From that, we guess he could still be swimming ashore or already in this area," he added, circling the area around Le Touquet. "We have the French covering this whole area and we're sending every asset we can get our hands on to assist."

"That seems like a very premature descent," said Carson, tracking the oval out to the twenty miles off shore point.

"It's exceptionally early," confirmed the Lieutenant.

"Almost like it was planned?" suggested Carson.

Turner looked up from the map. "What, are you saying he jumped twenty miles from shore?"

"It's one of the busiest waterways in the world with many large vessels that a competent parachutist could easily land on."

Turner looked at the lieutenant. Up until Carson's arrival, he had been his aviation specialist. The lieutenant nodded that it was possible. "It would explain the very early descent towards Le Touquet."

Turner shook his head in despair. Every time he thought he was gaining some ground, it was lost. "We're going to need a lot more resources," he said, turning to Carson.

Carson nodded his head and took out his cell. He had contacts in the British and French navies that he knew would be more than happy to assist.

As the net expanded across the entire English Channel, Turner realized once again that Nick may have slipped through their fingers. "Frankie, are you okay to talk now?"

Frankie nodded.

Turner led her through to the adjacent room where a team of suited agents were working. The walls were covered in just about everything they knew of Nick Geller. Photos of his childhood were pinned to the wall next to photos of Nick with Frankie.

"Frankie, I know this isn't going to be easy," Turner said sincerely, "but we really need to know everything you know about Nick, no matter how insignificant."

Frankie nodded again and took a seat. Turner introduced her to the six agents in the room, three from the FBI, two from CIA and one from DIA, a colleague of Nick's that Frankie had previously met. She smiled at a friendly face who, like her, was shell-shocked at Nick's betrayal.

Special Agent Sarah Reid kicked off proceedings. "Can you tell me what you know of Nick's background and family?"

Frankie took a deep breath and a sip of water. "His parents were Jewish Americans having moved here from Tel Aviv just before Nick's birth. Unfortunately, they both died when Nick was a teenager and he spent a few years in various foster homes before joining the forces as soon as he could."

Agent Reid nodded her head as she ticked off the numerous points with the information she had before her.

"How did you meet Nick Geller?"

"Wait a minute," said Flynn, the DIA agent who had been a colleague of Nick's and whom Frankie had met previously. "As hard as this is for Frankie, I think it's only fair that we bring her up to speed with what we know so far. It's certainly helped me focus on catching him."

"Like you needed an added incentive? He shot the President and blew up the White House!" said one of the CIA agents angrily. Interagency cooperation was alive and well.

"Don't be an asshole, Barry, you know what I mean."

"Okay guys, cut the bullshit," intervened Turner, nodding for Special Agent Reid to continue.

"His parents weren't Jewish. After a lot of digging, we discovered they were originally from Lebanon. It looks like they managed to escape the civil war and made their way into Israel and from there, came here to America. They were Shi'a Muslims."

Frankie was shaking her head. "But he's not Muslim, he talked about his Jewish heritage a lot."

"All a sham," Reid replied, producing some photos of a teenage Nick in a mosque with his parents. "We found these in a safety deposit box at his bank. When his parents died in an auto accident, he was cared for by three different foster families."

Frankie nodded and another photo was set before her, a slightly older Nick with an Imam. Frankie recognized the Imam as a radical preacher that the US had spent years fighting to deport.

"His last foster parents were neighbors of the Imam," said Reid.

"Jesus! They've been planning this all these years?" asked Frankie, trying to comprehend what it all meant.

"We don't think so. We believe his parents began the pretense of being Jewish in order to gain entry more easily and once in the country, we can't find anything to suggest that they were anything but hard working citizens. They attended and made donations to their local synagogue. They did secretly attend a mosque, but it has no history of radicalism. It was after their death that we think Nick may have turned to a more radical doctrine."

Frankie sat with her mouth agape. If she had thought she couldn't be any more surprised, she was wrong. Nick was the least religious guy she had ever met. As a Jew, he was terrible. His favorite sandwich was ham and cheese. She was constantly reminding him that he wasn't supposed to eat pork. A radical Muslim? It just didn't make sense, at least not on its own. But along with everything else that had taken place that day, it made perfect sense.

Chapter 20

Nick followed the street cleaners and refuse collectors through the almost deserted streets of Paris. When he neared the Seine Saint Denis Departement, a large suburb to the northeast of Paris, the number of street cleaners and refuse collectors began to dwindle. This was the forgotten corner of Paris. The high-rise apartment blocks had been quickly erected in the 1970s to house the ever-growing immigrant population and were now falling into disrepair. The blocks secured the gentrification of the jewel in the French crown, central Paris, but left the immigrant communities on the outskirts of society. Crime and violence flared, as did the radicalization of youth.

Nick stopped the car and parked outside a large block of flats that loomed over the skyline. Graffiti besieged the ground floor while the upper stories would have benefitted from the paint afforded by the vandals. He reached into the glove compartment and, despite the darkness, opted to alter his hair and to wear spectacles. He combed in white powder that speckled his dark and youthful hair into that of a mature man with graying temples. The glasses added another five years. It was the simplest disguise but more than enough for the casual passerby to consider Nick a man in his forties rather than early thirties.

Reaching under his seat, he retrieved a Berretta M9 pistol. A few more weapons were secured in a locked box in the trunk but Nick opted for the subtle approach. The Berretta could be easily hidden and would give him the chance to gain entry without too much alarm being raised. He stepped out of the car and stuffed the Berretta into the back of his belt under his shirt, grabbed the metal briefcase, and approached the apartment block as the first rays of sunlight began to creep through the dark sky.

The entrance door hung on its hinges and its glass portions were replaced by graphitized plywood. The entrance lobby stank of stale urine and the elevator door sat unwelcomingly open. Nick looked at it briefly and went for the staircase. He opened the door to the staircase and began his climb to the tenth floor.

When he reached the fifth floor, he rounded the corner into a welcoming party. Three young men blocked his way to the higher floors. Obviously roused from their beds in a rush, one had no shoes or shirt on, while another's hair stood on end. The third was yawning.

"Bonjour," said Nick jovially.

"This building is private, fuck off," replied the tousled hair youth in French.

"Not for me," remarked Nick in Arabic, catching them all by surprise.

"For everybody," insisted the tousled hair youth again in French, though with a little more respect.

"I have business with Mohammed Farsi."

The shoeless youth stepped forward. "He does not have business with you." He was the largest of the three and it was obvious why his shirt was left off. His muscle definition was impressive.

Nick made a point of looking at the youth's naked feet, before looking up into his eyes. "He does, he just doesn't know it yet. Tell him I come with a message from the Caliph," ordered Nick with a menace in his voice that had the youth stepping back, particularly given Nick's inordinate interest in his feet.

The yawner watched Nick closely for a moment, then turned and retreated back up the stairs. The two others waited awkwardly, watching Nick lean casually against the wall. His demeanor was such that they had no illusion this was not a man they should be very wary of. The yawner returned and nodded to his colleagues.

"Next time, take the time to put your shoes on," advised Nick, brushing past the shoeless man.

Nick was led up to the tenth floor and met at the door by Mohammed Farsi. The man was flanked by another two youths, although these two had guns drawn, ready to use. They tracked Nick as he walked towards them. Mohammed Farsi's expression changed from confusion to bewilderment, once he realized who was walking towards him.

"I don't know if I should hug you as a brother or shoot you as a traitor!" exclaimed Mohammed.

"A brother," said Nick handing him a copy of the DVD he had shown the prince. "I will wait here while you watch it," he said, then turned to Tousled Hair and tossed him his car keys and asking him a favor.

The hug that followed the watching of the DVD meant that all weapons were withdrawn and Nick was invited into the home of the most senior member of Al Qaeda's French network. Nick had one goal over the next few days - securing the support of all the European fundamentalist groups.

He had an army to build and a war to begin.

Chapter 21

After three hours, during which Frankie related to Special Agent Reid her entire history with Nick, the questions finally stopped. Ultimately, she had nothing that would assist in the search for Nick. This equaled the grand total of what the search of her guesthouse had revealed. Nick had left clues about neither his secretive life nor his plans. Frankie felt the coolness towards her wear off when it became clear that she was not an accomplice or in any way involved.

"Thanks, Frankie, I appreciate that was not easy," concluded Turner. The rest of the group filtered out of the office, and once the last of them had left, he stood up and closed the door, keeping Carson and Frankie in the room.

"Just a couple more questions," he said, taking his seat again.

Frankie looked at Carson, aware of how he wanted to control information. "Of course."

"I'd like to know a little more about your family."

"I'm not entirely sure how that is relevant," interrupted Carson.

"I have no issue discussing my family," Frankie said. "My father is Albert Franks, born and raised in Houston, Texas. He went to college, then joined an oil firm as an accountant. In the late seventies, he was working in Saudi Arabia where he met my mother."

"Do you think Nick meeting you was planned?"

"I doubt it. We met at the White House and since no one there, except for President Mitchell and my boss, is aware of my heritage, I can't see how he could have known."

Carson bit his lip. Nick Geller was a highly trained intelligence officer and probably one of the best they had, if not *the* best. He would have known exactly who she was. However, telling Frankie that would make her feel even worse than she already did. He opted to let her think that she was bearing the child of a man who had loved her and not used her.

Unfortunately, Turner was not as thoughtful. "I highly doubt that, I'm afraid. Nick Geller had access to any personnel records he wanted. It is inconceivable that a man of his training would not have checked your history before making a move."

Frankie remained impassive at the thought that she had been used for some ulterior motive.

"Tell me about your mother."

"She was the twentieth child of my grandfather, born to his fourth wife. She was ten years younger than her closest sibling and was the baby of the house. She was my grandfather's favorite. She could do no wrong and as she grew up, he took her everywhere with him. From the stories I have been told, he was a hard man to his older children and alienated most of them. Having my mother in his fifties had softened him and made him appreciate his children far more. Although he was a prince, he was far removed from the king. He owned a lot of land in the oil rich desert and as a result, he had many interactions with American oil companies. It was on a trip to one of the oil fields that my parents met. By that time, my grandfather was dying and he saw the spark in my mother's eye when she met my father. My grandfather knew that when he died, her life would be nothing in Saudi Arabia. She'd bear children for a man who may take numerous wives. She was very intelligent and highly educated. Publicly he forbade their union, but privately he encouraged it. A letter from him tells of his proudest and saddest day, the day she got married to my father and the day he couldn't be with her to celebrate. He died shortly after her marriage."

"If he publicly forbade the union, I assume he left her nothing?" questioned Turner.

"Publicly yes, privately no."

Turner let the silence hang, waiting for more. Frankie didn't elaborate.

After a minute of the two looking at each other, Carson intervened. "Well I think that covers everything," he concluded.

"I'd like to know where your mother's money came from," Turner said.

"I don't see how that is relevant or any of your business," replied Frankie.

"Neither do I," replied Carson, standing up to leave.

"Prince Abdullah bin Fahd al Khaled, the man who smuggled your boyfriend out of the country, is your mother's cousin!"

Both Frankie and Carson laughed, much to Turner's chagrin. Before he could respond, there was a sharp knock on the office door and it opened. Special Agent Reid stepped in.

"We've got a lead on a car," she announced.

Chapter 22

Turner followed Reid out onto the gangway and looked down onto the operations floor below. The huge screens on the wall showed an aerial view of a small car travelling along a road in an urban area. Reid led Turner, Carson and Frankie down into the main center, filling them in along the way.

"We've been scouring whatever CCTV images we could get from France. There isn't much thanks to it being a weekend. They seem to close down on weekends."

Carson sighed knowingly. The French were a nightmare to work with. If they weren't on lunch, they had already left for the day or were on vacation whenever you tried to reach one of them.

"Anyway, what we have managed to retrieve has turned up a car at numerous locations between Le Touquet and Paris over the last few hours. The darkness has meant most images are very grainy but we did get one that confirmed our suspicions."

On cue, an image of Nick driving the Clio through a junction in a small French town was displayed on the screen.

"Excellent!" Turner exclaimed, congratulating everyone in the center.

Carson hit the dial button on his phone at the confirmation that Nick Geller was in France. He had two navies to stand down.

"We followed the images and have him driving through Paris for around one hour at around four a.m. local time. Unfortunately, we lost him just as he headed towards southern Paris."

Frankie looked at the image; it was definitely Nick. She looked across at the numerous locations that were being highlighted across Paris on a separate screen. Carson ended his calls and joined them and he too began to study the pinpointed sightings.

"Can that system draw a route, taking the time stamps of each sighting into account?" he asked. Frankie looked at Carson. He was thinking the same as her.

Reid nodded for the analyst to do what had been suggested. It'll just take a few minutes," confirmed the analyst.

"It appears from the image on the screen that we've just reacquired him?" she asked as much as told.

"Yep, we've got him on a KH-11 now," said Barry from the CIA, pointing to the live image on the main screen. "Heading south out of Paris."

"Why didn't you tell me sooner?" asked Turner.

"We just got the image ID. As soon as we knew it was definitely—"

"Okay, okay," waved Turner. He'd made his point.

"I have a SOG team inbound from Ramstein. ETA is about forty-five minutes at the airfield here, just North of Auxerre," said Barry, pointing to the airfield on the map. "The road here is the A5 which becomes the A6 and it's the road we're tracking him on. Our team will be in place just as he approaches Auxerre."

"What's a SOG team?" asked Frankie.

"Special Operations Group," said Carson. "A bit like a SEAL Team or Delta Force."

"Only better," said Barry, smiling and ignoring the looks of disagreement from Carson and Flynn from DIA. "Nick Geller is history. We've got a ten man team with an attack chopper and two Range Rovers on board."

"We could have a team there in an hour," suggested Flynn.

Turner understood his point; they'd rather deal with their own. But the CIA team would be on site first and it may be better for another agency to deal with the problem. "I think it's best we let the SOG team take him down."

Flynn nodded. "What about the police stopping him?"

"Too risky," said Carson. "It's going to be hard enough for the SOG team to take Nick down."

"Piece of piss, pardon the French," said Barry disdainfully.

Carson had had enough of the rhetoric and bullshit. "Be very clear and warn your guys that Nick Geller was one of our best. Make no mistake, this will not be a piece of piss, a walk in the park or any other fucking cliché you want to spout out."

Barry nodded halfheartedly, more a 'whatever' than a 'yes'.

"Barry, do you know our biggest problem in Defense at the moment?"

"Your boy just tried to kill the President?"

Carson ignored the cheap and rather pathetic shot. "Who is the guy we'd send to track and deal with Nick Geller, when he is the guy we'd send after himself?"

Barry struggled to understand what Carson had just said.

"He's saying that *Nick* is the guy that can catch Nick," explained Flynn succinctly. "Don't be so cocky, Barry, you'll just look all the more of an ass when he hands it to you."

"I've got the route," announced the analyst, breaking up the machismo display.

Frankie and Carson were first to move to the screen, keen to see if their thoughts were correct. It was what they had predicted. Flynn walked over and saw the same. Turner looked at the screen and saw a route that circled around on itself a number of times before dropping off the screen.

"He was lost?" asked Turner.

"Do you know how many CCTV cameras there are in France?" asked Carson.

"Millions?"

Carson shook his head. "In the UK, God yes, literally millions. In France, maybe a hundred thousand, probably less." He turned back to the analyst. "Can you show the placement of CCTV cameras on that map of Paris?"

The cameras appeared almost in sync with Nick's route around and around the French capital.

Barry reluctantly joined the group, and instantly saw what the others had noticed. "Shit, he wanted us to track him."

Carson and Frankie nodded in unison. "In all the time I've known Nick, he's taken the fastest and most direct route to anywhere," Frankie said ruefully. "Even when we're going places he's never been to, he checks it out and knows the route in advance."

"And that's exactly why your input is critical to this investigation," said Turner, almost congratulating himself for Frankie being there, despite having nothing whatsoever to do with her involvement.

They all looked back at the screen as the little Renault Clio continued its journey towards Auxerre and its imminent interception by the SOG team. Carson checked his watch. It was midnight.

"I'm going to call it a night," he said, much to everyone's astonishment. "It's been a long day!"

"We're about to catch him!" said Turner, perplexed.

"Let me know when you do. Frankie do you need a lift?"

Frankie nodded.

Chapter 23

Sunday 6th July.
France

The C130 landed just after 7:30 a.m. local time in Auxerre and taxied to a cleared area of the apron as requested. The team of flight mechanics dragged the MH-6 Little Bird attack chopper out onto the apron and set about preparing it for takeoff. Meanwhile, the two Range Rovers wasted no time. Their five liter supercharged engines kicked into life and propelled eight of the SOG team out into the early morning sunshine. Their communications screens synched seamlessly with the satellites overhead. Their target was twenty miles to their north.

They raced off. Their job was to get around and behind the target vehicle and in place, ready to take it down. With their arrival, the motorway was being shut down. The police, following a signal from NCTC, had begun to block all entrance ramps to the southbound carriageway and had a rolling speed block in place, well out of sight, behind the target. As the SOG team got in place, the traffic around the target would have thinned, allowing them a clear run to capture him and minimize civilian casualties.

With the helicopter up and in the air, the 'go' was given. The two Range Rovers stationed at an overpass had just watched the target speed past. The traffic around him was almost nonexistent. With the 'go' signal, both drivers accelerated hard and joined the motorway, gaining fast on the small Clio. By the time the first Range Rover drew level, the helicopter was hovering off to the left with its mini gun and rocket pods hanging menacingly underneath.

The road ahead was clear and from behind the target, the driver of the second vehicle gave the order to move.

The first vehicle accelerated sharply, cut in front of the Clio and slammed on the brakes. The second Range Rover closed to within an inch of the Clio's rear bumper and matched the braking. Even if Nick had wanted to escape into the next lane, it was impossible, the Clio had become as one with the Range Rovers. The three vehicles connected and the Clio drew to a stop wedged solidly between the two SUVs, each of which weighed three times the tiny Clio.

Even before they had drawn to a compete stop, the passenger doors of both Range Rovers were open and six of the SOG team members, dressed in full tactical assault suits with bio-hazard protection, rushed to take down the target.

***

Turner watched the images the SOG team's head-mounted cameras beamed back to them. Barry stood smiling as the CIA team performed the maneuver perfectly. Stopping a moving car at 80 mph was no mean feat. Stopping it as well as the SOG team had just done was remarkable.

"Looks like he's given up," announced Barry. They could just make out the driver sitting still, keeping his hands visible on the steering wheel.

Turner nodded; it was looking very good. He turned around to look at Flynn, who stood shaking his head slowly.

"I know it's tough," said Turner. "He was one of yours."

Flynn shook his head even more and sighed. *They just don't get it.*

"Here we go!" shouted Barry, as the SOG team member reached for the Clio's door handle.

***

Nick grabbed his 9mm Berretta the instant the door opened, causing immediate panic amongst the intruders.

"Don't shoot!" screamed the yawner, dropping the tray with a selection of breads and pastries on the floor. Shoeless, who had graduated to just being shirtless, having heeded

Nick's advice, dropped a small pot of coffee as Yawner fell back into him.

"*Putain!*" he shouted as the hot coffee burned into his naked chest.

"You know… you should wear a shirt," advised Nick, smiling and lowering the pistol.

"You were right about your car," said Yawner, bending down to pick up the pastries and breads. "It's on TV right now."

Nick followed them through to the living room to the television set, where the news helicopter filmed the action from afar. They could clearly see the two Range Rovers wedge the small Clio and bring it to a stop before the SOG team approached the car.

"Who's in there?" asked Nick.

"Not sure," Yawner said. "Amir arranged it."

"Any chance of any comeback?" Nick asked.

"Absolutely none."

***

A range of expletives exploded in NCTC when the youth was pulled from the car. When the SOG team had him prone on the ground, they searched the car but a close-up of his face showed him to be eighteen at most.

Flynn grabbed his jacket. "Guys, do you get it now?"

Turner snapped. "What, Flynn? Do we get *what* now?!"

"You're not dealing with a fucking amateur. He'll always be a step ahead of you and when it looks like you're closing in, he'll jump to three steps ahead."

"We'll make that little shit talk!" said Barry pointing to the youth on the ground 3,000 miles away.

"Barry, he won't know shit!" Flynn sighed and picked up his jacket. "I'll see you guys in the morning." "Are you going to update Carson?" Turner called after him.

"Jesus, Turner! Why d'you think he left? I only hung around to see Barry fall on his ass!"

And with that, he was gone.

Chapter 24

Frankie woke up in the unfamiliar surroundings of the guest room of her house. She had taken one look at the bed she had shared with Nick and decided against. The meticulous search that had only just finished when Carson dropped her off had revealed nothing and fortunately had been done with great care and attention. With no mess to clear up, Frankie had called her mom. Obviously, the 'I'm fine' SMS hadn't appeased her mother's concerns, judging by the thirty-seven missed calls that had amassed throughout the day. After a long and tearful conversation, she had gone straight for what turned out to be a fitful night's sleep.

She checked the clock, 6:00 a.m., just forty minutes since she had previously checked it. Sunday afternoon was barbecue day. At least that's what had been planned with a few friends. She was going to have to cancel, although it was probably unnecessary given the only news that was filling the channels centered on Nick. The man who should have been their host was the most wanted man in the world, hardly a guy who'd be hanging around to fulfill his barbecuing duties. Just in case, she sent a group SMS message. A few responded immediately despite the early hour, asking if there was anything they could do and saying they hadn't contacted her before etc…

All bullshit, she thought. It was at times like these that true friends rose up and showed themselves. She checked her phone from the previous day. A couple of messages she had ignored, given they weren't work related, sat waiting for her. Her real friends. She sent a message back thanking them for their kind words.

Frankie grabbed a bathing suit and swam her morning twenty lengths, then jumped in the shower in the master suite. The water poured over her as she gently increased the heat.

The dial stopped turning. This was where Nick usually jumped out. He couldn't take the heat like she could. She thought of him as she pressed the button and turned the heat up beyond the safety level imposed by the manufacturer. The steam filled the entire bathroom, the water almost sizzling when it hit her skin. She stopped the water and almost pinched herself, it couldn't be true, it must have been a dream. Stepping from the shower all such thoughts immediately evaporated.

I'm so sorry - it was real
N x

The message had appeared on the mirror above the sink. Written by finger, the steam had clouded the entire mirror except for the message. She had been asked constantly whether Nick had left her a massage. Nothing had been found during the search, yet this was the simplest but oldest trick in the book. Frankie stared at the message, not knowing what to feel or do. The man she knew was dead. This was a message from dead Nick. The Nick that still lived, she didn't know. She smiled. He had loved her. Dead Nick had loved her. Live Nick didn't. Live Nick was going to be stopped— even if that meant killed— with her help. She grabbed her phone and snapped a photo of the message. Carson would know what to do.

Dressed and ready, she walked across the driveway and unlocked the Prius, the car she used for work. She looked at the beautiful clear blue sky and the 911s cloth top. *Fuck it,* she thought. She went back into the house and, grabbed the Porsche keys, retracted its roof and pulled away. Her life was an open book now. Hiding her background was irrelevant. Everyone at the center was going to know everything about her as part of the investigation. She had nothing left to hide.

Carson's car was already in the lot when she arrived. She smiled. He had taken the Director's spot, the spot which Turner had used the previous day. Turner arrived while she waited for her roof to close, and he tried not to show annoyance as he drove past 'his' spot to find another.

Frankie waited for him, pondering whether to tell him about the message. She decided against. She'd tell Carson first.

"Good morning," she said brightly.

"Is it?" was the gruff and unfriendly response.

Frankie was initially taken aback until she remembered. "What time did you find out?"

"We left here just after 2:30 a.m." he replied, marching towards the entrance. Frankie had to jog to keep up.

"So who was in the car?"

"A teenager who'd been approached by 'some guy' in the street to deliver the car to Marseille for 500 euros."

"What? And he was doing it?"

"He lives in a tough part of town and they made it clear they knew who he was and where his family lived."

"Deliver the car or we'll pay you a visit?"

Turner nodded holding the center's main door open for her. "He didn't recognize the guy?" she asked.

"The description fits every dark haired young man in France and I don't know if you've been to France, but they're almost all dark haired!"

"So he was scared?"

"Shitless. He assumed there were drugs in the trunk and still wants to deliver the car, just in case they do come after him."

"Dead end?"

Turner nodded. "Just as you thought," he added pointedly.

"Would you have done it differently had we told you he wasn't in there?"

Turner pondered for a couple of seconds before shaking his head. "Fair enough," he said, much to Frankie's surprise.

Carson was waiting for them in Turner's office.

"Good morning, Mr. Carson," he said, knowing Carson preferred Harry.

"Morning, Paul," he replied. Touché.

Before they had a chance to talk, the night supervisor knocked and entered. His update was short and succinct. They had had little progress overnight. Even the black box they had retrieved from the prince's jet on landing at Riyadh had offered nothing. It had mysteriously developed a fatal electrical fault and had failed to record any of the journey.

"Any ideas?" asked Turner once the supervisor had left the room.

"Other than work through the leads, I'm struggling," said Carson.

"We know the prince, my mother's cousin, is lying," said Frankie.

Turner smiled at the reference to his comment the previous evening. "I know, your mother has thousands of cousins. I'm sorry, it was a long day."

"That's okay, and anyway, not one of those thousands of cousins has spoken to her since the day she married my father. So what about the prince?"

"We're on him," Turner acknowledged. "NSA is monitoring everything he does and CIA has a team watching him. If he so much as farts or sneezes funny, we'll know about it."

Chapter 25

Nick checked the luggage that the youths had removed from his car. Everything was in place. He stripped down the guns and gave them a much needed cleaning and lubrication. He checked the metal briefcase that had remained by his side. The seals were intact. He had become accustomed to the constant checking. Timing for the use of the virus was key. Any inadvertent release could significantly weaken the impact of the plan.

A coded knock preceded the opening of his door. Without it, Nick had made clear, he would shoot first. Following the earlier incident, the message had travelled quickly and any further mishaps were deemed highly unlikely.

"He will see you now," said Amir as he opened the door. His unkempt and tousled hair was now groomed.

Nick nodded and, taking the briefcase but leaving the weapons, followed Amir out of the small apartment he had been allocated and along a corridor to Mohammed Farsi's far larger apartment. The entire top floor had been taken over by the group. The building stood in the center of the complex amongst a number of other high-rise apartment blocks. Nick assumed lookouts were stationed in all of the surrounding buildings and any suggestion of a raid or assault by the authorities would be spotted well in advance. The apartment block had numerous exits and roads leading away from it. It was, in his expert opinion, an excellent and safe base, certainly somewhere that would suit his needs should it be needed.

Nick entered what he assumed to be the main place of worship for the group. A disproportionately large room had been created by knocking together three smaller rooms. A wash area, the *wudhu*, was set into the far wall opposite the *Mihrab*, which denoted the *qibla* wall and the direction of Mecca. Nick removed his shoes and placed them on the wooden slats by the doorway before entering. He proceeded directly towards the *wudhu* and under the eyes of the group already in the room, performed the ritual washing routine before prayer. Once completed, he stood up and joined the group.

"Would you lead us?" asked Mohammed Farsi.

"Of course," he said, smiling to the group of twenty men that hung on his every word.

Nick turned and faced the *qibla* before leading the most senior Al Qaeda members in France through the Salat al-Zhur midday prayer.

With the prayer complete, the questions began to rain down. The group had been summoned and had spent many hours travelling through convoluted routes to meet the man who brought a message from their Caliph and who had so nearly killed the living embodiment of Shaytan (Satan) on earth.

Nick raised his hand to silence the group. He had much to tell them and then he would take their questions.

He outlined the plan he had formulated with the Caliph. Specifics would be divulged when required to ensure the operational security and ultimate success of their mission. Nick apologized throughout as he skirted over details and the numbers of jihadists that he would utilize. It was vital, he explained, for the security of the plan, that the Caliph's dream be protected until the last moment. If any jihadist or member of the leadership were captured by the authorities, the plan would be protected. As of that moment, all that was important was delivering the Caliph's dream for Allah. Nothing else mattered. The jihadist groups had to come together as one to fight for the Caliphate that the Caliph and Allah deserved. When he finished, no one spoke. The scale of the plan that had just been described to them was beyond anything they had ever dared to imagine. Even without the fine details, the devastation it would cause would dwarf 9/11, which had up until that moment been the pinnacle of their efforts.

With his audience speechless, Nick told them what he needed from them. He needed an army of true believers, not just from Al Qaeda but from across the Muslim world. He needed men who were willing to give their lives to the cause but not those who simply offered those words vacuously. He needed men who had proved their worth, trained soldiers ready to fight and give their lives to Allah.

The group nodded as one and began to leave in a hurry. They had work to do. They had the jihadists within their groups to select for the Caliph's plan - the men who matched Nick's exacting standards and who would make their leader proud to be part of Nick's army.

Nick took Mohammed to one side as the rest of the group left the building. "Have you got everything I asked for?"

Mohammed nodded and led Nick out of the prayer room and along the corridor to an exit staircase. One floor down, he led him to an apartment door being guarded by another two youths. The youths stepped aside and let the men enter. A bed sat in the middle of the room, enclosed within a plastic tent. A small generator ensured that filters cleansed the air leaving the tent.

Nick surveyed the room. "That was very quick," he said, impressed.

"A lot of the people around here work at the local hospital. We immigrants are good for cleaning," he said bitterly.

"And the guinea pig?"

Farsi led Nick through to the next room. Two women in full burkas and a man sat on the floor, bound and gagged. Fear raged in their eyes as Nick and Farsi entered the room.

"What are the charges?" asked Nick.

Farsi pointed to the first woman, her eyes pleading. "This one, adultery". Moving to the second one. "This one, also adultery."

Nick noted the area around the eye of the second woman was bruised.

Farsi moved to the man. "This man, rape," he said with disgust for all three.

Nick walked forward and removed the veils that covered both women's faces. They immediately dipped their heads to avoid his gaze but not enough to hide that they were both severely bruised.

"Did he rape them?" asked Nick.

Farsi nodded. Nick took a step closer to the rapist and forced his knee into the man's genitals and pushed hard. The man tried to scream but the gag stopped him. Nick pushed harder and removed the gag. "How many others?" he asked.

"None!" said the man struggling against the pain. Nick pushed harder, feeling one of the man's testicles begin to burst. "Six!!!!" screamed the man.

"The Caliph did not believe rape was an adulterous act," said Nick. "It encourages scum like this to rape *our* women! There are six other women who have been too scared to tell what this man has done to them for fear of reprisals against them for his acts. Do what you wish with the women, the rapist will be my guinea pig."

Farsi shouted for the youths to escort the women back to a holding room where their ultimate fates would be decided by the Al Qaeda-led council that ran the local community under strict Sharia law.

The youths returned after depositing the women and followed Nick's orders. They took the rapist to the bed and strapped him down. Nick checked the camera that he had requested was in place and had a good view of the bed and the rapist. He also checked that the field of vision offered no peripheral insights into the location. Likewise, the names of any branded products were taped over to offer those watching no clues as to where or even in which country the recording was made. The man was stripped bare except for a small pair of medical pants to cover his genitals. His face was partially covered with a mask to stop any facial features being recognized.

Nick combed the specks of powder out of his hair with water and removed the spectacles. He double-checked everything then hit the record function and stepped into the camera's field of vision.

"Ladies and gentlemen of America…" he began, then proceeded to spill out a hate-filled rhetoric of how disgusting and ashamed the Americans should be of their lives, how unworthy they were of Allah and how they were to be punished. Leaving the plastic tent briefly, he appeared back fully dressed in protective gear. His face, although behind a mask, was visible enough to confirm that it was still him.

Safely ensconced in his protective gear and within the tent, Nick opened the metal briefcase. A small hiss accompanied the seal being broken on the airtight case, revealing rows of vials with small amounts of liquid inside. Nick removed one, then took a syringe and removed the liquid. The rapist was fighting desperately and futilely against his restraints.

"This, ladies and gentlemen, is the Ebola Zaire virus," said Nick, holding the syringe up to the camera, "one of the most deadly viruses known to man. It is highly contagious and has a 95% mortality rate. It acts fast and travels through the air with ease. If you wish to see how deadly and how fast it acts, this feed will continue live until the man lying here dies a horrific and painful death."

Nick plunged the syringe into the man's arm. With the virus delivered, Nick left the tent and sealed it behind him, leaving the man to his fate.

Farsi and the youths stepped back as he removed his suit. "It's okay," said Nick. "That was just for effect. The virus isn't contagious until after about four hours in the bloodstream. Now let's get that tape uploaded and put some terror into terrorism."

Chapter 26

"You need to see this!" said Colonel Barnes, barging into Turner's office and taking control of his TV remote. She selected the Al Jazeera channel and was rewarded with an image of the plastic tent holding a man strapped to a bed. Frankie gasped when Nick appeared in the shot. The anti-Western diatribe that followed was shocking in itself and overpowering, particularly given that it was delivered by an apparent white American, the same white American who had been the subject of newscasts for the previous twenty-four hours.

"How long do we have to find him?" asked Turner, watching the syringe infecting the patient on the screen.

"He's dead already," said Barnes shaking her head. "There's no cure. The moment you're infected with the strain, it's a death warrant."

"Jesus! Can we stop this getting onto American networks?" asked Carson.

Turner shrugged, he didn't know. However, when the website address scrolled across the bottom of the screen, any attempt to block the broadcast was deemed futile.

Turner rushed out onto the gangway and shouted to the floor below. "I want that IP location traced asap!" he shouted.

A number of nods from the techies below told him they were on it.

"He's not that stupid," said Carson.

Turner nodded. "I know, I know, you taught me that lesson yesterday but we have to try."

The room dropped back to silence as the image of the man struggling against his restraints played out on screen. It was straight out of a horror movie but the desperation and fear shown by the victim was no act.

Colonel Barnes broke the silence. "In twenty-four hours, the fever and headaches will start, followed by diarrhea and vomiting shortly thereafter. A rash will precede open, bleeding wounds, and then death. This man will die a horrific death before our eyes in the next forty-eight hours."

Turner hit his intercom and was instantly connected to his assistant. "Get me someone from Justice up here now!" he shouted.

An out of breath and very young looking man burst into the office. "Dan Gimenez, sir," he said, "I'm from Justice."

"Son, no offense, but I was looking for someone with a little more clout." Tuner turned back to his intercom.

"Sir, I work directly for the Attorney General. I graduated first in my class from Yale and spent two years clerking for the Chief Justice."

Turner turned back round. With those credentials, there was every chance he'd be working for Dan Gimenez in a few years. "My apologies, Dan," he backtracked seamlessly. "Have you seen this?" he asked, pointing to the website address on the screen.

Dan nodded.

"I want it blocked on Google, Yahoo, Bing or Bong or whatever you call it now, whatever providers we know and have some influence over, do you understand?"

"Ah, there may be a problem," said Frankie, looking up from the laptop she was working on.

She turned the screen to Dan for him to read. There was a warning page. Dan scrolled down it as though scanning it and turned it back to Frankie.

"Did you read it?"

Dan nodded. "Miss…?"

"Frankie, just Frankie," she said.

"Frankie's correct. We have a problem. According to the notice on the page, they have a room full of patients. Any provider or search engine that blocks access to the website will have a new patient infected and added to the website wearing a T-shirt stating that provider or search engine killed them!"

Frankie nodded, impressed. "You read fast!"

Dan smiled. "Very."

"Shit!" said Turner. "One step ahead," he added under his breath.

"All right, thanks, Dan."

Dan returned to the floor below, his ego and confidence leaving a little while behind him.

"We need to start preparing for the panic this video will cause," said Colonel Barnes.

"Somebody does," agreed Turner, "but what we need to do is catch this evil son of a bitch before he does something we can't stop."

"I think Paul's right," Carson said, "we can't do both. We need to focus on catching and stopping him. I'll give the President a call, get FEMA involved, and get the ball rolling."

"I'll prep a team for them," said Barnes, who rushed out of the office, almost knocking Barry over in her haste.

"We're certain the driver doesn't know anything," he said, entering Turner's office uninvited. "Are you okay for us to release him?"

"Yes, yes," replied Turner dismissively. He had forgotten all about the Clio driver.

"Also, we've pulled in a few more teams and stationed them around the EMEA area," Barry said, referring to Europe, the Middle East and Africa. "We have six teams available. We can have a team at most major cities within an hour."

"Thanks, Barry," said Turner.

"Excellent. We have a lead he may be headed to Cape Town," said Carson.

Barry was about to answer when he noticed the wicked grin on Carson's face. He was playing with him. "Okay, North Africa. We can cover North Africa in about an hour," he said, leaving the room and closing the door firmly behind him.

"You shouldn't wind him up," Frankie snickered.

"It's too easy and those shits are loving this. They'd love to bring the DIA guy down and show us how it's done."

"We don't have time for playground nonsense," chided Turner. "Frankie, did you notice anything in the video that could help us?"

"Like what?"

"Phrases you recognized, gestures, movements, what he's wearing. I don't know, anything that reminded you of a time or a moment you were together."

Frankie didn't hesitate. "I have no idea who was in that video. Physically, I recognize him as Nick Geller but that's it. There's nothing about that man that I recognize. Jesus, we just witnessed him murder an innocent man strapped to a hospital bed!"

"Well, we're assuming he was an innocent man. We don't know who he was," corrected Carson, drawing surprised looks from Frankie, Turner and Reid.

"I'm just saying," he protested. "You never know."

"Did you hear him? Did you hear what he said about the infidels not being fit to breathe Allah's air?"

Carson held up his hands in defense. "Fine, forget I said anything."

"So where does that leave us?"

"Where we were, only with the panic of a killer disease spreading fear across the nation and world," summed up Reid.

With the meeting at an end, Carson, Reid and Frankie left Turner's office. Agent Reid continued back to the main floor below, while Frankie followed Carson into his office.

Frankie showed Carson the photo of the message left by Nick.

"Where did you get that?" he asked angrily.

"On my mirror this morning," she said defensively, pulling the phone away from Carson's reach.

"Sorry," said Carson. "I'm just a bit rattled with what Nick's done. Best just delete it. He's gone."

"I know, I just thought it might help," she said quietly, and left Carson's office, making her way to a desk that had been set aside for her on the main floor below.

When the door closed behind her, Carson lifted his phone and dialed a number very few people knew existed.

"Target?" answered a voice on the other end of the line.

"Aisha Franks," replied Carson.

"Purpose?"

"Background and surveillance," he responded, ensuring he would know every detail of her life from that moment on.

Chapter 27

With the video complete, Nick was free to change his appearance. His dark, wavy hair was cut shorter, bleached and then dyed a sandy brown color with gray streaks. Tinted contact lenses were a must. The one feature that stood out beyond all others was his piercing blue eyes. They had fascinated Frankie and were one of the first things she had spotted when they noticed each other. A pair of glasses completed the change. His two-day stubble would normally have been removed but further added to the disguise. Nick Geller was a changed man in every way.

Mohammed Farsi responded to Nick's summons and entered his apartment by observing the knocking code. The surprised look on his face was all Nick needed to confirm that the disguise was successful. The athletic, handsome, dark-haired Nick Geller had become a middle-aged professor type, complete with corduroy jacket.

"Remarkable," Farsi said.

"The fewer people see me like this, the better," said Nick.

"Of course," replied Farsi.

"I leave tonight."

"But I thought—"

"I have an army to raise and a war to win, brother," said Nick.

Farsi nodded and was reminded of their first meeting a year earlier. The selfless act by the Westerner had saved the family of the local Al Qaeda leader's family in Afghanistan. Mohammed Farsi had been training with the Afghans when Nick Geller had fallen into their laps. A gift from Allah himself. He thanked Allah that they had not killed him. It had been so close. On awakening from his concussion, he was to have been beheaded. The filming of a Special Forces soldier being beheaded would have made news around the world for at least a day, if not more. But he spoke of Mohammed, of Allah, in a way that only a true believer could. He lived and fought with them for three months, trained them as he had been trained by the infidels. He had proved himself many times to them.

He had promised to continue the fight from within. His return to America had once again proved his trust. No attacks targeted Taliban or Al Qaeda strongholds that he had been told of. Defenses were not bolstered where he knew they might attack. Nick was one of them, a true believer at the heart of the enemy. The Caliph's grand plan had been merely whispers when Nick became involved but with his help they had grown into a powerful force. However, Nick's status changed when he betrayed them all and slaughtered the Caliph. That was one of the darkest days of Farsi's life. However, this day was one of his brightest. From darkness had come light. His faith was strong and with Nick's help, the Caliph's grand plan would win the day.

Nick stepped forward and drew Farsi close. "He was dying brother. Cancer was killing him."

Farsi stepped back, confused.

Nick drew him back. "The Caliph, he wanted to die a warrior, not a sick old man."

Farsi smiled as Nick shed even more light on the darkness.

"Allahu Akbar!"

"Allahu Akbar," agreed Nick.

"Now my brother, please clear the corridor and staircase. I don't want to be seen leaving. And remember, have your men ready for me. Prepare your warriors and yourself for what will be our finest hour. But only the truly faithful. This is Allah's war. They must want and need to die for Allah. We have no room for the weak or those lacking the courage of Allah!"

"We will be ready!" he promised as he left to clear Nick's exit.

Nick checked his weapons were safely stored. He then removed his Berretta and placed it in his satchel along with the small metal briefcase. He grabbed the walking cane that he stored with his weapons and waited a further five minutes for the coast to be clear before leaving.

On exiting the building, he gained a limp and with the help of the walking stick, he disappeared into the night.

Chapter 28

Frankie stared at the screen, watching over and over again Nick spewing his vile hatred and plunging the syringe into the man's arm. Each time she watched, a shiver ran down her spine and a knot in her stomach had her reaching for her womb. She bore that monster's child; it was growing inside her. She opened up a new search window and typed 'abortion clinic' into the address bar. A number of options appeared. She closed the window without looking. It wasn't the baby's fault, the baby was an innocent.

The best thing she could do for the child was to make sure its father was stopped. Frankie pulled up her calendar. She kept a note of everywhere she had been with Nick. Their whirlwind romance over the last five months had been just that, a whirlwind. Every moment they had was spent together.

Three months earlier, they had been to Paris. Nick had an assignment that would take him away for a month. It would be the first time they were to be parted since they had started dating and included a few days of business in Paris before moving on to Afghanistan. Frankie had taken a week's vacation and surprised him. She thought back to how shocked he had been when she had appeared at his hotel room. She tried to pull up the memory of his face, the image of shock. She had forgotten about it but the shock had been such that she thought she might have interrupted him with another woman. However, his room had been empty and she had just pushed it to the back of her mind. The next few days had been some of the most memorable of her life.

As the memory came flooding back, the image sharpened. It was shock alright, not at the surprise, but at being caught out. Nick hadn't been with another woman. He had been planning his escape all those months earlier and she had interrupted his plans.

She had surprised him at a small hotel near one of the main railway stations, the Gare de Lyon. After her arrival, they had moved to the recently refurbished Hotel De Crillon, one of the most salubrious Parisian hotels and her mother's favorite. While he worked, she shopped and in the evenings, they spent the most wonderful time together enjoying Parisian nightlife. It had been a special few days prior to his departure for a month. The same month that had propelled him to becoming a secret superstar by assassinating Zahir al Zahrani, the head of Al Qaeda.

On the second day of their Paris trip, she remembered something strange had happened and again she had just set it aside. He had left early and returned late in the afternoon. She had spent the morning shopping and then went for a run. She had told him in the evening of how she had run seven miles that lunchtime. He had joked about how funny that was as he had had lunch with a Mr. Rahn. He then expressed concern about her being caught in the terrible hailstorm. There had been no hailstorm in Paris; it had been a beautiful clear day until after three. Only then had any clouds appeared.

She picked up the handset and asked for the NOAA, National Oceanic and Atmospheric Administration. She gave them the date, a rough timescale and asked them if they could look into it. The operator was helpful but pointed out numerous times that it was a Sunday and that he'd do his best.

Armed with the little she had, she approached Special Agent Reid, the head of the Joint Terrorism Task Force and as the hunt for Nick had overshadowed every other terrorist activity, she was Turner's Number Two and lead agent on the operations floor. Frankie explained the trip to Paris and the probably innocuous weather reference. Reid listened, one eye remaining on her screen as the updates from thousands of agents and law enforcements agencies scrolled continually across her screen.

"I know it's crazy but I just remembered it because when I said I had run that day at lunchtime, he had laughed as he had had lunch with a Mr. Rahn," added Frankie to put a bit more context around why she had remembered the weather being different.

Reid's second eye left her screen and stared at Frankie, giving her her full attention.

"He had lunch with a Mr. Rahn?"

Frankie nodded.

Reid stood up. "Charlie?" she called across to another female FBI Agent a few desks away.

"Yes?"

"What was the name of the bank that the prince made the transfer to, earlier this morning?"

Charlie rifled through some notes. "Rahn & Boderman, but it was just from one internal private account to another."

"Thanks," said Reid, her excitement building. They were onto something.

"$250 million dollars," added Charlie.

Reid nodded. That part she had remembered.

"Frankie, sorry to interrupt, but I've got a guy from NOAA holding for you, he said it's urgent," said an agent who had come to find her.

Frankie thanked him and took the call on Reid's phone. After listening to the NOAA operator, she thanked him for his quick work.

"There were heavy hailstorms on that day in Southwest Germany and Northeast Switzerland," said Frankie, updating Reid on the latest intel.

Reid pulled up a map on her computer and found what she expected.

"Northeast Switzerland, Zurich. The location of the Rahn & Boderman private bank."

Reid called Dan Gimenez over. An internet search and a call to Interpol resulted in the home phone number of a Mr. Paul Rahn, one of the main partners of the Rahn & Boderman Bank. After numerous inquiries into whom he was talking to, would do nothing more than confirm that the prince was an account holder. As for the money transfer, he was far more interested in how the US authorities were aware of the transaction. Getting nowhere, Dan informed Rahn that the US government would do everything within its power to ruin his bank should he fail to cooperate. Rahn hung up.

"Shit," said Reid.

"He'll call back," said Dan assuredly.

"I don't think so."

Dan pulled up a web page and pointed to the entry for Rahn & Boderman. "That's why he'll call back. Unlimited Liability."

Reid looked confused.

"Very few Swiss banks still operate on that model. Basically, the partners have full responsibility for any losses the bank incurs. Just look up Wegelin Bank, they were the oldest private bank in Switzerland," said Dan. "I emphasize *were.*"

Before Reid or Frankie had a chance to look it up, Paul Rahn called back.

"I have a meeting scheduled tomorrow morning with the recipient account holder."

"Do you have a name?" asked Dan.

"In a safe in my office. All I have is the account number in my diary."

"Can you get me the name?"

"Of course, when we open the bank in the morning," he replied, ending the call again.

"Thanks, Dan, you're a star," said Reid. She grabbed Frankie's arm. "Let's go," she said, taking her notes and heading up to Turner's office.

Frankie popped her head into Carson's office on the way. "Come on, you'll want to hear this!"

Once in Turner's office, Turner and Carson both listened as Frankie and Reid updated them on the latest discovery.

Carson checked his watch when the two finished. "Twelve hours until the bank opens its doors."

"Plenty of time to get there," replied Turner. "I'll get the jet prepped."

Carson shook his head. "Mine's bigger than yours, we can take a team with us." He walked onto the gangway and shouted down to the floor below. "Flynn, my office! Oh and I suppose you'd better bring Barry," he added, noting Barry's interest peak.

"Ladies, can you hold the fort?" asked Turner.

Reid nodded.

"Frankie, you're coming," said Carson, walking back into the office, answering for Frankie before she could respond.

Chapter 29

Monday 7th July

After a circuitous route checking for any tails, Nick retrieved his second planted vehicle just a mile from Farsi's stronghold. The small Peugeot had seen better days but the simplicity of its engine ensured it started instantly on reconnection of its battery. Not a soul on the planet knew of his new mode of transport or where he was headed. He checked the mirror and didn't recognize the face looking back at him. So far, everything had run perfectly to plan. He tuned the radio to Beur FM, an Arab radio station, and headed south.

His meeting with the banker was penciled in for 8:30 a.m., which gave him plenty of time to avoid the main routes and once again take the less obvious ones. It was a long drive but he'd rested well through the day and would have plenty of time to sleep after his meeting.

***

The C-32 landed at 6:30 a.m. local time in Zurich. The military version of the Boeing 757 was designed for VIP travellers and so delivered a fresh and energized team ready for the task ahead. One of Barry's SOG teams met them at the airport with transport for the thirty operatives Flynn had brought with them. Another SOG team was already in position, preparing the ground around the bank and scoping out positions for the rest of the team.

A car awaited the rest of the team. Their role was to meet with Rahn at his home and explain what was required of him. If possible, Nick would be taken down before reaching the bank. However, should the opportunity for a clean takedown not be available, they would take him during his meeting with Rahn.

Their arrival at Rahn's home had been less than welcoming. Their visiting him at his private residence at any hour was outrageous and at 7:00 a.m. even more so. He had insisted that they leave and would meet them at his office at 8:25 when he normally arrived for work. Turner and Frankie had complied with his request and turned to retrace their steps to the waiting car. Carson, however, had not.

Five minutes later, he called them back to a far more receptive Rahn, who invited them in.

"What did you say to him?" Frankie whispered to Carson.

"I just told him he wouldn't be the first banker I had arranged to disappear in Lake Zurich." He smiled wickedly. Frankie had a horrible feeling that there was far more truth to that statement than should have been the case. It certainly had transformed Paul Rahn and begged the question of how many Swiss bankers had vanished over the years for Carson to be taken at his word.

Turner explained to Rahn what they expected. However, a call from Barry and Flynn soon changed all of that. The street was empty. A team would be spotted far too easily. The takedown would have to be in the bank. Rahn's face fell further. A look from Carson ensured his compliance.

"When do you normally leave for the bank?" asked Turner.

"7:57," replied Rahn, "which gets me into the office between 8:23 and 8:25 a.m. Leaving at 8:00 adds an extra ten minutes to the journey." "The most important thing is that you keep to the routine," said Turner.

"How many entrances and exits?" asked Frankie.

"One main entrance and one fire exit," said Rahn. "And one exit from the vaults below. But there are a number of security doors that only open outwards. It also links to a building behind which was the original bank building."

"Can we get in that way?"

Rahn made a call and wrote down the address.

"Call Flynn and give him the address," said Carson to Turner. "Mr. Rahn, we'll meet you inside the bank and don't worry, we'll make sure you and your staff come to no harm."

***

Nick's drive through the night had gone far quicker than he had anticipated and he arrived almost two hours early for his meeting. He drove along the waterside, admiring the boats in the warmth of the early morning sunshine. His Peugeot was old enough to know a time before air conditioning and as the sun rose, the temperature responded.

Although confident that not a soul knew where he would be, old habits died hard. He parked the car in one of the many vacant spaces and walked back towards the bank, thankful of the early morning breeze. The waterside location meant there were many coffee shops that would allow him to sit and watch the goings on without drawing attention to himself.

With the time approaching 8:30 a.m., bank staff began to arrive. So far, everything appeared normal. He had noted a slight increase in joggers, particularly male ones but, given that the weather was far better than when he had last visited, that wasn't unexpected. He finished his last mouthful of croissant and limped across the road with the aid of his walking stack, entering the foyer at precisely 8:31 a.m.

***

One of the oldest and most prestigious banks in Zurich, Rahn & Boderman was one of the few to benefit from a lakeside position. Zurich sat at the top of Lake Zurich, a stunningly beautiful lake that stretched off into the distant hills and mountains of the Swiss Alps. Unfortunately, the secret rear entrance had not afforded any of the visiting Americans the stunning views to the front of the property. They had had to make do with the old entrance of an obviously poorer time.

The aging guard that met them at the old entrance guided them back through a mind-boggling number of security doors, nearly all of which put the single vault door protecting the President's emergency operations center to shame. Flynn and Barry had tossed a coin for the takedown team and much to Flynn's disappointment, it would be an SOG team that would accompany Frankie and the investigative team.

By the time they were in the building, it was already 8:00 a.m. A quick tour confirmed the takedown had to be in Rahn's office. The grand entrance and banking hall offered Nick far too many options. On the other hand, Rahn's office had one entrance, was two floors up with bars across the window, and had as a bonus a secret sub-office hidden behind a bookcase. The team would be able to hide in there and the plan was that Rahn would leave Nick in his office to 'deal with something', and the team would come out from behind Nick and secure him in the enclosed environment.

After running through the scenarios, Barry instructed two of the bank's security staff to be replaced by two of his men. The other eight SOG team members would be located in the sub-office.

Carson, Turner, and Frankie would wait in one of the other partners' offices just along the hall. When Nick arrived, an assistant would inform Mr. Rahn of his arrival and then take him up in the private client elevator. All was standard procedure in the bank and would give everybody ninety seconds' heads up.

At exactly 8:24 a.m., Paul Rahn arrived and proceeded to his office. He had been told to act as normal and so spent a few minutes chatting with staff. It was a Monday morning and this was the opportunity for staff to tell him what they had been doing over the weekend. Not that he was at all interested. However, his father had done it before him, just as his son would do it in the future.

He reached his office right at 8:30 a.m. Rahn ignored the entourage in his office and opened his calendar. The numbered account due at 8:30 a.m. was the first thing on it. He opened his bottom drawer, revealing a safe below. He keyed in a number and withdrew its only contents, a large ornate and very old leather bound and gold leafed ledger.

"What are you doing?" asked Turner, surprised at how cool the banker was, given the situation.

"I was asked for the name when you called yesterday. I told the young man I would get it when I arrived at the office."

Turner shook his head. The name was irrelevant. It wasn't as though the account was going to be in Nick Geller's name. A bank of small screens on his desk allowed Rahn a view of the banking hall below and his eyes flicked between the ledger and the hall as he looked to match the number he had obviously memorized.

"Ah, there we are. It appears my 8:30 a.m. has arrived."

***

Being the first customer in the bank, Nick was attended to immediately. His meeting with the director was confirmed against the diary and he waited to be taken through to the offices. His hand rested on the satchel and the reassuring outline of the Berretta below the material gave him comfort.

The director walked into the banking hall and warmly welcomed Nick.

"Monsieur Guillon, it is a pleasure to see you again," he said, hugging one of the largest depositors at the Crédit Agricole branch of Marseille, France.

***

"Mister Harry Carson, number 652348190-235, you are Harry Carson, no?" asked Rahn.

"Yes, but…" said Carson, his face ashen.

"Passport number is…"

Carson raised his hand for Rahn to stop speaking. Turner looked at Carson, not fully understanding.

"He set us up! He's not coming here. It's a joke. It's a fuck you!"

"The account is a fake?" asked Turner.

"We do not *do* fake accounts at Rahn & Boderman," insisted Rahn, insulted at the suggestion.

"So you do have an account here?" asked Frankie.

Carson nodded. "From many, many years ago. There's probably nothing in it."

"Other than $250 million you mean?" she said mischievously.

"Let's wrap this up. I'm not discussing my private details here. Obviously that money needs to go back to the sender. It's a mistake!"

"So you wish me to send the money back?" asked Rahn.

Carson nodded, although every muscle in his body fought him. That $250 million sat in his account: it was therefore his. Whether the prince had made a genuine error or not, which of course he hadn't, Nick Geller was fucking with him. The money was his and under Swiss law to do with as he pleased.

"Is that a yes?" asked Rahn, wanting a verbal response.

Turner and Frankie looked at him. "Yes," he grumbled.

With two strokes of the keys, Harry Carson's rainy day fund dropped from two hundred and fifty million dollars to three hundred thousand dollars. It hadn't even been in his account long enough to gain a day's interest.

Chapter 30

Nick smiled as he placed the items in the safety deposit box. He also couldn't help smiling at the thought of what may have been happening in Zurich. They would have pieced the clues together he was sure. Carson would be furious. He always liked to be the smartest guy in the room. Closing the box, Nick's smile dropped. What if they *hadn't* found the clues? He had just given the cantankerous old bastard a quarter of a billion dollars! He shook his head. The prince's transactions would be looked at with a fine toothed comb. Not a chance. Although Harry Carson was as sly as they came. *Shit*, he thought, leaving the bank behind, that was one scenario he hadn't thought through properly. However, if that were his only mistake, Harry Carson wouldn't enjoy his new-found wealth for very long.

Money was not an issue for Nick. That had been arranged many months before under the assumed name of Monsieur Jacques Guillon, a former diamond merchant, who had moved to Marseille from Tunisia after selling his business. Seven million euros, almost the equivalent in dollars, had been deposited at the local bank and with all the paperwork in order, no questions had ever been asked of their newest cash rich customer.

Using the funds over the last six months, on his travels he had purchased and loaded numerous pre-paid credit cards in various currencies. All transactions relating to the cards had been made in cash, rendering them anonymous and totally untraceable. His first transaction was for a ferry ticket to Algiers, departing in a few hours from Marseille, France's largest port and gateway to North Africa and his African army of believers.

Chapter 31

Manhattan, New York
Hunter College

Rafik took his seat as the 8:00 a.m. class in General Chemistry was due to begin. The six seats to his left remained vacant. His friends had not shown up yet. He called them friends but 'acquaintances' was probably more accurate. They never fully welcomed him into their fold. They seemed wary of his background, a Muslim immigrant from Iraq. His family was killed during the insurgency and he was left alone in the world. Bitter and unhappy with life, he had tagged onto the group and it seemed at times that he was accepted and at others excluded. He looked at the vacant seats and wondered what it was today that he had been excluded from.

Perhaps he had pushed his anti-American rhetoric a little too much and had frightened them off? It was a beautiful day and there were better options than being stuck in a classroom for the morning. However, they were very serious students, like him, and keen to learn as much about chemistry as possible. He looked around the lecture theatre and noticed that all of the normal seats were occupied. Just the six to his left remained vacant.

The clock above the blackboard at the front of the lecture hall clicked to 8:01 and like clockwork, the lecturer entered the room. Rafik had voiced his disgust to his friends at being lectured by a female. He watched with disdain as she placed her coffee cup on the desk and bid them good morning.

Rafik looked out for his friends, but still they didn't show. He thought back to the previous Friday. Had he said something that may have scared them off? He had tweaked the rhetoric up slightly but not dramatically. He was playing the long game, gaining their trust. At 8:10, they had still not arrived. Perhaps he had pushed it too far. He began to consider that he might be in danger. He looked around and recognized all the faces. The exits appeared to be unmanned. At 8:15, Rafik got up from his seat. Something was definitely amiss. He made his way out of the lecture hall and, checking the corridor carefully, to an exit. There was still no sign that he was being watched.

He crossed the street and walked the short distance to Central Park, losing himself amongst the early morning joggers, tourists and sun worshippers. He withdrew a cell phone from his backpack and swapped the SIM card with another from his backpack. A pre-programmed number on the SIM required him to dial a code to access the number. He entered the code number into the cell, hit the dial button and waited.

***

NCTC

Special Agent Sarah Reid had arrived at 6:00 a.m., having left only five hours earlier. Many joked that she had no life. It wasn't a joke; she didn't. She lived for her work. She was forty-five years of age, single, a little too short for her weight and not a looker. She was the stereotypical definition of a plain Jane. If there had been a pictorial example in the dictionary, her picture would have fitted perfectly. However, her personal lackings were the Bureau's gain. Special Agent Sarah Reid was without doubt one of their best and most talented investigators. When Deputy Director Paul Turner put his team together, there had never been a doubt he would select Reid as his number two. There was not a more hardworking or tenacious investigator in the Bureau. She had refused promotions into management and training many times. She lived to catch criminals, particularly terrorists. Her father had died in the North Tower on 9/11. It was one of the many reasons she lived for her work.

There were over a hundred Joint Terrorism Task Force Centers across the country, all feeding into the main National

Task Force at the NCTC where any patterns could be noted and analyzed. Resources could be shifted as and when required at any particular hotspot.

Updates throughout the day were normal. The regional centers were encouraged to notify the National Center of anything out of the ordinary.

By 8:00 a.m., the phone lines at the National Centre were struggling to cope. By 8:30, Reid had secured additional resources and lines to take the sudden and unexpected increase in calls.

***

Rafik's listened into his cell, it rang once. A pause followed and a connection was made. He waited, ensuring he was out of earshot.

"ID?"

"Rafik Al-Basri," replied Rafik quietly.

"Go ahead."

"I need the Watch Commander asap."

After a few seconds, the line clicked and another voice came on the line. "Come home, bud, they've gone, flown the coop."

"Shit! They made me?" asked Rafik.

"No, son. Rafik was perfect. They've all gone. Come home, Ricky," replied the New York JTTF Watch List Commander, using undercover FBI Agent Ricky Hernandez' real name.

***

Reid didn't know whether to be ecstatic or more nervous than ever. Across the board, the phone calls were informing them that the radical Muslims— jihadists— on their watch lists were booking flights and heading out of America. If this continued as the sun rose and the west caught up with the east, there wouldn't be a jihadist left in North America.

Reid picked up the phone and called Turner. Like her, he was nervous. She heard him update Carson and could have sworn he shouted at the pilot to fly faster. Whatever the case, they were already heading back after their wild goose chase.

Chapter 32

After twenty hours on board the packed ferry, Nick was glad to stretch his legs properly. The small Peugeot had been left with keys in the ignition not far from the Marseille terminal. He doubted it was there five minutes later. Marseille had improved dramatically from its less than illustrious reputation. However, like any large city, there were areas best left unexplored. In Marseille, that was the area around the ferry terminal. Nick had felt his pockets brushed a little too closely twice while he was waiting to board the ferry. If it happened a third time, he wasn't sure he was going to be able to restrain himself.

Algiers was an African city with a very mixed heritage. The various buildings from its history of empires stared back at Nick as he left the ferry; it was loud, chaotic, smelly and beautiful all at once, the way only ancient cities could be. Nick wasn't interested in any of it. He checked his watch and approached a passport checkpoint. This was a mere formality but the facial recognition system of any camera in the hall was certainly to be avoided. An increased exaggeration of his limp ensured a perfect view for the cameras of the crown of his head.

Nick placed himself two thirds of the way into the line, not keen to get off but not keen to appear he didn't care, just a normal guy getting in line. His passport in the name of Jacques Guillon scanned perfectly and Nick walked freely onto another continent. While the noon call to prayer echoed across the city, Nick headed towards the Casbah area of Algiers. The traditional walled quarter was a maze of alleyways and buildings built on a steep incline, some preserved beautifully, others falling dangerously into disrepair.

The call to prayer quieted, and Nick found himself in front of the Ketchaoua Mosque, a beautiful entrance to the old city behind. Nick entered and paid his respects to Allah. His western appearance drew a number of disapproving looks from fellow worshippers, particularly the younger men. Nick continued unperturbed.

Being one of the last to enter, Nick was one of the first to leave. He entered the Casbah by climbing the steep staircase and, owing to his limp, he was soon overtaken by many other worshippers. As he moved deeper into the Casbah, the tight alleyways stole the sunlight and shadows became longer and darker. Nick had a rough idea of where he was going, although he had a feeling the four youths who had followed him from the Mosque had other plans. Nick turned a sharp right and, out of the youths' sight, bounded up a short flight of stairs. As he neared the center of the Casbah, the walls closed in further. The alleyways tightened and darkened with each step and they climbed further and further up the hillside.

Nick stepped back into a doorway, just before another sharp turn in the alleyway. He needed to lose or deal with his admirers, whoever they were. His meeting was far too important to be put at risk.

He heard them at the base of the staircase, wondering where he had gone. Their cockiness was diminished a little at the ease with which the cripple, their easy prey, had eluded them. Nick pushed himself further back into the shadows and their footsteps raced to catch up and find him. Nick let the first three run past, reaching out and grabbing the fourth by pulling him towards him. The youth attempted to cry out, so Nick clamped his hand over his mouth, then slammed the youth into the stone wall. The sickening crunch made far less noise than the wooden door would have. It would also mean that the youth was far less likely to die from his injuries. Nick opened the door and was rewarded with a magnificent arched courtyard that led off to various apartments. Fortunately, the courtyard was empty. He dumped the youth's unconscious body on the floor and moved back to his original position, closing the door behind him. He took up position on the opposite side of the doorway. When the youths came back, they would not see him unless they looked behind them.

A clatter of steps suggested they had discovered the loss of one of their own. They charged back down the steps and once again, as they passed, Nick repeated his previous actions. Unfortunately this time, the youth screamed the moment he was touched. The loss of their compatriot had obviously spooked them. Nick powered the screamer into the wall, and his two friends ground to a halt. The screamer's lifeless body slumped to the ground. Nick, without his cane, limp or stoop cut a far more imposing figure and not the easy target the muggers thought he would be. The two hesitated, looking at one another for support. Nick had a meeting to get to. He stepped towards them. They turned and ran.

Nicked carried the second unconscious youth into the courtyard and checked their pulses. Weak but there. He emptied their pockets, removed the battery from their cells and pocketed the lot. They'd live but they'd certainly think twice about chasing cripples in the future. He placed them in the recovery position to ensure they didn't choke on their own vomit and hurried off to make his meeting on time. He cut across a number of alleyways as he worked his way to the far side of the Casbah. He had led the youths in an opposite direction. Ten minutes later, he approached a nondescript wooden door in a nondescript alleyway, just as it had been described to him. He thanked Allah that his directional skills were as good as they were and he knocked on the door three times, once, then twice. It opened and a gun was forced into his face and the trigger pulled.

Chapter 33

"Did you see that? Did you see his face?!" shouted the gunman to his followers behind him.

Nick pushed the gun away from his face and walked into the room.

"He didn't even flinch! Not even a flicker of his eyelid!" said the gunman excitedly. Handing the unloaded pistol to another man, he hugged Nick.

"I've warned you before, Shaheed," said Nick. "One of these days your practical jokes will get you killed!"

"Brother," said Shaheed whispering in his ear, "I needed to show these men how special you are. You are a gift from Allah. Truly, you are."

Nick hugged him back. It wasn't the first time Shaheed had played the unloaded gun trick in his face. The first time had been back in the hills of Afghanistan. Although that time, Nick had not known he was joking.

"Come eat," called a voice from the back of the room. The voice belonged to an older man who was instantly obeyed. The room silenced and the thirty men that had been gathered for the meeting moved to a table at the far end of the room. Shaheed led Nick to the top of the table and introduced him to the head of the Maghreb wing of Al Qaeda, Mustafa Ghazi. The welcome was warm but cautious, a normal response on meeting a new member of the leadership for the first time. Nick was everything they despised, at least, on the outside. Nick joked that if he were a sweet in a wrapper, he'd be the last one chosen but whoever chose him would be in for the most delicious treat of their life. The message was loud and clear: Don't judge him on his looks. Mustafa accepted his words and introduced him to the hierarchy of the jihadist fighters from across Northern Africa. Leaders from Mali, Niger, Sudan, Morocco and many more were introduced to the man that had brought a plan to unite them in a common goal.

"Shaheed," said Nick as the lunch was coming to an end, "do you have the laptop I asked for?"

Shaheed reached behind him, produced a laptop and handed it across to Nick.

Nick opened the Tor browser, the browser of choice for the world's criminals, untraceable and hidden behind thousands of anonymous relays. Although not perfect, it certainly was better than the commercial options.

The website opened to reveal the man Nick had injected with a lethal virus just over thirty-six hours ago. It was not a pleasant sight. The man had been suffering from a high fever, vomiting and diarrhea and due to his contagious status, had not been tended to. Large sores had appeared across his body to add to the horror of the image.

Nick turned the screen around to his audience. "Friends," he said, "this is the disease that will rid us of the infidels! In less than eight hours, this man will literally bleed out on live TV. His writhing in pain right now is nothing compared to what it will be just a few hours from now."

A cheer erupted. the group began to understand just how grand the plan before them was.

"But how do we protect our lands?"

"We don't need to. All travel to and from North America will cease after we introduce the virus. No country on earth will accept a plane or boat from America or Canada once we release this. Mexico will close its borders. A military buffer zone will keep the virus in. They will be isolated as the virus eats through the fabric of their corrupt society."

Another cheer erupted.

"What do you need from us?" they asked, almost as one.

"I need your men. I need your warriors. I need the men who want to fight and more importantly, are not afraid to die for Allah."

"Then you want every man in this room!" shouted Mustafa proudly.

"I want an army. I want to strike fear into them like they have never known. The virus is just part of the plan. I want to take the battle to their streets. I want them to see the army of Allah running down the streets killing their policemen and soldiers without fear. I want to destroy their hospitals before the virus takes hold. I want their hearts and souls to die before they do."

The resultant cheer almost lifted the roof.

"The Caliph set the groundwork. He wanted a one true Islam to rule over us, for us all to unite together against the infidels. Together we can defeat them. That is what the Caliph died for and has asked me to help you deliver."

Another cheer erupted.

Before Nick left, he laid out the detailed instructions of what each man needed to deliver. He was clear and precise. He wanted the true believers, only those who, if caught on film, would smile as they pressed a detonator that would send them to paradise. He warned that many would be tested and if one man failed, all of those leaders' men would be sent home in disgrace. It was a threat that ensured only the true would be delivered to Nick's army. Once selected, the jihadists' names would be added to his army and their instructions sent to them thereafter. Each jihadist would receive his own instructions. Again, Nick emphasized the importance of compartmentalizing the plan. The fewer people who knew the final details, the less chance the infidels had of stopping them.

Some, the most courageous and talented warriors, would have the honor of taking the fight to the streets of America. Others would have the honor of taking the virus into the heart of America and would be responsible for killing millions of infidels.

Just as individual fighters would wait to hear their fate, so would the leaders. Not all could make the trip. Not all would have the honor of taking the fight to the Americans. Some would have to stay and fight for the future, ensure that those who had sacrificed themselves for the cause would be rewarded by the creation of the one true Caliphate.

Not until the morning of the attack would each jihadist learn of his final destination and role in the plan. It would ensure that even if fifty were caught by the Americans before the attack, the Americans would have no idea whether they were trying to find one hundred jihadists, one thousand jihadists, or even twenty thousand. A huge cry of 'Allahu Akbar!' from his audience sealed the approval he required.

Nick retraced his steps back through the alleyways of the Casbah and grabbed a taxi on the outskirts of the old quarter. He headed towards Blida Airport, a small airfield to the southwest of Algiers. Between Farsi in Europe and Mustafa Ghazi and his African compatriots, Nick's army was already growing into the thousands and he hadn't even yet been to the heart of Islam. He was going to deliver a blow of such a magnitude that the world would struggle to understand what was happening.

Chapter 34

Frankie struggled to sleep on their return from Switzerland. She took a shower and stared at the message that Nick had had the nerve to leave on her mirror. She had taken her towel and swiped through it. He was gone. The deception had started four months earlier. Only six weeks after they had started dating, he was already weaving her into his plot. He had definitely used her.

The words played on her mind throughout the night, every waking moment. It hadn't been real. The detail he had gone to, even dropping in the hailstorm. It had been so natural, so well acted. But it didn't make any sense. How was he so sure they'd be together all those months later? Without that clue, they would never have followed up on the transfer. The prince moved money constantly between accounts and that scale of transaction had been far less suspicious than one a hundredth of the size.

At 5:00 a.m., she gave up. Sleep was not coming, not in her state of mind. She lifted the handset and called the Rahn & Boderman bank in Zurich. After the discovery of Harry Carson's account, Mr. Rahn had all but ejected them from the premises. He had a business to run and they had interfered far too much in his business as it was.

"Mr. Paul Rahn, please," she said. It was 11:00 a.m. in Zurich and she knew that he took tea at eleven and forbade meetings in his diary at that time.

"I'm afraid Mr. Rahn is busy," replied his secretary curtly.

"Tell him it's Aisha Franks, from yesterday."

"Please hold," said the secretary. Frankie was hopeful, but she came back a moment later and said, "I'm afraid he's still busy."

"Can you tell him it's urgent and perhaps he should be aware that my mother is a Saudi royal?"

"One moment please."

"Miss Franks," said Mr. Rahn warmly and almost immediately. Money opened doors and diaries in Swiss banks.

"Mr. Rahn, can you please check this date in your diary?" asked Frankie, giving Rahn the date and time that coincided with hers and Nick's trip to Paris and the hailstorm. While she had been waiting, she had sent him an email.

"Yes," he said. "A quiet morning and then lunch with a prospective client."

Frankie's pulse raced. "Can you check the email I've just sent you, please?"

After a minute or so of waiting, Rahn came back on the line. "It was a few months ago but if I had to say what the client looked like, I'd say number four."

"What name did he use?" she asked excitedly.

"Frank Hilton. I remember, that's right... I initially wondered if he was linked to the hotel group but he wasn't."

"Did he say what he did do?"

"If he did, I'm afraid I can't remember. He was supposed to call me the following day but never did. I made a note in my diary to expect his call."

And I know why he didn't call, thought Frankie. *Because he had let slip with me he had left Paris.*

"However," Rahn said, cutting into her thoughts, "I remember he had sold a business and had around seven million euros to deposit. I don't forget numbers," he laughed.

"Thank you, Mr. Rahn," said Frankie, about to the end the call.

"You mentioned your mother...?" he said quickly.

"Yes, I'll pass on your details. Good day, Mr. Rahn." Frankie replaced the handset and flicked through the images on the email she had sent to Rahn. They were images created of how Nick would look in a number of disguises. Number four was graying temples and a beard. There would, of course, be a persona and documents created for "Frank Hilton" but they would have been ditched long ago, along with his plan to use Rahn & Boderman Bank.

Being the ex-girlfriend of the world's most wanted terrorist was not an ideal situation. Being the ex-girlfriend, used as part of a plot, was even less ideal. Being the ex-girlfriend that your ex had respected enough to change your plans due to the tiniest slip-up months earlier, strangely enough, gave Frankie great comfort. He hadn't used her after all. He had respected her.

It was 5:20 a.m. She picked up the handset and called Carson. He answered before the first ring ended. It appeared he hadn't slept either, although his problem was far more basic. He had just lost a quarter of a billion dollars.

Chapter 35

Blida Airport was just a short taxi ride to the southwest of Algiers. The small airfield was almost entirely stocked with helicopters. One corner of the apron had been set aside as a scrapyard for two aging fighters that sat alongside an old and past its best transport aircraft. Nick was initially worried that the aircraft he had hired was nowhere to be seen. However, as they drew closer to the small main building, a little corporate jet sat gleaming within the only hangar. Nick proceeded to the info desk, as directed by Shaheed, who had arranged Nick's transport. The friendly young lady manning the desk asked him to wait while she spoke to an elderly gentleman in an off-white and ill-fitting shirt and tie who eventually made his way towards Nick.

"Monsieur Guillon?" asked the man.

Nick returned the gentleman's handshake and couldn't help but notice his coffee-stained tie and almost white shirt.

"I'm Nasim, your pilot."

Nick's handshake became more tentative. The elderly handshake wasn't the most steady.

"I've been flying for almost fifty years," Nasim said reassuringly and led the way outside to the runway.

Nick followed behind and slowed down further on reaching the hangar. The elderly gentleman ignored the shiny new corporate jet and proceeded purposefully to an old propeller plane. Its white paint, like the pilot's shirt, had seen far better days.

"There may be some mistake," Nick called after Nasim. "I chartered a VIP aircraft!"

"No mistake," Nasim smiled back. "He's a little beauty. I opted for all the VIP options when I bought him. King of the skies!"

"And how long ago was that?" asked Nick, approaching the small turbo prop plane that didn't look like it would reach the end of the runway, let alone the other side of Africa, almost two thousand miles away.

"Let's see, my son's forty," he began, "and it was a few years before he was born… so, maybe forty-three years ago? Beechcraft King Air, never let me down yet…unless I wanted it to, of course," he added, laughing.

He opened the door and the interior did not look any different than the external condition. Four seats lined each side of the fuselage and the cockpit area was open to the rest of the plane. The seats were badly worn and the controls were from a whole different era, before computers. It would have been an excellent museum piece.

Nasim turned to face him, instantly losing his joviality, directing the discussion to money. "So young man, payment. Return to Sudan, no questions asked, $12,500 as agreed."

Nick pondered the situation. He looked back at the gleaming corporate jet, a small Learjet. It would be twice as fast.

"A quick call to Net Jets and I'm sure, with all the docs and flight plans in order, you'd be good to go. Of course, it needs a good tarmac runway for landing," said Nasim, tapping his nose and pointing to his tires.

Nick looked at them. They were oversized with a chunky tread. The plane could land anywhere.

Nick handed over his pre-loaded credit card. Nasim looked at it carefully and then pulled out his cell to connect to the credit card's website. He checked the balance. $15,000 was showing. It seemed Nasim was more than familiar with this type of transaction, somewhat surprising Nick, who thought he was going to have a hard sell.

"I don't have change," said Nasim.

"If we get there alive, consider it a bonus. If we don't, it doesn't really matter," replied Nick, stepping into the small plane and taking one of the seats.

Nasim climbed in, removed his tie and started the engines, which immediately fired up. Being the only aircraft on the field, they were given immediate clearance. Nasim wasted no time in powering the small twin prop plane down the runway and with a prayer to Allah, lifted off.

Mustafa Ghazi was arranging Nick's next meeting, just as Mohammed Farsi had organized the meeting with Mustafa. It wasn't an ideal plan, and involved a significant risk should the meeting details fall into the wrong hands, but it also built a significant level of trust. Trust was lost far more easily than it was gained. Having killed the Caliph, Nick had a mountain to climb but with overwhelming evidence for his actions, the trust was coming back. That and a plan that would strike back and destroy America in the name of the Caliph certainly helped.

"Do you have the exact co-ordinates?" asked Nasim.

Nick handed Nasim a slip of paper Shaheed had given him.

Nasim punched the details into a small GPS locator. "This can't be right," he said, looking at the destination displayed by the coordinates.

"Why, what's wrong?"

"It's directing us into the desert in Northern Sudan, hundreds of miles from anywhere."

"No, it's right," said Nick, closing his eyes and grabbing some sleep.

Chapter 36

Carson and Frankie arrived at NCTC minutes apart, well before Turner but not before Reid. Reid had already gone through the previous night's updates from across the world by the time they arrived. The situation was, as she informed them on arrival, unchanged. Nick Geller had vanished.

Reid pointed to a screen on the bottom left of the wall of screens showing the infected man. "They reckon eight hours at most, if the poor guy lasts that long." She shivered.

"We may have a lead," announced Frankie, not wanting to linger any longer than necessary on the Ebola victim's image.

Reid perked up. Leads over the previous twenty-four hours had been either nonexistent or false-starts.

Frankie was bringing Reid up to speed when Turner arrived. She started from the beginning again.

"He'll have ditched the identity too," said Turner.

"Seven million Euros to deposit though, what are the chances of that amount being deposited in one go at around that time?" explained Frankie.

"It's a long shot," said Reid. "If he changed everything else, why leave the amount of money the same?"

"That's what I thought and then I thought maybe he'd think the amount was irrelevant given how many transactions are made daily."

Turner looked at Reid and nodded. "Worth a try?"

"Fair enough, we've got nothing else," said Turner. "Frankie, grab Dan and check out all the other private banks."

Frankie grabbed a pad and rushed off to find Dan.

"So where are we on the fleeing radicals?" asked Carson.

"Four hundred and eighty-two to date and they were just the ones on our watch list. We have another seven hundred or so who were being watched and haven't gone anywhere."

"I'd bet my left testicle that that's because they shouldn't have been on the list in the first place," said Carson bitterly. "How many of them are we still tracking?" he asked.

Reid coughed. "Twenty-three," she replied, embarrassed.

"Jesus! Four hundred and fifty-nine lost, just like that?!"

"It was a very coordinated move. Most of them had no bookings. They just headed to the airport without notice, paying cash for flights leaving within the hour. The Security Services in England are tracking ten of the twenty-three after they landed in the UK. Six are being tracked by the Germans, four by the French and three by the Spanish. Most took flights but never arrived. They must have booked transfers under different names when they arrived at their first destinations, thereby avoiding having to leave the airport."

"What are the twenty-three doing?"

"So far, nothing. They've just visited family or friends."

"Had they pre-booked their flights?" asked Turner.

Reid checked down the list of names. "They were all pre-booked," she said.

"Shit! How can we lose four hundred and fifty-nine potential terrorists so fucking easily?!" shouted Carson to no one in particular.

"It was hours before we realized what was happening and by that time, we were desperately trying to coordinate resources to be where they were landing but they never arrived where they were supposed to," replied Reid defensively. "We're going through footage and passenger lists and bookings, but it's taking time."

"I'm not criticizing you, Jane," replied Carson. "It's just frustrating. They're handing our asses to us on a silver platter!"

"What about the twenty-three?" asked Turner.

"Keep a watch on them. If they come back, I suspect they should be off the watch list. If nothing else, we've freed up a hell of a lot of resources."

Frankie and Dan spent the day calling every Swiss bank they could find. A number of transactions of similar amounts at around that time were found. It would take some time to track them all back to source and identify the owners but they were getting somewhere, or at least it felt as though they were.

At 6:00 p.m., Carson approached an exhausted Frankie. "May I have a word?"

"Of course," she answered.

"In private," he said, looking at Dan.

Dan removed himself from earshot.

Carson leaned in closer. "I think you may have done it," he said happily.

"I haven't done anything."

"No, let's just say that the NSA can see and hear more than most people think they can. Anyway, I gave them a few parameters this morning and asked them to start a search," he said, pressing a piece of notepaper into her hand.

She looked down and read the note.

Monsieur Jacques Guillon,
Crédit Agricole Marseille

"Nobody can know where you got this, especially Dan," emphasized Carson.

Frankie nodded while quickly calculating the time in France. Midnight. Too late to call the bank.

"I'll get on it at 8:00 a.m. French time," she said enthusiastically.

Carson shook his head and pointed to Turner and Reid huddled on the other side of the operations floor.

"There's a car waiting. You and Reid are getting over there tonight. Flynn will meet you at the airport with a team of Deltas. You need anything, you just call me, 24/7, and I mean *anything*! Nothing's too big or too small and I'm including aircraft carriers!"

"You're not coming?"

"No, Turner and I need to stay here. We're briefing the President tonight. The crisis planning is kicking into gear."

Frankie nodded nervously, feeling a huge weight shift onto her shoulders.

Carson noticed her mood darken. "Hey, we're here because of you. You tracked down this lead. Just remember you trained as an investigator with the Secret Service and from looking at your personnel records, you were a damned good one before you moved into protection."

Reid joined them. She too was apprehensive. Turner followed. "Best of luck and remember, don't come back without him!" he said unhelpfully.

Frankie looked down at the note again. Monsieur Jacques Guillon, aka Nick Geller.

You are caught, you just don't know it yet.

Chapter 37

Carson and Turner were among the last to arrive. Turner took the seat next to his boss, the Director of the FBI, while Carson took the seat next to the Secretary of Defense. A spectacularly grand room, the State Dining Room had been transformed with miles of cables into the temporary Situation Room. The President had made it clear he wasn't hiding in a bunker on his return from the hospital, ruling out the use of the emergency operations center deep below the East Wing.

Just four days on from the shooting and explosion, the West Wing had all but disappeared. The demolition crews had removed the debris and the site was being prepared for a new West Wing with plans being drawn up. However, the overwhelming suggestion was for the building to be rebuilt exactly as before with greater blast proofing protection. The only positive that remained was the fact that only one person had lost their life in the blast. The Vice President. His on-duty Secret Service detail had recovered his body shortly after the blast and all of them handed in their resignations for not having been by his side. The President had rejected every one of the resignations from his hospital bed but they all refused his rejection. A funeral was scheduled for later that week at which heads of state and leaders from around the world would pay their respects to a great man. He had served his country at war and in peace and whenever called upon, he always rose to the task handed to him. A widower with no children, he had given everything to his country. The President was going to give him a send off fit for the President he should and could have been.

President James Mitchell entered the State Dining Room, his arm still strapped to his chest. The First Lady escorted him into the room, fussing as any loving wife would, telling him that it was too early, he had just been released from hospital, was lucky to be alive. President Mitchell nodded to each statement as it was thrown at him but continued unperturbed. Sitting him down and making sure he was comfortable, she turned to the group assembled to update her husband. A strong and beautiful Southern Texan, she was a powerful force in her own right.

"Now y'all listen here!" she said, pointing to a photo of Nick Geller. "I want that man to feel pain before you kill his sorry ass!"

A few nods emanated around the table.

"Dead! I want him dead!" she demanded.

The nods grew stronger as they realized she wasn't leaving until they all agreed.

"Okay, good. You've got him for forty-five minutes," she ordered.

The group consisted of the most powerful individuals the world had ever known. At their fingertips were the mightiest forces ever assembled but they nodded meekly in unison, as though chastised by their grandmothers.

"Good," she said, kissing her husband on the cheek. "Forty-five minutes!" she reiterated and promptly departed.

"Let's make it quick people," smiled the President, making light of the First Lady's timescale, however, everyone knew she meant it. The meeting would be over in forty-five minutes whether the President had finished or not.

"Deputy Director Turner, why don't you kick off?"

Turner stood up and updated the group with their progress up to and including Reid and Frankie's departure back to France.

"So basically, we're nowhere near catching him?" asked the President.

"No, sir," replied Harry, saving Turner from answering.

"Do we know his plans?"

"No, sir," replied Turner.

"Colonel Barnes?" The President turned to the virus specialist. "I believe you're working with FEMA on a plan in case the virus is released?"

Colonel Valerie Barnes stood up and briefly updated the group with the outbreak plan.

"So if I'm hearing you correctly, the plan is that everybody goes into quarantine in their homes and stays there for weeks while hospitals are overwhelmed with millions of people they can't save? In short, America will grind to a halt until six weeks after the last death from the virus?"

"Well, I wouldn't put it quite like that," she protested to a roomful of looks that suggested that was exactly how she had put it. "Yes, I suppose it is that bad," she sighed, taking her seat.

"Ladies and gentlemen, I'm so glad I managed to get out of my hospital bed for this meeting," President Mitchell said sarcastically. "And we've not even touched on the four hundred fifty-nine disappearing radicals or the death of the Ebola victim streaming live on the internet!"

The Director of National Intelligence stood up. The DNI was responsible for all of the US intelligence services and gave a brief update on where they were on tracking the vanishing radicals. He also informed the President of the threat that for every search engine or service provider that blocked the Ebola victim's live feed, another victim would be added, also confirming that the Ebola victim had sadly died a few hours earlier.

The President banged the table with his good hand. "So now we're letting terrorists dictate to us?! We don't negotiate! And we don't let them stream live murders into American homes!" he shouted. "Chairman?"

The Chairman of the Joint Chiefs of Staff stood. "Mr. President, our forces have been placed on high alert and all leave is cancelled. We're calling up reservists and heightening security at all installations. We're coordinating with the National Guard and FEMA should a requirement for martial law occur. In short, Mr. President, we're ready when you need us."

"Thank fuck someone is." President Mitchell let that hang for a moment, then turned to CIA Director Carl Hunter. "I believe you've done some background on how they turned one of our guys against us?"

Both Carson and Turner sat up in their chairs. Barry, their CIA liaison and a member of their team, had not mentioned to them any work that was being done without their knowledge.

The CIA Director, however, offered little they hadn't uncovered themselves when it came to Nick Geller's secret family history of being Muslim and his potential radicalization after his parents' deaths as a teenager. What they had uncovered was the point at which Nick had reengaged with his radical youth. They had pieced together what had happened to him a year ago when Nick claimed to have been injured and lost in the hills for three months. Images were shown of Nick in various disguises meeting with Al Qaeda and Taliban hierarchy on various trips, all of which were new to Carson and Turner.

"Where the hell did you get these and why haven't we seen them?" asked Carson angrily, one of the few people in the room brave enough to go up against one of Washington's most feared power brokers.

"We need to protect our sources," said Hunter smugly.

"Perhaps if you hadn't, we wouldn't be sitting here now?" countered Carson.

"Our source had no idea who this was. Nor did we until the mock-up images of Nick Geller were released. "It was just luck that one of our image analysts recognized Geller and pulled up these old images."

"This is bigger than any source's confidentiality! We need those images and your source!" demanded Carson.

"Over my dead body!"

"Just make sure you put that in your will tonight!" threatened Carson.

"Okay, okay, enough," said President Mitchell, stepping in. "Carl, give them what they need. And I don't mean just what they ask for. They don't know what you've got." He glanced at the door. "Anything else? I hear my wife coming."

The room stayed silent and the President got up, signaling the briefing was over.

"Bob," President Mitchell said to his Secretary of Defense, "and Harry," he said, looking at Carson, "can you both hang back?"

Turner looked at Carson; they had shared a ride over. Carson signaled for Turner to give him ten minutes, and Turner stepped out into the hall.

When only the three men were left, the President turned to Carson. "Honestly, what are your thoughts? And no bullshit."

"I'll know better when I see what the CIA has on Geller and what the source has, but at the moment it's not looking good."

Chapter 38

Nasim, as directed by Nick, flashed the aircraft landing lights every ten seconds as they neared the GPS location. Nasim kept an eye on the fuel gauge; its warning light had already begun to blink. With every second that passed, Nasim could have sworn it began to blink more rapidly. He flashed the landing lights again and began the count, *ten, nine, eight…* He stopped. The dark desert floor had just sent a bolt of light off into the distance. Approximately a mile ahead, a line of light suddenly appeared. As they neared, Nasim began to descend, the light separated and became two - their makeshift landing strip.

Nasim called out their imminent touchdown. Nick braced himself but needn't have bothered. The oversized tires and Nasim's many, many years of experience produced a near perfect landing.

"You certainly earned your bonus with that landing," said Nick, looking out at the uneven desert floor highlighted by the meager landing lights.

"That's a far better runway than I'm used to," Nasim replied, making Nick wonder exactly what the pilot usually transported. Nasim opened the door and was met by an unwelcome sight of six men pointing AK-47s at him. They gestured with the barrels of their guns to get out.

While Nasim blocked the gunmen's view, Nick reached around and extracted his Berretta. He checked the safety, placed the pistol on the seat opposite him, along with his satchel and metal briefcase, and followed Nasim out into the darkness. The fires that had lit the runway were slowly dying. Only dim lights from a truck illuminated the area around the plane.

"What is the meaning of this?" barked Nick in Arabic as he stepped from the plane.

The gunmen looked at him. It was clear that they hadn't understood a word of what he'd just said. He tried a similar message in French. Again, they looked at him with obviously no idea what he was saying. Nick's gestures began to grow more wild as the gunmen, all of whom were in their early twenties, looked on. Nick could see they were nervous and, more worryingly, poorly trained. Their fingers were on the triggers of their weapons and not the trigger guards. Their gestures were so erratic that they occasionally pointed their weapons at each other.

"It's not them dude, shoot them!" said one of the gunmen to another. Again, poor training was evident. The talker was frightened to take the shot but, just as importantly, Nick recognized a strong regional English accent.

"Whoa, calm the fuck down!" shouted Nick in English.

"What the fuck? You're American? Dude, we nearly blew your motherfucking head off!" replied the gunman in barely recognizable English.

"What's with all that mumbo jumbo, mate?" another said, lowering his weapon. The rest followed, lowering their weapons. A mumble of discontent rose as they bragged how close they had been to 'popping' the American. The truth was that none of them had come close. They were embarrassed at how badly they had handled the situation and were trying to big themselves up after a dismal showing.

"Are we going to stand here all night?" asked Nick, taking command, something these guys desperately needed.

The gunman pointed to the truck and gestured towards the open back. Nick looked at him with contempt. "Nasim!" he said loudly. "You and I in the front with the driver. The rest of you in the back."

The driver pulled away when the last of the gunmen climbed onto the back for a bumpy ride ahead of them.

"How far?" asked Nick.

The driver shrugged his shoulders. Nick repeated his question in Arabic.

"One hour."

"How long you been here?" asked Nick.

"Five months."

"And these jokers?" Nick gestured to the six in the back.

"Not long enough!" the driver said, perceptively.

Nasim agreed wholeheartedly. Nick nodded. He was worried. This was one of the major training camps that would prepare his warriors. Deep in the Sudanese desert, hundreds of miles from the nearest living soul, they all had the space and privacy they could ever want. With millions of square miles of bland, featureless terrain, the chance of being spotted even by satellite was so remote, it wasn't even a concern. However, if the men who were training there were of the caliber of their reception team, it was a wasted journey. Nick needed only the best and most dedicated followers of Allah for his plan.

After an hour, they arrived. The light on the horizon began to creep into the darkness at the impending dawn. The camp was impressive. The huts and buildings were colored to blend in with the surroundings. Even the equipment was painted to ensure it blended seamlessly with the environment. It was an impressive sight but not as impressive as the men who were filling the area ahead of them. Nick stood and watched. Proud, strong and well-disciplined soldiers. Their exercise routine would have been worthy of any forces Nick had ever served with. They were hardened men, whose faces bore the determination of true warriors.

Nick had expected about fifty good men at the camp. What faced him was a small army of almost three hundred men, ready to fight and die for Allah.

Nick smiled.

Chapter 39

Thanks to Carson, a slightly smaller VIP aircraft of the USAF touched down at 07:30 at Istres-le Tubé Air Base in the South of France, twenty miles northwest of Marseille. The C40B Clipper was a military version of the Boeing Business Jet based on the Boeing 737 and had more than enough room for Frankie, Reid, Flynn and the Delta team.

"Bonjour, Madame," greet Captain Leclerc when Frankie stepped onto French soil at the bottom of the steps.

"Bonjour, Monsieur," she replied politely, shaking the offered hand.

"Captain Jean Leclerc at your service, Madame. We have been asked by our Minister of Defense to offer you whatever assistance you require."

"I'm Frankie, this is Sarah, and this is Flynn," she replied, introducing her colleagues in turn. "And Flynn's team," she added as the Delta team began to emerge from the rear of the plane after gearing up.

"Can we offer you breakfast, coffee or any refreshments?" asked Leclerc.

"No thank you, we just need to get to this Crédit Agricole, asap," said Reid, handing over the address written on a slip of paper.

Captain Leclerc looked at the address and motioned them onto a small bus that awaited their arrival. A two-minute ride had them on the other side of the airport and surrounded by helicopters.

"At this time in the morning, traffic is horrendous for getting into the center of Marseille. This will be far easier." He motioned towards the smaller helicopters, Eurocopter Fennecs. "I believe time is of the essence?"

"Absolutely," replied Frankie, moving towards the small chopper.

"Three of these should fit us in," he said, holding the door for Frankie, Reid and Flynn to board the first chopper before jumping into the pilot's seat.

Frankie listened intently to the captain instructing French police to clear a section of road on the Vieux Port. Her Swiss finishing school training, taught almost entirely in French, insisted on by her mother, was finally paying off.

"The Vieux Port?" she asked, once Leclerc had ended his call.

"The old port," he replied in English for the benefit of the others. "It's a large harbor, mainly leisure boats now but it's in the heart of Marseille, the oldest city in France. The premier port of France and the gateway to the world," he smiled, proud of his native city.

With a history lesson en route, the journey was over in no time. They neared the magnificent sight of the port and a police cordon was already in place to allow them to land on the road outside the Crédit Agricole. Reid reached into her bag and gave Frankie and Flynn each a small white facemask. They both looked at it and then at the crowd that had already gathered around the perimeter of the cordon.

"I'm not so sure that's a good idea, nor whether it will make any difference" said Frankie.

"Good idea or not, we should take precautions," insisted Reid.

"I agree with Frankie," said Flynn handing his mask back. "This will cause panic and to be honest, I'm not sure it would do much good anyway!"

Frankie handed hers back too.

Reid looked at them both and shook her head in disgust but also replaced her mask in her bag. "But I'm keeping them close," she said, laying them carefully at the top of her bag. "One whiff of disease and you're putting them on!" Flynn told the Deltas to wait in the helicopters while they followed Leclerc into the bank. The General Manager of the bank had already been alerted by the police of their arrival but, as he had been given no information other than senior investigators were about to arrive to speak to him, he was a bag of nerves by the time Frankie and Reid approached him.

"*Vous parlez Anglais?*" asked Frankie.

"*Oui*, a little," he replied nervously.

"Please don't be worried," said Frankie, reassuringly. "You have done nothing wrong, we just want to ask you about a customer of yours."

The bank manager relaxed slightly but given banking laws and the requirements to vet customers' identities, his concerns were not entirely alleviated.

Reid took the photo of Nick Geller from her bag and showed it to the manager. Relief flooded across his face. "*Non*," he said emphatically. "He is no customer of mine."

Reid produced some of the mock-ups. The manager paused briefly at one of them.

"You recognize this man?" prompted Frankie when she noticed the pause.

"*Non*, just a little familiar," he said.

"Familiar how?" she pressed.

"One of my clients, a rich man, Monsieur…"

"Jacques Guillon?" "*Oui*," he replied. "But if you already knew, why—"

"We wanted to put a face to the name and not the name to a face," replied Reid. They had agreed in advance that an independent verification of Nick was going to be far more convincing than giving the name and seeing if Nick's disguise matched one of the mock-ups. Plan A was to see if the manager recognized Nick. Plan B was to give him Jacques Guillon's name and hope it was Nick.

"But Monsieur Guillon is older, with a limp," he said.

"Older? His hair is graying at the temples?" asked Frankie.

The manager nodded.

"And the limp, Flynn?" she asked.

Flynn limped across the room, almost identical to Nick's limp. "Street Surveillance 101. One of our first lessons in how to change our appearance."

"*Merde!*" exclaimed the manager.

"We need every transaction he's made. Locations, times, amounts, currency, anything you have," Reid urgently requested.

"Of course, Madame," replied the manager. "And his safety deposit box?"

"He has a safety deposit box?" asked Frankie.

"*Oui*, he arranged it yesterday when he was here."

"He was here *yesterday*?!" they said in unison.

"*Oui*. He had a small metal briefcase with him. I didn't see it when he left, I assume he left it here."

Reid reached into her bag and withdrew the small white paper masks, including one for the manager.

"I suggest you tell your staff to wait outside the branch while we check the safety deposit box," suggested Reid, handing out the masks.

The manager's face suddenly paled at the realization of what the mask meant. "You think he could have given us that disease? Like the man on the video?"

"No," lied Frankie. "We just have to take precautions, health and safety laws."

From the expression on the manager's face, acting was not a line of work Frankie could fall back on. He tentatively and after some persuasion took them down to the basement and into the vault that housed the safety deposit boxes, his mask fixed tightly to his face.

Flynn pulled the box out of the wall and with all three of them looking on, each holding their breath, he opened the lid.

Chapter 40

With sunrise just minutes away, the training camp came to a standstill for Salat Al Fajr, the morning prayer, to be said in unison by hundreds of trainees. Nick felt at one with the group as they faced Mecca to the east and the words of the Quran echoed around him in a predawn chorus. As the final words died away, the sun peeked over the horizon and gave the worshippers a hint of the power that Allah possessed. It was as though he had heard their thanks and praise of him and rewarded them with a sunrise in their honor.

"Nick, my brother," said the man who had led the prayer, embracing Nick warmly.

Nick stood back and held the man at arm's length smiling into the face of a fellow warrior. "Ibrahim, my brother."

"You broke my heart, brother," he continued somberly. "But then," he smiled, "you put it back together and now it is much stronger!"

Nick knew he was referring to his killing the Caliph and then the shooting of the President. One act explained another.

"I wished I could have told you, but the Americans needed to believe I was their hero. I needed their trust and I needed my shot at the President. Why my bullet didn't fly true, only Allah can know."

"Allah wants the man to witness the disaster that will befall his corrupt and evil empire. Death would have been the easy route. Allah wants to punish him more," Ibrahim said.

Ibrahim had been another of the men he had met on that fateful night in Afghanistan a year earlier; another man whose family had lived thanks to Nick's quick thinking. A former Pakistani soldier, Ibrahim had joined the cause to fight the infidels who were destroying their world. Meeting Nick had been a turning point for Ibrahim, a young raw soldier.

He'd been destined to join many of his friends and family in an early grave. Under Nick's tutelage, however, he had grown to become a feared warrior, leading and training warriors of the future. It was thanks to Nick that he had been sent to the Sudanese camp to train their newest and most promising recruits to continue the struggle.

"Impressive!' said Nick focusing on the many men before them in the desert.

"Thanks to you, my brother, we select only the most devoted and most capable, just as you instructed us," replied Ibrahim proudly, watching the men go through a further exercise routine before they would be rewarded with breakfast.

Nick turned towards the body of the camp and spotted the group that had met him at the aircraft and gestured toward them, squinting his face in question.

"Hmm, yes, a rich benefactor's wayward son and friends," he explained. "Even within our cause we have to play the political game."

"Send them home. They have no place in our army," said Nick.

Ibrahim shook his head. "I have tried, brother. The boy's father is too powerful. They are here on the request of the new Caliph."

Nick paused. He had not known a new Caliph had been selected. A number of candidates had stepped forward to fill the shoes of Zahir Al Zahrani, the Caliph he had assassinated. These candidates would follow Al Zahrani's path of uniting the jihadist world to form one united and far stronger army. A few far more radical candidates favored a much more insular approach, by increasing the number of low scale attacks to initiate a war of terror from within America. They all seemed to agree that the war needed to be taken to the Americans; it was just the methodology that differed. Nick's plan rested on the grand-scale approach. He had hoped to have achieved consensus before a new Caliph was announced, during the mourning period, and ultimately in the memory and honor of Caliph Zahir Al Zahrani. Nick had made promises to Caliph Al Zahrani that he had every intention of keeping. A new

Caliph could put an end to everything, particularly if he disagreed with unification.

"I am speaking out of turn, the decision has not yet been finalized," said Ibrahim, regretting his indiscretion.

"I must meet with who you believe will be the new Caliph and I must convince him to follow Caliph Al Zahrani's plan," said Nick, his concern growing over the potential for a major upset to the Caliph's plan.

Ibrahim smiled. "Well you are in the right place, my brother, he will be here tonight."

"Here? In this camp?"

"Yes and I don't think it is a coincidence. I've only just been told of his arrival. I imagine he wishes to meet you too."

Nick felt a sudden lump in his stomach. The list of candidates was long and illustrious within Al Qaeda with many men more than capable of taking over the head of the organization. However, one name stood out and Nick began to panic.

"It's not…no it can't be… He's too young?" said Nick, trying to rule it out.

Ibrahim realized he had guessed and smiled, not realizing just how devastating the appointment could be for Nick.

The Caliph's plan was dead in the water. Nick was a dead man walking.

"Al Zahrani's son?" said Nick. His face remained impassive as his internal organs convulsed.

"Yes, can you believe it?" replied Ibrahim excitedly. "He is desperate to meet you!"

Nick couldn't believe it, and was very sure that his victim's son was desperate to meet him. Unfortunately, not for the reasons Ibrahim thought. Nick prayed for some divine intervention. Otherwise, he would never see another sunrise.

Chapter 41

"Son of a bitch!" shouted Flynn, slamming down the lid on the safety deposit box and removing his paper mask. He flipped it back up so the others could see the contents and walked away in disgust.

Frankie retrieved the contents: a debit card and two credit cards in the name of Monsieur Jacques Guillon, along with a driving license and passport in the same name. The metal briefcase was nowhere to be found.

The manager looked on, confused. "I don't understand," he said.

"He knew we would find the Jacques Guillon identity. He's telling us that he's not using it anymore."

"Ahh," said the manager, his smile widening.

Reid spotted the smile and knew exactly what the manager was thinking. "Which means we'll need to seize the accounts and any monies still in them," she explained quickly before the manager's imagination got the better of him.

The manager's smile stayed fixed on his lips but died in his eyes.

"What I don't get," Frankie said to no one in particular, "is why lead us here in the first place if he just planned to ditch it? Why even bother?"

"Let's grab some images off of their security systems and get moving," said Flynn, agitated at another wasted trip.

Reid didn't move. She was still pondering Frankie's question. "Why *is* he doing this?" she asked out loud. "Frankie's right, it doesn't make any sense. He only came here to show us he knew that we knew. But why?"

"He's just showing us he's smarter," said Flynn.

"But that's just it, that's not Nick. He doesn't care whether people think he's smart or not. They assume, because he was a soldier, that he's not. But as we both know, he's usually the smartest guy in the room," said Frankie, following her logic. "He laughs at guys who try to show how smart they are."

"So, if he's not showing off?"

"He's playing with us, keeping us busy and out of his way," surmised Frankie.

Before they could consider what that meant, Frankie's cell buzzed. The caller id told her it was Harry.

"Harry?" she answered.

"We've got a lead on Nick."

"Timbuktu?"

"Not quite," he said surprised by her attitude. "Right continent though. Sudan."

"What did he do, send you a postcard?" she asked.

"No, he's just used a cell phone."

"I'm sorry, Harry, but we'll get there and he'll be gone and we'll have just wasted another day. He's playing with us."

"Not this time," said Harry.

"Seriously, Harry, from all the increased chatter, out of all the billions of calls that take place every hour, you've managed to identify his voice on a phone call? Bullshit!"

"Good point. But I didn't say we identified his voice. Two youths were assaulted in Morocco yesterday. Their phones were taken and both of those cells were recently turned on briefly in the desert in northern Sudan. The attacker who stole those two cells fits the description of Nick as Jacques Guillon."

"He's not that stupid, Harry."

"We all slip up now and then. He's in the middle of a desert with no cell signal, he'd not think for a second a brief power up of the cell would pinpoint his location. The phones were on for less than a second, not even time for the SIM cards to register a network if there even were one to connect to. He doesn't know we can do this, hell *I* didn't even know we could track cells from what he just did. Anyway, we've pinpointed the location and have a satellite pass set up in the next thirty minutes."

"Okay, we're on our way! But Harry?"

"Yes?"

"You and I both know, Nick doesn't slip up!"

Chapter 42

After breakfast, Nick took Ibrahim aside.

"My brother, I need to test your men," he said apologetically.

"Of course, brother. Please, it would be my honor."

"I don't think you understand. I need to test that they are ready to fight and die for Allah."

"Of course, I expect nothing less," Ibrahim said.

"Some will die during the test," explained Nick.

Ibrahim's heart sank. These were men he had trained and honed to perfection. They were men to whom he had promised a fight against the infidel. Dying in the desert sands for no reason other than to test their resolve was unworthy of the warriors he had produced for Allah. However, he was not going to question Nick. He was there with a plan direct from the Caliph and therefore from Allah himself.

"I understand," he said, trying to hide his disappointment.

"On the plus side, I'm sure I can get the benefactor's useless son and friends out of your way."

"You can't kill them!" Ibrahim said in a panicked voice.

"No, but I can show them what is expected of them if they stay here and fight with us for Allah!"

Ibrahim nodded reluctantly. "What do you need?"

"I need a lift back to the plane to pick up a few things that will assist me."

Ibrahim pointed to the benefactor's group and instructed them to take him back.

Ninety minutes later, as the sun was beginning to heat the desert floor, they arrived back at the plane. Nick told the boys to wait while he jumped aboard the plane. His Berretta, satchel and the metal briefcase sat where he had left them. There wasn't a living soul within three hundred miles of them;

it was probably one of the safest places on the planet. He checked the Berretta and removed the two stolen cell phones from the satchel. He reinserted the batteries and turned them on briefly, pleased to see both had juice. There was every likelihood he'd be needing them sometime soon.

"We're getting toasted out here, man!" shouted one of the boys from outside the plane.

Nick put the cells back in his satchel, grabbed everything he needed, and jumped back down to the desert floor.

"What's in the fancy briefcase?" asked another of the youths as Nick approached the truck.

"You'll find out soon enough," smiled Nick climbing into the passenger seat. "Now get us back and quick!"

Nick settled in for the wild ride across the desert at twice the speed the truck was meant to travel in rough terrain. Not that he had any intention of complaining, the further away from the plane the better as far as he was concerned. He had calculated that the camp was about fifty miles from the makeshift runway. They'd have to search an area of roughly two thousand square miles to find the camp. Even then, the camp was well camouflaged and not easily visible. He closed his eyes and fell into a deep sleep.

"What the fuck's up with these dudes?" asked the driver as they bounced over the entrance ramp.

Nick woke up, not sure what had woken him first, the driver's voice or the bang on the head as he bounced into the air. However, on opening his eyes, it became far less important to know the answer. The soldiers that had been happily training when they left were still training on their return. Unfortunately, about twenty of them were training their weapons on the truck and Ibrahim was standing amongst them, pointing at Nick.

Fuck, thought Nick, *this doesn't look good.*

Chapter 43

Carson and Turner paced the operations center, waiting for the satellite to get into position over Sudan. At 3:00 a.m., the staffing levels were reduced but with most of the investigative work being done in time zones outside of the US, the building was still relatively busy. The image on the main screen suddenly changed.

"Deputy Director Turner!" shouted an analyst unnecessarily. Turner's eyes were already fixed on the image.

Whoever was controlling the satellite image knew what they were doing. The image sharpened quickly revealing a barren beige landscape.

"Are we on the coordinates yet?" asked Carson into the speakerphone that was connecting them to the National Reconnaissance Office operator, controlling the satellite image.

"No, sir, we're a few degrees short. We should be on the precise coordinates in about thirty seconds."

Carson muted the call. "What did the NSA say was the margin of error on those coordinates?" he asked Turner.

"Ten miles."

Carson unmuted. "We've got a ten mile radius of those coordinates," he advised.

"Yes, sir, I'm factoring that in. My colleague's looking at a wider range than I'm sending to your screen. He'll feed anything of interest from that on to me and onto your screen."

With every second that passed, their hopes faded. The land was utterly desolate and the rocky and rough terrain was not conducive to tracks being laid that could be followed. Unless they were still there, it was going to be like looking for a needle in a haystack the size of Rhode Island with a limited time frame.

"We've got something. I'm just changing the image now," informed the NRO operator though the phone line.

Everybody watched as the image changed to that of a small propeller aircraft sitting in the middle of the desert. The faint lines of two tracks running parallel to one another made it clear that there was a runway of sorts in place.

The excitement level increased significantly within the NCTC when the plane came into view.

"I'm afraid our infrared suggests it's empty," said the operator.

Carson was already on his cell when Turner turned to him. He waited and listened.

"Yes Admiral, thank you, I'm good," said Carson. He noticed Turner watching and grabbed a pad and pen and wrote '*Commanding Officer CSG2*'

Turner shrugged. He had no idea what CSG2 meant.

"How quickly can you get assets in place?"

Turner looked on in frustration. He had no idea what was happening.

"Excellent, I'll call you right back." He hung up and looked at Turner. "That was the Commander of Carrier Strike Group 2. They're based in the Eastern Mediterranean. I was just arranging a welcome party for whoever comes back to that plane."

"How long?"

"Two F18s will be on station within twenty minutes and will remain out of sight and sound but just five minutes' striking distance away."

"How long can they remain there?"

"Until they're needed, or at least until they're relieved by another two planes and we'll keep that up until we get them," replied Carson confidently. "We've got a Hawkeye inbound as well, so we'll see what's going on down there long before they get back to their plane," he added.

"Hawkeye?"

"It's an early warning aircraft, like an E3 Sentry only smaller and able to operate from a carrier," replied Carson.

Turner had a rough idea of what he meant. "So how are the F18s going to capture them?"

"Who said anything about capture? As soon as we have him in our sights, the two F18s will swoop down and blow him the fuck away."

"I'd rather capture him."

"And I'd rather be thirty years younger and dating a supermodel," replied Carson.

"I'd still prefer we captured him."

"Be my guest, capture him if you can," replied Carson.

"Let me call the Admiral," said Turner, reaching out for Carson's cell.

"Oh no, if the FBI want him captured, you capture him. The DOD will end this the first chance we get. Those are the Admiral's orders and they stand."

"But—"

"They are seven hundred miles deep in the desert. We don't have a chopper that flies that far and our planes on the carrier don't have the range to get there and back. Beyond that, Nick Geller is trained to evade and defend with the best of them. You try and capture him, lives are going to be lost. I'm not sending any men to their deaths over this. If we get the shot, we're taking it," replied Carson, ending any further discussion.

Turner walked back to his office and called Reid's cell. She answered by the second ring.

"What took you so long?" he blurted when she answered.

"Sorry, my lightning reactions have been dulled by a lack of sleep over the last four days."

"How long until you land at the coordinates?"

"Four hours, but I'm not sure we can; it sounds like it's a dust strip in the middle of the desert and we're on a fairly heavy plane!"

"Shit, I didn't think of that, so what's the plan?"

"Hold on," she said.

He heard her hand go over the microphone as she talked to the pilot, their muffled conversation unintelligible to him.

"We're landing at Abu Simbel Airport, it's in Southern Egypt about two hundred and fifty miles from the coordinates. We'll pick up jeeps or a ride somehow there to take us into the desert."

"I'll try to get a smaller plane to take you in. How long until you land?"

"Three and a half hours."

"I'll have something waiting!" he promised and hung up.

He picked up the handset and dialed Barry, who answered on the first ring. "Can you get one of your CIA teams to Southern Egypt in three hours?"

"I can get you more than one!" said Barry excitedly. Having been sidelined by Carson, Barry was more than happy to rejoin the fold. More importantly, Turner knew Barry wanted the chance to interrogate Nick as well.

Chapter 44

Nick stepped down gingerly from the truck. The weapons swung as one from pointing at the truck to pointing at him. The benefactor's son and friends, it appeared, were not the issue. Ibrahim stared at him through impassive eyes.

"What's going on, Ibrahim?" asked Nick, his voice measured with a tinge of anger.

"The Caliph has ordered us to keep you under guard until his arrival."

"The Caliph is dead," replied Nick.

"The new Caliph," said Ibrahim.

"I thought it hadn't been agreed yet."

"It was announced while you were away. We just heard and his first order was to keep you under guard."

Nick marched towards Ibrahim but was blocked by four men who stepped in front of him, their weapons trained directly on him. Nick stopped. He could see there would be no hesitation from them in shooting him.

One thing was for sure, he wasn't going down without a fight. He noted the distances to each before catching Ibrahim's eye once more. Ibrahim recognized the look. He had seen it in Nick when Nick had trained him.

"Whoa!!!" shouted Ibrahim. "Guys, stand down."

Nick stopped himself from moving. He had been about to strike as Ibrahim's face cracked.

"I was just fucking with you, showing my guys how a real hard guy deals with a tight situation."

The four gunmen who had squared up to Nick were perspiring heavily. They had all sensed how close it had come to action.

Nick looked at Ibrahim with utter contempt before walking away to the main building. He had his own training exercise to prepare for and deliver. Ibrahim thought better of following Nick and instead opted to debrief the group on what they had gleaned from the exercise. Ibrahim was not disappointed, every man agreed wholeheartedly: Nick Geller had not one ounce of fear in his body, even when faced with four gun barrels at close quarters and about to fire at him. He had stared back as if the guns hadn't existed and as a result, the gunmen feared the situation and not Nick. Ibrahim smiled as the men talked about a true warrior with the courage of Allah. He was an inspiration to them all and a man they would happily follow into battle for Allah.

Having given Nick fifteen minutes to calm down, Ibrahim went in search of his brother in arms. He found Nick in a back room huddled over a number of suicide vests. Small charges were packed tight inside the vests. They were small enough not to cause any peripheral damage but were certainly powerful enough to kill the wearer. The two cells stolen the previous day were in bits next to the vests, Nick having stripped them of a number of vital components.

"I'm sorry, brother, but it was a great success. They have seen that your heart is that of a lion," offered Ibrahim as an apology.

"Have all your men assemble outside and select twenty of them to take part in my exercise," commanded Nick, not looking up. Ibrahim wanted to object but Nick's tone suggested that was not an option.

Ibrahim began to walk away but stopped. "One thing that I did notice is that you weren't surprised the Caliph would want you under guard?"

Nick stopped what he was doing and looked up into Ibrahim's eyes. "Is he really the new Caliph?"

Ibrahim nodded.

Nick shook his head in anguish. "Then today I will die."

"But you killed his father on his own orders. You are a hero."

"He hated his father. He is a weak man, unfit to bear Caliph Al Zahrani's family name, never mind the title 'Caliph'," spat Nick.

"But why are you so sure he will kill you?"

"Because I promised him the next time we met, I'd kill him," replied Nick.

"You *what?*"

"You heard."

"Why?"

"It's a long story but let's put it this way – even his own father would have voted against him."

"Tell me," demanded Ibrahim, moving and closing the door to give them some privacy.

Nick shook his head. He didn't want to talk about it.

"Tell me, brother, please," insisted Ibrahim.

"It happened a year ago and I don't want to talk about it," replied Nick adamantly.

Ibrahim didn't move. He looked at Nick pleading him to open up.

Nick shook his head again. The memory of the incident was not one he ever wished to relive. A tear welled in his eye at the thought of what had happened. He turned his back to avoid Ibrahim seeing as he finished the final vest.

"Assemble your men, Ibrahim."

Ibrahim conceded and left Nick alone with his vests and went to assemble the twenty volunteers Nick had asked for.

The image of the young girl who had tended to Nick a year earlier flashed into his mind. Haseena's beautiful warm smile had radiated a purity that intoxicated everyone in its range. She was barely thirteen but spoke with maturity beyond her years and environment. Highly intelligent, she was a young girl who, in different circumstances, would have had the world at her feet. Before long, Nick had adopted her as a little sister and assured her that he would protect her as any brother should. Nick blinked as the smiling face of Haseena disappeared, just as it always did. The twisted and broken body of the young and prepubescent girl, her face contorted in agony for eternity stared back at him. The smile extinguished as the mouth that had so often shone had been beaten to a bloody pulp.

Nick's fists balled at the thought of the new Caliph, the man who had taken the light that was Haseena and extinguished it forever. He had seen how the new Caliph had looked at Haseena the night before her death. The predatory eyes picking out her purity and youth. He had not taken his eyes off her. When Haseena had looked over at Nick and smiled, hatred had burned in his eyes. He had not seen the innocence of the smile. The man was a monster.

Nick's nails dug into his palms as they balled tighter and tighter, cutting into his skin. Nick had been escorted back to his hut that night, watched by the new Caliph's men. The screams of Haseena's mother the next morning were the first sign something was wrong. When Haseena's body was found soon afterwards, it took a strong stomach to bear what the young girl had endured for what must have been hours. Nick had looked into the new Caliph's eyes and seen the killer that nobody else saw: the pedophile that had tortured and raped a young girl to death. Nick had wanted to rip the man's throat out there and then. However, it would have been suicide and, with no evidence, futile. Nick knew the day would come to reap revenge. Haseena deserved it and Nick would deliver. He just needed the right time and place. He had walked across to the man and made his promise –he was a dead man walking, and Nick assured him he would kill him the next time they met.

The tragedy had resulted in a request from the old Caliph to meet with Nick. The meeting had been unprecedented. An American operative meeting with the head of Al Qaeda was unheard of. It had been a difficult meeting, an old man admitting the shame and desperation he felt at his uselessness and inability to deal with the deviant that was his son. Knowing that Nick knew about his son's actions had for the first time allowed the Caliph to discuss the problem with someone else. The fact that there was no love between father and son was made all the more evident when the elder Caliph asked Nick for one favor, namely to follow through on his promise but not until after the elder Caliph's own death. If his son were to die while he was still Caliph, his son would be revered and honored and that was something he did not deserve, nor did the elder Caliph wish to see.

Nick had planned to deal with the young Al Zahrani during the buildup of the elder Caliph's plan. His being elevated, unwittingly by his peers, as the new Caliph meant that Nick would never deliver on his promise. There was only one reason the new Caliph was visiting the training camp and that was to kill Nick before Nick had the chance to kill him.

Nick piled the vests into a box and with a prayer to Allah for assistance, he lifted the box and continued on with the plan. He needed to show just how faithful the followers had to be to follow him into battle.

Chapter 45

Deputy Director Turner grabbed a few hours of sleep on the couch in the corner of his office. Going home just wasn't an option. Much like Reid, he lived for the job. He'd soon discovered that that did not sit well with marriage. Not many women were willing to be the second most important thing in their husband's life, certainly not the two who had tried to be.

A knock on his office door at 6:00 a.m. was accompanied by the morning newspapers. This particular wake-up call was guaranteed to get him moving. The front pages of the nationals were covered in the image of the Ebola victim's last breaths. It was a headline that would see America waking up to a vile reality if Turner failed to stop Nick Geller.

Turner grabbed the remote, turned on the TV and selected one of the 24/7 news channels. The scrolling bar had changed; it no longer scrolled the news of the Vice President's death or the President's recovery. Their leader's health was old news. The death of the first terrorist victim from a deadly virus that threatened the world, including America, was now scrolling the news banner. The newscast cut to a supermarket with a few people queuing for the opening of the store, not an uncommon occurrence. However, the headline was that lines were beginning to form as people digested the news of the upcoming pandemic.

The shit was always going to hit the fan. They had managed three days without too much pressure. The media had cooperated as requested, and played down the virus, and in any event, had more than enough to keep the airwaves busy with the Vice President's killing, the injury to the President and the destruction of the West Wing. Day Four, however, was obviously the tipping point. News had slowed down and ratings counted. Fear drove a need for knowledge, and hence ratings. What better than a disease about to kill us all in the hands of Al Qaeda and a mad American soldier?

Capturing Nick Geller and the virus would kill the story dead. Killing Nick Geller, along with the virus, would also kill the story dead. Killing Nick Geller without killing the virus would make the story more sensational. If Nick didn't have the virus, there were seven billion people on the planet at risk. With that thought, Turner rushed from his office. He needed to get Carson on board. They couldn't kill Nick without knowing if he had the virus on him.

Turner crashed into the DoD office that Carson had sequestered for his personal use. It was empty. There was a sofa in the corner and, much like his own office, there was a blanket cast aside. Carson had slept there too. He rushed back onto the gangway and looked down into the operations center, which had filled significantly since he had left for his sleep. Carson, however, was not hard to spot. He stood directly in front of the main screen with a number of operatives reacting to his every movement and command. More worryingly, the view on the screen was one similar to that of a computer game screen. A crosshair surrounded by circles was overlaid on the landscape of the desert floor. It didn't take a genius to realize that they were watching the view from the cockpit of one of the F18 jets.

"Harry!" shouted Turner, racing down the metal staircase, brushing aside those in his wake.

Carson turned around nonchalantly as Turner careened towards him.

"Don't shoot!" Turner said, pleading for him to call off the attack. "We need to know if he's got the virus on him."

"He will have," assured Carson.

"But you can't guarantee that!' wheezed Turner, catching his breath.

Carson shrugged. "Not 100%, granted, but enough to be comfortable to say 'fire' when we get the shot."

Turner looked at the screen, willing there to be no target. The crosshairs remained on a blank and barren landscape. There was still time. He grabbed his cell and dialed his boss, the FBI Director, at, home. It was just after 6:00 am. but he was an early riser. He could ask the President to stop Turner.

While the phone rang, Carson walked away towards his office.

Turner dropped the phone from his ear. "Where are you going?"

"To catch some sleep," replied Carson evenly.

An irritated voice was yelling 'Hello? *Hello??'* from the handset now at Turner's hip.

"But the attack?" Turner said, pointing to the screen.

Carson laughed, now understanding Turner's confusion. "That's the Hawkeye's camera, not a fighter's. Nothing's happened yet. Still plenty of time to try and overrule me," he added with a wink, pointing to the handset Turner was holding from which the irate voice emanated.

Chapter 46

The C40B taxied across the Abu Simbel runway and drew up next to the only other aircraft at the airport. The Boeing V22 Osprey had two oversized propellers and stubby wings. Frankie had seen one before but from the look on Reid's face, she hadn't.

"The wings rotate so it can work like a helicopter as well," she explained as they walked down the aircraft steps.

"Ah, I see," said Reid staring at the strange looking machine. "We're not going on it though are we?"

"Ladies, Barry sends his regards," offered the soldier that awaited them at the bottom of the stairs.

Frankie involuntary shivered at the mention of his name.

Reid noticed and just managed to stop herself from having the same reaction. However, Barry didn't look at Reid the way he looked at Frankie. "You've never met Barry, have you?" she asked of the soldier.

"No," he said.

"Trust me," she replied, "you don't want to be handing out his regards."

Frankie nodded wholeheartedly and the soldier got the point. "Ladies, welcome to Abu Simbel, your chariot awaits. I believe you have some amateurs that want to tag along?" he said with a smile, as Flynn appeared with the Delta team ready for action at the top of the aircraft stairs.

Smiles and high fives were shared amongst the CIA and Delta teams, many of them having worked together before. All joking and rivalry was set aside. As consummate professionals, they were on the same team and would have each other's backs. The twenty assembled men made up a fearsome team. They would die to save one another, irrespective of who issued their paycheck, DoD or CIA.

Frankie and Reid were suited up in body armor before being allowed anywhere near the Osprey. Once kitted out to the level required by the Delta and CIA team leaders, the Osprey took off. They were just over two hundred and fifty miles from the coordinates and thanks to the Osprey's capability, just under one hour away and able to land anywhere they wanted.

Flynn and the two team leaders pored over the charts that had been created over the previous few hours. The satellite imagery had been mapped and rises and falls in the landscape plotted to allow a 3D image of the terrain. A plan was formulated. Points were selected for fire teams and other areas selected for exit and entry of assault teams. With thirty minutes to spare, they repeated the exercise and were pleased to see that they still agreed with everything they had already planned. They were good to go.

Chapter 47

The training camp was spread along a valley on the desert floor. Its natural walls obscured the camp's structures, other than from above where their natural coloring ensured only the most observant viewers would see anything unless viewed in very high definition. At one end, the valley swept up on three sides from the desert floor, creating a perfect natural amphitheater and location for Nick to carry out his exercise to maximum effect.

Nick stepped into the center of the natural stage and surveyed the hundreds of jihadists crowding on the slope, desperate to prove their worth to him. He laid his box down and turned to face the twenty men Ibrahim had selected. As Nick suspected, Ibrahim, aware that some of his men may not survive, had selected men for their fanaticism, not for their ability. Nick had watched many of the groups train in the few hours he'd been there and none of these men had stood out in anything he had witnessed.

"Ibrahim!" he shouted. "You have selected well, my brother. All of these men, I am sure, are more than happy to die for Allah but that will not be today!"

Nick dismissed them with a wave and began to lay out the vests. Each vest was wired with a detonator switch which Nick carefully placed down on the ground, ensuring he didn't trigger any in the process.

From the bottom of the box he produced a small video camera that he set up on a tripod. He selected a view that offered no clue as to their location and tightened the bolts to stop the camera from moving. A further check offered a perfect view of the crowd as a backdrop. Nick paced forward and drew a cross in the desert floor with his foot. Once again, he checked the camera's view and, happy with his work, he turned to an audience that was transfixed by his every move.

"Gentlemen! Today I am going to offer a number of you the opportunity to strike fear into the heart of every American! You are going to join our founder and father, the Caliph and Allah in paradise! They are, as we speak, preparing your seventy-two virgins!" he shouted to a great cheer.

Nick, with his aging hair disguise removed, stepped in front of the camera and with a small remote, hit 'Record'.

"Ladies and gentlemen of America," he began, before once again spouting a hate-filled tirade at America's excesses and abuses and describing in detail how they had witnessed the death of the Ebola victim. This, he promised, was only one part of what was to befall America. He motioned towards the army of men behind him and promised they were coming to a street near them soon, armed with machine guns, explosives and a desire to die for their cause.

"It is that desire that I wish to demonstrate to you today," he said, ending his diatribe to the camera. He turned to his audience and asked for volunteers. Every hand in the audience was raised. Nick paused the recording.

He then selected, much to Ibrahim's disappointment, fifteen of the most impressive men he had witnessed during training, along with the benefactor's son and his four friends. Not surprisingly, the benefactor's son and friends were in no way eager to join the suicide party.

"I'm sorry, but these men are not ready," Ibrahim said, stepping closer.

"Then they have no place amongst us!" shouted Nick. "Only men happy to die for Allah and his cause should be amongst us!"

A barrage of abuse began to rain down on the five young men.

Nick held up his hands to silence their discontent. "We are the soldiers of Allah. For us to fight, we need food, we need clothes, we need weapons. We need others who can provide these for us so we can fight for Allah. They are still our brothers, just not our soldier brothers. I need soldiers willing to die for Allah! There is no shame in not having that courage—there are plenty who have. Please, if you don't have that courage, step forward now! We have many functions to fill, many areas where you can fulfill your promise to Allah. Look into your hearts as you watch these men strap the vests to their bodies," he nodded towards the fifteen men as a sign for them to begin putting on their vests. "Can you do it with the courage that these men do? Can you pull the trigger and prove your courage to Allah? If so, I want you here in my army for our march to victory. If not, we will find other jobs for you."

A silence fell and they all looked around at each other.

"I have five vests that need to be filled. If you can walk forward and happily wear one, then stay. If not, step forward now," commanded Nick, authoritatively but with compassion.

Slowly two men stepped forward at opposite ends of the slopes, then another two. After three minutes, twenty-three men had stepped forward. Nick looked on as a good proportion of the hundreds who hadn't stepped forward shook their heads in disgust.

"Do not be disappointed in our brothers admitting they are not true warriors! By doing so, they have shown as much courage as you have by staying! I would ask that they go and pack their belongings. They will be leaving this camp soon."

The men trudged off, their heads held in shame. They joined the benefactor's son and his friends and disappeared back into the camp.

"My warriors!" shouted Nick proudly and once again received a huge cheer.

"I have five empty vests," he said, lowering his voice.

A number of men broke from the crowd and rushed to grab one of the five vests. The five to win the race proudly donned the vests.

"Not all of the vests are live," Nick told them. "This is not an exercise in proving you can kill yourself, it is an exercise in proving you are worthy of killing yourself for Allah."

Blank faces looked back at him. Nick needed to show them what he meant. He pointed to one of the first fifteen men he had selected and asked him to step onto the cross he had created in front of the camera.

The man stepped forward proudly and on Nick's countdown, pressed his detonator, proudly shouting "Allahu Akbar!"

Nothing happened. The man stood on the spot and almost looked disappointed at not having exploded.

"You see! This man is happy to die for Allah! Today is not his time, but he has proved himself to all of us!"

Nick pointed to one of the last five volunteers to take his place on the cross in front of the camera.

Nick hit 'record' on the camera. The volunteer repeated the previous man's proud shout to Allah and pushed down on the detonator. This time, Nick pressed a small transmitter in his pocket and, thanks to the components from the cell phones, he triggered a small explosive charge in the vest.

A huge cheer erupted as the small explosion took the volunteer's head clean off his body. The image was safely captured for Nick's next video of terror for the American public. Nick repeated the process for the other eighteen men and in each instance only recording the four remaining volunteers for whom he triggered the device as they hit the detonators. None of detonators would have worked unless Nick wanted them to. The frenzy of the crowd by the fifth beheading was electric and would strike fear into the heart of any enemy.

Nick was waging a psychological battle on the American people. His army was coming and it was an army that would die with a smile on its face to further its cause. Being at war was frightening even for the most battle-hardened soldiers. Fighting a war against men who were happy to die for their cause was going to strike fear across the nation on the scale of the Ebola virus itself. He was also recruiting every likeminded jihadist and terrorist in the world. He was showing them that the Jihad was coming and if they wanted to be part of it they had only to join but the message was clear, true believers and warriors only need apply.

Ibrahim dismissed his fully energized army and joined Nick while he was dismantling the camera and tripod.

"Thank you for not killing my stars," he said.

"Allah's will," smiled Nick, pulling the small transmitter out of his pocket.

"What about the ones who left?"

"Send them home. They haven't got the heart to fight. We need to know that now, not on the battlefield when we need them."

"I cannot believe the energy, faith and excitement that your exercise has created. I have never seen the men so ready for battle, it's a shame it's not soon."

"It will be," said Nick. "Our time is near."

Ibrahim winced. "Perhaps not our time. A truck has gone to collect the new Caliph. He is landing shortly. I was instructed to send transport just as your exercise started."

"So he'll be here in…" Nick looked at his watch, "about an hour?"

"No, he's using a different landing strip. He'll be here any minute."

Chapter 48

"Harry!" Turner yelled through the doorway. "Something's happening down there!"

Carson, slowly awakening, stretched and joined Turner on the gangway looking down at his team. The image on the screen showed a small aircraft being tracked across the desert, flying at a low level. Harry took one look and ran down to the main floor at a speed belying his age.

"What have we got?" he called as he ran.

"One Antonov 24 flying low, approximately one hundred miles from the target location."

"Origin?" he asked, lowering his voice as he neared his team of specialists who had spent the night analyzing every piece of data from the Hawkeye and F18s that were circling the target landing area.

"The Hawkeye first picked it up on the Eritrean border to the East. From the aircraft's range, it could have come from there, Saudi or Yemen. It was already of interest due to a lack of transponder but when it dropped altitude, it obviously became far more interesting, given its origin and destination."

"Good work. It doesn't look like it's heading to the same spot though?" he asked, looking at the path being shown on the screen.

"No, and the altitude suggests he's getting ready to land."

"A meet?" asked Turner, having followed Carson down.

Carson nodded his head but continued to ponder what was happening. "Or maybe just coincidence?" he mused aloud. "How good is the camera on that Hawkeye?"

"Good but not a patch on the F18s, sir," replied the specialist.

"If they land, do a fly-by with an F18 and get me some faces."

"But that'll let them know we're on to them," protested Turner, looking at the time. His team was only twenty minutes away.

"I know, I know, but these sly fuckers have rabbit holes and warrens they'll bolt down and we'll need a thousand men just to find all the exits," replied Carson, ignoring the eyebrows being raised amongst his team, fortunately out of Turner's field of vision. "If these are high value targets, I'm not missing my chance."

"Jesus," replied Turner looking more closely at the screen. "I didn't know that!"

"Yup, they've spent years building tunnels throughout the desert to hide their camps," lied Carson convincingly, causing more than one coughing fit amongst his DoD team. "Anyway," he continued more honestly, "who's to say that Nick isn't being delivered back in that plane?"

"To a different location?"

"These landing areas get torn up. They're just dirt tracks, only good for a few landings."

Turner looked almost convinced which surprised Carson, who hadn't even convinced himself.

"Mr. Carson, it looks like they're going to make a landing."

"Sir?" a hand shot up a few desks over. "I have what could be a truck about three miles out from that location."

The specialist flicked the main screen to his colleague who had spotted a truck. The image was very poor due to the distance and quality of the Hawkeye's camera but something moving was indeed visible.

"Well spotted," said Carson. "Now people, let's time this right. I want a flyover with faces in the open!"

Turner grabbed his cell and desperately tried to call Reid. Her cell was switched off. He turned to Carson. "I need to contact the CIA team!" he said urgently.

"We're all DoD here I'm afraid," smiled Carson. "CIA don't trust us with their numbers."

"Will someone get me in contact with the CIA plane!" shouted Turner in frustration.

"Deputy Director Turner, I have Barry for you," called a voice from across the operations center floor. A CIA team member had heard Carson's bullshit and contacted Barry to update him.

Carson looked at his watch and noted the progress of the CIA team in their plane. They were fifteen minutes out. His orders were clear. A clean kill. Nothing else was acceptable.

Carson willed the AN-24 plane to land. He needed to know who was on it before the CIA team had a chance to complicate matters.

Turner watched the same screen, willing the plane to take its time. He had been informed that the warren holes and tunnels were utter nonsense. The desert was a dark hole in surveillance without the need for any burrowing. Camps came and went in the millions of square miles of barren and featureless terrain. Stumbling across one on satellite imagery was the equivalent of winning the Powerball every week for a year. It just didn't happen.

DoD had an agenda, one Turner was unaware of and one he certainly wasn't going to sit back and let happen. He wanted Nick Geller in custody. Period.

Chapter 49

The first moment Frankie knew there was an issue was when the CIA team leader started yelling at the pilots.

"Can't this fucking thing go any faster?!"

The answer was as succinct; they were travelling as fast as they could.

The CIA Team Leader jotted down the new coordinates and walked into the cockpit, handing them over to the pilot. He took the note and set it aside. He had already altered their course.

"ETA twenty minutes," he said, before the team leader could protest.

The team leader made his way back into the main body of the V-22 Osprey and was met by a sea of faces keen to know what was happening.

"Well?" prompted Frankie.

The team leader opted to let Barry update them. He dialed his number and hit the loudspeaker, explaining who was listening in.

"They've picked up another plane. We don't know who's on it but it seems Carson is hell bent on shooting the shit out of it," said Barry, bringing them up to speed.

"And?"

"And there's a chance it's your boyfriend," he said, immediately regretting taking out his frustration on Frankie.

"Uncalled for," said Flynn, shaking his head in disgust.

"Pathetic," said Reid.

Frankie remained unphased. Her boyfriend had died four days ago. The Nick Geller they were chasing was just a man she had known in a previous life.

"So what's the rush, they'll beat us—" she halted in mid-speech when she was suddenly thrown across the cabin and slammed into the side of the Osprey as it was blown across the sky, rocking wildly from a blast.

***

"You have a go," said the DoD specialist from NCTC into the headset of the F18 pilots, thousands of miles away, above the Sudanese desert.

"Roger. Commencing reconnaissance run," one replied, throwing the afterburners forward and rocketing towards the target. They had a two-minute window to catch the disembarking occupants while they waited for their inbound truck.

Staying just out of sight, they sped in low and would slow down over the area to ensure the best possible angles for the reconnaissance cameras to pick up even the tiniest detail on the pass.

"Watch the friendly ahead," warned the first pilot to his wingman.

Both of their headsets buzzed to life. "Make sure they know you're there," ordered Carson, listening in and watching the scene play out thousands of miles away. "We wouldn't want them getting in your way."

Both pilots tweaked their direction slightly, thereby reducing the distance by which they would clear the Osprey. Within a second, both had blasted past the Osprey on either side at almost four times its speed. It rocked wildly and dangerously behind them.

"Shit! We may have cut that a little closer than we should," said one of the pilots.

"Are they still in the air?" asked Carson.

The pilot looked back, just to make sure. "Yes."

"Then you didn't."

Nearing the target, they began to slow down, aiming their cameras at the group of men scrambling on the ground to find cover at the sight of the US warplanes. A couple of bullets buzzed past the planes but it really was the equivalent of taking a knife to a gunfight, a very large and powerful gunfight.

"Okay, hang back while we check the images we have," instructed Carson to the pilots.

***

With the new Caliph due to arrive any minute, Nick felt it was a good time to make a move. He had his video and the next phase of the plan was in place. The new Caliph was an issue but he was hoping that an enlightening conversation with his next group might elicit a change in the Caliph and a further endorsement of Nick and the original Caliph's plan. Everything came down to money, and for Al Qaeda and a number of the fundamentalist groups Nick was looking to unite, that came from Saudi Arabia and the Emirates.

The four armed guards protecting Nasim's small bunkroom were not a welcome sight. Nor was the information that Nasim would not be flying Nick anywhere by order of Ibrahim. Nasim was far easier to imprison than Nick and without him, Nick was trapped. It was a clever move by Ibrahim and far less confrontational than trying to imprison Nick.

Making his way to 'discuss' the situation with his 'brother', Nick heard a noise he shouldn't have.

"Ibrahim!' he shouted as loud as he could in the center of the camp.

Ibrahim appeared warily, a hundred yards away from the main building. He had no business being there other than to avoid Nick.

"Thunder," he said, strolling casually towards a furious Nick.

Nick shook his head. "That, brother, was a fighter jet's sonic boom."

Ibrahim looked around the sky in a panic.

"Where is the Caliph's landing strip?"

Ibrahim pointed to the area the clap of noise had emanated from.

"How far?"

"Twenty, thirty miles."

Nick looked out across the empty sky. "They must have tracked him. Tell them to stay away from here!"

"I have no way to contact them," Ibrahim shrugged despondently. "We will stand and fight!"

"They will massacre us. How can we fight warplanes!" replied Nick. "You have an evacuation plan?"

Ibrahim nodded.

"Well, let's GO!"

***

Almost as soon as the faces were extracted from the images being beamed back by the F18s, the facial recognition software had identified them. Hit after hit confirmed the faces as the son of the former head of Al Qaeda Zahir Al Zahrani's son and his bodyguards who were well known to the authorities.

Carson had a decision to make. With no identification of Nick and, as far as they could tell, every individual accounted for amongst the twenty two men that had landed in the AN-24, should he send in the jets or let Barry and the CIA and Delta team deal with them?

He checked his watch. Barry's team was still ten minutes away.

"What's the ETA on the truck?" he asked.

"Two minutes," came the reply.

"Take it out."

Twenty seconds later, a flash in the corner of the main screen was all the confirmation they needed. The truck was out of the equation.

"Mr. Carson?" One of the CIA analysts attached to the team had ventured over to the DoD area.

"Yes?" he replied distractedly.

"We're hearing that Al Qaeda has chosen the young Zahrani to take over as leader."

Carson spun back and stared at the collection of men cowering in the desert thousands of miles away, looking down like some kind of god deciding if they were to live or die. "Are we 100% confident that Al Zahrani is the new Caliph?"

The resounding answer was yes. *To kill or not to kill?* he asked himself.

"Turner, it looks like you may just grab yourself a genuine live and nasty Al Qaeda leader. If you don't fuck it up!" Carson turned back to his team. "Tell the F18s to offer whatever support the ground team requires."

***

"Holy shit!" Barry exclaimed as he was fed the news of their teams' 'Go' to capture the new head of Al Qaeda. He called the V-22 Osprey and gave them the news. "Lock and load boys," he said, adding quickly for Reid and Frankie's benefit, "and girls! Ten minutes!"

Chapter 50

Thanks to the F18s' fly past, the Osprey pilot had an excellent image of the assault area. He altered course on their approach and came in behind the hill that obscured the landing site. A brief touchdown deposited the CIA and Delta teams out of sight of the terrorists before the Osprey continued up and over the hill. Armed with a mini-gun and M240 .50 caliber bullets, the Osprey could stand off in hover mode and lay down cover fire while the CIA and Delta teams initiated the assault on the ground.

Two snipers, one from each of the teams, were sent to the top of the small hill. They would provide targeted fire support for the two teams who would work their way around either side of the hill and perform a pincer movement. With the snipers on the hill and the Osprey on the other side of the landing zone, the terrorists were already boxed in, they just didn't know it yet.

The snipers reached the small summit and were pleased to see almost half a mile of clear, open ground between them and the landing zone. Not great for their colleagues but for the snipers, they had the gift of an open field for targeting the terrorists. Just like the rest of the teams, they had all been shown the photo of Al Zahrani. He was the only target they had to avoid killing. Every other target before them was open season.

As a result of spotting the F18s, the terrorists had not ventured away from the landing area. None had braved the open ground, staying close to the plane instead, no doubt hopeful that the F18s would disappear and let them reboard their plane and depart.

The Delta sniper set up his AX338 sniper rifle, alongside his CIA counterpart's McMillan TAC-338. Both approved each other's choice with a nod before zeroing in on the terrorists before them.

"Target acquired," the Delta sniper said into his mic, quickly adding, "Target down."

"Target acquired. Tango down," said the CIA sniper.

Delta sniper: "Target acquired. Tango down."

The commentary continued. Ten jihadists ceased to exist before the other jihadists had managed to squirrel themselves away into safer positions, outside of the snipers' view.

CIA sniper: "Osprey, could you please stir up the nest?"

The V-22 Osprey had been hovering just outside the terrorists' small arms' fire range and had stayed out of the fight. The pilot swung the Osprey around and the M240 opened up. The 0.50 caliber bullets tore into the ground and had a number of terrorists running for cover, the very cover that protected them from the snipers. The snipers, once again, began their duck shoot.

"Jesus, guys!" shouted Flynn into the mic, as the Delta and CIA team were about to enter the battlefield. "Leave something for us!"

With the snipers and the M240 pinning the terrorists down, the CIA and Delta teams had an easy run into the killing zone. Working in four four-man squads, two CIA and two Delta, the teams approached the last few entrenched terrorists. A small cluster of rocks had proved an excellent defensive position for Al Zahrani and his last four bodyguards. Impervious to the long distance fire, it was down to the assault teams to break down their resolve.

Flynn directed the two Delta teams who converged from the east while the CIA team leader directed his two four-man teams from the west. The bodyguards, armed with AK47s, tried in vain to halt the advance but the onslaught of the highly trained operatives converging on them was overwhelming. The individual teams worked in tandem. Two men laid down cover while the other two moved forward and repeated the procedure. The teams literally walked across the open desert floor without so much as a single bullet in response from the pinned down bodyguards. As the teams reached the opposite side of the rock cluster, a number of flash bangs preempted the final assault into the small area that held Al Zahrani, further neutralizing Al Zahrani's loyal bodyguards. Despite the overwhelming odds, two of the bodyguards were suicidal enough to try and stop the capture. Both fell to the ground, three bullets apiece, double tap to the chest and a kill shot to the forehead just to make sure. His other bodyguards dropped their weapons, just as Al Zahrani had done himself. Al Qaeda had just lost its newest leader, even before the world knew who he was.

Once the area was announced clear, only two additional jihadists were alive, although barely, alongside the new Caliph and his loyal bodyguards. The rest were all killed in action with no casualties among the CIA or Delta teams. A number of high fives were exchanged throughout the ops center. Even the F18s were allowed in on the action. Their job was to destroy the AN-24 aircraft that had been left in the landing zone. A short burst of their M61 Gatling guns saved the US tax payer a few thousand dollars, destroying the plane without the need for any missiles. All in all, the operation had proved an overwhelming success.

"What about the other plane?" asked Carson of the smiling Turner, bringing him back down to earth with a bump. Their job was not to capture Al Zahrani, their job was to catch Nick Geller.

"Oh yes, I suppose we continue to watch it."

Carson shrugged. "I doubt there's much point. I'm sure if Nick were somewhere in that desert, he wouldn't go anywhere near that plane again, given the noise we just made."

"Sir, I have Special Agent Reid on the line, she says it's urgent," announced one of Carson's DoD team.

"Put her on speaker," said Carson.

"Frankie, it seems, was right." Reid said.

"About what?" asked Turner.

"Geller doesn't slip up!"

"Would you mind explaining?" said Carson irritably.

"Al Zahrani is laughing at us, telling us how we fucked up big time,"

"We just captured his sorry ass!" said Turner.

"Yes we did. However, we captured him on his way to killing Nick Geller!"

"What?!" asked Turner.

"He was coming here for one reason and one reason only – to kill Nick Geller!"

"Son of a bitch played us again!" Turner brayed.

Carson shook his head, a slim smile across his face; it was hard not to admire that level of ingenuity. "Did he tell you where they were heading?"

"Flynn's asking him now," she said, wincing at the sounds coming from the rear of the plane as Flynn 'questioned' Al Zahrani.

Ten minutes later, Flynn reported that Al Zahrani did not know the meet location, all they had were the co-ordinates for landing. The truck that was to pick them up was to take them to the secret camp.

"Well let's get looking for that camp!" Turner urged.

"We have been since we found the plane," said Carson. "There are hundreds of thousands of square miles to search. But even if we do find it, I guarantee they'll be long gone."

"So he's done it again."

"Yep, we saved him and not only that, we removed the only man on the planet who could stop him from within Al Qaeda."

"Perhaps we should let Al Zahrani go?"

"If it wasn't for that," replied Carson, pointing to the breaking news banner on one of the news channels announcing Al Zahrani's capture, "I may have agreed with that quite ridiculous idea."

"How the hell did they know already?"

"Wouldn't surprise me if Geller hadn't tipped them off himself," sighed Carson.

Chapter 51

"So, what do we think...where will he go next?" mused Reid. She and Flynn were poring over a large map of the desert. Exactly the same conversation was happening back at NCTC, only with a far larger map and group of specialists. They all came to the same conclusion: they had no idea. There were just too many variables.

Frankie had accompanied Al Zahrani back to the US on the C40B, insisting that Flynn and Reid were far more valuable in the hunt for Geller. Her job was back home, trying to look for clues from the last few months. Flynn had argued initially, but ultimately, he was a soldier and was more than happy to stay at the sharp end of the hunt with his Delta team. Reid just wanted to catch Nick and if Frankie felt she could help do that better from the States, she had no complaints. With no objections from Carson and Turner, Frankie, along with four of the CIA Special Operations operatives, waved the V-22 Osprey off at Abu Simbel and took off in the C40B for the US, most likely via Guantanamo Bay, although that was still to be decided.

"Port Sudan," said Reid, tracing her finger east across the desert to the coast of Sudan.

"Any particular reason?" asked Flynn.

"He came from the west and headed east. I expect he'll keep going east."

"There are lots of ports to choose from," Flynn noted, looking at the coastline.

"Yes but Port Sudan's the biggest, easiest to get lost in, and will have the greatest flow of traffic," countered Reid, judging the size of the ports by the diameter of the circles denoting their locations on the map.

"As good a call as any," said Flynn, hitting the dial button to reach Turner and Carson back at NCTC. "We're going to head down to Port Sudan to see if we can pick up anything," he said when he had them on the phone.

Turner looked at Carson for a hint of his thoughts. Carson traced the route and considered the option. "With nothing else to go on, I don't see why not."

"Okay, make your way down there. If we get anything, we'll be in touch," he said, killing the connection to the V-22 Osprey.

Carson's cell buzzed. He looked down and read the message. "Turner, we've been summoned."

"By whom?"

"There are only two people left on this planet who can summon me," replied Carson, leading the way.

Turner didn't need to be told twice. He knew Carson was a widower, so that left the President and the Secretary of Defense.

"Any ideas why?" asked Turner when he caught up with Carson.

"Nope but it's not usually to say 'well done'. In fact, scrub that, they *never* summon me to say 'well done'."

"Al Zahrani?"

Carson nodded. He had a gut feeling that he should have just blown the man back to his Allah. He should have known from Bin Laden and Al Zahrani Senior that the fallout of killing a leader was minimal. However, capturing one gave the jihadists a reason to react. They had someone they could save. A cause.

Thirty minutes later, Carson and Turner were ushered through to the President's private lounge in the main White House residence. He did not look happy, nor did his guests – the Secretary of Defense, the Director of National Intelligence and the National Security Advisor. Turner moved to close the door behind him but was stopped by the Chief of Staff, who was rushing in to join the meeting. Carson swore under his breath. The Chief of Staff and Carson rarely agreed. His absence in the last few days, due to preparations for the Vice President's funeral and the organization required to rehouse the West Wing staff, had been most welcome by Carson.

"Jeff," said Carson, greeting the Chief of Staff coldly.

Jeff Lewis looked at Carson as though he had stepped on something unfortunate on his way into the office. He did not return the greeting. Jeff was the political genius behind the President. He had gotten James Mitchell into the White House and it was his job to make sure he stayed there for a second term. He understood the need for the Carsons of the world but was never comfortable with them.

"Mr. President," Jeff said, "I'm sorry I'm late, just finalizing the details for tomorrow," he said somberly. The Vice President's funeral was to be held the next day with hundreds of dignitaries from across the world due to attend.

"Not a problem, Jeff. So what's up?" he asked.

Carson shifted uneasily in his seat. Jeff Lewis had called the meeting, not the President. And if Jeff had requested Turner and Carson to attend, it wasn't going to be good news. Turner, he noted, was sitting blissfully unaware of the shit storm that was about to hit them. Jeff Lewis looked like a warm cuddly bear to the outside world. His rotund waistline and cheery smile hid a manipulative, devious and stunning intellect that had dismembered political foes with ease over the years.

"Cluster fuck, SNAFU, FUBAR, just a few expressions I could use for the incompetents over there," he said, pointing to Carson and a stunned and suddenly fully alert Turner.

"Now, come on, Jeff, those are rather strong words," warned the President, leaning back in his chair and supporting his strapped arm.

"Who authorized the capture of the Al Qaeda leader?" asked Jeff of the cabinet level members in the room.

All shook their heads, while Jeff pointed to Turner and Carson.

"Those two. And thanks to their efforts, the President is being torn a new asshole by Speaker Lopez! It seems she got a taste for the top spot and is looking far more likely to stand against the President now at the next election!" He paused for added impact and then continued.

"For those of you not in the know, that's seriously fucking bad news! Up until now, she was in her box but she's ripping into us over the incompetence of one of our own doing this to us," he spurted furiously, waving his hand to where the West Wing used to stand. "And now she's got us having to pay millions to house the new leader of Al Qaeda! Not forgetting that every American on the planet will now be a hostage target to trade for the fucker! There was a fucking reason we shot Bin Laden!!!" he screamed.

"I'll tell you what, Jeff. If you're so fucking clever, you catch Geller. Sorry, you *kill* Geller!" suggested Carson, his temper rising by the second.

"If I didn't have an administration to save, I might just have taken you up on that offer!!"

"It's my fault," said Turner stepping forward. "I pressured Carson into letting me capture rather than kill Al Zahrani."

Jeff looked at Turner with incredulity before he bent over with laughter. "That's a classic!" When Turner failed to react, Jeff stepped in again. "Seriously?! You believe that?!"

Turner looked around the room. They all avoided his eye contact. He looked at Carson who simply shrugged.

"You're playing with the big boys now, Turner. Harry Carson's not been pressured into anything since he stopped needing his mother's tittie!"

Carson had a reason for wanting Al Zahrani captured, it just wasn't one he cared to share with the audience before him.

"Okay guys, enough," said the President. "Jeff, you deal with the politics. Harry, you know what you've gotta do. I understand, Jeff, you are pissed and Speaker Lopez is going to hit us no matter what we do. Christ, if we had killed Al Zahrani she'd be spitting blood!"

"Sir, I believe Jeff has a point regarding Americans being taken hostage. We should issue an alert," advised Liz Roberts, his National Security Advisor.

"The already heightened chatter has exploded," added Mark Nelson, the DNI. "We've had heightened levels for eighteen months. They increased again thanks to Geller and it's just gone ballistic since Al Zahrani was captured. The terrorists are talking. We just don't know what they're saying at the higher levels. Some of the low level stuff we can break and there have been a few comments regarding hostages…"

Before he could finish, a knock on the door preceded the President's secretary who entered and turned on the TV. "Mr. President, I've been asked to put this on for you."

All turned to the screen as Nick Geller once again hit the news headlines. Al Jazeera, the Middle East news channel, was running new footage with an 'Exclusive' banner running across the screen. Nick's diatribe had not changed but his location had. He was now in a desert amphitheater surrounded by hundreds of fanatics. He stopped speaking and the image cut to a smiling man wearing a suicide vest. The man shouted *Allahu Akbar*, then looked to the heavens and with a smile of anticipation, blew himself up.

"Oh my God!" shouted Jeff, when the man's head separated cleanly from his body.

The crowd in the amphitheater went wild. Another four happily suicidal men met the same fate to huge cheers from the fanatical crowd.

"Dear God!" said Liz. "This is going to create serious panic."

"In America, yes," corrected Carson. "It's also created a legend," he added, pointing to Geller who had just reappeared on the screen.

He was still in the desert but without the crowd. He faced the camera somberly: "Brothers and sisters of the cause, I bring you bad news. Our new Caliph has been captured by the American infidel. However, I call on you not to act rashly. Together, united, we can make a difference. I ask all true Islamic warriors to join our cause and let us free our Caliph as one united people, fighting for Allah. You have seen the video of the believers who fight for Allah, happy to die for him. If that is you, come and fight for Allah, join his army and help us destroy America."

The screen went blank before cutting back to the Al Jazeera news anchor.

Inside the President's lounge, nobody spoke. They were all digesting the horrors of the video and the impact it had on themselves and ultimately what it meant for America.

Finally, Carson broke the silence. "Well *that's* not helpful," he remarked, summing up perfectly how everyone felt.

Chapter 52

"Jeff Lewis is a grade A asshole," said Turner, as he and Carson exited the White House residence.

"Practice makes perfect and he's been practicing being an asshole his entire life," joked Carson. "Although, to be fair, if you want to run for office, there is no better guy to get you there."

Turner opened the driver's door. "I can't believe you give that guy any credit!" "It was me that recommended him to President Mitchell," said Carson, climbing into the passenger seat and leaving a speechless Turner holding the door handle. "He does his thing and I do my thing."

"But what exactly is it you do? I mean, what is your title?" asked Turner, sliding into this seat. He realized then just how out of his league he really was.

"Titles are just something people get hung up on. Did you know it's the number one cause for labor disputes? If I don't have one, people can't pin me down on an organizational chart. For example, you have the FBI Director above you, the Deputy AG above him, the AG and then the President. You're four steps removed from the President. Lots of people are more senior than you. Every person at Justice who reports to the Deputy AG is more senior than you, according to the organizational chart."

"So what *do* you do?" pushed Turner.

"I do what's needed," Carson replied mysteriously.

"And Al Zahrani needed to be captured, why?"

Turner pulled the car out of the White House gates. He had been keen to know why since Jeff Lewis had belittled him over it.

"You wanted him and I couldn't think of a reason why not," replied Carson with a smile.

"Bullshit!" said Turner. He was beginning to think there was another agenda at play, one he was most definitely not in on.

Carson stayed silent, further antagonizing Turner. The silence hung in the air until they arrived back at NCTC. Carson, it seemed, was very comfortable with silence. Turner was not. He slammed his door and marched unhappily into the center, barking orders at anyone below him on the organizational chart, essentially everyone in the center.

"Power is something you earn, it's not something you're given," said Carson as he followed Tuner into his office.

"Who said that?" asked Turner, his temper barely holding.

"I read it on a fortune cookie," said Carson. His cell rang, interrupting his fun. Few people knew the number to that cell. He exited the office quickly and jogged down the hall to his own.

"Yes?" he answered, closing his office door behind him, something he never did.

"We've carried out an exhaustive background check," said the voice.

He was about to ask on whom but realized it was Frankie. He had meant to cancel it the following day; it had been a kneejerk reaction.

"I meant to cancel that request," he said apologetically at the thought of the amount of man hours and work that would have been expended.

"It's just as well you didn't, we found something interesting."

Chapter 53

"Say that again," said Carson, hoping he had misheard what had been said.

The caller repeated exactly, word for word, what he hoped they hadn't said the first time around.

He ended the call and sat for a moment as the implications of the news hit home. Had Nick Geller known? And if so, why had he chosen her? It seemed inconceivable that he *didn't* know. The chances of it being a coincidence, something he didn't believe in to begin with, were so remote that Nick must have known.

All the time Carson was thinking, he wasn't doing anything. The easiest course of action would be to go down to the operations center floor and alert everybody. That, however, would be such a betrayal of Frankie's right to privacy that he couldn't do it. He had grown fond of her and was not going to destroy her publicly. He needed help and bizarrely there was only one person who *could* help. He picked up the phone and called Barry.

Barry rushed into the room a minute later, more than happy to help a cap-in-hand Carson. The idea that Harry Carson would 'owe him one' was not something he was going to pass up.

"Thanks for coming so quickly, Barry," said Carson, motioning for him to shut the door behind him.

"Anything I can do to help," Barry offered cheerily.

"I need you to contact your lead CIA guy on the flight with Al Zahrani and order him and his team not to leave Al Zahrani's side."

Barry squinted, reading between the lines. "Is there a problem on the plane?"

"Not if you do as I say."

"I should warn my guys if you think there's a problem... they can land and –"

"Look, just do it and I'll owe you one, okay?!" insisted Carson.

Barry picked up his cell and contacted his CIA counterpart on the flight. After a short conversation catching up, he turned the conversation to Carson's request and put the phone onto speaker. "Steve, would you mind babysitting Al Zahrani all the way here?" he asked.

"Not a problem, he's going nowhere," said Steve confidently.

"Excellent," said Barry looking at Carson for approval.

"Is he with him now?" asked Carson.

Barry repeated the question.

"Yes," replied Steve.

"Good, just don't let him out of your sight," reiterated Barry.

"What, literally?"

"Jesus!" barked Carson, grabbing the phone. "Can you see Al Zahrani at this very moment?"

"Who is this?" asked Steve irritably.

"It's fine, Steve, it's Harry Carson, just answer," said Barry.

"Not physically, but he's in the rear cabin and no one can get to him without going through us."

"Would you mind putting Frankie on the phone with me please? And then I want you and your team not to let Al Zahrani out of your sight. Go into the rear cabin with him and don't leave his side, *literally*."

"Should I interrupt her?"

"Is she sleeping?"

"No," he said a little confused. "She's questioning Al Zahrani as per your orders and we weren't to disturb her."

"Disturb her!!!" Carson yelled, panicking now.

Barry's stunned face looked at Carson while the shuffling and door opening noises came through the phone line as Steve rushed towards the rear cabin. A bang on the door went unanswered and was followed by the sound of a door being smashed open.

"Oh fuck!" Steve bellowed.

"What? What is it?" said Carson.

He was desperate to know what Frankie had done with the pedophile who had raped her when she was twelve.

***

When the image of the man who had raped her when she was a child appeared on the screen, Frankie had almost fainted on the spot. It was an image she had never been able to visualize in her mind but one she instantly recognized. The new Caliph, although many years older now, was the man who had crept into her bedroom late one night. Frankie and her parents had been visiting relatives in Riyadh, Saudi Arabia, and the main purpose of the trip was to introduce Frankie to her mother's heritage. It would be the only trip and contact she would ever have with her Saudi relatives.

The new Caliph had done things that no innocent twelve-year-old could comprehend or be able to forget. As he pinned her to her bed, she had vowed she would one day have the strength and resolve to fight back. When he had stepped onto the Osprey, bound and gagged, she had stayed out of sight, not wanting to alert him to her presence. Not that she looked anything like the young child he had abused and defiled. She wanted to scream and shout "rapist!", "pedophile!" but that would deprive her of her chance. Despite her stomach being tied in knots, she remained calm and argued why she should accompany the monster home.

Waiting until he was secured in the rear cabin, she boarded the C40B. Shortly after takeoff, she had advised the rest of the team that she was to question Al Zahrani. The CIA operatives very kindly offered to assist. However, she wasn't sure they'd have the stomach for what she planned and certainly wouldn't have allowed it.

Eventually walking into the room and coming face to face with the monster, after all those years, was a great disappointment. He didn't recognize her. He didn't even show the faintest interest in her. Frankie was a stunningly beautiful woman. She turned heads wherever she went. When she walked into a room, she was noticed. Sickness swelled in her stomach as the realization hit her. He didn't find women attractive, he only found young girls attractive. She sat down and stared into his eyes, willing him to recognize her. His hands were bound and his mouth gagged. He looked back at her uninterested. However, the faintest hint of recognition flickered in his eyes. Her deep blue eyes, inherited from her father, somehow betrayed her Middle Eastern looks. The more he stared, the more he began to remember something and the more sick and disgusted Frankie felt. She nodded at him, letting him know his memory was correct.

Tied and gagged, he suddenly realized the danger he was in. The tables had turned; the abused was about to become the abuser. Frankie stood up and tightened the gag, adding another one just to be safe. Once completely silenced, the struggling Al Zahrani put up a fight as Frankie secured his legs to legs of his chair. She smiled as he sat, his legs slightly spread, at her mercy. Al Zahrani wore the traditional *thawb*, a long white robe that fell to his ankles. Given the summer climate, he had elected not to wear cotton pants underneath and instead, as she fought the struggling Al Zahrani, Frankie found only a pair of boxer shorts.

A phone ringing in the other room caught her attention for a second, but only for a second. She looked down on the wretchedness of the man who sat naked from the waist down in front of her. His manhood lay limp and frightened, unlike the day it had met the far younger Frankie.

Her anger swelled again and fear flashed in Al Zahrani's eyes when Frankie produced a knife and without a moment's hesitation swept the razor sharp blade across the top of Al Zahrani's scrotum. A second and third slash ensured that Al Zahrani would never again harm a child and never again need to use a standing urinal. Zahrani passed out from the pain and blood flowed freely from the wounds. Frankie picked up the offending articles and deposited them in the restroom before flushing them away deep into the chemical waste system that would render them useless for any attempted reattachment.

The door flew open as Frankie was pushing towels against the wounds in an attempt to stem the blood flow.

"Oh fuck!" shouted Steve.

Frankie removed the towel, sending Steve's own testicles running for cover as he convulsed at the sight before him, dropping his cell to the floor.

Frankie calmly stood up and retrieved the cell.

"Hello?" she said.

"Christ, Frankie, what have you done?" asked Carson.

"Don't worry, it's still alive."

"Does he need medical attention?"

"Well I wouldn't exactly call him a *he* any longer and medical attention probably wouldn't be a bad thing if you want him to reach the US alive."

Carson killed the line and contacted the pilot. The nearest stop with decent medical facilities that they could use safely and secretly was the Princess Royal Medical Centre in Gibraltar, a UK overseas territory that was nothing more than an outcrop of rock measuring 2.6 square miles on the southern tip of Spain.

A one-hour emergency stop had the less than perfect Al Zahrani stitched and in a condition that would ensure he survived the Atlantic crossing.

Carson just needed to work out what he should do with Frankie, who had not one ounce of remorse for her actions. It was, however, out of his hands. Frankie was on the case at the request of the President. Having sworn the CIA team to secrecy over the matter, they were the only people, except for the surgeon, who were aware of the extent of Frankie's handiwork.

Carson climbed into his car for a private meeting with President Mitchell. A meeting he was not looking forward to.

Chapter 54

Nick had spent the day travelling across the desert. The evacuation plan was executed to perfection. Over twenty different routes were in operation ensuring that even if the Americans did spot some of the terrorists escaping, the impact to the cause would have been minimal. However, with trucks and vehicles camouflaged to blend in with the environment and speeds restricted to ensure minimal dust disruption, only the keenest eyes looking from close range would have spotted any of the escaping terrorists.

Nick and Ibrahim had traveled throughout the day and half the night to reach their destination, a small port to the south of Port Sudan. Suakin Port was once the main Port of Sudan but over the years had become usurped by the far larger port to its north. On an ancient natural inlet, the original city sat in ruins within the harbor. In its day, it would have been a spectacular sight but like many Third World cities, it was merely a reminder of the great place it once had been.

Ibrahim led Nick onto the small freighter that would take them onto their next destination, Sana'a, the Yemeni capital, via a small port on the northwest coast of Yemen.

***

Having landed at Port Sudan airport, Flynn, Reid and the teams spent the evening and very early morning in the main port where it became abundantly clear that the chances of finding Nick Geller amongst the hustle and bustle of one the region's busiest ports and where the majority of the locals earned their living were negligible.

"This isn't going to work," Flynn said, looking at the vast port area and the thousands of people swarming around them. "But I still think he's heading east."

"He's probably already there," sighed Reid.

"I'm not so sure. He'd know we had AWACS up as soon as we intercepted Al Zahrani. If I were him, I'd have gone to ground, literally."

Reid wagged her finger excitedly. "And you had the same training as him!"

"Yes," agreed Flynn without enthusiasm.

"So what would you have done?"

"I wouldn't have come here, too obvious. I'd have picked a smaller port, still busy enough to lose myself if I needed to and board a vessel that wouldn't look out of place making the crossing to Saudi Arabia or Yemen.

"I have no idea how far that is," Reid admitted. "Is it a thousand miles or so? In which case it'd be a fairly big ship, no?"

Flynn shook his head. "No, it's about 150 to 200 miles and no, it wouldn't need to be that big a ship."

"Oh, okay, so where to?"

Flynn hit the transmitter on his two-way radio and spoke into the small, discreet mic. "Guys, back to the airport," he announced. Turning to Reid, he said, "I'll know when we see the charts."

Back on the Osprey, Flynn grabbed the charts and maps, his finger tracing up and down the coastline of Sudan and Eritrea to the south.

"There," he said, his finger stopping on Suakin. "That's where I'd go if I were being chased." *Shit,* he thought. Why hadn't he been thinking like that earlier?

"There's no airport there though," said Reid.

"We don't need one," he said, making a swirly helicopter motion with his hands.

He walked through to inform the pilot of their next destination, just forty miles to the south. With immediate clearance, they were on their way and landed at the main port in the mouth of the harbor less than fifteen minutes later. The local time was 6:37 a.m.

Nick heard the Osprey before he saw it. It was a noise you didn't forget once you had heard it, especially when it had been your ride home from some hairy situations. He looked out of the freighter's cabin and watched the propellers rotate to allow the oversized helicopter and small plane to land at the mouth of the harbor.

The door opened and the first of a squad of heavily armed men rushed out to take up defensive positions. With the Osprey's mini-gun pointing into the narrow outlet, no ship was going to get past them without being searched. It was an impressive move and Nick, using the binoculars on the small bridge, recognized a kindred spirit. Flynn, an old colleague and excellent operative, stepped down from the Osprey. Nick watched as Flynn organized his men for a thorough search of the port area.

So near, yet so far, thought Nick. They had cleared the narrow outlet into the main waterway five minutes earlier. As far as anyone looking now was concerned, the small freighter was just one of many, bobbing along, transporting wares around the area.

"That was close," said Ibrahim, looking over Nick's shoulder.

"A little too close and I was a little too obvious." Nick chastised himself. His purpose was far too important to be ruined by not doing his best. Allah deserved his best, as did the old Caliph. He had promises to keep.

Chapter 55

"Come in," said the President without looking up, at Carson's knock. He entered the President's private study, which had most recently been the Lincoln Sitting room until the destruction of the West Wing.

"Mr. President," replied Carson nervously.

"What's happened?" asked President Mitchell, looking up immediately. Carson didn't do nervous.

President Mitchell waved him to the chair in front of his desk impatiently.

Carson sat, then described in detail what had happened. The President sat emotionless while Carson talked. Carson wrapped up the update with the stitching of Al Zahrani's wounds. The President remained speechless.

"She sliced off his balls?!" he asked after a minute, making sure it wasn't a joke.

"And his penis, Mr. President," clarified Carson.

The President nodded, pondering. "And we're certain it was Al Zahrani that raped her as a young girl?"

"It appears so. There is a file on Al Zahrani in Mossad. A number of incidents have been compiled but no charges have ever been brought against him. Mossad thought they were in luck when he was made head of Al Qaeda. They were going to use it against him."

"But we captured him almost as the announcement was made."

"Yep and as you can imagine, they're a little pissed that we didn't consult with them. They think that with the leverage they had against Al Zahrani, we should have left him in place."

"Well that'll teach them not to hold out on us," replied President Mitchell, equally pissed.

Carson nodded in agreement. "What do you want me to do with Frankie, sir?" he asked, moving on to the main purpose for his visit.

"Is she sorry she did it?"

"No, sir," replied Carson. "Not at all."

The President smiled. "That's my girl," he said proudly. "If he had raped my daughter, I'm not sure that I'd have stopped at the genitalia."

"As much as I agree, it doesn't eliminate the fact that he was a prisoner in our custody," said Carson.

"Fuck it, throw him in Gitmo. Nobody will ever know. He's not going to tell anyone a woman cut his dick off! Especially not when they find out he's a pedophile."

"Are you sure? If this ever gets out…"

"What?" asked the President with a smile.

"We'll probably gain five points in the polls," said Carson, understanding.

"I'd bet fifty bucks it would be nearer ten!"

"Sir, that's the easiest fifty bucks you'd ever win from me. And Frankie?"

"Stays on the case," insisted the President. "Did Geller know?"

"About the rape?" asked Carson. "I don't know. But I can tell you it was more serious than we knew between them."

"How serious?" Carson made an arc motion over his stomach.

"Jesus, Harry," he said shaking his head. "Once this is all done, she can't come back on the detail, you know that. She's on the investigation because otherwise she'd be in an office pushing papers across a desk and she's too damn fine an agent to do that. And you're telling me she's pregnant with his child?! What the fuck is Geller doing?"

Harry shook his head. "Mr. President, he didn't know she was pregnant."

"Do you think he would have done this if he had known?"

"Honestly, Mr. President, yes, I think he would have."

Chapter 56

Two lights flashed brightly on the shoreline lighting up the blackness of the horizon and another three followed shortly after, signaling all was well. Ibrahim and Nick thanked the freighter captain who, over the course of the day had ferried them across the Red Sea and boarded the small ribbed inflatable that had been launched for them. A short, fast run deposited them on the beach just south of the main Yemeni Red Sea port of Al Hudaydah. Nick stepped ashore and helped the unsteady Ibrahim from the inflatable, both nearly falling into the warm Red Sea waters as Ibrahim proved just how uncomfortable a seafarer he was. A mountain fighter, born and bred, Ibrahim was very happy to be reacquainted with dry land, kneeling down and kissing the sand beneath his feet.

The almost moonless sky offered little natural light but a further two flashes followed by one short flash guided them towards their welcome party who awaited them at the far end of the beach. Nick led the way as they approached the seemingly lone representative of the Yemeni branch of Al Qaeda. Stepping forward to offer his greetings resulted in an expertly trained and well-maneuvered appearance of a further ten heavily armed and masked men. Unfortunately for Nick and Ibrahim, their weapons were raised against them.

Caught entirely unawares, Nick and Ibrahim had little option but to surrender, such was the precision and professionalism of the move. Nick's heart fell. The US or the Israelis must have intercepted their landings and hijacked the situation to catch him.

The sack over their heads and binding on their hands, all done in total silence by their captors, certainly enforced that belief. The subsequent marching towards a group of vehicles and the careful guidance into the back seats of separate vehicles gave Nick some hope. Had it been Americans, he most certainly would have not been treated with such care after shooting the President and killing the Vice President. And if it had been the Israelis, he'd have more likely been bundled into the boot, probably breaking a few ribs in the process.

Nick tried to engage in conversation with his captors to no avail. During what Nick guessed to be around a two-hour drive, not one word was uttered from any of the four men accompanying him in the vehicle. By the time they arrived at their destination, Nick was no further forward in understanding who had captured them. However, the level of professionalism of his immediate watchers was once again leaning his guess towards a government of a yet to be determined country. Of course, given Nick's position, there were very few countries that would be friendly to his cause and he had already ruled out the most likely of those. All of their captors stood at least six feet tall, blowing every statistic out of the water for the vertically challenged North Koreans who, on average, stood at five and a half feet.

A metal shutter clattered behind them when the vehicle doors opened. Nick listened intently for any clues as to their location. Beyond the metal doors, he heard busy street noises. If he were correct and it had been a two-hour drive, that would mean it was 5 a.m. local time and he guessed he was hearing the morning street traders preparing for business in Sana'a, the capital of Yemen. However, there was always the chance they had driven him around aimlessly for two hours and they had actually stayed in Al Hudaydah and he was hearing the busy port area. Whatever the case, wherever he was, it wasn't good.

Led once again carefully through a number of doorways and corridors, Nick was guided into a chair. A door then closed behind him, leaving Nick alone with his thoughts. Worryingly, a TV was playing in the corner, tuned to the English language version of CNN. Nick feared the worst. He had failed.

Seconds became minutes, which became hours. The TV kept him up to date with current headlines from across the world. Despite being the CNN worldwide edition, it seemed that little else was happening other than Nick's exploits and the impact they were having on the United States which, in short, was devastating. Panic buying had led to major shortages across the country while air travel had plummeted to post 9/11 levels. Hospitals were inundated with people convinced they were suffering from the Ebola virus.

Nick smiled beneath his hood as he listened to the impact of his videos and actions, exactly as they had predicted and planned.

Almost on cue, the door opened and Nick's hood was removed. The brightness of the room pained his eyes but they soon focused on the masked man who sat across from him.

"Nick Geller?" the masked man asked rhetorically. His accent was English, upper class English. The Secret Intelligence Service, Britain's CIA, employed more than its fair share of well groomed gentlemen, many having been recruited from the two premier British universities, Oxford and Cambridge.

Nick stared more closely at his captor. The eyes were brown, Arab brown. Those same Universities educated many of the oil rich Arabs. Nick put his feelings of despair on hold. All may not be lost.

He nodded his head in acknowledgement of his name.

"You have made quite an impact in your few days on the run, haven't you?"

Nick stayed silent.

"But it can't be ignored that we lost our leader in that time," said the man pointedly.

Nick thanked Allah. He was in the hands of friends. He just had to prove to them he was a friend.

"My brother, you have me at a disadvantage. You know me but I do not know you," said Nick, his tone friendly and warm.

"And nor will you until I know you are trustworthy," came the reply. "Bring them in!" he shouted.

The door opened and two men were brought into the room, both dressed in full length black gowns. They were also hooded and appeared to be struggling against the bindings holding their hands behind their backs. Another masked man joined them holding a video camera.

"Start recording," instructed the well-spoken terrorist.

A small red light began to blink on the camera.

"Mr. Geller, before you are two men. One is the man you arrived with, a man you claim as a brother, Ibrahim. The other is an American, a member of staff from the American embassy who we kidnapped earlier this morning. You don't know which is which."

The man laid a pistol down on the table and stood up, walking slowly around Nick until he stood behind him. He then produced a knife and cut off his bindings, freeing Nick's hands.

Nick wrung his hands briefly to regain the blood flow and then snapped forward, catching his captors off guard with his speed and retrieving the pistol. Feeling for the safety, he ensured it was off and then pointed the pistol at the hooded men, shooting them both cleanly through the head. Both fell to the ground as Nick replaced the pistol on the table in front of his captors, engaging the safety in the process.

Chapter 57

Turner heard the sirens. He had failed. Nick Geller and his army of suicidal terrorists were attacking Washington D.C. Turner ran to the White House. He had failed to defend the country but he wasn't going to fail to defend his president. The Army and police had their defenses in place as the hordes descended upon them. Thousands of Arabs charged towards the White House on camels, their curving swords slashing the air as they rode to their death. The sirens blared again.

Turner opened his eyes, his phone ringing. He looked at the bedside alarm clock. It was 1:00 a.m. He had barely been asleep for an hour. The phone's ringtone must have been the siren in his dreams. He lifted the handset.

"Yes?"

"Deputy Director Turner, I'm sorry to have woken you but I think you need to see the video we've just received. I've emailed it to you," said the night supervisor at NCTC.

"Hmm, yes, okay," he replied.

Opening the attachment and seeing Nick Geller being held captive had him wide awake instantly. Watching him execute the two men, one of whom was supposedly an American, was one of the most chilling things he had ever seen in his life.

Turner dialed the supervisor back.

"Get everyone in now!" he demanded. "Have you sent this to Carson?"

"Yes but I've not been able to reach him!"

"Keep trying! Do we know who the American was?"

"No details yet but we're looking."

"News blackout. I don't want this getting out until we know who it was and the family has been informed."

"I'm afraid that's not possible, sir. This one went viral instantly. Whoever posted this knew what they were doing."

"Shit! I'll be there in twenty!" He hung up, grabbed some clothes, and dressed himself as he ran to the car.

Frankie's was the first face he saw as he walked into the center. She was pacing nervously across the reception area. She looked at him in anticipation of a reaction. He rushed past her while asking, "Have you seen the video?"

Frankie nodded gloomily.

Turner pushed on towards the center's operations floor, holding the door for Frankie, who hadn't moved. He paused and looked back at her. She looked like a child who had just broken something and was waiting to be yelled at.

"Is there something wrong?" he asked.

"Al Zahrani?" she asked.

He shrugged.

"What I did to him?" she asked, almost irritated, not understanding why he wasn't reacting.

"You took him to Gitmo?"

"Well yes and—"

"Good morning, people!" bellowed Carson, rushing into the middle of the conversation, grabbing Frankie by the elbow and propelling her with him towards the door being held open by Turner.

"So they found you?" asked Turner questioningly.

"At the White House, with President Mitchell," replied Carson. "I just need five minutes with Frankie."

Turner nodded and followed them into the operations center, taking his place in the center of the room while Carson escorted a silenced Frankie up onto the gangway and into his office.

Once again, he uncharacteristically shut the door behind him; it was becoming a habit, one he didn't like. Open doors allowed him to hear what was happening outside his office.

"Nobody knows about," he looked down to his crotch area, not wanting to say the words.

"Not nobody!" argued Frankie. "The CIA team, the surgeon in Gibraltar, Al Zahrani, you and me."

"And President Mitchell."

"Oh God! What did he say?" she asked, slumping into a seat and burying her head in her hands.

"That's my girl." Carson smiled. "That's what he said, or words to that effect."

Frankie's head snapped up. "He's not furious?"

"He's amazed you left him alive. He's not sure he would have."

"So who *knows* about what he did to me as a child?"

"Only me and the President. I guess the CIA guys may put two and two together but they've not been told why you did what you did."

"Obviously I'll resign unless, of course, you're firing me, which I'd completely understand."

Carson shook his head. "You'll do no such thing. The President wants you to stay on the investigation team."

"That makes no sense! I'm Nick Geller's girlfriend," she said, adding quickly, "well, *ex*-girlfriend. And I've just mutilated a prisoner in our custody!"

"All true, as is the fact that you're a damn fine agent who, through no fault of her own, fell for a man who has betrayed his country. As I told you before, Nick has fooled far more people than just you. As for Al Zahrani, nobody is talking and he certainly won't be."

"And if he does or people do?"

"The President personally called each of the CIA agents and the surgeon. They are not talking and if by any chance anyone ever did, Al Zahrani is a pedophile who was the head of Al Qaeda. You'll be a national hero and the President would gain points at the polls, not lose them."

"It still doesn't feel right."

"You'd rather be at home?"

She shook her head.

"Do you want to help catch Nick?"

"I want to stop him!"

"Good, well get down there and help. You know him better than anyone."

"Well I thought I did," she said, opening Carson's door. "Open or closed?" she asked as she went through the doorway.

"Open, thanks."

Frankie arrived back in the heart of the center as the video of Nick executing the two robed men was once again playing on the large screen.

"Any idea who the American was?"

"None. We've not had any kidnappings and as far as we're aware, there are no Americans missing anywhere."

"So they're lying?" asked Frankie.

"It would appear so," replied Turner. He turned towards the night supervisor. "So are we absolutely sure it's not an American then?"

"We know one hundred percent that it wasn't an embassy staffer. We've accounted for every one of them and all of their family members."

"But it could still be an American?"

"We can't say one hundred percent but we have no reports of any person missing. There's always the chance they've picked up a lone backpacker but they clearly stated that the American was a member of staff from the embassy. And that is not true."

""Alright then," said Turner, "let's get a statement out there that they're lying."

"I've just spoken with President Mitchell and Defense Secretary Hammond. We're not putting a statement out," said Carson loudly, joining the group.

"Why the hell would we not show them to be liars?" argued Turner to a number of nods from around him.

"Two reasons. First, they'll deny it and suggest *we're* lying, meaning no one will know who is telling the truth and before you know it, everyone thinks someone's died and that we're trying to cover it up and even our own people won't believe us. And secondly, more importantly, if we do say they're lying, there's every chance every American in the

Middle East will become a target to be kidnapped, killed and portrayed on TV as the person that they killed, just to prove us wrong."

"Reason one is bullshit. We should always tell the truth!" said Turner, holding up his index finger, before raising his middle finger. "Reason two, yep, they would and as such, fuck reason one. Shit!"

"So they didn't kill an American but we will let the world believe they did?" asked Frankie, clarifying the position to nods from both Carson and Turner.

"So was that real or a set up with Nick?" she asked.

"I think that was real," replied Carson. "I think Nick was being tested by the group to check he was legit. The tape being broadcast material is a bonus. Nick certainly shows how ruthless and cold a killer he is on that tape and how devoted he is to their cause."

"By killing one of their own?"

"No," answered Turner. "You have to think like them. He has told the jihadists he has been given a mission. This video is more powerful because he cold-bloodedly killed someone he cares about. He's showing that no one man is bigger than the cause, that sacrifices are part of that cause and he just made one to prove himself and to allow him to complete the path he laid out with the Caliph and Allah."

"Exactly," said Carson. "The American is immaterial. The far more powerful message is killing a man he called a brother, at least to the faithful that they're recruiting. By disputing an American died, we'd not only *not* water down the message, but we'd likely get a few Americans killed."

"And you think they knew that from the start?" asked Frankie.

"Who knows? But I can tell you one thing for sure, Nick would have."

"So you think there was a chance it was staged," surmised Frankie, grasping onto the hope that the man she had already written off was not as coldhearted as the tape showed.

"No," replied Carson.

Chapter 58

"Stop taping!" ordered the masked man as Nick placed the pistol back on the table.

The man who had just freed Nick from his bindings removed the gun from Nick's reach, finding it difficult to take his eyes off the two bodies that lay on the floor to his right. The speed with which Nick had acted had surprised him. There had been no time taken to consider what the course of action should be, he had just acted. He took two lives without a second thought for who they were or whether they deserved to die. He had just simply extinguished their lives like swatting a fly.

Taking his original seat and ensuring the camera had stopped rolling, he removed his mask.

Nick stared into the man's face. He had no idea who he was.

"I am Prince Abdullah bin Fahd Al Khaled's nephew. My name is Walid," he offered as a greeting. "My uncle sends his greetings."

"Your uncle is a great man and true believer in the cause," Nick stated. "It was his help that secured my escape from America."

Walid nodded, indicating he knew all about it.

"He wasn't too inconvenienced after I jumped from his plane I hope?"

"Between you and me, he loved every minute of it, although the Americans are watching him very closely now. I will be your contact now. Anything you need from him, I will arrange for you. I believe you returned the monies he sent you?"

"Just a little diversion," smiled Nick.

Walid smiled briefly before moving the conversation on. "He apologizes for the need to test you. However, after the new Caliph was tracked and captured, suspicions were raised and it was agreed that a test of your allegiance was required."

"Your uncle wasn't worried I would kill you and the cameraman?"

Walid shook his head. "My uncle never doubted you. He assured me I would be safe in your presence, that you would understand the test and pass it with ease. He did not tell me just how easily, however," he said, once again looking at the two bodies on the floor. "It was others, more powerful in the leadership, that were worried you may have led the authorities to Caliph Al Zahrani."

Nick looked at the bodies, both were still covered in black robes but Ibrahim's feet were clearly visible, as were the feet of the other body. "Perhaps another room would be more appropriate," he suggested, noting how often Walid glanced down at the bodies.

Walid almost leaped out of his seat at the suggestion, keen to remove himself from the unpleasant smell that had invaded the room following the killings and the ensuing bodily fluids that had slowly leaked onto the floor around them.

"This way," he said, leading Nick out of the room and along a series of corridors to an elevator. Arriving at the top floor of the building, they stepped out into a palatial corridor that led to an extravagant apartment overlooking the city below.

Nick moved towards the feature floor-to-ceiling windows and looked over a city he recognized. "Sana'a?"

Walid nodded, pouring Nick an Arabian coffee from an extremely ornate gold coffee jug.

"I see you have your uncle's taste."

Walid shook his head. "No, this is one of my uncle's apartments. He throws his wealth a little too much in your face for my taste."

"Yes, he does," agreed Nick looking around at the gaudiness of the apartment, exactly as you would expect the inside of an Arabian palace to look like. The only problem was that they were in a modern apartment building.

Walid took a sip of the coffee. "I'm sorry about your friend Ibrahim."

"He was a good man, a great warrior and a good friend," reminisced Nick. "But he died for the cause. As pointless as his death seems, it was for the greater cause. I must complete the Caliph's plan. That is why I am here and it is what Allah wants me to do. Whatever has to be done to achieve that is part of his greater plan. Ibrahim is with the Caliph and Allah and that was the path Allah wanted him to take."

Walid nodded as he spoke. "And the American?"

Nick smirked. "He's with Allah too, isn't he?" he said to a surprised Walid.

"No, he was an infidel!" Walid insisted, a slight tinge of anger in his voice.

"If you mean the *American* you had me kill, no. Any other American, I would agree but not that *American.*"

Walid took a step back. "You knew?"

"Only when the man fell to the ground. His feet gave him away. Those were not the feet of an American who worked at the American embassy. Those were the feet of a man who wore sandals his whole life, a poor Arab man's feet."

"A thief that was captured in the market," explained Walid.

"May I see the video?"

Walid shrugged, seeing no reason why not. He made a call and the video card was brought to them, already inserted into a laptop.

Nick hit 'Play' and watched the scene play out. "What were the plans for this?"

"It was to be sent to a number of high ranking leaders across the various organizations that you are trying to bring together."

"You mean the leaders that the Caliph and Allah wished to bring together. I am merely the conduit," corrected Nick. "I would not want to take the Caliph's grand plan as my own."

"Of course not."

"I have a better idea for this video, which will strike even greater fear into the Americans," said Nick, watching the shootings again.

"But we didn't shoot an American from the embassy."

"Irrelevant. If they dispute it, we shoot an American and display the dead body for the world to see. We'll prove the Americans to be liars."

"And if they don't?"

"The American people will fear us even more!"

Walid nodded as he thought through the logic. "I will tell the leadership of your plan and see what they say."

It had not taken long for the OK to come back for the video to be sent out to news agencies.

"Excellent. Send it to Al Jazeera," said Nick.

Walid spun the laptop back to himself. "I can do better than that," he said. "I have a doctorate in Computing Science from Oxford."

Nick was not surprised, and guessed that most of Walid's youth had been spent in the more expensive establishments of the British education system. His accent certainly suggested it. He was, however, surprised at the doctorate, he would not have put Walid at more than twenty-five years old.

Walid's fingers flashed across the keyboard for the next few minutes until he spun the laptop back around to face Nick. A number of screens were open: Facebook, You Tube, Twitter and many others that Nick had never heard of.

"The video is now the top trending video on each of these sites," he announced proudly.

"But how did you do that?" asked Nick. He knew enough about the internet to know that was no small feat.

"As I said, I have a doctorate in Computer Science."

Nick looked at him, unconvinced. Many people had a similar doctorate and couldn't do what Walid had just done.

"It helps that my billionaire uncle is a major shareholder in all of these companies. It allows his nephew, who manages his tech stocks, a little more access than the average user."

"But traceable?" asked Nick urgently, wondering if Walid had forgotten himself in his quest to impress him.

"That's where the doctorate comes in," he smiled.

"So what's the plan now?" asked Nick.

"It would appear that your dreams have come true. Sorry, the Caliph's dreams," corrected Walid. "I am to take you to a meeting of the leaders of all the jihadist groups. It looks like the plan to create one army fighting for Allah is becoming a reality!"

Nick beamed.

Chapter 59

With no American apparently having been killed, the center quieted as the team, roused from their beds, tried to grab some much needed shuteye. Most of them had worked almost non-stop since Nick Geller had started his crazed plan to destroy the western world. However, any time any of them felt as though the pace or working hours were too much, a trip home made it clear just how vital their role in catching Nick Geller had become. America was a nation living in fear.

Food and fuel was scarce. Hospitals were overrun with perfectly healthy people convinced they were dying. Shopping malls and cinema complexes were suffering as the general public avoided places that involved large gatherings, unless absolutely necessary. The country was suffering and the terrorists hadn't even begun their attack.

Carson was in no mood for sleep. His conversation with the President had not gone as well as he had implied. Once discussion had turned to the dire issues facing the nation, it became apparent that the President was under severe political pressure for an early resolution to the threat.

With just about every available asset across the US' Intelligence community being put to use in the hunt for Nick Geller, it was beyond Carson as to what more they could do. Although Geller posed the most overwhelming threat to the nation, other threats still had to be monitored. Carson was reminded by the intelligence community of that exact issue every time he drafted more resources into the hunt. Ass-covering emails from heads of department littered his inbox. For decades, Harry Carson had avoided just such a situation. If the shit hit the fan, he would be nowhere to be seen. In the Nick Geller hunt, if the shit hit the fan, Harry Carson would be buried up to his neck in it, *if* he was lucky and way beyond if he wasn't.

With another day of disappointment looming, Carson headed back to his office and lay on the couch. He hadn't even had time to pull the blanket over himself when he was disturbed.

"Harry?" said Turner, rushing into Carson's office.

"Yes," he replied, not bothering to open his eyes.

"Speaker Lopez—"

"I'm just catching a few minutes rest."

"No, you don't understand, she's here."

"Here? As in, *here*?" Carson asked, sitting up sharply.

"Not in the building yet but she's outside and she's brought the press with her!"

Carson, defying his age, jumped off the sofa and rushed out of the room, almost knocking over Turner in the process. Speaker Maria Lopez had been one of the main topics of conversation with the President. She was making huge political gains against him. It seemed inevitable that she would contest the presidency at the next election.

The President had had to make cuts across the government and although the intelligence community had been one of the least affected, in real terms – as Speaker Lopez made sure everyone was aware – the budget had been cut. As a result, they had lost a Vice President, the West Wing, and the President had been injured. They also faced the greatest threat to the American people since the Cold War. She was already promising an inflation-busting increase to the intelligence community to ensure the safety of each and every American. Where she was going to find the money was anyone's guess because it just wasn't there. However, her poll ratings were looking good and she wasn't going to let reality spoil her opportunity.

Carson hit the gangway and looked down on the sleeping masses that filled the center below.

"Fuck!" He whirled around to Turner behind him. "Delay her! I need to get this place buzzing! They'll crucify us if pictures get out of half the agents asleep at work!"

"But they shouldn't even be here! They were pulled in through the night to help, they're just catching some sleep before their shifts!"

"I know that and you know that and I'll bet Lopez knows it too, but do you think the American people will ever get to know that when they see the footage?!" Carson was taking the steps three at a time as he rushed to the main floor to wake up the staff. He could see how Lopez would claim that she was coming to offer her support but instead found the center half asleep and failing in its duty to protect the American people.

"And Turner," he said, as they passed each other, "we need to find the fucker who contacted Lopez and set us up!"

***

"Deputy Director Turner," beamed Speaker Lopez, as Turner walked calmly out of the NCTC main entrance into the warm darkness.

"Madame Speaker," he offered with an equally radiant smile in return.

Turner noted the Secret Service agents that surrounded her, which reminded him that no Vice President had been announced. He hadn't had time to keep up to date with the national news.

"Let's walk and talk," she said, aiming for the center with the camera crews in tow.

"Have you been here before? I could give you a tour of the complex," he offered. However, she continued unabated. She definitely knew the center was half asleep.

Steamrolling through the reception area, she checked the camera crews were ready and filming her entrance through the main doors into the operations center.

Turner cursed. He hadn't been able to stop her and give Carson the time to get all the staff up and at their stations. She'd walk in to half the staff in the process of being woken up. It was not going to play well and the President was going to get hammered even further for lack of progress. And

Turner, more importantly, would not see the inside of the building, nor any federal building ever again.

Pulsing sound waves in his ear were the first sign that things hadn't gone as planned for the Speaker. The blaring sirens drove everybody out of the building for fear that their eardrums would explode such was the overwhelming and piercing noise. Turner was met by a wave of fleeing staff and a quietly smiling Carson.

Carson shouted at the security staff to apprehend every journalist that had accompanied the Speaker. The Speaker was rushed to her car by the Secret Service, her feet barely touching the ground. Before she had a chance to say a word to camera, her car was already speeding her away from whatever potential danger existed in the center.

With the press corralled into one area by security and the building emptied, the sirens were eventually and much to everyone's relief silenced.

Carson marched over, fury etched on his face as he approached the waiting press. "Every one of you will be searched and your equipment confiscated!" he shouted as the cameras rolled. "Our explosives sensors just went wild and caused an evacuation! We don't have time for this bullshit! What the hell was Speaker Lopez thinking?!"

Walking back towards the building, Turner caught up with him. "What explosives sensors?" he asked quietly, out of earshot of anyone else and well away from the very distressed looking press pack.

"The ones that we'll install very quietly later today," smiled Carson. The Speaker was going to be back in her box for at least a little while. The press was going to destroy her for her attempts at politicizing the crisis and impacting the search for the terrorists.

Chapter 60

Saturday 12ᵗʰ July

The journey after leaving the apartment block was far more comfortable than Nick's journey on the way there. A blacked-out Bentley Continental chauffeured them in comfort to Sana'a international airport. The Bentley pulled up next to a Cessna Citation X jet that was fueled and ready to fly. Nick walked the short distance to the jet, obscured from any potential onlookers. His ever-present small metal briefcase took a seat next to him, while Walid took the one opposite.

"Your uncle's?" asked Nick, noting the garish and extravagant décor.

"A cousin's, actually. My uncle's aircraft are being heavily monitored at the moment."

Nick turned his attention to the featureless view outside the window. Looking out onto the desert around them, his mind quickly returned to the Caliph's plan. The meeting of the main leaders of the jihadist groups was happening much quicker than he had anticipated. He had expected a far more difficult sell, given his history and background. However, his actions and the impact they had had on American society could not have been predicted, nor could they be questioned. America was living in a fear even greater than it had experienced after 9/11 and it was not a chance they wished to pass up on.

The small jet rocketed down the runway and leapt into the sky. Nick closed his eyes and the next time he opened them, the vast expanse of desert had been replaced with the vast mountain ranges of Spin Ghar, towering above the jet as they made their final approach into Parachinar airport in Western Pakistan. The jet landed on the floor of the Kummar valley, enclosed on three sides by the snowcapped mountains of Afghanistan.

"Stunning, aren't they?" asked Walid, his face pressed against the window.

"Yes," replied Nick halfheartedly, not looking out again. The mountain ranges brought back memories he'd rather stayed in the past. The Battle of Tora Bora had been fought on those very mountains not long after 9/11 and had been the first time Nick had had to engage Al Qaeda and the Taliban. It was not a period in his life he wished to remember for many reasons.

"Have you been here before?" asked Walid.

"Yes." He stood up, lifted his metal briefcase and walked towards the exit, not waiting for Walid.

Walid grabbed his things and joined him. "Bad?"

"Not something I want to talk about," replied Nick. "But let's just say it's one of the reasons I'm here today."

"Understood," said Walid. "You'll be pleased to hear that we're staying in the valley this time," he said, leading the way as the door opened to reveal a SUV awaiting their arrival.

Nick kept his face pointed to the ground as he covered the short distance to the SUV, which wasted no time setting off. The road soon disappeared as the driver favored an off-road route which, as Walid had said, headed south. It took less than an hour for them to arrive at a desolate looking farmhouse on the banks of the Kurram River. The SUV drove beyond the farmhouse and was guided by a waiting man into a large and just as shabby looking barn. The barn was already packed with a number of other vehicles. The driver squeezed in the SUV and, safely out of sight of any passing satellite or drones, he unlocked the doors for his passengers.

"Larbi will take you across to the meeting," said the driver, pointing to the man who had guided them into the barn.

Nick stepped out of the SUV and took a gulp of air. The enormity of what he was about to do finally hit him. He had promised the Caliph he would deliver and he now had the chance to do that. The men that could make the plan a reality were sitting, waiting for him, just yards away.

Larbi ushered them on, raising a hand to stop Walid when they neared the farmhouse door while beckoning Nick forward.

Nick looked at Walid, who looked as confused as Nick did.

"Walid?" asked Nick.

Walid shrugged. "I was told to come with you."

Larbi ushered Nick forward towards the door where a number of guards surrounded the entrance.

Nick's plan was foolproof up to a point. The point being that he had to stay alive to deliver it. A crushing feeling hit him when the door opened to reveal a wooden block in the center of a large room. An executioner stood by its side brandishing a gleaming scimitar. That was not the sight Nick had hoped for. The men he had hoped to meet were in the room but rather than around a table, they were lining the walls smiling at him and beckoning him to join them in the room.

Before he had a chance to consider their offer, two guards grabbed him from behind and propelled him into the room. Nick considered fighting back but the odds were just too overwhelming. He didn't stand a chance.

Chapter 61

NCTC
Two weeks later, Monday 28th July.

Reid walked back into the center, having spent the previous two weeks in various locations across the Middle East with Flynn. All had proven to be wild goose chases. Nick Geller had quite literally disappeared off of the face of the earth. With no new videos having surfaced over that same period, the news stations had even managed to broadcast unrelated stories. Some semblance of normality was returning across America. Food supplies had been bolstered in stores, although there was still a significant minority insisting on bulk-buying and perpetuating food lines that weren't quite back to what they had been just three weeks earlier.

Gas stations, however, had recovered more quickly. There was only so much fuel people could fit in their gas tanks. Once full, they were topping up just as they had when they had run their car at nearly empty. People weren't using more gas, they just had more gas in their cars.

Reid knocked on Turner's door before entering. "Deputy Director Turner," she said, as she walked into the office.

"Special Agent Reid, good to have you back," replied Turner, delighted to see his number two. Without her on site, he had spent more time on the main operations floor than he would have liked. He had also realized just how much work she did behind the scenes that he had been blissfully and happily unaware of.

"Any news?" she asked hopefully.

"Nothing. Not a sighting. Not a whisper, anywhere, even of his name," he replied.

Carson, having heard Reid arrive, crashed the welcome party. "Sarah! Good to have you back," he said warmly.

"Thank you, Harry," she replied with a smile.

"Quite a trip you had. Is there anywhere you haven't been in the Middle East?"

"I don't think so. It was a fairly comprehensive trip but a complete waste of time."

"Nothing anywhere. Even the chatter has dropped to levels we've not seen in years," said Carson.

"The calm before the storm?" asked Reid rhetorically.

Both Carson and Turner nodded, the worry of that exact thought etched on their faces.

"Anyway, great to have you back," reiterated Carson, heading out of the office.

"I found Speaker Lopez's mole!" Turner called after him, causing Carson to stop in his tracks.

"You did?" asked Carson in surprise, closing Turner's door as he stepped back into the office.

"It wasn't easy. I had to call in a few favors at NSA. They tracked all calls from all cells from this location on the day in question."

"Good thinking."

"They've just come back and informed me that there was nothing. No calls to Speaker Lopez or anyone connected to her."

"But I thought you said you found the source?" said Reid.

Carson smiled, as did Turner.

"What's there to smile about?" asked Reid, looking at them grinning at each other.

"There's not a chance in hell the NSA would have run that check without Harry knowing. He already knew the result because he made sure that's what it was."

Carson put on his best offended look.

"Furthermore," continued Turner, "the biggest winner out of that debacle was the President. Speaker Lopez has been put firmly back in her box by the media. Her trip here was a public relations disaster that will be replayed for years to come."

Carson nodded in agreement. "Yes, Madame Speaker was shown to be a little naïve when it comes to dealing with national crises. Don't politicize or try to score points when people's lives are at risk."

"Emptying the center was genius and couldn't have played out better if it had been *orchestrated*," Turner said, looking directly at Carson.

"What, you think I set that up? Sending her a secret message from a '*friend*' and telling her to bring a press pack and catch the center having a nap?"

"Did you?" asked Reid, finally catching up.

"If only I had thought of that!"

Turner shook his head as Carson walked out of the room.

"You think he did it?"

"Of course he did. The son of a bitch plays us like a grand pianist plays the piano!"

"Should you not tell someone?"

"Who?" asked Turner, walking over to the door and closing it, something Carson seemed incapable of doing.

"The Director? The President?"

"My proof is a lack of it. I only guessed the NSA would run it by him first. He didn't deny they had. Even then, what are they going to do? Speaker Lopez is back at her day job and keeping her head down."

"I guess that helps us too."

"I know," said Turner, reluctant to admit that Carson's maneuver, however wrong, was helpful.

"So anyway," said Reid trying to lighten the mood and change subject, "what leads are we working?"

Turner pointed sullenly to the white board at the back of his office. Nick Geller's name was written in large letters across the top. The board below was empty.

"Nothing?" she said, unable to hide her disproval.

"Not nothing. There are little snippets, sightings down on the floor. I leave this board for the leads I think are going to come to something. Leads that might actually help us catch him."

"Shit," she said despondently, dropping onto the sofa. Silence filled the room and then she said, "What about Frankie?"

Turner shrugged. "The same, nothing new."

"But she was hunched over her desk and too busy to even say hi when I came in."

"To be honest, she's been a bit strange all week and come to think of it, ever since she got back with Al Zahrani."

"Strange how?" asked Frankie from the doorway.

Startled, and a little embarrassed, Turner said, "I didn't hear you come in."

"Secret Service training. We open doors very quietly," she said before pressing her question. "Strange how?"

"Quiet," said Turner.

"After what Frankie's been through?!" Reid snapped.

"No, he's right. I have been a bit off this week," Frankie admitted. "I'd be buried under a blanket! I can't tell you how in awe I am of how you've coped," said Reid, patting the sofa next to her for Frankie to join her.

"I appreciate that but I'm not here for sympathy," she said. "I'm here because I've got something."

Chapter 62

Sarande, Adriatic Coast
Albania

Gary Truman grabbed his camera and headed out. Daylight was still a half hour away but he planned to hike north into the hills and capture some dramatic early morning shots as the sun crept over the hills that framed the Adriatic Sea below. Albania was still relatively untouched by tourism, certainly from a European perspective, and offered miles of deserted beaches and coves that elsewhere in Europe would have been crowded during the summer.

A keen photographer and wildlife enthusiast, he was also hoping to catch a few shots of the Mediterranean monk seals, one of the most endangered mammals in the world. Thanks to the tranquility afforded by the quite coves and bays of the Albanian coastline, the seals were residents in some of the underwater caves just to the north of Sarande, the tourist town in which Gary's hotel was located.

Gary walked out on to the street and followed the road as far as it took him into the hills, which wasn't far. Albania was a country with a checkered history. During the communist era, it had all but closed itself off from the rest of Europe and due to successive regimes favoring a rail network for the people, roads were neglected and private transportation even into the 1980s was mostly limited to a horse and cart. Albania had come a long way in the two decades since the fall of the communist regime but had a lot of building to do to compete with other European countries and economies.

Whatever the case, Gary was delighted when the road disappeared to be replaced by a dust track. It meant that he was travelling the less trodden path and the chances of catching a shot of the seals increased.

He couldn't have been happier. The warm air of dawn was promising another beautiful day ahead. He was alone in the world. His view from the hillside stretched down into the deserted coves and along the coastline. The only sounds he could hear were his footsteps brushing through the dust. This was in stark contrast to his working life. Although being armed with a camera was no real change, the subject of the photos was somewhat different. He was a crime scene investigator with the Metropolitan Police Force in London. His work shots were not ones he would ever care to share on his Blipfoto account, unlike his holiday snaps.

Gary witnessed daily what one human could do to another. Fortunately, he had always preferred his own company, and had always been regarded as a bit strange by his colleagues. However, no one doubted his diligence when it came to work. Gary Truman was a perfectionist and noted the tiniest of details that many others in his profession would miss. Mildly autistic, Gary was blissfully unaware of any of the idiosyncrasies that set him aside from the rest of the team.

Having captured his sunrise shots, Gary trekked down towards Krorez Beach. He had heard from a local that the seals sometimes spent the early morning swimming in the bay. Snapping off shots as he went, it was only as he neared the beach itself that he noticed for the first time that he wasn't alone. Still on the hillside above the beach, he spotted something in the water.

What he had initially thought might have been a seal's head when it emerged around the headland was, when he zoomed in, revealed to be that of a man, a swimmer enjoying an early morning dip in the warm seas. Gary had snapped a couple of shots before he even realized it wasn't a seal. Slightly irritated, he packed his camera back in his camera bag. Any chance of seeing the seals had been thwarted by the selfishness of the swimmer. Gary turned and headed back for Sarande. He would just manage to catch breakfast if he hurried.

Nick Geller felt invigorated as he walked out of the waters and onto Krorez Beach. His sunrise swim was his one outing each day. The deserted coastline offered a beautiful change from swimming laps in a pool and with the added current, a lot more of a workout. Swimming with the dolphins and seals that had accepted him as a non-threatening addition to their habitat was a very welcome bonus.

He grabbed his towel and spotted the man in the distance, halfway up the hill. He was too far to be able to make out Nick's features but he was climbing up the hill so had been closer when Nick swam ashore. The man's pace was normal which suggested he was not rushing away after identifying Nick but he was, nonetheless a risk. Nick swept the hillside. The man was alone, or at least not with anyone he knew. Nick noted a slight movement a few hundred yards behind the man.

Larbi, his ever-present companion since the meeting in Parachinar, was on the man's trail. The meeting had gone exceptionally well. His arrival at the farmhouse had been marked by the sacrifice of a goat, expertly and ceremonially killed by the executioner armed with the scimitar. A celebratory meal in Nick's honor had been prepared and a lavish feast was enjoyed by all. Leaders from across the jihadist world had congratulated him and offered their undying desire to be part of the Caliph's plan.

Nick had been exceptionally pleased to see two men in particular - the first was the highly reclusive leader of Jabhat-al-Nusra, the Syrian wing of Al Qaeda, a man with thousands of battle hardened and experienced men under his command. Whether they all fit Nick's exacting criteria to participate in the Caliph's plan Nick did not know, but the leader's presence was a massive boost to the cause. The other man was the leader of the Iraqi wing of Al Qaeda, another man with thousands of jihadists under his command. Between just those two of the many leaders in the farmhouse that night, Nick would have been more than able to deliver for the Caliph.

Nick had warmly greeted them all, again emphasizing that only the truly devoted were welcome. The point, it seemed, had been well made. The leaders, ready to produce lists of names there and then were stopped in their tracks. Once again, Nick made the point. The Americans had to be kept in the dark as to the scale of the attack. Names would be collected after the meeting, in secret and each leader should keep the list to themselves. That way, even if they themselves were captured, the greatest damage they could do was give away their own group. They all agreed, appreciative of the diligence with which Nick was protecting the plan.

Nick explained how each man would receive information to be at a set location at a set time. Each jihadist would receive his own instructions. Only on the morning of the attack would they learn their final destination and role within the plan, fighter, infector or protector. The fighters would be taking the fight to the infidels, a great honor. The infectors, the chosen few, were given the even greater honor of taking the virus into the heart of America, killing it from within. And finally the protectors, they would protect the future of the Caliphate. As for numbers, he refused to be budged. He would not disclose a number. If the Americans caught anyone, they would have no chance of understanding what they faced.

In all, over the previous two weeks, the leaders had offered over ten thousand names from across their groups of highly trained and experienced soldiers who had pledged their lives in support of the Caliph's plan and were ready to take the war to the American streets.

Nick had his army. The true warriors of Allah from across the Muslim world, irrespective of their individual allegiances— Al Qaeda, Taliban, Hezbollah, Hamas or any one of the smaller groups— had come together. The Caliph's dream, eighteen months in the making, had been realized. A dream that would see all ten thousand men take the role of fighter. Nick would take all ten thousand jihadists with him, none would be left behind, fighters and leaders alike. This was a grand plan befitting Allah and the Caliph. To protect the plan, he had to keep the details of its scale as quiet as possible. Misleading the leaders meant none would know just how massive the attack would be until they were on their way to America. Compartmentalization of the detail was key to the success. The fewer people who knew, the less they could tell and the less chance the Americans would find out until it was too late.

Larbi had escorted Nick back to his SUV after the meeting and the waiting Walid. He had surprised them both when instead of guiding them out he had joined them in the vehicle. Larbi was to be Nick's bodyguard and constant companion. Wherever Nick went, Larbi would watch over him. He was a highly experienced Mujahedeen fighter and was at home on the hillside.

Nick had never witnessed such a master at work. He blended into the hillside and followed the man above Krorez Beach with ease, remaining out of sight of his target.

When they disappeared over the hillside towards the next bay, Nick could only speculate as to the man's fate. He grabbed his robe and slipped on his sandals to begin his own trek back up the hill towards the luxury villa that housed Nick and his many assistants as he planned the downfall of America and the rise of the Caliphate. The word 'villa' did not, however, do the property justice. Built into a hillside of commanding views across the sea, it was more of a complex than a villa. Stretching out across the hill, the walled perimeter offered complete privacy from the various buildings that made up the summer home for one of Walid's many cousins. The main house was over twenty thousand square feet in size, with many smaller properties on the grounds for housing servants and guests alike, should the need arise.

***

Larbi sped up. He had spent hours walking the area over the last week and knew every stone and path that surrounded the complex. He knew the man was taking a route that offered a shortcut into the next bay. A narrow ledge with a treacherous drop deterred most walkers but to Larbi it was the second quickest route. There was another more direct route that was more suitable to mountain goats, the ledge so narrow that it was only possible to walk sideways, while looking down onto rocks over five hundred feet below.

Larbi walked along the ledge without a second thought of falling. His feet were as certain as they were walking a paved sidewalk. His shortcut would allow him to overtake the man and double back, in order to meet him coming from the opposite direction.

***

Gary was agitated. His plan for the day had been ruined by the swimmer. At that time of the morning, he should have had the beach to himself and the seals, he was sure, would have been there. He removed the camera from its bag and scanned through the photos as he walked. The images of the sun rising calmed him down. He had captured some great shots and was sure to get some fantastic comments from his Blipfoto admirers when he posted them online later that day. His Blipfoto followers were as close to friends as Gary had. Their comments, no matter how brief, always made him feel calm and more relaxed.

Pausing as he neared the narrowing path, he came across the photos of the swimmer. Photography was Gary's only hobby, his only outlet outside of work. Therefore, the quality of his equipment was second to none. His zoom lens picked up every detail the naked eye could not see from several hundred yards away. The image viewer on the back of the camera was clear enough to zoom into the face of the man who had disrupted his day. The image was that of a face that Gary had seen many, many times over the previous three weeks.

He gasped at the realization of who the swimmer was. The face that had appeared from the water belonged to none other than Nick Geller, wanted terrorist.

Gary placed the camera back in the bag and with renewed purpose, strode towards his hotel room, a phone and the authorities. He hadn't even noticed the man approaching him nervously, tucked against the inside wall of the path, as far from the drop as he could get. Gary had no fear of heights and was happy to pass the man on the outside, uncharacteristically smiling a good morning to him. He understood just how big a discovery he had just made. Finding evidence was his job. Finding evidence that would catch the man at the center of the largest manhunt in history was something he had really not expected.

***

Larbi approached the narrow pathway as the man stopped at the other side. He needed to meet him on the pathway. His plan was to fall into the man, making him drop his camera bag over the ledge while saving him. The camera would be lost but all the man would care about was that he had survived. However, he needed the man on the pathway for that to work.

He pushed himself up against the side of the hill, as far from the ledge as possible and began to edge across slowly, trying to show genuine fear of the drop just a yard or two in front of him. Larbi slowed almost to a stop as the man seemed totally entranced by whatever he was looking at on his camera. Eventually, he put it away and walked towards Larbi, only far quicker than before. Larbi was going to have to time his maneuver perfectly, just in case anyone was watching.

The man drew alongside him and smiled. Larbi feigned a slip and fell forward into the man, grabbing out for him as the man fell towards the ledge and the five hundred foot drop.

***

Gary felt the weight of the man against him as his footing gave way. The ledge loomed and he felt sure the man was reaching for him but he continued to fall. Gary felt a weight pull against him and realized it was the shoulder strap of his camera bag. The leather strap stretched and strained but the weight exerted against it was too much and it gave way.

Gary reached out but it was too late.

***

Larbi watched the man plummet to his death. He was certain that from the landing on the jagged rocks below there was no chance the man had survived but he had to be sure. From five hundred feet up, it was too far to be certain. He unzipped the camera bag and used the camera's zoom lens to check. He decided against taking a picture; the sight was too gruesome to be seen again. The man was most definitely dead.

Whether Larbi had saved the camera or the man was irrelevant. He had to protect Nick Geller. Seeing the recognition on the man's face of whatever he had seen on the camera was what had resulted in the camera being saved and the man dying.

Larbi grabbed some loose twigs and spent a few minutes wiping away any sign of his footprints. If they did have anyone check the scene, only one set of footprints would show up. A tragic accident would be recorded.

Unfortunately Larbi was not aware of how advanced modern cameras were. If he had been, he may have noticed, on the camera's viewfinder, a bar on the upper right of the screen showing the upload progress to Gary Truman's Blipfoto account.

Chapter 63

NCTC

Frankie produced a sheet of paper, placed it on Turner's desk and beckoned for Reid to join them.

"Remember Nick's French bank account?"

"Monsieur Jacques Guillon, I don't think I'll ever forget that name," said Reid.

"I've been going through the detail of all his transactio—"

"Dead end," Turner cut in.

"Maybe not," said Frankie.

"He's never going to use that account again, he knows it's burnt," agreed Reid.

"Not the account but what about the cash he withdrew?" she said teasingly.

"Unless the French have developed some super GPS impregnated paper that we know nothing about, how in the hell do we track cash?" asked Turner.

"It's what he bought with the cash that we can track," she said triumphantly pointing to the sheet of paper on the desk.

"What's that?" asked Reid looking at an array of numerals written across the page.

Turner stared at the page before recognizing what they represented. "Are those credit card details?"

"Yep," announced Frankie, struggling to hide her excitement. "Pre-paid credit cards."

"But there must be millions of them, tens of millions," said Reid, wondering how that could help them.

"I know. I thought they held about a hundred bucks maybe five hundred max but no, you can put thousands on them, a few even take fifteen thousand dollars and that was the breakthrough."

Both Turner and Reid stared at the numbers on the sheet as Frankie talked. There were four card numbers, one with a tick at the end.

"The transaction history for the account was either ten or fifteen thousand dollar transactions at each location. Not all at once but when you add them up, they're always around that amount. I had a chat with some of the specialists at Treasury and they told me about these high value pre-paid cards."

"And this one with the tick?" asked Turner.

"The proof. Transactions on the Guillon account amounted to fifteen thousand dollars in the Chicago area where a pre-paid card was loaded with the same amount. That card was purchased in Chicago at around the same time and that card has just recently been used in Algiers."

"Nick Geller was in Algiers! He took those cell phones in Algiers a couple of weeks ago!" said Reid excitedly.

"Wait," cautioned Frankie, "I've checked. Nick didn't use the card. I It was used by a pilot who is known to the authorities as a smuggler. They have his image from the aircraft leasing company where he just put down a payment on a plane he needs to rent."

"Because we blew the shit out of his in the desert in Sudan, I'll bet!" Turner chuckled.

"Which means that even though he knows we know about the account, he thinks the prepaid cards are still safe," said Reid, looking at the other three card details. "Do you think that's all there are?"

"No, but this was just taking two locations. Two of these are probably innocent or, according to my friends at Treasury, not Nick. As far as they're concerned, anyone with a pre-paid card with fifteen grand is trying to hide something. But anyway, not many people have the cards loaded to the max and if we tie withdrawal locations to the dates, we just need to find how many pre-paid cards were loaded to the max in that area and get the numbers from the companies."

"Have we asked the Algerians to pick up the pilot?" asked Reid.

"No, I thought if we did, Nick might guess that we know about the cards," replied Frankie.

Both Turner and Reid nodded their agreement and admiration. Turner picked up a marker and walked over to his empty white board and wrote four words: 'Pre paid credit cards.'

"Special Agent Reid, I think we have a lead," he announced. "Great work, Frankie!"

"Thank Harry," she said. "He told me to follow the cash!"

Turner didn't know why but Harry's involvement somehow soured what had been a very good moment, probably not helped by the fact that every time Harry was involved in anything, it was very seldom what it appeared to be at face value.

Chapter 64

St Albans City
Vermont

Mary Williams had to negotiate through a line of shoppers to make her way back out to the parking lot. She usually only needed a few hours' sleep and so found being at the store at 5:30 a.m. no great hardship. She secured a good position in the growing queue for the 7:00 a.m. opening. She had argued with her mother against the need to stock up but had eventually caved. The government would protect them and ensure they were looked after but in the meantime, she just wanted some peace and quiet at home.

With the shopping secured, the next task was to fill up with gas, which fortunately proved far easier than the food shopping, although Mary couldn't help but notice that the price had increased by nearly twenty cents a gallon. A letter would have to be sent to Exxon. Profiteering during a crisis was un-American and unbecoming of any US company. She expected that type of behavior from BP but certainly not from Exxon. She filed the receipt and would match it with the one she had from just three weeks earlier as evidence of her complaint.

By 8:15 a.m., Mary was back at the small home she shared with her mother and had done since her birth sixty-two years earlier. She unpacked her shopping. Everything had a place and there was a place for everything. That was her motto.

Her mother sat and watched. She had learned many years earlier to let Mary do it herself. Helping just led to huffs and puffs and ultimately Mary reorganizing it all anyway. Her daughter liked things in the right place. By the time Mary had turned sixteen, her mother had known she was going to be stuck with her. There wasn't a man on the planet who would put up with her. She was, as much as it pained her mother to say, a person only a mother could love.

At 8:22 a.m., Mary fed her two cats. They purred at receiving the food, not at Mary; even they struggled to love the woman. At exactly 8:24 a.m., she kissed her mother goodbye and got behind the wheel of her Ford Focus. She purchased the same car, brand new every year, always American made and built. Just like everything in their lives had to be. Mary believed in her country and appreciated just how important it was to support the nation's industries, to the extent that she insisted on paying full list price. She had served her country for over forty years and was proud to be a member of the government's civil service.

Mary hung a left on South Main Street and journeyed the one mile to work in approximately two minutes and thirty seconds, give or take ten seconds. Mary's short commute ensured her yearly car purchase generated significant interest in her trade-in. Had it not been for the fact that the car was a year old on the license documents, nobody would ever have believed it. The salesmen even joked that it was cleaner when it came back a year later than it was when it had gone out brand new.

Mary drew to a stop outside the two-story redbrick United States Post Office and Custom House and parked beneath the flag of the United States of America that proudly flew on the flagpole just outside. She walked through the right hand archway and entered the door marked 'US Passport Agency' at precisely 8:29. This was her domain. Mary was at her desk as the clock on the wall clicked to 8:30 exactly.

A number of her fellow agency officers were still engaged in conversation but when the clock hit 8:30, Mary was already processing her first application. She was a machine. Her job was to process applications and that was exactly what Mary did, with meticulous efficiency. If Mary rejected an application, it was often checked surreptitiously by another officer who, in the interests of customer service, would dot an 'i' or change a check to a cross. Despite this, Mary processed more applications than any other agent in the history of the office. Her daily total seldom changed. She was paid to do a job for her country and she did exactly that, to the best of her abilities, every single day.

At 9:30 a.m., a parcel arrived for Mary. She never received personal mail at work, unlike her colleagues who were constantly receiving parcels from Amazon or any number of mail order companies. This parcel was special and one she had been waiting for a number of months. A code on the top right corner of the parcel identified that this was a parcel that required special attention.

Mary relocated to the meeting room, something that she usually did when handling sensitive or high profile applications. Her colleagues wished she worked on sensitive and high profile applications permanently. Mary's constant hushing of her colleagues when they tried to engage in general conversation throughout the day was tiresome and a cause for regular complaint. They were pleased to see her and her parcel disappear into the room.

Mary cut the parcel tape carefully and withdrew the pile of applications for US passports. They all needed to be expedited and sent overseas. Sorting the applications into alphabetical order, she was surprised at the number of them. Her first estimate was over four hundred. It was more than had been suggested at the meeting she had had a number of months earlier but she had a job to do and Mary Williams was not going to let her country down.

Mary had been selected as a member of the top-secret elite in the Passport Agency. Her diligence and hard work for her country had been recognized at the highest levels. Promotions had passed her by because patriots like Mary were needed on the frontline to protect the country. She had never been more proud. Her country needed her. Her skills would help protect the nation. She had been approached by a man from the government at her home several months earlier. He was the Under Secretary of State responsible for a special division of the Diplomatic Security Service, the agency responsible for passport security. He asked her to sign a top secret clearance agreement prior to their conversation, thereby securing her absolute discretion about the processing of passports which he might require her to issue at some point in the future. They would be issued to individuals who would be working to protect America in the fight against terror and having them issued at the regional offices, rather than head office, added a level of legitimacy that ensured even greater protection for the men and women who spent every minute of their lives in danger to protect the American people.

***

Nick Geller had selected Mary Williams carefully, just as he had selected similar candidates at the twenty-four other branches of the US Passport Agency. His disguise was worthy of Hollywood. He had transformed himself into a sixty-year-old man, the stereotypical WASP, dressed head to toe immaculately in Brooks Brothers. His air of authority had added greatly to the pretense. He looked exactly as you would have expected a very senior member of the State Department to look. The chauffeured Executive Town Car that waited for him outside each house, added further to the charade. Each of his candidates was a loner, each one was a patriot and each one would do whatever they could for their country. Each one would remain true to their promise to keep their work for Nick a secret. Each one could issue legitimate US passports for his army. All he needed to provide were the names and photos.

With his own exclusive US passport agency, Nick felt sure that his plan would go without a hitch. The consequence of any recruit discussing their actions would be treated as treason, punishable by execution. All he had to do now was the small matter of arranging transport for over ten thousand soldiers.

Chapter 65

Nick unlocked the door to his domain. His office was in a villa that nobody was allowed to enter. He had made it abundantly clear to all within the confines of the grounds that to do so would be construed as an attempt to retrieve information about the plan. The only reason this would be done would be to foil the plan and so anyone who entered the office would be shot as a traitor. The threat was all encompassing. Nobody, not even Walid or Larbi, was exempt from the threat.

Compartmentalization was key to the security of the plan. If nobody knew all the details, no matter what, no one could stop the plan. Even if ten percent of his men made it to America, the devastation they could cause would be overwhelming. In theory, they only needed one man infected with Ebola to cause chaos. Ten percent would still be over one thousand warriors. Although Nick had no intention for all of his warriors to be infected, a small portion would carry the virus while the vast majority would terrorize the civilian population, taking the fight to the streets of every major city and town in the continental US. The scenes of death and violence that had plagued their TVs from Iraq, Afghanistan and Pakistan over the years were about to get local.

Nick sat at his desk and pulled the map of the US from under the paperwork. A number of crosses marked the locations of weapons depots that he had arranged over the last year. The crosses were located close to the major airport hubs that served the continental US. The volume of guns, ammunition and explosives in each depot would more than satisfy the needs of his ten thousand plus warriors. He pulled out the corresponding flight timetables. Hundreds of flights from across Europe and the Middle East fed into the airports. Getting the men in place was not going to be a problem. Nick even had the benefit of choosing almost exclusively from American airline companies - United, Delta, American or US Airways. With his men carrying US passports, their passage would be even easier, particularly when they landed in the US.

Across the villa complex, Nick had a number of individuals arranging travel. They were working independently and were separately housed. They were each given lists of bookings but were unaware of any of the other lists. Again, a threat had been made. Any attempt to discuss or find out what others were doing would be for no other reason than to scupper the plan. As a result, they all remained quiet and did as they were asked. They spent their days booking individual flights and preparing instructions for over ten thousand men. Only Nick knew who was on which flight and where each man would depart from and the time at which they would arrive.

Travel plans were only required for fighters and infectors. The infectors were the Ebola carriers and the fighters were the jihadists who would take the fight to the streets of America. The infectors' job was far simpler. They would infect hundreds of people on the plane so a large part of their job would already have been done. However, once they landed, they were to visit as many mass population facilities as possible and to draw little attention to themselves. They were to visit shopping malls, train stations, subways, churches, wherever they could go to spread their germs to the maximum number of Americans.

The fighters' tasks were a little more complex. Nick wanted them to form fifty-man strong teams. Each team would have a number of key targets to hit in their assigned geographical area. The destruction of hospitals, schools and transport hubs were to be their top priorities, along with the elimination of any law enforcement establishments. Nick planned to have almost two hundred of these teams striking at exactly the same time across America. It was no small task but with months of preparation behind him, it was a simply a case of putting the plan into operation.

The passports were on their way. The tickets were almost all booked and the instructions for each man were ready to go. The final instructions would only be available to them on their arrival in America. Each man would receive a cell phone with his passport. His instructions would be sent by SMS on his arrival in the US. The most any one individual could compromise would be one fifty-man team or one flight, of which there were potentially hundreds.

Nick tried to think of any areas he had failed to consider. He evaluated the risks many times. The passport issuers were a risk but extremely low. In their minds, they were helping to make their country stronger, not destroy it. His flight bookers knew at least a portion of the flights. But none would be allowed to leave the complex before the attack was underway and all communications were restricted to hardwire, thanks to Walid having installed a scrambler that would ensure nobody was sneaking messages out and exposing their position. The bookings themselves were being charged to hundreds of different and legitimate credit cards, whose billing dates were after the flights were due to depart. This was another brainwave of Walid who had stolen the details of the cards, once again thanks to his computing skills. They were all company credit cards with high credit limits, further minimizing the likelihood of them being queried.

The fighters themselves were a risk but the most they would ever know would be the individual flight they were boarding. Whatever the case, for the whole operation to be blown, the risks were minimal.

A loud knock on his door interrupted his thoughts.

"Yes!" he snapped angrily. He was not to be disturbed when he was in his office.

"It's Walid, I must speak with you urgently!"

Nick pushed the map under the papers on the desk and made sure nothing of importance was visible.

"Come in!" he called, maintaining an angry tone and walking over to the door.

Walid rushed in with a camera, once the pride and joy of Gary Truman, in his hands.

"Larbi took this from the man who saw you swimming."

Nick shrugged, uninterested; the man had been some distance away and not a threat.

Walid showed him the viewfinder and the clear image of Nick's face.

"Don't worry, the man's no longer an issue," Walid assured him. Nick's interest level dropped. "But this is," said Walid, holding out a SIM card. "Larbi isn't used to technology so didn't realize that the camera could be sending out pictures to the world on its own."

"Shit! Do we need to move?"

Walid shook his head. "No, it's fine, by the time I pulled it out, it had only managed to upload one photo out of hundreds. The signal around here is shocking. I'm surprised it even managed to find one!"

"What about tracking the SIM?"

"The signal is so weak it's not an issue. Also it's not like a cell phone, it's far harder to track. Larbi will dump the camera minus your images into the sea near where the man's body is. They'll find the camera and not even bother trying to track it."

Nick shook his head. "Where are we with the bookings?" he asked.

"All done," replied Walid.

"Albania has served its purpose," Nick remarked. "Prep the jet and assemble the bookers in the courtyard."

Nick packed everything meticulously, ensuring no trace of the plans had been left behind, even down to destroying the desk blotter that he may have inadvertently leaned on while placing crosses on his map. With the room cleansed, he made his way out to the courtyard and addressed the men that had helped him make the plans a reality. Thirty eager and bright jihadists soaked up the praise he bestowed upon them and joined him in a prayer to Allah, praying for the success of the mission that would rid the world of the great infidel and also confirming their allegiance to Allah, Nick, and the cause for which they fought.

Nick asked them to wait while he went back into the main villa and appeared a minute later with Larbi and Walid.

All three were armed with silenced assault rifles. Nick began shooting the men one by one systematically ensuring they were dead. The men understood this was their sacrifice for the cause. They knew too much and their knowledge was a risk that Allah could not afford for others to uncover. As with everyone he worked with, Nick had ensured the men doing his bookings were ready and prepared to die for the cause. All thirty men sat and waited silently and patiently for their turn to travel to paradise and enjoy their 72 virgins.

An hour later, Nick was settling into a deep sleep while the jet took them towards their next destination. The fire that engulfed the Villa complex below was so intense that it would take months to identify the number of bodies there, let alone their identities.

Chapter 66

The White House

Money, thought Carson. It was always the money. Follow the money and it inevitably leads you to where you want to go. He looked at the list of pre-paid card numbers that had been highlighted as ones that may have been purchased by Nick Geller. Over two hundred and fifty prepaid cards were loaded with various amounts in dollars, sterling and Euros, all equivalent to between ten to fifteen thousand dollars. They equated to more than the two million Euros taken from Jacques Guillon's account but not all the cards would be Nick's. There were some unsuspecting individuals who had bought cards and were about to discover that the anonymity of the cards wasn't quite what they expected. Any transactions on these cards would soon have the full might of the US looking into them.

The news of Frankie's discovery had resulted in a summons to meet with the President and Secretary of Defense Hammond. The request, or more appropriately the command, had been for Carson and Carson alone. Turner had unsuccessfully tried to hide his disappointment at not being included. Frankie and Reid were too busy to care. They had been coordinating the efforts of the majority of the team to track down the other card numbers.

"The President will see you now," said his secretary.

Harry entered the private study and took the seat next to the Secretary of Defense, as instructed by President Mitchell.

"Great work," began the President much to Carson's relief. He had been nervous, not something he was accustomed to. But he had felt like a schoolboy summoned by the headmaster while he waited in the hallway.

"Thank you, Mr. President."

"Is this the break we needed?" asked Secretary Hammond, not one for mincing his words.

"Yes, Bob, this is exactly what we needed," replied Carson.

"What about timing?" asked the President.

"It's good," said Carson. "We have time to put our assets in place. That's if you're happy for me to do so?"

"Definitely," replied the President. "Do you need me to make a call?"

"No, Mr. President, it's fine, I think they'll act on my orders."

"Well, any nonsense, you just throw mine and Bob's names around like candy and if that doesn't work, I'll go visit them myself."

"Thank you, Mr. President, but I'm sure it'll be fine. I've been dealing with Colonel Travers for over a year. He's a good guy."

"Excellent. Gentlemen, I think we deserve a Scotch!" announced the President.

"Mr. President," cautioned Bob, saving Harry, whom he noticed was squirming as uncomfortably as he was, from speaking up, "I think you might be a little premature."

"You've just told me you have what you need and you wish to position our assets to deal with the terrorists, correct?"
"Well yes, but—"

"Guys, we've had enough bad news to sink most governments. Let's enjoy at least one piece of good news."

The President swiveled his chair around and hovered his hand over a selection of different Scotches before finally swooping down and pulling out a bottle of Johnny Walker Blue Label.

"This was the VP's favorite," he said, pouring three large measures and handing them around.

"The Veep!" they said in unison, raising a toast to former Vice President Donald Brodie.

"Have you chosen a new VP yet?" asked Carson.

The President moved his eyes to the Secretary of Defense, Bob Hammond, who sat bolt upright in his chair.

"Me?!" said Hammond incredulously.

The President nodded.

"An excellent choice, Mr. President," Carson said.

"A blood stupid choice!" said Bob, not amused in the least. "Who the hell's going to be my successor?"

President Mitchell's eyes swiveled to Harry.

"Never going to happen," said Harry and Bob at once.

"Already done," said the President, checking his computer screen as he spoke. "It's amazing what you can get done during a crisis. Both the House and Senate have just confirmed Vice President Hammond. And the Armed Services Committee has just ratified Secretary of Defense Carson."

"That's bullshit!" said Harry, standing up in frustration. Holding office was something he had successfully avoided for over thirty years.

President Mitchell turned on the TV screen and the news channel banner displayed the breaking news of the appointments.

Carson sat down and gulped the rest of his Scotch. He had to hand it to the President, it was a masterful move. Carson was an outsider who knew far too much. Placing him in one of the highest offices in the land had just secured Carson's secrecy beyond all doubt. The ultimate political player had just been outplayed and if you were going to be outplayed, it should be by the man you work for.

"Thank you, Mr. President," said Carson reluctantly but with great admiration.

"Mr. President, Mr. Vice President," he said as he exited the room.

Walking away from the President's study, Harry was met by four men he recognized very well.

"Mr. Secretary," said Jack Miller, head of Bob Hammond's security detail.

"Hello, Jack," said Harry, as he walked past him.

"Mr. Secretary," Miller said again before Harry realized that Jack now headed up his security detail.

"Ah shit!" he said, resigning himself. "Come on then, I need to go back to the NCTC."

Chapter 67

Carson was met by cheers of congratulations as he walked back into the NCTC. A much happier Turner than the one he had left was waiting for him.

"I suppose you'll be moving over to the Pentagon?" asked Turner happily.

"I hadn't thought of that," said Carson mischievously. "But no, I think this is still the single largest threat to our nation, so I'm staying right here."

"Oh... o-of c-course," Turner stammered, surprised by the answer.

"Don't worry, Paul. I'm not going to take over your investigation," said Carson reassuringly.

Turner's eyebrows rose slightly and he bit his tongue.

"What?" asked Carson, agitated. He had just inherited, against his will, one of the largest offices and workloads in the country.

"Nothing," said Turner, turning to leave.

"You sure?" asked Carson, knowing exactly what was wrong. It had never been Turner's investigation since he had joined the team.

"Yes and once again, congratulations," said Turner.

Carson couldn't help but feel sorry for Turner. Turner's big chance had come, only to be sidelined by him. The problem was that Turner could not be privy to everything that was underway. Very few people could. One of those very few commanded an airbase 2,500 miles away and it was someone with whom Carson needed to talk to urgently.

"Could you shut the door please?" asked Carson, as Turner exited the room.

Carson lifted the receiver and dialed Colonel Travers at Creech Air Force Base.

"Ian, it's Harry," said Carson when the Colonel answered the phone.

"Mr. Secretary, my congratulations, sir," replied Ian Travers formally.

"Just Harry, thanks, Ian," said Carson, already fed up with the formality of the new role. Life was so much simpler when there was only your name on the door and no title. Ian's silence told Carson that his protestations over being called Mr. Secretary were pointless. These were highly disciplined military men who believed wholeheartedly in the chain of command, a chain in which Carson had just taken the number two spot.

"How are things progressing?" he asked.

"Good to go," replied Colonel Travers.

Carson had first met Colonel Travers eighteen months earlier. He had been conducting a review into the use of drones overseas and their effectiveness. Huge numbers of innocent casualties were being claimed by various insurgency groups but Carson found that ninety percent of the claims were either totally false or had been self-inflicted to put pressure on America. In short, the unmanned aerial vehicle program was a resounding success and saved many American lives.

Fascinated by the possibilities of the program, he had posed a challenge to Colonel Travers. The E3 Sentry AWAC aircraft were one of the key elements of the air force. However, as their mission was simply to fly over a designated air space and stay aloft as long as possible while the technicians looked at computer screens, would it not be possible to automate them, thus allowing the aircraft to remain on station without worrying about the crew tiring? He similarly argued that aerial tanking was also an area that could be considered in the same way. Once in position, the plane required little more than to remain steady, with no real skill being required of either pilot.

Colonel Travers had risen to the task and had, within a matter of months, created two test planes. One E3 Sentry modeled on a Boeing 707, which had four engines and one K46A tanker, based on the soon to be deployed Boeing 767 version of the tanker. The E3 was entirely automated and required no crew or technicians aboard. All communications and equipment could be controlled from the ground, anywhere in the world, as effectively as they could be onboard. Updating the four engines to more modern versions, the plane could happily cruise on just two engines at any time, allowing it to burn fuel far more economically and efficiently. It also allowed the E3 Sentry to stay aloft with almost continual in-air refueling.

There were hundreds of tankers and thirty-two E3s in the Air Force that could benefit from the upgrade. Those, however, were just the tip of the iceberg as far as Carson was concerned of what Colonel Travers and his unmanned Aerial Vehicle Battlelab team could deliver.

"How many have you got ready?" asked Carson.

"Twenty."

"And controllers?"

Carson was referring to USAF Combat Controllers, some of the most highly trained Special Forces soldiers in the US military. Their motto, 'First There', said it all. They were invariably amongst the first US troops on the ground and would pave the way for a larger force. Multi disciplined, they were skilled fighters, air traffic controllers and communications specialists.

"More than enough," replied Travers confidently.

"Excellent. Get them prepped and ready. I want them in Europe and the Middle East in the next couple of days."

"Yes, Mr. Secretary, sir," replied Travers. Carson would have sworn he heard a salute as well.

Carson still had some concerns, though not related to the unmanned vehicles. Those, he felt sure, would perform admirably. The controllers were about to be thrust into a role none of them had signed up for. Trained for the most dangerous missions imaginable, nobody could ever predict how some men would react in certain situations and it was that fallibility that could threaten the success of the mission. Computer-controlled vehicles, as had been proven many times, did exactly what they were told, every time.

Chapter 68

Frankie tried to grab some much needed sleep. She and Reid had worked around the clock to track down every possible card that Nick may have purchased. A second hit had proven her theory even further – a card had purchased a ferry ticket from Marseille to Algiers. At the time, they knew that Nick was in Marseille and that the ferry's arrival coincided with the timing of Nick being in Algiers.

He had done exactly what he didn't do; Nick had slipped up. He hadn't connected the cards with the cash and he was now just a purchase away from being tracked down.

The single biggest problem they had was where that purchase would be and how they would react. With a finite resource of Special Operations teams and equipment, there were only so many places that were reachable in a short time. If Nick surfaced in Europe or the Middle East, they'd be on him in minutes. Asia, depending on where, could be minutes, hours or days. South America and Africa were also sparsely covered across the vastness of their continents but well covered in the major cities. It had been the largest mobilization of Special Forces in US history and an absolute nightmare for the mission planners and logistics experts. There had been some positives as well. Flynn and Barry were pulling together and working as a team rather than counterparts.

Frankie jumped when her phone rang. Her head had been lying right next to it since she had fallen asleep at her desk. She grabbed the receiver, expecting a notification of a purchase. Her phone had only recently been installed and its number remained unpublished. Reid wheeled her chair over in anticipation. She too had woken up when the phone rang.

"Hello?"

"Frankie, can you pop up and see me? And bring Reid too," said Carson, one of very few people who knew her desk extension.

"Of course, Mr. Secretary," she said, as much for Reid's benefit to let her know it was a false alarm.

"It's Harry, just Harry, okay?!" replied Carson irritably and hung up.

When they arrived, Turner was already there. The room was silent and Frankie could only assume it was because Carson only wanted to say what he had to say once.

"We've just had a call into the Pentagon from the Albanian Deputy Minister of Defense. They've an incident that they believe may be related to Nick Geller."

"Albania?" asked Turner, trying to picture where it was.

"Just north of Greece in the Eastern Mediterranean," offered Carson helpfully, before continuing. "A fire has swept through a villa complex killing in excess of twenty people. From local reports, they were all devout Muslims and kept to themselves, at least until recently. A car was seen leaving just prior to the fire and from everything they've pieced together, it drove to the airport where three men dressed in Arab robes boarded a jet and left the country."

"Nick?" asked Frankie.

"We believe so. The jet landed shortly afterwards on a deserted runway in Northern Italy where it was also torched."

"All of this points rather ominously to the conclusion of at least some part of their planning, if not the complete conclusion."

"Any way to track them from Italy?" asked Reid.

"We've no idea if they picked up a car, a train, or even another plane. He could be anywhere but I believe Europe is most likely to be the jumping off point for them and so I've moved a number of assets into place, including two Carrier Groups to cover the Atlantic on the European side and another two on this side. A further two groups will cover the Pacific."

"You really think he's going to do it?" asked Frankie. Up until that point, she really had thought there would come a point when Nick would see sense.

"I have no doubt in my mind," replied Carson. "I have advised the President to begin enacting any recommendations that Colonel Barnes and FEMA deem appropriate to minimize the risk of the Ebola Virus in the mass populous. An emergency broadcast is going out this evening."

"Oh my God, you think it's that imminent?" asked Turner.

Carson nodded. "At least twenty men have been executed. I can only assume this was to ensure they did not disclose what they knew. From the positioning of how they were found, they died without a struggle, while praying. As for timescales, I think we're down to hours, maybe days away from their attack. I've advised Homeland to double their checks on all US bound flights and particularly all non-US citizens boarding flights bound for the US. We're effectively closing our borders to non-US citizens. The Coast Guard and Navy will be checking every boat that enters US waters. Anything they don't like the look of will be turned away and they have orders to shoot first and ask questions later, if need be.

"What can we do?" asked Frankie.

"Pray that he uses one of those pre-paid cards," said Carson. "I'm afraid that's probably our last hope."

Chapter 69

Frankfurt
Germany
Friday August 1st

After months of preparation, the day had finally arrived. Plans put in place as promised to the Caliph were about to become a reality. Those promises had been cemented with Allah, and Nick was just hours from making them come true. Despite the knowledge that his life would soon end, he was elated. The legacy he would leave behind would create a new and better world.

The image of a laughing Frankie lying on the bed flashed into his mind. It was a beautiful memory that he couldn't and had no intention of erasing. It remained his only regret. He could never forget the first time he had seen her, sweeping through a corridor in the White House with the President. Her beauty shone across the room, her piercing blue eyes clashing with her Arabian looks. Looks that only ever seemed to exist on TV shows or on the movie screen. Her command of the area only added to his captivation. Her eyes scanned constantly, checking positions, people, her colleagues, while never taking her eyes off the President.

Despite their eyes only connecting for a fraction of a second across the length of a corridor, he knew there was something there. She had paused just slightly longer on him. It was then that a hint of recognition had sparked in his mind. He recognized something familiar about the eyes. The devastation of that recognition came many weeks later. Long after the consummation of their relationship, the image of the eyes of a much younger Frankie suddenly visited him. A photo that had been shown to him by the Caliph as he shared the deepest darkest secrets of his son, the victims that the Caliph had been aware of and had managed to suppress. Frankie, a much younger Frankie, had been the victim of a pedophile.

Nick had lain awake that night, questioning his motives, his desires, his actions towards the victim Frankie. Had he subconsciously wanted to protect her, keep her safe? Those feelings had grown over time, not immediately. They were feelings that were futile in any event. Frankie could more than look after herself. She had never once acted like a victim. She was a strong, career-orientated woman, the poster woman for positive attitude and desire. She was captivatingly beautiful. It was that simple. He had fallen for a woman for her looks, personality, courage and strength. Not one day had he ever felt sorry for her. He had asked himself a question: If Frankie hadn't been a victim of the Caliph's son, would he still have made a move? *Hell yeah.* Would he still have fallen in love with her? *Hell yeah,* he thought, realizing for the first time that he had in fact fallen in love. It was the best and worst moment of his life, a life he knew was coming to end just as the potential for a new life had begun.

Nick opened his eyes with the image of Frankie's flawless body seared into his eyelids. It was not the time to reminisce, he chastised himself. A cold shower revitalized his body and mind for the task ahead.

After disembarking from the plane in Northern Italy a few nights before, they travelled by car across the Italian border through Switzerland and soon entered Germany. The racetracks, known as autobahns, were a wondrous motorway system. Nick had been on them before but never in a car that could cruise at almost one hundred and ninety miles an hour legally. The first two hundred miles of the journey took almost three hours as they stuck religiously to the speed limits to avoid unnecessary attention. The second half of the journey, once they crossed into Germany was covered in half the time, as Walid was keen to show them what the Porsche Panemera Turbo S could do. Not that Nick or Larbi were in the least bit interested.

Over the previous two days, his army was mobilizing across Europe. The first instructions sent each jihadist to a hotel in one of many European cities. Each would travel alone, unaware of his compatriots' or leaders' whereabouts. Were they intercepted, they would know nothing of their final destination or the whereabouts of any other jihadists. Nor would they have any idea of the numbers involved. Even the leaders knew only of their own individual group's input. Even then, they did not know how many of those Nick would ultimately use in his plan. Those details would only be made known to the individuals in the final hours before their flights.

Over ten thousand hotel rooms had been rented across the various cities that would be used as the departure points for Nick's army. Over ten thousand jihadists ready to fight and die for Allah. They were the most vehement supporters of the various sections within the Islamic faith. Sunni, Shi'a, Wahhabi, Sufi, amongst many other smaller factions had joined as one force, sending their most devoted and devout followers to fight for the cause. Those prepared to die for their cause, Allah's cause, were waking up on a day that would change the world for Islam and the infidel.

Each of the ten thousand would log in to an email account and receive their e-ticket and learn their ultimate destination. The emails were pre-set to be delivered at 7:30 a.m. Central European Time (CET). The logistics of the operation were mindboggling but had been expertly carried out by the Albanian bookers. Ten thousand passports had been sent to ten thousand separate locations. Ten thousand hotel rooms had been organized and allocated to ensure men who knew each other were separated and unaware of each other's locations. It was vital to ensure that the compartmentalization of the plan was followed through until the last moment. If any man were an impostor, his knowledge of the plan and of others involved would be minimal. Ten thousand cell phones had been pre-delivered to each of the rooms for use on arrival at their destination, along with Western style clothing. All the jihadists would be dressed from head to toe in American made and branded apparel. Messages were pre-set to be delivered on arrival at their destinations, detailing the next steps to meet up with their fifty-man strike team or to maximize the delivery of the virus they carried.

Nick checked the time, 8:03 a.m. CET. The couriers that had been sent out across Europe would be delivering the special containers that housed forty-nine vials of Ebola Zaire virus. Those who would carry the virus would discover their fate with the arrival of the vial. Their fate would be sealed before the operation commenced but with the knowledge that they would be responsible for more infidel deaths than any other Muslim in history. Their suicide would be greater than any suicide in history.

Nick, like every other member of the jihadists, had received his email at precisely 7:30 a.m. CET. However his email information was incorrect. He had changed his destination but the booking still showed the destination he had originally planned: Washington, D.C. As much as he wanted to take the fight to the heart of the infidel and Washington, he had decided against it. Even with the best disguise, the security at Dulles Airport would be far greater than at any other target airport. Even though he wanted to lead from the front, the dangers of him never even arriving were too great. Washington, New York, Chicago and L.A. were too high profile and his arrival at any of those was too great a risk to the operation.

Nick logged into a travel website and looked for alternative routes from Frankfurt. The nearest to Washington and New York that he could use to meet up with others was the Frankfurt-Philadelphia route. Another less obvious but slightly further route was to Charlotte, North Carolina. He tried to remember which flight Walid was on. He knew Larbi was definitely on the Washington Dulles flight. Walid was flying into Charlotte or Philadelphia. Not wanting to be on the same flight, he booked both while there was space and he'd use whichever one Walid wasn't on. He used a separate pre-paid card to ensure as much anonymity as possible for each purchase and thinking what the hell, he went for business class tickets. First class was, as far as he was concerned, just a step too far, no matter whose money it was.

Nick Geller had just made his second mistake.

Chapter 70

Within one minute of the first transaction, Frankie's phone rang, along with many others in the center. *Frankfurt.* A hotel near the airport was being pinpointed as the location of the transaction. Frankie contained her excitement. All of the card numbers on the watch list were not Nick's. Some belonged to innocents whose purchases coincided with Nick's. Three false alarms had already been triggered over the last few hours. However, this was the first transaction on the watch list of cards outside the US. Frankie was still rubbing sleep from her eyes when the transaction details came through. A business class seat on US Airways Flight 701 to Philadelphia leaving at 11:00 a.m. which she quickly realized was in just over three hours' time.

Flynn was already at her desk. "Ramstein Airbase is just 80 miles away," he told Frankie while simultaneously talking into his cell phone.

"We've got a Defense Clandestine team there and…" he stopped talking, once again focusing on what was being said to him on his cellphone.

Reid moved across to hear what was happening. She watched as Frankie's screen opened to reveal a copy of an e-ticket purchased for "James Smith".

"Holy shit! Result!" he grinned as he relayed his news. "There is a full Marine Special Operations Battalion on the base. They're on a stopover on the way to Afghanistan. That's about two hundred and fifty kick ass Marines ready and itching for some action!"

"Let's just make sure it's not another false alarm before we go starting a war in Germany," said Frankie.

"James Smith is one of the most common names in America. It's about the best pseudonym he could use."

"As you said, it's also a very popular name which means it's more likely to be legitimate," cautioned Frankie.

Flynn squinted at her. "How does that make it more legitimate?"

"If more James Smiths exist than any other name, statistically, it's more likely a James Smith will book a flight than someone with another name," she explained.

"But it's also the reason you'd be more likely to use that name," said Reid.

"Exactly," said Frankie, confusing Flynn further.

"So what we're saying here," said Reid, "is that we're both right. There's a good chance it is Nick using the common name. But there's a good chance it is just somebody with a common name booking the flight."

"Clear as mud," said Flynn. "Am I sending the troops or not?"

"How quickly can they deploy?" asked Frankie.

"The DCS team can leave now and are about 45 minutes away. The Marines a little longer but they're already gearing up and prepping the Hercules. I'd say they're an hour and a half, two hours max, to have the full force on site."

Frankie turned to Reid who, in turn, looked up at the gangway. Turner was appearing from his office, having been awakened at Reid's request. He joined them, rushing to catch up with the last few minutes' manic activity.

"So what do you think? Send in the DCS team and hold the Marines until we're sure?" he asked, looking for thoughts.

Two nods from Frankie and Reid had Flynn hitting the speed dial button and shouting, "Go!" into his cell.

"Do you think they heard you okay?" asked Turner, rubbing his ear.

"Sorry, but they were in the chopper with the rotor blades on."

Frankie's phone rang again. The second purchase had just been made. US Airways Flight 705 to Charlotte, North Carolina, departing 12:0 p.m. It had been made on another card, which had been purchased 1,500 miles away from where the first card was purchased. The chances of an innocent having purchased two cards at the locations Nick had withdrawn funds from the Jacques Guillon account were so close to nil they were inconceivable. Both flight purchases had been made on the same computer IP address, the Sheraton Hotel at Frankfurt Airport. The name was once again James Smith.

"That's definitely him!"

"Or at least someone with one of his cards," corrected Reid.

Frankie didn't want to say it but she just knew it was him. She felt it. The fact that they were business tickets just added to her intuition. Nick wouldn't fly first class, no matter how much money he had at his disposal. She had found him.

Flynn looked at Turner, who was still soaking in the relief that they had found him or least someone linked to him. However, he was of the same opinion as Frankie, something was telling him it was Nick Geller.

"What?" he asked the staring Flynn.

"The Marines?"

"Send the Marines."

Chapter 71

Omar woke up for prayers just before dawn. It had been a terrible night's sleep. More accustomed to the North African desert, the sound of the air conditioner chilling his room, much like the clear desert skies, was unbearable. The unit rattled and dripped with such irregularity that it wasn't even possible to follow its rhythm. With the air off and the window open, there was nothing more than the noise of passing traffic and the temperature building relentlessly to the point that it, impossibly, was far hotter than the day had ever been. Even without the heat, it seemed that every other person in the hotel had taken turns to bang a door in the hall or stroll along the corridors talking excessively loudly.

Whether he would have slept anyway was another matter. The excitement about what was in store for him would surely have kept him awake. He had been chosen to fight for Allah against the infidel. His courage, bravery and fighting skills had been rewarded, as had his faith in Allah. He was one of the select group that had proven their faith to Allah beyond all others. Only the truly faithful and willing to die for Allah without a moment's hesitation had been chosen and Omar was one of them.

He walked down to the hotel lobby and entered the small business center where a number of computers were provided for customers. It was 6:30 a.m. UK time, 7:30 a.m. CET. He checked his email. He stopped himself jumping for joy when he found that he had been selected to take the fight to America. He was a Fighter not a Protector. His job was to take the battle to America and show the Americans the strength of Allah and the jihad. He wondered how we would have felt had he been a Protector, ensuring the Caliphate was created and protected after the fall of America. He would have been disappointed but still proud. He checked the screen again, the booking was there, he was definitely going to America. United Airlines flight UA35, departing at 10:45 a.m. for Los Angeles, the home of Hollywood, the home of the Muslim haters. Their portrayal of Muslims was abhorrent. He smiled. They didn't know what was about to hit them.

He hurried back to his room and dressed in the Chinos and polo shirt that had been waiting for him on arrival the day before. The socks and boating shoes completed the look and Omar stared into the full-length mirror at a stranger. His beard had been removed two weeks earlier for his passport image. The whiteness of the skin underneath the beard had initially been covered with make up for the photo but after two weeks, the skin had blended to hide any evidence of a beard. Omar stared back at an infidel, not a proud Arab warrior, but not for long. The pretense would soon be over and, armed with his trusty Kalashnikov and as many explosives as he could carry, he would be taking the war, at last, to the streets of America.

It was now all about timing. His instructions were clear. He should remain in his room for as long as possible, minimizing his contact with the outside world. If he were to leave the room, it was only to be for a few minutes after 7:30 a.m. CET to pick up his travel details. Once at the airport, he was to proceed directly to his gate, keep to himself and not talk to anyone unless absolutely necessary. Once on board the plane, he was to take his seat, strap himself in and close his eyes as though he were sleeping. Sleeping, it was advised, was the best thing to do. Whatever the case, he should avoid interactions with other passengers wherever possible and under no circumstance should he acknowledge any other jihadist that may be sharing the same flight.

At 7:05 a.m. (8:05 a.m. CET), Omar found out why he needed to remain in his room. A knock on the door initially panicked him but when it was announced in hushed Arabic that there was a parcel to sign for, Omar opened the door. Omar accepted the parcel and opened it carefully. A small vial sat protected in a stainless steel case. Omar couldn't have been prouder, he had not been chosen as a Fighter, he was an Infector. He was going to kill *millions* of infidels, not just a few hundred. He jumped about the room as though he had just discovered the last golden ticket and then remembered how fragile the vial was.

A small note described in detail how he was to administer the injection and when – the when being the most important. It was imperative for the safety of Islam that the injection be administered as near to his departure time as possible. He would be contagious within four hours of injection. The contagious stage must happen while airborne. Otherwise, the disease could spread across Europe and the Middle East and beyond. The details even described what he should do if his flight were delayed to the point that he would still be in Europe at the point of contagion. He read the detail but was sure that Allah would ensure it was not needed. Omar had a destiny that Allah had pre-ordained along with forty-eight other lucky jihadists who would share his honor in taking the virus into the heart of America.

***

Across Europe, the other ten thousand jihadists who would take the fight to the streets of America were discovering their fates, unknown to each other that they were all selected as Fighters or Infectors. Nick was leaving nothing to chance. He was taking every man who met his criteria into the battle. In hotels in Paris, Amsterdam, Zurich, Rome, Madrid, Barcelona among many others, those same ten thousand jihadists were preparing for their flights and a day that would see them immortalized in the history of Islam.

Chapter 72

The UH-72 helicopter touched down as close to the terminal as possible while remaining out of sight of the public windows. It was on the ground for less than six seconds while the eight-man Defense Clandestine team disembarked. The UH-72, although slower and smaller than the UH-60 Black Hawk, was far less recognizable as a military helicopter. Based on the extremely popular Eurocopter EC145, the UH-72 would not raise any concerns from its shape in the sky.

Dressed casually to blend in with the passengers in the terminal, the team members were armed with MP7A1 submachine guns hidden under their jackets, along with their side arms. Silencers were available for both should the opportunity for a quiet takedown occur. The Team Leader signaled for the men to speed up; it had only been fifty minutes since the transactions had occurred and there was still a chance to take Nick down in the hotel that was located directly across from the terminal building.

The security door opened as they approached the terminal building and the head of Airport Security introduced himself. He was a former commander in the German Federal Police Service and was very accustomed to dealing with Special Forces. He kept his information short and to the point, talking while he walked.

"Karl Brunner," he said, shaking the hand of the Team Leader.

"Simon Klyne."

"We've identified the room from the internet connection and the images that have been sent to the hotel," said Karl, walking briskly towards the airport exit and hotel entrance.

"Excellent, let's hope he's still there."

"We've checked the hotel lobby footage since the transactions and he hasn't been seen. I have three men stationed in the lobby."

"He is extremely dangerous," cautioned Simon.

"They are former GSG 9 officers," replied Karl. "Their orders are to follow and detain only if absolutely necessary."

"Well, whatever the situation, we can handle it. We even have a Marine Special Forces battalion coming in behind us, should we need any more back up," said Simon.

Karl stopped walking, causing the DCS team to stop abruptly to avoid walking into him.

"I have not been told about that. Who authorized it?!" asked Karl angrily. "I have called in the GSG 9 team. If there is any fighting to be done in a German airport, it will be done by German officers."

"Time is of the essence," argued Simon. "The Marines are probably thirty minutes behind us."

"The GSG 9 team is based in Bonn, only eighty miles from here. They're due in the next ten minutes. I'm only letting you attempt the hotel takedown since you are already here," informed Karl curtly.

"Well let's hope *he* is," said Simon to the team behind him as Karl began walking once again, engrossed in an angry-sounding phone conversation.

On entering the busy hotel lobby, Simon and the team spread out. Wandering aimlessly amongst the hotel guests, they all headed in the same general direction but to the casual person did not appear to be together. Simon noticed the nod Karl gave his three men. He had to hand it to Karl, they were good. None stood out as overly observant to what was happening around them, although on closer inspection, they were totally attuned to everyone around them.

Four men waited in the lobby while Simon and three of the DCS team members joined Karl in the elevator. Karl hit button '4'.

"How did they know his room from the IP address?" asked Simon, as they ascended.

"Worried hotels know what you're looking at, boss!" said one of the DCS team members, laughing as they prepared their weapons.

"Each floor has a number of Wi-Fi stations that cover a number of rooms. That way, everyone gets a good signal in their room. The IP he was using is the Wi-Fi station that covers about ten rooms on the fourth floor. From that, we knew the possible clerks who had checked those guests in and the cleaner who cleaned those rooms. Each were shown the photos of the various disguises and we pinpointed the room," said Karl, ignoring the laughter from the DCS team. The imminent arrival of a battalion of US Marines at his airport had resulted in a complete and total humor bypass.

Simon placed a hand on Karl's chest and stopped him exiting as the elevator doors opened to reveal an empty corridor. Two DCS team members eased out, their MP7A1 machine pistols, complete with attached suppressors and stock expanded, looked far more menacing than the slightly oversized handguns they had looked like previously. Simon followed with the third team member holding a hand up to instruct Karl to hold where he was. Moving quickly and silently down the corridor, they approached Room 416. The door was closed. A 'Do Not Disturb' sign hung from the handle.

Simon turned his comms system onto the channel that would allow the NCTC center to listen into the team. Up until that point, their conversation had been localized to the eight team members.

"NCTC, can you hear me?"

"Loud and clear," confirmed Flynn from three thousand miles away in the NCTC.

"Blow it?" the DCS team member at the door whispered to Simon.

Simon looked back at Karl near the elevator. He had a funny feeling that blowing it would make an already pissed Karl exceedingly more pissed.

"No, let's try the card,' he said, handing over the room keycard that Karl had given him.

With their weapons up and ready, the card was inserted and a green light on the handle appeared.

"Go!" said Simon.

Karl watched as the four-man team disappeared expertly into the room.

"Shit!" said Simon.

The room was empty.

Chapter 73

Nick finalized his disguise to match his passport photo. Almost twenty years older, even Frankie would struggle to recognize him. He would have loved to have undertaken the day as himself but there was no way Nick Geller would get past the hotel lobby, let alone airport security. Although still early, he left his room and joined Walid in his room. It was the last time they would probably see each other and Walid had been an invaluable assistant in the planning of the operation. A true believer and warrior, Nick wanted to thank him and wish him well before they left. He also, selfishly, needed to know which flight he was on.

He left his room making sure he had taken everything with him. There was no need to go back. Walid was just three doors further along the corridor in Room 410. He knocked quietly. He noticed the eye appear at the viewer but the door did not open.

"Walid, it's me," he said as loud as he dared, realizing Walid hadn't recognized his new disguise.

The eye appeared again at the viewer before the door opened slightly for Walid to get a better view. Walid stared but did not open the door any further.

"It's me, Nick!" he hissed, wanting to get out of the corridor.

Walid opened the door wide and stepped back.

"That's amazing!" said Walid, looking at a man he knew but could not recognize.

"Thanks," said Nick, brushing past him and into the room.

"No seriously, I can't recognize any part of your face," said Walid, studying him more closely.

"That's the idea. Up until now, a simple disguise was all I needed. To get through security and the cameras that will be analyzing my every feature, it needs to be a little more robust."

"Well it certainly works!"

To prove the point, Nick reached down into the back of his mouth and fished around at the inside of his jaw line. He pulled out a small pink mass and held it up to Walid, his jawline settled back to its more normal state. "I've got a few of these stuffed into my jaw and cheeks. They alter the shape of my face," he explained, moving across to the mirror and replacing the filler back into his jawline.

"I've also injected a serum that loosens my skin. It's like the opposite of Botox but wears off much quicker and rather than hiding wrinkles, it causes them. The effects will be gone in a day or two but in the meantime, it makes me look far older."

"It's fantastic! You'll breeze through security. What time's your flight?"

"Ahh, hold on," said Nick, rummaging through his small bag for the details. "When's yours?"

"12:30 p.m."

"11:00 a.m.," said Nick immediately in response. He did not have to check either. He just didn't want to admit to having changed his flight booking and not wanting to fly on the same flight as Walid.

Walid checked the time, it was almost 8:30 a.m. "You should make a move, no?"

"Probably," said Nick. "Although we're practically in the terminal building," he said, looking across at the terminal and runway beyond. "I suppose this is farewell then."

Walid nodded, his eyes glistening as the emotion of the moment began to build.

"Yes, I suppose it is. I guess this is the last time we will see each other?"

"Never say never, my friend," said Nick. "If not in this life, there will always be paradise."

Walid smiled and nodded as he walked, speechless, to the door. Nick took him by the shoulders.

"Remember, the plan has a number of leaders that will be landing in areas without Ebola carriers. Those leaders will seek shelter until after the contagion does its worst."

"Am I one of those leaders?" asked Walid. He had no issue with fighting and dying for Allah but to be classed as one of the leaders would be an even greater honor. He would be one of the few that would rise from the ashes of the Americans and build a new future grounded in Islam.

"Keep your cell close, you'll find out when you land." Nick had grown fond of Walid.

Nick opened the door and as always, since the first day of training, checked the area he was about to enter. He glimpsed down the hallway and saw all he needed to see to snap the door closed as quietly and quickly as he could.

"What's wrong?" asked Walid.

"Four-man team at my room!"

"But how? We've been so careful!"

It hit Nick like a sledgehammer. He slumped on the bed. The pre-paid cards. It was the only mistake he had made. They were untraceable unless, of course, you had the full resources of the US government to cross-check withdrawals against card purchases.

"What do we do?" asked Walid, pacing the room.

"We don't panic. We all checked in separately so there's no link to anyone but me and my room."

"But what about the flights?"

"This has nothing to do with your flight," replied Nick confidently. He was certain that the two flights he had booked that morning had raised the alarm.

Walid continued to pace as his mind began to consider whether, after all their planning, they might have failed.

"Will you stop pacing? I need to think," said Nick. After a minute of stressful silence, Nick spoke. "I need to make a few calls."

Chapter 74

Frankie's phone ringing stopped the murmur of disappointment that had befallen the center. They had thought they had him.

"Are you sure?!" said Frankie loud enough to catch the attention of everyone around her.

Frankie wrote down what was being said to her:

> *UA133 Munich to Dulles departing at 11:40 a.m. – James Smith. Transaction made in Munich airport.*

Flynn grabbed a map of Europe and a ruler, quickly measuring the distance. "That's nearly two hundred miles away!"

Frankie replaced the receiver. "It's definitely one of his pre-paid car—" and was interrupted by her phone ringing again.

She answered curtly, then began scribbling again:

> *US717 Munich to Philadelphia departing at 12:15 p.m. – James Smith. Transaction Munich Airport.*

"What the hell?" said Reid.

No sooner had Frankie replaced the receiver than the phone rang again:

> *UA953 Munich to Chicago departing at 1:00 p.m. – James Smith. Transaction Munich Airport.*

Turner leaned forward across Reid's desk and hit the comms button that connected with the DCS team in Frankfurt.

"Simon, when was the last sighting of Nick Geller?"

"I'll check," he replied. A minute later he answered. "Late last night, the turn down service. Why?"

"It may be a diversion," said Turner.

"What do you mean?" asked Simon, unaware of the Munich purchases.

"He might not be in Frankfurt."

"What do you mean he might not be in Frankfurt?" asked a heavily accented voice in reply.

"Who is this?"

"Karl Brunner, head of Airport Security."

"I'm sorry, Mr. Brunner, but there's a chance he may have tricked us."

"So what do I tell the GSG9 team that is inbound as we speak?" asked Karl, struggling to hide his frustration.

"We should continue as though he may still be there."

"Is he or isn't he?"

"At the moment, there's a chance he may be in Munich," said Turner, further inflaming Karl.

"So I should alert GSG9 to go there as well? Anywhere else?"

"I'm sorry, Mr. Brunner, but we can only go on the information we have and since there has been a sighting in Frankfurt, we have to assume he may still be there."

"So why do you think he's in Munich?"

"I'm afraid that's classified," said Turner, receiving a torrent of what he assumed were German expletives in response.

"I'm very sorry, Mr. Brunner."

"No, I'm sorry, Mr. Turner," replied Karl, calming down a bit. "It's just that today is not a good day. We seem to be far busier than normal."

"Busier how?" asked Reid, leaning across in front of Turner.

"Plane spotters, thousands of them. In the terminal and around the perimeter."

"Why?"

"I'm not sure. I was called away to meet your team as the influx started."

"You don't have any experimental or new aircraft type arriving today?"

"No, we're always advised of those events and well prepared. The arrival of the airbus A380 was the last really big event here."

An urgent shout cut across the operations center floor.

"Deputy Director!"

All heads turned to the corner of the room where the shout had originated. Turner left Reid appeasing Brunner and headed across to the young computer specialist from the NSA who was sitting at a screen that seemed to be scrolling a huge amount of text.

"What's that?" asked Turner.

"E-mail addresses," replied the NSA agent.

"For who?" asked Tuner, a sickening feeling forming in his stomach.

"I don't know but they all went out at the same time and from the same account as the one that went to Nick Geller's IP address this morning."

"How many?" asked Turner.

The NSA agent looked at the bottom of the screen and shrugged. "Hundreds."

"What do they say?"

"Not sure yet, they're password protected. I need to break the code."

"How long?"

"I'll know once I have a chance to look at them. I thought you'd want to know how many there were first."

"No, no, that's great work," he said, patting the NSA agent on the back. "How's it going?" he asked, approaching Frankie, not wanting to disturb Reid's conversation with Karl.

"We think we may have found the source of the plane-spotting rush." "What?"

"A Boeing 747," she said, pointing to the main screen. It was on a website called airliners.net and had over 2,400 comments. The number of comments seemed to be increasing by the second.

"Who the fuck called in the Marines?" shouted Harry Carson, bursting into the operations center and killing all conversations and noise dead.

"Me," said Turner confidently.

"I've just had a new asshole reamed, thanks to you, by the Secretary of State, who in turn just got reamed by the German Foreign Minister," said Carson, marching over to the group.

"We've been trying to contact you," said Turner.

"I know!" said Carson. "I've been busy."

"We're closing in," said Turner.

"Deputy Director, I've got it!" shouted the NSA agent.

"Got what, son?" asked Carson.

"I've cracked the email code."

Turner rushed away to see what it was and missed the slashing motion that Carson made across his own neck.

By the time Turner reached the NSA agent, every computer screen in the building had gone blank. Phone lines stopped working and Reid's conversation with Simon and Karl in Frankfurt stopped.

Frankie had spotted Harry's cutting motion just before the computers died.

"What are you doing Harry?" she asked confused.

"What happened?" asked Turner, looking up at the blank bank of screens that towered over the room.

The sound of boots running into the room answered Turner's question as the outer perimeter of the room filled with military personnel.

Turner looked at Carson with great confusion and betrayal.

"People, I want to thank you for all the hard work you have put in over the last few week—"

"What in the hell are you doing Harry?" protested Turner.

"We have arrived at a point in the investigation when this has become a military matter. As such, I would ask all non-military personnel to vacate the building immediately."

"No fucking way! We've just cracked the emails!" screeched Turner.

"*We* cracked them thirty minutes ago," said Carson.

"We?"

"Defense," replied Carson.

"What are you going to do?"

"Whatever we need to, to protect the United States of America," replied Carson before adding. "And her allies."

"What *are* you doing, Harry?" asked Frankie quietly.

Carson looked at her. She could see he was struggling. He turned back to face the main center.

"Ladies and gentlemen, once again, I thank you for all your efforts. But action will be taken here that none of you have signed up for. I must ask you to leave now, or you will be removed forcibly."

"Oh Jesus, you're not, Harry. Tell me you're not?" pleaded Turner.

"What?" asked both Reid and Frankie.

"He's going to shoot the plane down!"

"Just stop it from taking off!" said Reid.

"They won't, they want to make sure they get rid of the virus and any carriers that may be aboard. If they stop the plane they may not get them all and risk a European outbreak," Turner worked out.

"Harry?" asked Frankie, looking for confirmation.

"Everyone out *now!*" screamed Carson.

Chapter 75

"There must be something we can do!" said Reid as they walked dejectedly out to the parking lot of the NCTC.

Turner looked back at his center where a ring of very serious-faced young soldiers stood guard. "He's the Secretary of Defense and I'm fairly sure he'll have informed the President of what he's doing."

"Shooting down an American airliner?!" said Frankie in disgust.

"That's if it's just one. We've got five different flight bookings for James Smith," reminded Reid.

"Where's that NSA guy?" asked Turner urgently looking around the hundreds of agents that were pouring out of the center.

"He's probably still there. NSA's part of the DoD," said Frankie.

"Well, not the right part," said Turner, spotting the young agent amongst the crowd. He pushed through the crowd with Frankie and Reid in tow.

"The emails, what did they say?" asked Turner.

The NSA agent looked behind him. "I'm sorry Deputy Director, I can't say."

"You got kicked out just like us though?!"

"Only because I don't have the correct clearance to stay."

"What clearance are you?"

"Top secret," he replied. "To be honest I thought I was cleared for anything."

"So what clearance level is left in there?" asked Frankie.

"Top Secret, SAP."

"SAP?"

"Special Access Program. Only those cleared for the program are allowed to stay."

Turner looked back at the center. "How many was that?"

"There were only about ten left in the Operations center when I left. They checked my clearance and kicked me out."

"Ten?!" said Reid. "That's hardly enough to man the front desk!"

"But you cracked the email?"

"Yes but I can't tell you what was in it."

"Can you tell us how many there were?"

"Hmm, probably not," he said, looking back once again to the center.

"Was your guess right?" asked Turner.

"Way off."

"One zero?" asked Turner.

"Two, sir," he said.

Turner paled at the understanding of how big the number was.

"How many?" asked Frankie.

Turner didn't want to say it out loud in case the Agent confirmed it. He was still hoping they had crossed wires. "Ten thousand?" he said tentatively, hoping he'd be corrected. A faint smile from the NSA agent told him he was correct.

"That can't be right!" said Frankie. "That'd need hundreds of flights. They'd be on every flight leaving Europe for America!"

"He can't shoot down every plane heading for America," said Reid.

"What's a hundred thousand lives compared to over three hundred million?" questioned Turner.

"Just cancel all the planes!" shouted Frankie.

Turner shook his head. "They're assuming the jihadists aren't going to be contagious in Europe. Nick threatened America not the rest of the world. If Europe gets Ebola, the Middle East and the Muslim world gets it. The carriers will plan to become contagious during their flights. Remember what Colonel Barnes said, there's a four-hour window from infection to being contagious. They need the flights to go ahead as though nothing's wrong. They need the carriers in the air when they become contagious. Otherwise, hundreds of millions or even billions would be at risk."

"So they'll just massacre tens of thousands of innocent passengers?" asked Frankie sharply.

"They'll already be dead, they just won't know it yet. Shooting the planes down will save them an excruciating death. Remember that poor guy in France?"

"If we stop the planes, they won't be exposed," argued Frankie.

"They will. And all of Europe will be exposed if the planes don't take off. The terrorists are probably already taking their injections. Some of those flights are probably already in the air, or at least boarding, and they'd need to take the injection before the security gates."

"Do you need me anymore?" interrupted the NSA agent. He did not want to be seen talking to the group. Carson had told him personally not to divulge what he had discovered.

"Anything else you can tell us?" asked Turner.

"No," he said, leaving quickly thereafter. As desperate as he was to tell them about the incorrect assumption they had made, Secretary of Defense Carson had made it very clear that his life would not be worth living if he ever discovered the young agent had divulged what he had uncovered.

Chapter 76

9:30 a.m.
Frankfurt

Walid checked the corridor as per Nick's instructions. It was clear.

"What do you think?" he asked, his head still outside the door.

"I think you should come back into the room before you speak!" said Nick.

"Sorry," said Walid, quickly closing the door.

"I think we'll go ahead as if nothing has happened."

"But if they know your room, they'll know your flight."

Nick shook his head. "I've got a booking on the Washington flight at 12:20 p.m. in a different name."

"But they'll be looking for you?"

"It's a different airline using a completely separate area of the terminal and I don't look anything like Nick Geller."

"But what about the name you were going to use?"

Nick pulled out the passport for James Smith, opening it at the photo page. It looked exactly as he currently did - a man in his late fifties, with a heavily wrinkled face.

Nick picked up his small bag and disappeared into the bathroom. A far younger and rounder faced man appeared shortly afterwards. The gray streaks that had added maturity to the aging James Smith were gone and his eye color had also changed, once again, to complete the new look.

Small red dots covered Nick's face, onto which he was applying concealer.

"Botox to tighten the slack skin and a bit more filler in the jawline and cheeks, along with some heavier clothes and voila, five years younger than I normally look and a lot heavier thanks to a fat face," he said, pulling out another passport.

"Kyle Johnson, pleased to meet you," said Nick to Walid, holding out his hand in greeting, as though for the first time.

"You're very good at that," said Walid, thoroughly impressed.

"They trained me very well."

"Unlucky for them."

"Time to go," said Nick.

"Are you sure?" said Walid. "It's still quite early."

"Security is going to be tight and lengthy. If we go now, we'll blend in with the mass of passengers. Waiting until last would attract more scrutiny."

"Good point," said Walid nervously.

"You go first and I'll follow on in a few minutes. And remember, they don't know you. They're not looking for you, just me. Act casual."

Walid checked himself in the mirror, picked up his bag and with a hug, wished Nick Allah's blessings for the operation.

With that, he was gone, leaving Nick alone with his thoughts. Nick checked himself once more against the image in Kyle Johnson's passport. It was a good match. Not a perfect one but whose passport photo ever was?

After waiting five minutes, he followed Walid's lead and exited Room 410, without even a passing glance back towards Room 416. He pressed the 'Call' button and waited for the elevator. The doors opened, two passengers were already inside - a woman and a young boy. Nick stepped forward and smiled a good morning to them.

"Hey, Mister?" said the young boy, his American accent catching Nick's attention more than it should have.

"Hey there," said Nick, not wanting to appear unfriendly.

"Where you going, Mister?"

"Zach!" chastised his mother. "Don't be so nosey."

"Sorry," said Zach. "We're flying home to America."

"Nice," said Nick.

"We fly to Charlie…ot…"

"Charlotte?" said Nick helpfully.

"Yep, that's it," the boy said excitedly.

The doors pinged open in the lobby and his mother threw Nick an apologetic look as she rushed her out of the elevator.

Charlotte, thought Nick. Walid was flying to Charlotte. Everyone on Walid's flight was going to die. It was one of the reasons Nick wanted to ensure he wasn't on Walid's flight. He couldn't remember where every vial had been delivered but he did remember that one jihadist who had received a vial was on Walid's flight.

Nick returned the wave to the young boy as his mother pushed him out of the hotel's main doors.

Chapter 77

NCTC

The first thing Carson had done, after clearing the center of all non-military and cleared personnel, was to call off the Marines. On their final approach towards Frankfurt airport, he had called just in time to avoid the sight of three C130 US Military Hercules coming into view of the terminal building. His next call was to stand down the DCS team and get Karl Brunner on board with the plan. The plan being to let the terrorist Nick Geller, if he was indeed in the Frankfurt airport, board his plane and leave German soil. The conversation had been brief. Karl Brunner was delighted to let the arrest of the highly dangerous criminal happen somewhere other than in his airport.

The NSA agent had been incorrect in his guess at how many people were still in the center. There had been nine when the NSA agent left but another four left shortly after. Their clearance also fell short of the requirements to stay behind. Ideally, Carson would have carried out the rest of the operation from the Pentagon but with time critical, it was decided to stay and complete the mission from the NCTC while the investigation data that was never again to see the light of day was deleted by the program members who had accompanied Carson.

Even those who had been trusted with deleting the data were not fully aware of the scale of the operation underway. Carson retreated to his office and closed his door, then connected the video-conference equipment to Vice President Bob Hammond and National Security Adviser Liz Roberts.

"Harry," greeted Vice President Hammond.

"Liz, Bob," said Harry, acknowledging them and checking the line.

"How'd it go?" asked Bob.

"As well as can be expected," said Harry. "They've worked around the clock, as hard as any team I've ever worked with."

"Had to be done," said Liz.

"How was Turner?" asked Bob.

"Pissed, with a capital P-I-S-S-E-D."

"We'll make it up to him," promised Liz.

"So where are we?" asked Bob.

"If everything goes as we expect, Geller will be boarding in the next couple of hours. All assets are in place. On confirmation that he has boarded, I will, with the President's final approval, initiate Operation Takedown."

"Anything you need from us?" asked Bob.

"Just make sure the President's ready and available to take my call."

"Will do."

Harry sat back in his chair as the screen went black. Taking a human life, no matter whose, was never an easy decision to make. Killing thousands was even more difficult but beyond that, the number just became a number. The decision to kill vast numbers had already been made.

The greater good, thought Carson, *the greater good.*

Chapter 78

Terminal 4
London Heathrow Airport

Omar joined the line for flight UA35 to Los Angeles. A large number of desks showed the flight number, ensuring quick progress as the amount of desk agents prevented the build-up of queuing passengers.

Approaching the desk, Omar handed over his passport and his booking reference, as instructed.

"Thank you, Mr. Perez," said the check-in agent.

The man typed in Omar's reference and hit a key that resulted in Omar's boarding pass printing. A young woman to his left was checking in at the adjacent desk and looked across at him. She smiled, liking what she saw. Omar wasn't sure if it was he or the very muscly desk agent that the young woman was smiling at. However, rather than be flattered, he was angry at the inappropriate way in which she was dressed. Her short skirt and low cut top were no way for a young woman to dress in public. Remembering his instructions, he forced a smile back.

The check-in agent had other ideas. He could hardly take his eyes off of the young woman. Neither, it seemed, could most of the men in close proximity. *Pathetically weak*, thought Omar, *and exceptionally disrespectful*. He would be teaching their whole kind a lesson they'd never forget. There was only one true God and the world was about to find out once and for all who that was.

He smiled at the check-in agent, pulling his eyes away as the young woman bent forward to place her bag on the scales.

"This is your boarding card. We're having a few problems with the departure boards. This is the gate number you should go to, ignore what's on the boards. The flight's on time, so be sure to go straight through security as boarding will start very soon," he said, pointing to the number 25 he had written in thick red ink on Omar's boarding pass.

Omar felt uneasy until he overheard the same conversation about the gate numbers with the young woman. He was checked in. He had his boarding pass and the flight was on time. That was all he needed to know. He spotted the sign that directed him to the restroom. He waited in a short line for a cubicle and, when he closed the door behind him, he withdrew the vial containing the virus. He noted the time and without a second's pause for thought, injected the deadly virus into his body, whispering 'Allahu Akbar', as he pressed the plunger down.

As instructed, he flushed out the vial with a small bottle of bleach he had been given and then wrapped them both in toilet paper. He deposited the package in a bin as he exited the restroom. Next stop was security, where he breezed through without so much as a search. His US passport was working perfectly. Without it, he felt sure that his skin color would have elicited a body search.

Omar proceeded directly to the gate on his boarding pass where the plane was already filling up. He kept his eyes down and again was surprised at just how efficiently the line was moving. He spotted the young woman from check-in sitting nearby. He wondered why she wasn't boarding but was quickly interrupted when the check-in agent called him forward.

"Mr. Perez?" he said, recognizing Omar and taking his boarding pass. "First aisle, second row on your right, window seat," he said with a smile.

Omar stepped on board and avoided eye contact with anyone, just kept his head down and his eyes to himself.

"Excuse me," he said, climbing over two men who were occupying the seats next to him. Both had their eyes closed as though they were sleeping. He wondered if they were jihadists like him. He doubted it. There were only supposed to be a few on each plane. It was still early in the morning and not surprisingly, most people would be trying to catch some more sleep. He sat down, buckled his seat belt and, as instructed, he closed his eyes like everyone around him and tried to get some sleep.

Chapter 79

Narsarsuaq
Greenland

A small town at the Southern tip of Greenland, Narsarsuaq, had a lot to thank the US for. Its very existence in modern times had been a result of the US building a refueling station to transport aircraft from the US to Europe during the Second World War. Over four thousand American service men had been stationed there at its peak, assisting over ten thousand aircraft to make their transatlantic journeys. Even into the cold war years, Narsarsuaq and Bluie West One, the US name for the base, retained its strategic importance.

By 1958, the US had closed the base and moved most of its personnel to Thule Air Base on the eastern coast. However, benefiting from the legacy of the US airfield, the town of Narsarsuaq had grown, albeit not dramatically, but enough to offer a living to a small number of inhabitants who benefited from a flourishing tourist trade. The town (and its small airport) provided easy access to the southern tip of the glacier that covered over 80% of the world's largest island.

Almost sixty years later, the inhabitants were once again thanking the United States. The impromptu visit by a collection of fighters from across the different branches of the US military, accompanied by the significant support crew required to maintain and prep them had led to a bustling few days in the small town. The collection represented just about every fighter currently flying and due in service across the USAF, Marines and US Navy.

The official reason given for the impromptu visit was a fault experienced on one of the transport aircraft that happened to be carrying the majority of spare parts for the accompanying fighters. They were therefore all required to land. The ultimate destination was alleged to be a number of trade shows and air shows across Europe. However, a quick search would have revealed that no air show or trade show was due to see a US Marine F-35 Lightning fighter of which there were two sitting on the Narsarsuaq runway.

Whatever the reason, it was an impressive display of the US forces' flying power and was bringing back fond memories to many of the older inhabitants in town.

After two days of relative inactivity, the airfield had burst into life. The various crews that would prep each of the aircraft were busy preparing the planes for their pilots. As varied as the fighter types, the maintenance crews were from squadrons based all around the world. Few had met any of their counterparts before, nor would they ever see them again. Similarly, hardly a pilot amongst the fighter pilots had ever met any of the colleagues they were about to fly with.

The man who had been tasked with commanding the operation had described the groups of men as an amalgam of strangers, crew, pilots and aircraft, all passing in the night. There would be very few personnel in attendance who would even remember the event a year from then, some probably would wonder in a week whether it had actually taken place. However, for the Commander, Major General Howard Carter, it was a day he would remember for the rest of his life. For the first time in ten years, he would be behind the controls of a fighter plane. That would not be the reason he'd never forget. Despite having been drafted in from every corner of the world, from different branches of the US Military, and despite having never met one another before, on paper, not one of the pilots had one thing in common. Unless and until you dug a little deeper. Each of the fighter pilots at Narsarsuaq had lost a mother, brother, father, sister, wife, son or daughter on September 11, 2001.

The first two planes to take to the runway were a USAF F-22 Raptor and a US Navy FA18 Super Hornet. The Raptor pilot had lost his twin sister in the North Tower and had joined the Air Force a week later. The Navy Pilot had lost his father on American Airlines Flight 11 travelling from Boston to Los Angeles. Four years later, on his seventeenth birthday, he had walked into the naval recruiting office.

Both fighters leapt into the sky and headed east.

"Harry?" said Major General Howard Carter on connecting his call to Secretary of Defense Harry Carson. "Birds one and two are airborne."

"Thanks for the update," replied Harry somberly.

"Just remember, Harry, this is for Jackie," he said, remembering his wife who had died in the South Tower.

"For Jackie," agreed Harry, a tear welling in his eye, as he remembered his own sister fondly. And many, many others.

Too many, thought Harry to himself.

"God bless America," said Howard to his brother-in-law, trying to regain his composure.

"God bless America," said Harry. Never had he meant it more.

Chapter 80

Nick was stunned at how easily he had walked into the terminal. The anticipated additional security had not materialized. He approached the United Airlines check-in line, having barely seen a security officer and certainly none that appeared to have been advised of a potential terrorist in the area. His bookings for Munich-bound flights had obviously worked.

The line for the check-in was surprisingly short but he noted the large number of check-in desks being used for the flight. The staff were moving through passengers quickly, meaning the build-up was minimal. Unfortunately, not minimal enough as Nick spotted Larbi when a passenger in front of him moved, unblocking his view of the passengers in front.

Nick checked his booking. He had a business class booking. He just had to hope that Larbi hadn't been afforded the same luxury. He had no issue with sitting near Larbi; it was Larbi sitting near him that Nick was worried about. Larbi was a mountain warrior. Airports, airplanes and technology in general were all new to him. There would be a significant risk that Larbi would look to Nick for help if he knew Nick was there.

Larbi turned and looked back down the line and straight at Nick. He looked right through him. Nick was impressed. For a fish out of water, Larbi was coping admirably but then Nick remembered that Larbi would not have recognized him. Nick looked nothing like the man Larbi knew as Nick. Larbi was also doing something he had been told not to. Look around. His level of English, like many of the jihadists, was basic to nonexistent. However, all had been taught the very basics they needed for the trip. Most would have no ability to speak any more than, 'please', 'thank you' and 'good morning'. American Passport holders who didn't speak the language posed the greatest risk. However, they had all been taught to answer 'yes' to packing their own bags and 'no' to any dangerous items. Other than that, all they really needed to know was their departure/boarding gate. All of which had been explained to them prior to their journeys.

Nick watched closely as Larbi, probably as bad an English speaker as 95% of the jihadists who spoke no English, walked forward to the check-in desk. He handed over his passport and Nick could see him nodding his head to the first question and shaking to the second. The check-in agent then wrote something on Larbi's boarding card and pointed, directing him to the security gates. Larbi smiled and without a look backwards proceeded to the security gates.

Nick was pleased. If Larbi could do it, all ten thousand could.

Nick felt a knot in his stomach as the check-in agent called him forward. The young man looked at him closer than Nick would have liked but made no sign, at least outwardly, that he had recognized Nick. Nick answered the normal security questions and was rewarded with his boarding pass with instructions to proceed directly to the gate that the agent had written clearly on the boarding pass.

Nick smiled at the young family checking in for the flight at the desk next to his and as instructed, proceeded to the gate. Security was quick and seemed uninterested in him. Again, Nick had no doubt that he was safe, thanks to the Munich bookings. He passed a group of excited passengers taking pictures of two US Airways planes. He looked at them and couldn't see anything notably different. They certainly weren't a new model, just a pretty standard looking Boeing 747 jumbo jet to him.

"What's the excitement?" he asked one of the men, snapping shots like there was no tomorrow.

"It's a US Airways Boeing 747," the man said, as though that meant something to Nick.

"And?"

"They don't exist!" he said, somewhat negating his previous statement.

Nick looked out of the window at the very large plane that they both could see very clearly.

"Well obviously it does," he said.

"Obviously, yes," said the man. "But nobody knew they had any until they arrived here this morning!"

"Okaaay," said Nick, thoroughly underwhelmed. Plane, train and bird spotters were a special bunch of souls.

He walked through, checked his boarding pass, and proceeded to his gate. He noticed the board was showing a slightly different gate and made a detour towards the one displayed on the boards. Arriving at the gate, he noted the boarding had not started, something the desk agent told him had begun. A United Airlines staff member, one of the staff from the check-in desk, approached him and checked his boarding pass, then directed him to the gate on his pass.

"I apologize, sir. We're having a nightmare this morning, gate numbers, flight numbers everything's gone crazy," explained the agent, directing another two men behind Nick to the same gate as Nick.

Nick arrived as one of the last to board.

"If you just take the stairs to the upper deck, sir, your seat's on the left hand side."

Nick followed the instructions and tiptoed through the cabin where it seemed everyone was keen to catch up on their sleep from the early morning start.

He sat down and looked out at the other aircraft which seemed far below, given his position on the upper deck of a Boeing 747. Another United Airlines jet sat alongside and Nick recognized the young girl sat in the window seat. She had been with the family checking in next to him. They had checked in at the desks for the UA988 flight to Dulles, the flight he was supposedly on.

A steward was stationed just two rows in front. Nick waved him over.

"What flight is that?"

The steward looked out the window. "Not sure, there are a few that leave around the same time as us."

"This is the Dulles flight, right?"

"Yes, sir," he said confidently, allowing Nick to settle back and relax.

Chapter 81

They had agreed to convene at Frankie's house, being the nearest to the NCTC and providing more space than either Reid or Turner could offer. They owed it to the innocent lives at risk and to themselves to try whatever they could to stop the massacre. They had one major problem. Until the flights started falling out of the sky, they had nothing. All the evidence to back up their theories of the impending mass slaughter was back at NCTC, now under military control and lockdown.

They needed something. Unfortunately, the only thing they had would be after the first plane went down. The race would then be on to ensure that Carson was stopped before he massacred tens of thousands of innocents. They understood the reasoning. The Ebola virus had to be contained, but that didn't mean they had to kill everyone. Not everyone would contract the virus on the flights. They all hit the computers. They needed the details and flight timings for every flight inbound to the US from overseas that day. Turner and Frankie took on that task and were stunned at just how many there were - hundreds. With each plane they found they couldn't help but think it was another planeload of innocents flying to a certain death. It was madness; the hundreds of flights inbound to America now neared a thousand.

While they researched flights and details, Reid looked at potential solutions. Her job was to find remote facilities that could accept inbound flights and allow those who had not contracted the disease a fighting chance to survive while protecting the rest of the nation. With the rising number of flights that Frankie and Turner were logging, so too rose the number of potential locations required for the quarantine of passengers.

After three hours of research, the two lists were ready. They looked at them and realized that the scale of the task was monumental and not something that was going to be achieved in the space of a few hours.

"But were there only fifty vials of Ebola stolen?" asked Frankie, scanning down the vast numbers of flights.

"Yep," said Turner.

"Minus the one he used," Reid reminded them.

"So that means there are only forty-nine flights that are carrying the virus," concluded Frankie.

"At most," Turner remarked.

Reid sighed. "Unless they've infected each other before they left."

"Not without infecting everyone they met prior to boarding, which would have infected most of Europe."

"Does anyone really believe they can contain it in America anyway?" asked Frankie.

Both Reid and Turner nodded and Turner said, "We've seen the papers, it's not easy but possible, as long as you know where and when the infection started. Obviously, we've done it in reverse, protecting us from a virus released in Europe or Asia, not protecting the rest of the world from a virus released here. But the principle would be the same."

"Although it was North America, not just America," added Reid.

"Yes, the Panama canal, the narrowest point would be closed and any attempt to cross met with deadly force. Likewise, all shipping and air transport would be sent back or face being shot down. Thereafter, the Navy Coastguard, Air Force and Army would simply shoot anyone who attempted to enter our waters or airspace."

"So not dissimilar to what Carson's doing?"

"I suppose come to think of it, no. He'll say he's protecting Europe and North America with his actions."

"Hard to argue against," pondered Reid.

"Except there are only forty-nine flights inbound that may have carriers on board."

Turner splayed out the flight details. "But which forty-nine?"

"The emails!" Reid exclaimed.

"You mean the ten *thousand* emails?" asked Frankie dejectedly.

"There may be some flights that aren't in the emails."

Turner shook his head. "And what if there's another list of emails we haven't found?"

"Good point," said Frankie. "So where does that leave us?"

"Wondering if what Carson's doing may be the right thing?" ventured Reid.

"How many people on a plane?" asked Frankie.

"Depends on the plane," said Turner, looking at the list at the types they had noted down. "On a Boeing 767-300, maybe three hundred. On a triple 7, maybe nearer four hundred and on a 747, over five hundred. And as for the Airbus A380s, I think there can be over seven hundred."

"We've got hundreds of flights."

"But they won't all be full," said Reid.

"Let's pray to God they're not," said Frankie. "But even half full, that's still over a hundred thousand people if they're all on the smaller planes."

"For forty-nine carriers?"

"Not by the time they land here. That's forty-nine times, say an A380's planeload of passengers..." she said, punching the buttons on the calculator. She whistled. "...over thirty-four thousand carriers."

"So what do we do?" asked Reid.

Franking began collecting up their papers. "There's only one person who can stop Carson."

"Stop him doing what though, saving the nation?" asked Turner.

"President Mitchell's a good man. I can't believe he'd allow Carson to do this," she protested. Whatever the case, whether justifiable or not, she couldn't help but feel partly to blame. This was all because of a man she had loved, trusted and whose child she was carrying. Her child, no matter how innocent, would have the genes of a man responsible for the needless deaths of over a hundred thousand lives. She was not giving up while there was still something they could do.

"You don't just walk into the White House and see the President?"

"I'll call Bill, he'll get us in," she said confidently.

"Bill?" Reid asked Turner, as Frankie grabbed her cell.

"I assume she means Bill Jameson, the head of the President's Secret Service detail."

"We've got ten minutes, an hour from now," said Frankie.

Chapter 82

Saint-Jean-Cap-Ferrat
France

Prince Abdullah Bin Fahd Al Khaled stretched out on the lounger by his poolside Cote D'Azur retreat. The luxury mansion, one of many dotting the small outcrop of opulence on the spectacular French coastline, was a favorite of royalty and the new Russian Oligarchs. Prince Abdullah looked out to the crystal clear waters of the Mediterranean and was able to see the super yacht that awaited him, should he wish to spend a day at sea.

It had been a torturous few weeks, constantly under surveillance by the Americans who, although unable to link him with any involvement with the fugitive Nick Geller, had insisted on watching him quite openly day and night. Despite many protests to a number of Senators and Congressmen, many of whom would find far smaller campaign pots, nothing had been done until that very morning.

The prince had woken up to his head of security informing him that the cars stationed outside the mansion had gone, as had the speed boats that had sat permanently off shore. The Americans were gone. His watchers had finally gotten the message. He wondered which Senator had actually managed to grow a pair. The letter of apology from the United States of America's Secretary of State that arrived by special courier shortly after 9:00 a.m., offering a personal apology from the United States, was as unexpected as it was welcome.

Despite the watchers, the prince had still managed to stay in touch with the preparations that would see the Americans on their knees. They could monitor e-mails, phone calls, listen in to everything – even through walls – and photograph everything he was doing, but they couldn't stop the small handwritten notes that had been delivered to him on regular intervals over the last few weeks. His nephew, Walid, like himself, a true believer, had kept him in the loop. Very few people had any idea of the scale of the operation that was underway. It was part of the compartmentalization of the plan. Nobody would have any idea what they needed to prepare for, nor if any individual were captured would they know there if were one hundred others like them, one thousand, ten thousand or one hundred thousand. The authorities, even if one man were captured, would be as in the dark as they had been before. It was quite brilliant.

Of course, Walid was aware of the number due to his helping prepare the final details and had explained how vital it was for his uncle to keep the number to himself, detailing how Nick had killed every one of the bookers to keep that number from ever getting out. As far as the jihadists were concerned, they knew they were part of an army but none would have any idea just how large.

Prince Abdullah checked his watch, just after lunch. The final plane would be boarding, the final flight carrying the greatest warriors of Islam and their leaders to fight for Allah. Taking his word and his sword to the infidels, he couldn't have been prouder. He almost wished he were joining them, boarding one of the flights, just as Mohammed Farsi was. Just as Mustafa Ghazi was, just as any one of the many leaders that would take the battle to the streets of America. He had his role, just as Nick had promised. He had received the letter just a few days earlier. He was to fill the leadership void that would be created by the attack. Prince Abdullah bin Fahd Al Khaled was to be the new Caliph.

Prince Abdullah bin Fahd Al Khaled, as the new Caliph, would broadcast to the world the commencement of the war in America. He would tell the world of the virus that Allah had sent to plague the infidels. He would preach to them and tell them to pray to Allah for forgiveness for the sinful lives they had led. He would lead the jihadists who had not made the grade. Without a leader of his strength, Nick and the former Caliph had feared for the future of the jihadists. But they owed it to Allah to take his greatest warriors and leaders into battle. Many would return but in the meantime, Prince Abdullah held the future of the true believers and faithful in his hands.

Up until that morning, with the Americans watching everything he did, it would have been impossible. Their leaving was another sign that Allah was watching over them. Allah was ensuring that his will and the will of the Caliph, peace be upon him, would be delivered.

He stretched once again and stood up. He had a video recording to prepare for and a cause that needed a strong and powerful leader.

***

Flynn paddled the surfboard further out to sea. He checked that his three colleagues were still with him. It had been a lucky break, quite literally, for only five days each year the surf broke in the way it had that morning when they had arrived. Up until they had spotted the wave, they were struggling to see a way to get close without being too obvious. He looked around and spotted Prince Abdullah's mansion. The house was exceptionally well protected. Walled on three sides, motion sensors and cameras covered every square inch. If there were any weaknesses in the system, Flynn hadn't been able to find them, nor had the CIA team that had been permanently camped watching him for the previous few weeks. Even if there had been a weakness, the twenty-plus man security force, almost all ex Spetsnaz troopers, would have more than filled it.

The only access was the open sea front which itself was well covered by motion sensors and cameras. However, it did offer a clear view up to the pool area and the spectacular house beyond. What it didn't offer was any view from land, as the house was pointing south towards the open Mediterranean and the spectacular super yacht that the egomaniacal prince had called 'Abdullah'.

"Well?" asked Flynn's number two as he paddled alongside.

"Piece of cake." "Seriously?" he asked.

"Well yeah, if we didn't have to cover our tracks and make it look like an accident or it was natural, piece of cake; one cruise missile right through those beautiful French doors and right into the motherfucker's living room."

"And given we can't do that?"

"How good a shot are you?" he joked, as they bobbed up and down on the swell that broke into some quite fabulous surfing waves another fifty yards to their right.

"Whoa! What the fuck!" the number two suddenly shouted.

Flynn turned back to look at the prince's home. The prince had seemingly slumped to the ground, for no apparent reason.

"Shall we catch some waves?" asked Flynn.

"What the fuck did you do?" his partner asked.

Both were out of earshot of other the two DCS team members.

"I may have given him a letter," said Flynn quietly.

"And?"

"Let's just say you wouldn't have wanted to be the first to open it. After a few seconds, no problem, but if you were to touch that paper before the light was able to break down the chemical coating it, a few hours later you might just keel over."

"Like that?"

"Perhaps," smiled Flynn. "Anyway, let's go catch some waves. Being a courier is stressful work, you know," he joked.

After delivering the letter, he had washed his hands incessantly for an hour, just in case he had managed to get any chemical on himself, which he was assured was impossible. The chemical coated the letter sealed inside the envelope, which itself was specially lined to stop any light getting through. The letter was a risk. A secretary could have opened it before the prince, but with the number of official government seals and stamps that declared the letter extremely private and confidential, it would have been a brave secretary that would have broken the seals. The chemical itself would be absorbed through the skin on contact and begin its work. Seconds after exposure to light, the letter would be free of any compound. Any tests would show it to be standard government issue paper. A few hours later, a cardiac arrest would ensue. Any autopsy would show death by natural causes, heart failure.

Piece of cake, thought Flynn, riding the wave.

Chapter 83

The call from Flynn confirming the package had been accepted by the right person brought a smile to Carson's face. He had wanted to deal with the playboy prince for years. His funding had been aiding the jihadist cause across the world for years while he partied and socialized with the very people he was fighting against.

The call from Bill Jameson had been slightly less welcome. Frankie wasn't giving up. Her phone call with Bill had been overheard by the President and a meeting was consequently arranged, something Bill Jameson would never have allowed. But President Mitchell had always had a soft spot for her. They all did. It was the reason she had been put on the investigation in the first place. Her career was over. Her link to Nick was too toxic for her to remain with the Secret Service. The rumblings were already beginning as the news spread of her involvement with Nick. The President had already had three Senators ask him if he were mad having the girlfriend of the world's number one terrorist on the team hunting him down. "*Ex*-girlfriend" was the President's response but that would only work for so long.

If she remained in the Service, her pregnancy, a pregnancy she was not in the least interested in aborting, would be public knowledge. It would be the child and not just Frankie who would be labeled. A decision had to be taken, a tough one but it was for the best. Carson called his security team. He needed to get to the White House.

***

Frankie drove while Turner and Reid prepared the papers in the back seat of the Prius to show the President. They had ten minutes, and in that ten minutes the lives of tens of thousands of innocent civilians were in their hands. They not only had to lay out what they believed Carson was doing, they also had to offer an alternative solution. They would have to be concise, clear and convincing.

"I think you should do the talking," said Turner, looking at Frankie from the back seat.

"No way, you're the professional investigators."

"I agree with Paul," said Reid, surprising Frankie.

"What the hell? My job was to protect one person, not make cases that would hold up when put before a jury. You guys are the professionals," she replied, looking into the mirror and seeing fear etched across both their faces. "These are the lives of thousands, *tens* of thousands of people," she argued to them both.

Fear stared back.

Reid squirmed awkwardly. "We're not used to meeting with the President."

"The last time I met him, I was a quivering wreck," admitted Turner. "Too many lives are at stake for me to start stumbling over my words because of nerves!"

"He's just a person like we are," Frankie said.

"He's not, he's an office, he's an institution, he *is* the United States encapsulated in one person," Turner expounded.

"He's also a hell of a nice guy."

"Who *you* know and can talk to easily," said Reid.

The pleading eyes of two of the most senior members of the FBI from the rear seat were too much.

"Seriously, you guys need to grow some!" She sighed. "Make me good notes," she said as she turned in towards the security gate at the White House.

"Hey, Joe," she said, greeting the guard.

"Good to see you, Frankie, we've been missing that smile around here."

"Not for much longer, I hope," she said.

"Good news," he smiled. "Head on up, Frankie, they're expecting you in the residence."

'Thanks, Joe," she said, blowing him a kiss, as she had done for all the years she had known him.

"He's lovely," said Reid. "Can't imagine he's much good as a security guy though. Bit old and heavy," she mused.

Frankie laughed. "Don't ever let anyone hear you say that. When you talk about institutions, Joe is one. Don't let his age or weight fool you either. That man has more medals for bravery and has seen more action than nearly any other Marine alive. We rest easy knowing Joe's on the gate. If anyone ever got past him, we'd know we were in trouble."

Turner and Reid each looked back with a newfound admiration for the cuddly looking old guard who was still watching them drive towards the White House residence.

Frankie stopped as directed and was pleased to see Bill Jameson, her old boss, had come down to greet them.

"Hey, Bill, looking good," she said.

"Hi, Frankie," he replied without the warmth of his normal his tone.

"What's up?"

Bill didn't answer, he just led the way into the main residence towards the elevator which sat ready and waiting for them.

"Bill?" she pressed. They stepped into the elevator.

"It's nothing," he said gruffly, pressing the second floor button.

By the time they reached the second floor and home of the President, Frankie was worried. Bill was her mentor. He had guided her through the ranks, taken her under his wing, seeing the potential in her. He had never been like this with her before.

The tension that had built up on the short journey from the first floor exploded out into the hallway when Bill exited and ushered them to follow him. He paused outside of the President's study. Opposite the study, across the East Sitting Hall, was the Queen's Sitting Room, the door to which opened and revealed the Director of the FBI and his boss, the Attorney General.

"Deputy Director Turner, Special Agent Reid," said the FBI Director, summoning them towards him.

Frankie stood in place next to Bill.

"We have a meeting with President Mitchell," said Turner, standing firmly beside Frankie.

"Not anymore," said the FBI Director.

"It's okay, guys, I'll do my best," she said, letting them be beckoned away.

Once left alone with Frankie, Bill walked forward towards the door that led through to the President's study, opening it gently.

"I'm so sorry, Frankie," he said quietly.

Secretary of Defense Harry Carson was seated at the President's desk and alongside him sat the Director of the Secret Service. There was no sign of President Mitchell.

Frankie's heart started to thump.

"Please come in, Frankie," beckoned Harry.

Fifteen minutes later, Frankie was walking back out of the White House for what would be her very last time. She had managed to avoid crying while in the room but as she exited the residence, the tears flowed freely. Reid ran over when she saw Frankie's heaving body exit the door.

"We realized you were still in there, so we waited for you," she said, holding Frankie as she sobbed. "What happened?"

"I'm no longer a Secret Service agent."

Turner walked over to join them. "What do you mean?" he asked angrily. "You're an excellent agent!"

"They decided that my relationship with Nick Geller was detrimental to the Agency and suggested I may wish to consider my position."

"Carson, that son of a bitch!"

"He did look upset at having to do it," she said through sobs. "Sorry, what about you guys?"

"Reassigned with immediate effect. I've got a flight to Miami waiting for me and Special Agent Reid is going to LA."

"Well good luck to both of you," she said trying to smile. "You okay for transport?" she asked, pointing to her car.

"Yes, thanks. Will you be alright?" asked Reid, fussing over her.

"I'll be fine, it's just sad, I loved the job."

Reid kissed her on the cheek and hugged her. "Keep in touch, Frankie."

"Yes," said Frankie, knowing she'd never see either of them again.

With a kiss and an awkward hug, Paul Turner wished her well and he and Reid walked towards the government sedan waiting to take them to the airport.

"By the way, you'd make a great couple," Frankie called after them with a grin.

"Frankie!" yelled Harry Carson, as he walked out of the White House entrance. "I was hoping you might still be here!"

"What?' she asked, wiping the tears from her eyes.

"I wanted to give you this," he said, handing her a card.

Frankie looked at it grudgingly. "Obstetrician?"

"He's very good, probably one of the best."

"He's in Colorado!" she said angrily.

"I don't think you should stay in Washington," Carson said evenly.

"Am I in danger?"

Harry shrugged. "For you and the child, please take the card."

"How do you know him?"

"I don't, this is from President Mitchell," said Harry. "He's already called ahead. The doctor's expecting you."

"Am I danger?" she asked again.

"I don't know but if you are, it's here, not there," he said, pointing to the card.

"What are you doing, Harry?"

"I'm making sure your child grows up safe."

"The child that will have the genes of a man responsible for tens of thousands of deaths?"

Harry turned without a word and walked towards his waiting car. It pulled away with a screech of tires, leaving Frankie to look back on her past.

Chapter 84

Walid boarded his flight with ease. Like Nick, he had an upper cabin business-class seat. Unlike Nick, he was a little more interested in aircraft. The fact that he had boarded a Boeing 747-400 was not missed on him. Unlike almost every other jihadist, Walid had spent his life traveling the world, if not by private jet, certainly in the first class confines of the world's better airlines. It was to be his first trip on US Airways and he had looked forward to seeing what comforts would take him across to America.

The aircraft listed for the Charlotte flight was an Airbus A330-200, of which he had noticed at least one on his way into the terminal. There had been no mention of the airline owning or even operating Boeing 747-400s. Envoy Class, the US Airways business class, was a cubicle-style seat with the ability to lie flat, a large screen TV and a selection of excellent on demand newly released movies. What he had, however, was a business class seat from a decade earlier, with a small screen that was almost unwatchable due to a large number of scratches and a movie selection that was playing on a loop, something he hadn't experienced for a very long time.

"Excuse me?" he asked the steward, a man he recognized from the check-in desks.

"Yes, sir?" said the steward courteously.

"When did US Airways get 747s and why are they so poorly kitted out?"

"I'm sorry, sir, they've been rushed into service today to replace a number of aircraft that had to be grounded due to a recall by Airbus."

"There's an Airbus there," Walid said, pointing down to the aircraft next to them.

"I believe the recall only affected about 30% of our fleet," replied the steward.

"This isn't what I paid for," Walid snapped, realizing as he spoke that he hadn't actually paid for any of it. Some unsuspecting company had paid for it.

"We're aware that it's not up to our normal standards, sir. If you call customer service on arrival, I believe compensation will be offered. Can I get you a drink perhaps? Champagne or orange juice?"

"Orange juice," said Walid. Something felt... off. He thought back over the odd occurrences: The boards were not displaying the correct gate; the area for check-in was very large; the steward who had been on the check-in desk was standing in front of him now. He knew the airlines were cutting costs – particularly the US legacy airlines –but that seemed ridiculous.

The steward walked towards the small kitchen area where a colleague had watched the interaction with the passenger.

"What was that about?"

"This fucking plane!" he snapped, pouring an orange juice.

"Thank God somebody spotted the fuck up and sent us through the script to cover it."

"I know but how fucking hard can it be to check an airline flies a particular type of aircraft?" he whispered, before turning back to the passengers with a fixed smile, just as he had been trained in the last few months.

***

Omar woke up when the plane lurched in the sky. The passengers next to him were as alarmed as he was. Omar had never been on a plane before and it was therefore his first experience of turbulence. The announcement over the P.A. system did not give him any comfort. He had not been taught, as part of his training for boarding the flight, what the word 'turbulence' meant. Another lurch and he quietly prayed to Allah, which the passenger next to him copied. They both nodded recognition but dared not say another word. They were both warriors of Allah. He wondered whether the man next to him knew that he would be, thanks to sitting next to Omar, one of the special select warriors, chosen to deliver the virus across America.

If he had thought about it more, he probably had a few jihadists around him. Sitting near him would ensure they contracted the illness. He checked his watch, just over three hours since they had taken off. Four hours since he had taken the injection. Omar consciously began to breathe more heavily, expelling as many particles of his infected saliva as possible. He smiled at the special gift he was giving the jihadist next to him. He just wished he could tell him but they were forbidden to speak until after they had exited the airport.

***

When Mohammed Farsi had received his travel details, he was not ashamed to say that he had had to check a map to find Salt Lake City. Flying from Paris, his home town, had not been his favored option. As head of Al Qaeda in Europe, the authorities were aware of his existence but not of what he looked like. At least to the best of his knowledge, his appearance was still unknown. Flying out of Charles De Gaulle was certainly putting that theory to the test; a test that he had passed with flying colors.

Nick had told him he would be sent to a relatively remote location where the leadership would wait and take charge once the situation allowed. Salt Lake City certainly fit that bill. He had also been aware that Nick was planning a large-scale operation, far in excess of the 9/11 attack. However, having just had to visit the restroom, Mohammed began to realize that the scale was far greater than the few hundred warriors he had envisaged. He had spotted at least five other high-ranking leaders on board the flight in that one section. And that had been while trying not to look at those on board and with more than half the plane asleep under their blankets.

Back in his seat, he considered how many men the five he had seen would have been able to muster. And of those men, how many would meet the exacting standards set by

Nick? Those standards had been absolute. The warriors had to be true believers, not followers, men with the heart and blood of Allah pumping through them. True jihadists. Not play jihadists who spouted words with no meaning, feeling or real conviction or who lacked the courage to act on their convictions. Men who would stand proud and shout Allah's name as a bullet rushed towards them or as they pulled a trigger that would send others or themselves to hell or paradise. Excitement began to build as he realized the number was probably in the low thousands just from those five men. He wondered how many other of leaders were on board his flight. Salt Lake City was not a well-served airport. If that were to be the base for leaders, there were very few flights that offered a direct route, something else he had discovered during his search, thanks to his reticence about flying from Paris.

"Mohammed," came a whisper from behind his ear.

Mustafa Ghazi, head of the Maghreb wing of Al Qaeda was standing by his seat, having walked quietly down the aisle. Mustafa was one of the leaders he had spotted.

"We should not talk," whispered Mohammed as quietly as he could.

"Meet me at the restrooms in five minutes," whispered Mustafa before gliding away silently.

***

Nick felt the first bump of turbulence and looked out of the window at the crisp, clear blue sky, only visible from that height. It was a beautiful day, one that would be remembered for a long time. The steward appeared by his side, having reacted to his movements.

"Are you okay, sir?" he asked.

"Yes, thank you."

"I think the captain may put the seatbelt sign on soon, if you need to visit the restroom."

A visit to the restroom was just what he needed.

"Thank you," said Nick. He stepped over the passenger next to him and decided to stretch his legs. He walked down the stairs and into the main body of the aircraft, then down the aisle. Passengers were crammed in like sardines in the coach section but all seemed happy to sleep their way across the Atlantic.

Nick spotted Larbi in an aisle seat and gave him a subtle nod of the head in recognition. Every seat Nick could see was filled. As he reached the restrooms, they were empty. Two stewards stood nearby, both nodded a hello as he approached them.

"Quiet?" asked Nick.

"Remarkably, they're all sleeping like babies," replied one of the stewards who was pressing a call button for an elevator to the galley storage below.

As the elevator's light announced its arrival, the P.A. system began an announcement. The sleeping passengers came alive in an instant and Nick had to move quickly, pushing the stewards into the elevator as he did.

Chapter 85

Frankie had played with the business card for hours. She just sat at her kitchen counter and flicked it around and around in her fingers. The news channel in the background was focusing on local news. As yet, no planes had started falling out of the sky. Her mother and father were in California, where they had been for the last two months on and off. She had only just realized that the only reason they kept the home in Washington was for her. They were never there. She had been so involved in her work that she hadn't realized they had moved. They obviously just hadn't had the heart to tell her and she had been so involved with work and Nick that she hadn't even noticed.

A baby in California, near her parents. They wouldn't approve of her keeping the baby, certainly not after what was about to happen. She couldn't abort the baby. They wouldn't accept it, at least not at first. She was sure they'd grow to love it but they'd always resent what it stood for - the child of the man who had ruined their daughter's life. She twirled the card again. Colorado. She had been skiing in Aspen a few times, it was one of the President's favorite ski resorts and Colorado was the state he had grown up in and represented in the Senate before becoming President.

With one eye on the news screen, she began to research Colorado as an option to build a future for her and the child she would be bringing into a world and who would hopefully be unaware of the monster its father had been. Even saying those words felt so wrong. The man she knew was no monster. However, the new Nick Geller had proved, time after time, that that was exactly what he was.

She picked up the phone and even though it was still early in California, she called her mother. She had a lot to tell her.

Halfway through dialing the number, the news channel suddenly changed to a screen she had never seen before.

EAS was boldly displayed in red on the left hand of the screen with a lightning symbol in the top right of the screen. Underneath, written clearly, was the explanation of the acronym, EAS - Emergency Alert System. She turned up the volume. A repeating message was playing: 'Please stand by for the President of the United States of America'.

Frankie changed channels. The other news channels had the same message. She tried a movie channel, a music channel and even a shopping channel. They all had the same message.

Her phone rang. "Frankie?"

"Yes, Mom."

"What's happening?"

"I don't know," she said.

"But you're involved in all this, you must know!"

"Mom, I don't know." She didn't really think that it was a good time to tell her mom she had been fired. Her mom had been desperate to visit ever since the Nick thing had blown up but Frankie had told her to keep away; it would just complicate matters and she was too busy anyway. Reluctantly, her mother had agreed but only because she knew Frankie would be more annoyed at her if she had come, after being told not to.

"Should we come to you?"

"No, you're safer there, Mom."

"I don't care about safe, I care about being with you, honey."

"Mom, I'll come to you if need be."

"But your job, honey. You can't leave with everything that's happening."

Frankie broke down at that point. She couldn't blatantly lie to her mother. She told her about losing her job and being pregnant with Nick Geller's child. Her mother did what any mother would. She consoled her child and kept her opinions for a more appropriate moment.

"There's a countdown clock that just appeared," said Frankie's mother.

Frankie, feeling a lot better having unloaded her troubles to her mother. looked at her TV set.

0:59

0:58

She looked up at the wall clock and then down at the papers in front of her, detailing all of the transatlantic flight details for that morning. The arrival times started at just after 10:30 a.m. EST into the East Coast airports. It was 11:00 a.m.

She started to panic. They had underestimated Nick throughout the investigation. Why had they suddenly been so confident? He had consistently proved to be two or three steps ahead of them.

The counter counted down to 0:01.

The screen changed to the President of the United States, standing proudly but gravely behind the podium.

"Oh my God," said Frankie's mom, beating Frankie to it. She had never seen him look so serious.

Chapter 86

Narsarsuaq Airport
Greenland

Major General Howard Carter climbed into the cockpit of the F15. It felt great to be back in the pilot's seat again. He had missed the adrenaline rush as he hit the afterburners. It was an amazing machine and although he could have opted for the newer and even more exhilarating F22, his wife Jackie had fallen for him as an F15 pilot and in her memory it was that pilot who would try to do something to avenge her pointless death.

He signaled to his wingman, A US Marine pilot flying a new F35 Lightning whose young son and wife had died on 9/11, victims on one of the hijacked airlines. Their flight, American Airlines Flight 77 from Dulles to LA, had crashed into the Pentagon.

Both pilots turned east, powered into the bright clear skies and followed the route set earlier by the rest of the ad-hoc squadron. Carter and his wingman were the last to leave. Behind them, the maintenance crews would pack up and disappear back to where they had unwittingly and unexpectedly been pulled from. They would have no idea what they had been party to. Only the fighter pilots with a very personal interest in the proceedings would ever know what had taken place over the empty skies and empty waters of one of the most northerly and least travelled parts of the North Atlantic.

Running from the southern tip of Greenland to the west coast of Iceland, the Irminger basin stretched over one hundred thousand square miles of the North Atlantic's ocean floor. Plunging to depths of almost three miles and well beyond the capabilities of any manned submersibles, it was the perfect location for the day's events.

Major General Carter fixed the photo of his long dead but never forgotten wife to the inside of his window. She would give him the strength to carry out the task that only a select few had been offered and none had refused. Taking five hundred lives, no matter who they were, was never an easy task; it was, however, somewhat eased by the knowledge that the lives of those on board each of those flights were already fated. The moment they had boarded their flights, they were destined to die.

Chapter 87

Omar heard the announcement and stopped in his tracks. It was far clearer and louder than any previous announcement. Severe turbulence lay ahead and all passengers were to remain in their seats with their seat belts fastened. Restrooms were locked and trolley services suspended. Omar checked his seatbelt, as did everyone else around him same. With it tightly fastened, he assumed his previous position. He had been about to tour the plane, breathing and passing his now contagious germs throughout the length and breadth of the aircraft, but that would have to wait.

He closed his eyes for a moment and then they snapped open again. He had clearly understood the entire message. He didn't speak English.

***

Walid had not settled since the flight took off and it wasn't just that the seat was so worn it offered little support, everything about the flight from check-in, to the aircraft type, to the stewards - there were no stewardesses - to the seats, to the entertainment system, everything seemed off. Even the route they were taking was bizarre. After three hours in the air since leaving Frankfurt, the only thing below them should have been the ocean but all he could see was land. To still see land, they had to be flying a very northerly route. The North Atlantic Track, which Walid knew to be like a freeway in the sky, did not fly that far north. Each day, a number of flight paths were selected based on the current conditions that would minimize headwinds, maximize tailwinds and ultimately reduce fuel burn and flight time. All transatlantic flights would follow those same paths. East and west bound flights had separate paths. It ensured that the chances of mid air collisions in the radar and air traffic control-free mid-Atlantic were nonexistent. Having spent his childhood in aircraft, he had learned a thing or two from the aircrew.

Also, from his own knowledge and with the help of the route map in the seat pocket, he knew that there was no logical explanation as to why, that far into the flight, he could see land below. Land which, as they were still flying in the correct general direction, according to the sun, he could only assume was Iceland. And Iceland was far beyond the North Atlantic Track and certainly not the most efficient route to Charlotte, North Carolina. He hit the call button. No steward responded. He hit it again and without waiting any further, he unclipped his seatbelt and went to find someone with answers.

Walking down and into the main cabin, the answer became abundantly clear, as the announcement that boomed out of the P.A. system confirmed his worst fears. Ignoring the instruction to fasten his seatbelt due to turbulence, he rushed back up to the business class upper cabin and made straight for the cockpit door.

The steward seat to the left of the cockpit was empty.

"Come and help me get through this door!" he ordered the men he had recognized as jihadists in the front row seats.

The rest of the passengers in the small upper cabin looked on, not knowing what to make of the actions of the men trying to break into the cockpit. After ten minutes of using a trolley as a battering ram, the armored door buckled slightly at one corner. However, without heavy equipment or explosives, the door wasn't budging. Luckily the small corner offered Walid the gap he needed. He placed his camera phone's lens in the gap and took a number of photos of the cockpit beyond.

"Mother fucker!" he screamed when he viewed the images.

***

As requested, Mohammed met Mustafa Ghazi at the restrooms located just in front of his block of seats.

"Have you not noticed?" he whispered urgently to Mustafa, careful not to be seen.

"Noticed what?" asked Mohammed.

"There are no women on this flight."

"No I hadn't," he said, surprised. He hadn't been looking. He had, as instructed, tried to keep a low profile.

"There are none, not one, nor any children," continued Mustafa.

Mohammed looked around at the seats that he could see. Mustafa was right. Everyone he could see was a man, some were under blankets asleep.

"And tell me, Mohammed, what is everyone doing?"

"Sleeping, keeping to themselves and not talking," he said, understanding dawning.

Mustafa nodded knowingly.

"But this is only one section of the plane," said Mohammed.

"I've checked the others."

"Do you think we're all jihadists?"

Mustafa nodded.

"Oh my God, how many of us are there?" said Mohammed excitedly.

"I counted about five hundred and twenty."

"I had no idea there'd be so many of us going to Salt Lake, he must have amassed a massive army," said Mohammed proudly.

Mustafa shook his head in bewilderment but any words were drowned out by the announcement of severe turbulence and a requirement for all passengers to remain in their seats and fasten their safety belts.

Chapter 88

Major General Howard Carter spotted the Boeing 747-400 first; it had just cleared Iceland. He signaled to his wingman, who had been scanning the sky to the south, that they would go up and over. With the Boeing flying like them at five hundred miles per hour, the closing speed as they hurtled towards each other was nearing one thousand miles per hour. Both pilots pulled back and lifted their jets higher into the sky going invisible, at least to the passengers below, over the United Airlines Boeing 747.

A quick turn and thrust of power and the two jets pulled in behind and just out of sight of the windows and, more importantly, the turbulence being created by the massive airliner.

Being one of the aircraft that might be carrying the man who had assassinated the Vice President and masterminded the attempt to spread a deadly virus across the United States, the United Airlines flight from Frankfurt bound for Dulles was a tempting target. However, amongst the jihadist passengers, one man stood out for Major General Howard Carter. He was one of the terrorists who had been instrumental in the 9/11 attacks and had been identified in the emails from his photo. He was the mastermind behind the plot to attack the Twin Towers. He was a man who had seldom seen daylight in the many years since the attack but had surfaced once again to threaten the United States. With a pick of the targets, Major General Howard Carter had, for once in his life, put his personal choice first and mission second.

He pressed the power button on the small TV screen that had been retrofitted especially for the mission. Within a thousand yards, the TV was able to receive, thanks to some wizardry beyond his technical knowledge, the video feed from the aircraft. He checked the map as the TV screen remained blank. They were still a hundred miles from the target location. He checked his speed and heading, ensuring they were staying just out of sight of even the most observant of the passengers on board the aircraft.

His screen burst into life, relaying what was being shown on the United flight ahead of him.

The grave image of the President of the United States of America, standing proudly behind the presidential podium, filled his screen. Unfortunately, the screen provided no sound. But he knew, from the President's image, that it was a fifteen-minute countdown. He hit the timer and watched it click slowly and painfully down towards zero. He checked the map, looking to see where they'd be in fifteen minutes, another one hundred twenty-five miles out to sea and over some of the deepest and most unreachable areas of the world's oceans.

When the timer hit zero, he signaled once to his wingman and they both powered forwards, slowly coming alongside the passenger jet and the helpless and defenseless passengers. Their slow progression ensured that every passenger had a clear view of the two powerful symbols of American might.

Howard Carter looked across and, as expected, panic had ensued. Windows were being hammered and soundless shouts of abuse were hurled at him. He checked his map as he drew level with the Boeing's cockpit. The location was perfect. Everything had been timed to perfection. With a wave to the Boeing, he pulled up and over looped back behind the massive jet. He had spent a long time thinking how he would approach this moment. The kindest action was to fire four missiles straight into the body of the plane. Whoever the explosions didn't kill instantly would be unconscious from a lack of oxygen and dead long before they hit the water forty thousand feet below.

That was precisely the reason the only weapon available to him was his M61 Vulcan 20mm Gatling gun. He had specifically asked for no missiles to be loaded just in case, in a moment of compassion, he took mercy and opted for the quick and painless option.

The first burst of fire destroyed the majority of the right wing. The plane lurched to the right, bringing the left wing round and into his sights. Another burst destroyed that wing and the Boeing tipped forward and plunged towards the sea below. With not one bullet having touched the fuselage, the Boeing would remain intact and its passengers unharmed until it hit the water, some seven and a half miles below, or ten point five miles, adding the distance to the ocean floor.

Chapter 89

Frankie increased the volume on her TV to hear President Mitchell speak. "My fellow Americans," he began. She could hear the same message with a slight delay coming from her mom's TV three thousand miles away.

"I'll call you when he's done," she said, and hung up.

"As you are painfully aware, we have been living under the threat of an attack by militant jihadists that would threaten the very core of our nation. These men claim they act for Allah but no god would ever condone their actions, and nor do the 99.99% of law abiding and peaceful Muslims who practice a faith that, at its core, is peace loving."

After a pause, he resumed speaking. "Nick Geller was man that I trusted. A man I believed was acting in the interests of our country when he visited the White House a few weeks ago. How wrong I was, how wrong *we* were. A man we trained turned on us and used that training to evade and destroy us.

"Today, Nick Geller launched an attack to devastate our country. An attack so heinous in its plan, it's hard to believe that anyone could be consumed by that amount of hatred. The plan to bring the fight to our streets and a virus to our people is so grotesque it's hard to comprehend the enormity of its impact on our nation. Today, the proud men and women who fight to keep us safe every second of the day, have once again *prevailed.*"

President Mitchell paused to let the enormity of his words sink in.

"The nightmare of the virus that had hung over us is over, the nightmare of men running through our streets strapped with bombs is over. Nick Geller, along with many hundreds of jihadists, is, as we speak, languishing with the deadly virus at the bottom of the Atlantic Ocean. A flight bound for America and loaded with virus-infected jihadists was intercepted and destroyed by our military."

"Many of you, I know, will be concerned for loved ones who may have been on the flight. Please rest assured that all families affected by this action have already been informed and support measures put in place. If you do still want to check the status of a passenger, a phone number will be displayed at the end of this broadcast. It is automated and all that is required is for you to give the name of the individual. If they were on board, you will be transferred to a support center. If not, you will be informed that everything is fine. It is never easy being President and being entrusted with the security and welfare of hundreds of millions of American citizens. Some days, you have to make decisions for the greater good. Today is one of those days. We have struck a blow that will make the world a safer place. Tomorrow will be safer than it was today. As President, all I can promise you is that I will do whatever is needed to make sure that the day after that and the days that follow are safer still. God bless America."

The screen faded to a telephone number. Frankie sat still, not knowing how to react. Nick Geller was dead. *Nick* was dead. Although she had to keep telling herself *her* Nick died a few weeks earlier. It wasn't a nightmare. It wasn't some bizarre and crazy mistake. The President had just confirmed that Nick was dead.

Her phone rang. "I'm okay, Mom," she said.

"Hi, Frankie, it's Paul."

"Paul?"

"Paul Turner, Deputy Director FBI?"

"Oh yes, Paul. How can I help?" she asked absently.

"One plane?" he asked. "There were ten thousand of them heading here!"

"Well, there were ten thousand emails."

"That's not what the NSA guy hinted at," said Turner.

"The President said one plane, that's a few hundred."

"So Nick Geller, the man who handed us our asses on a platter over and over again, injected forty-nine people with Ebola on one plane?"

"What are you saying, Paul?"

"He never said which plane. He said *a* plane and then didn't give the flight number."

"You think there's more than one?"

"I think there are a lot more than one. Have you still got all the flight details?"

"Yeah, they're here in front of me. I'll check which ones land and which ones don't."

"Excellent. I need to board my flight to Miami, I'll call you when I land."

Frankie logged on to each of the airports and ticked off flight after flight throughout the day as each one landed safely. By 5:00 p.m. and with a only a few flights due to land which, in fact, had not even left Europe until after the President's speech, she had yet to find a single flight on her list that had not landed safely.

Frankie checked the news websites and they all carried the story as their headline but listed the flight simply as a 'United Airlines flight'. All five hundred and thirty seven passengers and crew were presumed lost. A list of the victims who were on board the flight had been published. Over two hundred and twenty innocent victims had perished, yet not one relative was being interviewed. There were no scenes of mass weeping or anguish at the arrivals gate at the airport. The news was focused almost entirely on how the virus threat had been lifted and almost three hundred jihadists, the most radical jihadists alive, had been stopped in their quest to destroy America. The loss of two hundred twenty Americans was being downplayed. It seemed the belief was that the victims had already been infected by the Ebola virus and that it was almost a blessing that they had perished in a plane crash rather than die an agonizing death. No further details about the innocent victims had been released, no ages or addresses, just a list of names that the President had pledged would be immortalized forever in a memorial.

By 6:00 p.m., Frankie began to wonder how long it could take to fly to Miami, having still not heard from Deputy

Director Turner. At 6:30 p.m., she knew she would never hear from him again.

The breaking news that the man who had led the investigation and foiled Nick Geller's plot was to be appointed Deputy Attorney General flashed on Frankie's TV screen. A beaming, newly minted Deputy Attorney General Paul Turner stepped forward. Frankie spotted Secretary of Defense Harry Carson in the background of the shot.

She turned off her TV, packed a bag that would fit in her Porsche and drove out of Washington for the last time. Her destination: Colorado.

Chapter 90

EIGHTEEN MONTHS EARLIER

Harry Carson paced the corridor outside the White House Situation Room. His position was one that few knew and even fewer understood. He solved problems before they became issues. A new problem had arisen. One that was way beyond his normal remit and as a result, he had asked for a special meeting with President Mitchell and Secretary of Defense Bob Hammond. Finally, the meeting that was delaying his access began to break up. The attendees filed past him warily. Harry Carson was a man few ever wanted to see in their department. If he was there, something big was about to happen.

With the room finally empty of all but the two men he needed to see, Harry entered the room, closed the door behind him and ensured that any recording devices were switched off. President Mitchell and Bob Hammond watched the unshakeable Harry Carson fuss around the room checking the devices with some concern. Harry Carson was unflappable, emotionless, nerveless. But he was obviously worried, which could only mean one thing: They should be *very* worried.

"Jesus Christ, Harry! What the fuck is wrong?" asked Bob, unable to wait any longer.

"Gentlemen, these are chatter graphs," he said, laying out a number of charts on the large conference table. "And when I say chatter, it's the level of communication from areas of known terrorist organizations. It's a gauge of how active the terrorists are." Both members of his audience nodded. "This is the graph up two weeks ago." He tracked a fairly uniform pattern with his index finger, no spikes or curves, just a fairly flat straight line. Both nodded again.

Carson put down a new chart. "This is from then until today, Monday." He pointed to a massive spike in activity.

"Yes," said the President. "The CIA has told us it's to do with the Caliph Zahir al Zahrani announcing some new offensive. They expect the levels to drop back in the next few days. They don't have the support or power they once had."

"One part of that's correct. Al Qaeda is not as powerful as it once was and alone it's not the concern it once was."

"And the other part that's not correct?" asked Bob.

"That the levels will die down," he said somberly. "Zahir al Zahrani has a plan, a dream it would seem, to join with all of the other jihadist organizations across the radicalized world and create one army fighting for Allah."

"Never going to happen," scoffed Bob. "Too many factions and differences between them."

Harry pulled out another chart. "I asked some very clever guys to drill down into what they could of the chatter. There is one shit load of crosstalk between organizations that we would never have thought possible. This is real, gentlemen," cautioned Harry sternly.

"Okay, Harry, you've got our attention," said President Mitchell, sitting more rigidly in his chair.

"So what's the plan?" asked Bob.

"The plan?" asked Harry.

"The plan, Harry, you know, the one you don't enter a room without."

"Oh, that plan," he smiled, walking to the door and opening it. "You can come in," he said to someone in the hall.

"President Mitchell, Secretary Hammond, let me present to you the most traitorous son of a bitch this country has ever produced, Nick Geller."

Chapter 91

"Nick," said Secretary Hammond.

"Mr. Secretary," replied Nick.

"You know each other?" asked President Mitchell, still confused as to what Harry was proposing.

"Nick is one of our guys in Defense Clandestine Services, one of our very best."

Nick proudly squared his shoulders. "Thank you, Mr. Secretary."

"I thought you said he was a traitor?" asked the President.

"Not yet, but by the time I've finished with him, his own family, if they were still alive, would hate him," said Harry confidently.

"Perhaps I'm missing something or just being particularly stupid today but what exactly the fuck is it you're planning to do?"

"Hijack Zahrani's plan."

"Surely we want to stop it?" asked the President in frustration.

"And then we'd have to stop them again the next time, and again and again. And then what would happen the time we didn't stop them?"

"So, no offense, Nick," said the President before turning to Carson, "but that's it? One guy? We've got over one and a half million service men and women and millions more in law enforcement to take these guys down. One guy? Seriously?"

"One guy who they think is theirs."

"Geller…" President Mitchell mused, "that's a Jewish name, isn't it?"

"We've worked that into his cover. The religions have more in common than you'd think."

"Perhaps if you start from the beginning and just explain it to us," said Bob.

"Last week, I visited Creech Air Force Base in Nevada on a trip to LA," said Harry. "While I was there, I witnessed the amazing work they're doing with drones. Anyway, I wondered if they could do something similar with our E3s and tankers. After a chat with the commander of the unit, he promised he'd do some evaluations. On the flight down to LA, we passed over a couple of airport storage facilities which, given the information we have on Zahrani's plans, got me thinking."

"What did?" asked the President impatiently.

"The drones and the storage yards. It came to me. What if we could get all the jihadists into one controlled area in which we were free— and without risk to any innocent life— to do anything that was necessary?"

"Yes?" Bob pressed.

"Aircraft. If we get them onto planes, they'd be weaponless, totally defenseless and at our mercy."

"And how do we convince them to board these planes?"

'We make them think they're coming to destroy us. We make them think they're part of the one true army fighting for Allah, a holy jihad to rid the world of American evil."

"I'm not convinced," said President Mitchell.

"We're still at the planning stage. There's a lot we need to work out. How do we get them to trust Nick? How do we get them to believe he can take Al Zahrani's plan and make it happen? To be honest, we're struggling to make it work with Al Zahrani around. We need to control the timescale, not him."

"Sounds like an impossible dream," said the President. "Perhaps we should just focus on stopping them."

"We think it's possible. We just need to think like the jihadists. Remember, they'll sacrifice themselves for their cause. That's where they have the drop on us but we can use that to our advantage."

"You're losing me again," said the President.

"The key, we believe, requires four stages. Nick winning their trust, that's number one and perhaps the hardest but we believe we can create a scenario that will make that possible. Stage two is Nick gaining the trust of Caliph Al Zahrani, again difficult but under the right circumstances, possible."

"So far, all I see is Nick being executed very publicly to humiliate us," said Bob.

"Stage three," continued Harry, ignoring Bob, "is where it gets tricky. We remove Al Zahrani, or at least Nick does."

"You kill him?' asked the President.

"So he can receive a medal from you and in the process attempt to assassinate you," said Harry quickly. "And this room could do with an update anyway. In fact, the whole West Wing could do with a refurb."

"Attempt to assassinate me and blow up the West Wing? You've got to be fucking kidding me?!"

"Nick would then escape and, armed with a tape of Al Zahrani to prove that he is carrying out Al Zahrani's plan, the tape will show Al Zahrani sacrificing himself for the greater cause. Nick then steals a deadly virus and over a period of weeks causes utter and total panic in the US while gaining the trust, confidence and admiration of the jihadists across the Arab world. They will rise and fight with the man who very nearly killed the President and has in his possession a virus that will destroy the entire country."

"In the meantime, we kit out a number of planes that we then sucker them onto thinking they're coming to carry out their jihad and destroy America."

"It's absolutely fucking crazy!" said the President. "Nick will be dead in ten minutes and we'll have done nothing to stop them! You know there's no chance you'll survive this?" said the President, looking at Nick.

"Yes, sir," replied Nick without hesitation.

"Assassinate me? Actually shoot me?"

Harry nodded. "It needs to be real, everybody needs to believe it's real. We need to throw everything we've got into hunting him down.

"And what if our guys catch him or kill him?" asked Bob.

"They won't," said Harry confidently.

"But if they do?"

"The plan's dead in the water. It's a risk but to the world and the American people, we need to make it real. The fewer people who know, the better. So far, we're the only four people who are aware of the plan and I'd like to keep it that way."

"The VP and NSA Liz Roberts would need to be in on it. I'd want their input on the plan. Jesus! You've got me talking like this is possible!"

"It is," said Harry. "Laid out like I've just done it sounds a bit ridiculous but over time, we'll iron out the creases and finesse the details. If we do it right and Nick thinks like them, I believe we can do it."

"And what do we do with these planeloads of suicidal jihadists? Gitmo's not that big and I'm supposed to be closing it down."

"Sorry, I left that bit out. We blow them the fuck away and let their bodies rot at the bottom of the ocean."

"That bit I get," smiled President Mitchell, before turning to Nick. "How good a shot are you?"

"Not bad, sir," replied Nick with a smile.

Chapter 92

PRESENT DAY
The White House

President Mitchell looked out at the construction teams who were rebuilding the West Wing. He was still struggling to believe the audacious plan laid before him almost a year and a half ago had been successful. Harry, Bob and Liz had been camped out with him since 11:00 a.m. in the makeshift situation center that had previously been the State Dining Room. The one man not present, the former VP, had been sorely missed but not forgotten.

In great secrecy, they had kept in touch with the events of the day through the various disconnected parts of the operation that Harry Carson had concocted.

The agents who had so efficiently manned the check-in desks and who had subsequently acted as the stewards on board the flights, were all Combat Controllers, highly specialized and skilled members of the USAF's Special Forces. They were expert in many fields and most importantly for the mission, high altitude parachuting. They had more knowledge than most of what was likely to happen to the passengers on board the aircraft but ultimately could do nothing but guess.

The drone pilots who had been trained over the previous months on how to pilot the Boeing 747s, had been told that the planes were being rescued from imminent scrapping and were being used in a military exercise. None was aware that there were passengers on board the crewless airliners.

The fighter pilots who had left Narsarsuaq were the only people outside of the makeshift Situation Room who were fully aware of the mission. They had been carefully selected by Harry's brother-in-law, Major General Howard

Carter, and given their history and personal losses, it was highly unlikely they would ever talk.

In all, they had created twenty Boeing 747 drones from planes sitting in storage waiting to be scrapped or sold for spare parts. All had been allocated a real flight number and thanks to the Combat Controllers at check-in, the real passengers were separated and directed to their real flights, while the jihadists were directed to a ghost flight of the same number. The airlines had helped, throughout the months of training, by allowing the military to carry out its top secret exercise which required the use of their desks and allowed the forces' planes to use their livery. It had all gone perfectly to plan except for the US Airways Boeing 747 screw up. US Airways not having a 747 in service had created a buzz amongst a very observant plane-spotting community. A buzz that needed to be silenced to protect the operation and which was costing the US government an extra $400 million. The only way to cover their tracks was to make the planes that should never have existed, suddenly exist. US Airways was about to gain two free Boeing 747-400s, whether they wanted them or not.

Getting the five hundred plus jihadists on board each flight without them realizing what was happening had been a logistical wonder. Allocating the various jihadists to planes where they didn't know other group members had been difficult. When the groups were greater than twenty in size, luck and allocation of seating played a big part, as did the boarding. The instructions for each jihadist ensured that different areas of the planes were filled at set times. Meticulous planning had been involved in how Nick should instruct the timings of each jihadist, based on their seat numbers. Each jihadist's instructions on the day depended on their seat number but this meant spreading the check-in over three hours. The excessive number of check-in desks ensured that, on arrival, the jihadists were checked straight onto the flight and as the flight was sitting and ready to go, they were directed to board immediately. By the time the later jihadists boarded, most of the plane was either asleep or faking sleep, desperate to follow their instructions, to keep to themselves and not draw attention.

"Do we have all the updates now?" asked President Mitchell, turning his back to the West Wing and rejoining the group, whose enthusiasm and elation had waned dramatically.

"Yes, Mr. President, all flights have been terminated."

"Casualties?"

"All combat controllers have checked in safely. They jumped over a desolate part of Iceland and all have been picked up and are on board US Naval vessels that were stationed offshore."

"The fighters?"

"All have landed back safely in the US."

"Geller?"

Harry shook his head. "The video started playing early on his flight. Two combat controllers were still in the cabin. He threw them into the lift and with no more room, sent them down with orders to jump immediately. They just managed to parachute onto land from where they were. It's unlikely Nick would have gotten out the cabin alive once the movie started. Even if he had, he would have landed in the water."

President Mitchell nodded. The movie they had played on the planes was a very different version than the one played to the American people and pulled no punches.

Just like the announcement regarding turbulence and fastening their seatbelts, the video was in Arabic, ensuring that the majority of the plane would take notice. Some just did what the announcement had said, others had instantly realized that Arabic was not a language used for announcements on American flights. Whatever the reaction, the announcement had woken up everyone on the planes and ensured they were awake when the screens burst to life.

The video started with a grave President who then, with a smile, told them to 'watch this.'

The real video of Caliph Zahir Al Zahrani was then played to the captivated audience, not the Hollywood special effects version that had created a digitized reality that had endeared Nick Geller to the jihadist cause. The real video showed Nick Geller promising the Caliph that he was going to kill as many suicidal jihadists as he possibly could and in the process wipe out the fundamentalists once and for all, cleansing the Islamic religion and Allah of the hate-filled crazies that had no part in the peace loving Islamic world.

The President then reappeared and through an interpreter told the jihadists that their hunger for death was about to be fulfilled by the might and power of the American people.

On cue, the fighter jets would then fly alongside each of the planes, before pulling away and sending the pilotless and crewless planes to the depths of the Atlantic. One option had been to do away with the fighters and just let the planes run out of fuel or have the remote pilots fly them into the ocean. However, the fighters ensured the planes went down exactly where they wanted them to, the deepest part of the Irminger basin.

***

"I want every available ship and plane looking for Geller," ordered the President. He had no illusions at the beginning of the operation that the chances of Geller surviving were anything more than slim to nil. But as time progressed and he had, piece by piece, brought the plan and the traitor to life, the more he thought they would see Geller again and have the chance to congratulate him for what he had managed to accomplish, an achievement that was nothing short of monumental to the world. The selection criteria for the jihadists had been precise. Only the true believers who, without hesitation, would give their lives for the cause they believed in. A cause that was so warped that they would have to kill or be killed.

However, thanks to Nick, the lives and souls of the most devoted and experienced members of the jihadist organization were now rotting three miles below the surface of the ocean. Their leadership, structures and lifeblood were gone forever. Each of the groups had offered up their best men, their leaders, their number twos and their team leaders. None believed they would all be selected, none knew they *had* all been selected. Nick had hinted many times that only the best of best would be offered the opportunity to take the fight to America. Every man whose name had gone on the list was selected. They had all been so keen to take the fight to America, that none had thought to question what they were doing, or the effect of what Nick was doing would have on their organizations. None could see beyond their opportunity to take their war to America. The jihadists had been dealt a blow from which they would never recover. With Flynn killing the prince, their monies were gone, their leaders were gone, their organizations were gone.

And so was Geller. Although whatever had happened, "Nick Geller" could never have resurfaced. For the plan to work, his demise needed to be believed. Nobody could ever know the jihadists had been tricked. Nobody could ever know that Nick only had one real vial of virus. He had destroyed the other forty-nine even before leaving the medical research facility. Nobody could ever know that the Americans had designed and executed the plan to rid the world of over ten thousand jihadists. As far as the world knew, the Americans had intercepted one inbound flight of virus-ridden passengers and jihadists. They had no choice but to shoot the plane down to save the world.

As far as any individual jihadist groups were aware, the three hundred jihadists who were killed were all the jihadists they knew. That one plane, to each group, was their group of jihadists. Their leaders, their team leaders, their best warriors, all gone, along with the man who had promised them their dream, Nick Geller.

Nick Geller was dead no matter whether on the plane or in the sea. Nick Geller would live on as the greatest "traitor" in American history.

Epilogue

Six Months later.
Castle Rock, Colorado

Frankie had been in labor for over six hours. She breathed in between contractions. It had been a tough six months but Castle Rock had been welcoming and she easily found a job with the local police force and was promoted within the first three months to Commander of the Serious Crimes Division. Outside of work, she kept to herself. Once the baby was born, she told herself she'd become more sociable but she wasn't sure that would ever be the case.

Nick Geller had been something special. His betrayal had extinguished the spark in her. Trust had become a major issue for her. Not trusting other people, not trusting her own judgment.

Another contraction came and the obstetrician told her to breathe. Despite how her time in Washington had ended, she had accepted the presidential recommendation for her doctor. Recommendations didn't get much better. So far, he had been brilliant and had allowed Frankie the natural birth she wanted. Her mom was by her side, holding her hand and supporting her through a pregnancy she deeply disagreed with but would support nonetheless.

Frankie had kept in touch with Reid, although a few emails every now and then were hardly the foundations of a great friendship. The one thing they had worked out was that the list of innocent victims' names was bullshit. Not one person on the list of names appeared to correlate with a real person. People had shown up at the memorial service but the more Frankie and Reid asked questions, the more the bullshit fell apart. If the press were on to it, they weren't interested. The return of pre-9/11 style travel was on the horizon. The Islamic faith had been all but cleansed of its radicalization, earning a newfound respect across the world. Their numbers had in fact grown since the incident as more and more Muslims who had lost faith due to the radicals flooded back to the mosques.

Another contraction hit. This time, the doctor told her to push. And push again. Her mother vociferously encouraged her up until the first screams of a beautiful baby boy.

Nurses fussed around the room as Frankie lost herself in the wonder of motherhood, her perfect baby boy nuzzling into her.

Two hours later, mother and baby were finally alone. She soaked up every one of his features. His ten perfect little toes, his ten perfect little fingers. His dark mop of hair, his sallow skin and his piercing eyes, his father's eyes.

"Miss Franks," said one of the nurses, interrupting a precious moment. He had been one of the nurses she vaguely recognized as one who had helped during the delivery. "I have a Facetime call for you, shall I hold the baby for you?" He held out an iPad. He was missing the tips of a few of his fingers. She reluctantly swapped her baby for the iPad. He noticed she couldn't take her eyes off of his fingers.

"Exposure," he explained. "Not careless." Ensuring that Frankie could see her son was safe in his arms, he walked to the other side of the room to give Frankie some privacy during the call.

"Congratulations, Frankie," said a beaming President Mitchell, the crystal clear waters of a Caribbean beach in the background.

"Thank you, Mr. President. I see you're enjoying some winter sun."

"Just visiting a dear old friend," replied the President. "In fact, he wants to say hello." The image on the screen spun around and a hospital style bed came into view in what otherwise appeared to a beachside villa, one she recognized and had in fact visited.

The image revealed the supposedly dead Vice President of the United States, Donald Brodie, a shadow of his former self, painfully thin and gravely ill.

"Mr. Vice President?" she said gasping. "But...but..."

"Cancer," he explained breathlessly. "I didn't want to go through it in office. I took an opportunity and bowed out in a blaze of glory," he joked, coughing painfully.

The President joined him, sitting on the edge of the bed. "I can't explain everything but your son has a father to be proud of," said Brodie.

Frankie was speechless and became suddenly aware of the nurse in the room.

She lowered her voice. "Are you saying Nick wasn't for real?"

"Your Nick was, our Nick wasn't," said President Mitchell.

"So I tried to shoot my Nick?" she asked, suddenly realizing she almost killed him.

"But you missed!"

"I wasn't trying to miss and I'm damned sure Bill wasn't either."

The President's face suggested otherwise.

"Oh my God, why tell me now?" she said angrily.

"Everyone believes we killed him. Everybody believes Nick Geller the traitor was real. There's only one person who deserves to know that's not true. Only six other people know the truth about who Nick Geller really was. You and your son deserve to know he was one of our greatest heroes ever."

Tears welled in her eyes, which turned into a flood. The emotion of six months of anguish and doubt, about herself, the life her child would lead, about Nick, came flowing out.

"Thank you, Mr. President," she said through the tears.

"You've got a great guy there," he said. "Look after him for us."

"Of course I will," she said, reaching out for her baby.

"I think he actually meant me," said the nurse, a man she didn't recognize in the least until she, for the first time, caught sight of his eyes, the only things the plastic surgeon hadn't changed.

Printed in Great Britain
by Amazon

26974716R00199